TIL DEATH DO WE START

KATE CROW

Cover by: Molly Cornell

Edited by: Grace Cook

For all of my difficult women

AUTHOR'S NOTE

This book handles death in many different forms, including on-page suicidal ideation and on-page suicide by the female main character. While the female main character is brought back to life, please consider if this may be sensitive content for you. Mental health is important, and please protect yourself. More in-depth content warnings can be found at www.katecrowauthor.com.

AUTHOR'S NOTE

CHAPTER 1

*J*ane Montgomery was bent over a squirrel carcass with her scalpel in hand when she was delivered a note from her brother demanding her presence at a ball that evening. With only an hour's notice, she had been bathed, plucked, prodded, and stuffed into a dress. Somehow, she was still the first one in the carriage despite the clear orders in Robert's note.

The offending note lay crumpled in her gloved hand. It said she needed to be ready in the carriage by seven o'clock sharp, wearing her green dress with her hair up, or else she would face dire consequences. The presumption that her brother could issue orders to her as if she were an employee, rather than his sister, made her hands shake with rage.

The requested dress was a pale green silk brocade with swirls of golden thread around the bodice and hem. The wide neckline stopped just before her shoulders, framing her modest décolletage with a bit of lace. The sleeves were tight around her biceps, but flared out at her elbow like a cumbersome pair of wings. It had been made years ago for Robert and Sofia's wedding, but it was still her best dress, so her maid fetched it from the attic every time she needed a fancy dress. Her chestnut colored hair was pinned in a gravity-defying mound with flowers and feathers sticking out in every direction. The weight of her hair strained her neck, but when she tried to push back on the style, her maid told her this was the style Robert requested.

Complying with her brother's orders felt like swallowing glass, but she had no interest in discovering what he meant by "consequences."

Balling her hand into a fist, she watched her tendons move beneath her pale green glove that matched her dress. As she watched her tendons, she wished she had her sketchbook so she could detail each slight movement. Over one hundred muscles, tendons, and bones worked together to provide the ability to crumple the note in her hand. Opening her fist, she smoothed the white cardstock to repeat the action.

Jane's head popped up as gravel crunched outside to see Sofia waddling down the drive, stopping halfway to catch her as she rested her arm on the big belly that seemed to have grown overnight. The carriage door creaked as Jane swung it open to hold out a hand for Sofia, whose sweaty palm met hers as she leveraged both Jane and the carriage frame to hoist herself inside.

"Where's your husband?" Jane asked, attempting to keep her tone light. "Shouldn't he be here if he insists you attend the ball in your condition?"

"Robert will be out in a moment," Sofia said breathlessly before unsnapping her white lace fan to frantically wave it over the sweat dotting her forehead and upper lip. "He had to finish some correspondence."

Jane nodded absently. It wasn't one of Sofia's better excuses for her husband's behavior, but she would never say a word against him, no matter how hard Jane tried to goad her. "How are you feeling?"

"Good. Tired, but good." Sofia laid her hand on her swollen belly, the edges of her lips curving into a soft smile. "I felt the baby kick for the first time last night. I was nervous because I felt my others sooner, but this one kept me up all night to make up for lost time."

This new baby would be Sofia's fourth in four years, which

2

seemed like a punishment as far as Jane was concerned. A wriggling creature that only seemed to scream and defecate seemed like a poor reward for nine months of pregnancy.

"Are you sure you really need to go to this ball?" Jane's brow furrowed as she took in the dark circles beneath her sister-in-law's glassy eyes, the washed-out pallor of her skin, and her labored breaths. "Surely Robert won't force you to go if you tell him you truly aren't feeling well."

Her brother was an unmitigated arse, but she was his *wife*, carrying his *child*. Surely he could find some kindness for her.

Sofia frowned. "I'm not being forced to attend the ball. It's an honor to stand beside him as his wife." Burrowing into the seat, she tipped her head back and closed her eyes. "Besides, it's been years since I've been able to tear you away from your little experiments."

"They're not experiments, they're dissections," Jane grumbled.

Her dissections were crudely performed on an old sheet in the back garden until she was caught and chastised for making a mess. Sourcing bodies was a challenge, but she made do with any small animals she found dead around the grounds.

Sofia shrugged. "It will be good for you to be around the living, and your brother agrees. He thinks you're spending too much time alone."

Jane's eyes narrowed. Robert clearly had some scheme planned, but she couldn't figure out what it was. If she were younger, she would assume he was trying to marry her off, but she was too old to be a commodity in the marriage market at twenty-nine. Not that there had been a single inquiry after she had so successfully chased off her one and only suitor nearly a decade before.

"You know, an audience won't deter me from making a scene." Her words weren't a threat, but a warning.

"Jane, be nice. Robert does everything for you. He buys your books, gives you an allowance, and has always allowed you to continue your intellectual pursuits without asking for anything in return."

Sofia's rehearsed speech made Jane want to scream because her entire existence was dependent on Robert's goodwill. Jane had been born first, and if she were male, she would have been sent to Eton and then Cambridge to learn how to take over their family's coal mines. Even if she had been born a second son, she would have received a good education, so she wouldn't have had to resort to dissecting decomposing foxes.

Robert didn't do those things because he cared for her, but because she was another one of his assets.

"That's not kindness, it's an obligation."

Sofia lifted her head and raised a brow. "Any obligation he has to you is worth far less than what he has given you. You want for nothing; not only have you kept the same quarters for your entire life, but you have a full library, and there's no expectation for you to contribute anything."

Jane huffed and turned her head towards the window. Listening to Sofia speak, it sounded like she was nothing more than a spoiled brat, but the only thing she ever wanted was autonomy.

The front door of their grey stone manor opened, and Robert strolled out in his freshly starched suit, holding the silver-tipped black cane he carried for fashion and twirling his black silk top hat in his other hand. Jane's body stiffened in preparation for the imminent arrival of her brother.

The carriage rocked as Robert got in and threw himself down on the bench next to Sofia. The smell of whiskey wafted from him in waves that made her eyes water. While he was barely tolerable sober, he was a mean drunk who would relish the ability to torture her in such a confined space.

"I didn't believe the footman when he told me you were in the carriage since I didn't hear Miss Mary crying," Robert said with a smirk that made Jane's nostrils flare.

She only made Mary cry once when they strongly disagreed on Jane's hairstyle for her debut, but Robert would never let her live it down.

"I would say that I am happy to prove you wrong, but it has lost some of its shine since it's such a regular occurrence."

"Your overconfidence is staggering."

They were too old to fight like this, but it had been their

dynamic for as long as she could remember. Neither was willing to be the bigger person, so they would be stuck in this cycle until one of them died.

"Whose ball are we attending? No one's told me anything about this event."

"It's at the old Gardner manor, our governess took us there a few times for picnics when we were children." Robert looked at her as if he thought she remembered every home she had visited, but she nodded as if she did, so he continued. "Anyway, Dr. Gardner was cavorting around Europe until his brother died, and now he's returned to share some scientific discovery."

Jane shot up from her slouched position. "What kind of scientific discovery?" Robert shrugged, and annoyance shot through her. "Well, what kind of doctor is he?"

"He's a doctor."

Jane rolled her eyes. Of course, her brother wouldn't know the one detail she cared about.

"I would have agreed without hesitation if you told me the ball was about science."

"I know, but then I wouldn't have gotten to watch you squirm."

God, her brother was beyond insufferable. Sofia sat next to him with her head tilted back and her eyes closed, falling asleep to the familiar tones of the siblings fighting.

"Why are you so keen on this party? You have no interest in science, since I'm fairly confident you can't even spell that word." Jane slapped her knee as if she had an epiphany. "I've got it. Did he invent a new type of distillery?"

"I have no interest in the presentation, but he invited someone I'm quite keen on seeing, and we figured it was as good a place as any to conduct some business."

Robert removed his flask from his inner jacket pocket and took a healthy swig, smiling at her in a way that made her stomach churn. Robert wasn't easy to deal with on his best days, but drinking made him erratic. He never lost his temper in public, but he wasn't afraid to rage at her in private, yelling until his face was red and spittle flew at her. However, Robert became truly dangerous once he became quiet. That was when he truly relished in her punishment.

"What kind of business?"

"And ruin the surprise? You'll find out soon enough."

Jane tried to lean her head back to alleviate some of the weight of her hair, but the feathers poked her scalp, so she sat back up. She wished her brother would send her away. It would be nothing for him to set her up with a small cottage in the middle of nowhere with only her books for company. However, no matter how much she begged, he never agreed.

His excuse was his deathbed promise to their father that he would always take care of Jane, and he was determined to keep his word. Their father had died from a sudden illness when they were nineteen, and their mother had died in childbirth, so the siblings were on their own after that. Robert quit school to take over the business, and they had a ceasefire that lasted until Robert broke it by attempting to marry her off.

Robert's best attempt at landing her a husband had led him to Henry, England's most unremarkable man. His only interest was quail hunting, and he was set to inherit one of the stores in town. In a desperate attempt to make conversation, she had tried talking to him about the best way to complete an autopsy, but he responded that she wouldn't need such knowledge once they had children. They only kissed once because he tasted of porridge. With her back against the wall, she would have done anything to get out of the marriage.

She had tried appealing to Robert, but he wouldn't listen when she told him they weren't suited for one another. In return, he had told her that marriage was a duty she would learn to live with. Jane then asked if he really wanted to eat quail for Christmas dinner for the rest of their lives, but he ignored the question.

Jane had no choice but to create her own plan for freedom, so she seduced one of their footmen and carried out a sloppy affair. He had been a clumsy yet enthusiastic lover, but she made sure all of their trysts were in places where they could be easily found. It took a few weeks, but it paid off when Henry caught them in the parlor with her skirts around her waist and the footman's hand in her bloomers. Jane had put on the performance of her life, begging him to understand her numerous transgressions, but Henry broke off their engagement. She imagined he went on one sad quail hunt before he moved on.

Robert had been beyond furious when he found out. It hadn't been enough for him to fire the footman and run him out of town, but he also banned the male servants from speaking to her, with only their butler, Smythe, exempt from the order.

The cold shoulder hadn't been much of a punishment, but Robert had frozen her allowance and confiscated her pencils so she couldn't work. That alone had been hell, but he then forced her to attend every social event for months, making her live through the whispers about her broken engagement. She had never been popular, but it had turned her into a pariah.

The carriage rolled to a stop, and Jane reached for the door, but Robert knocked her hand away before she reached the handle.

"I just realized something," Robert said with the smell of whiskey thick on his breath. "You might actually enjoy this party."

"Perhaps you should have thought of that before you forced me to come out tonight."

"I remembered Dr. Gardner studied at Cambridge before going to Germany. I believe some of his old professors will be here. Perhaps you'll be able to ask your little questions about the human body."

Jane stilled. She didn't know what Robert wanted from her. Did he want her to beg, or should she act like it was no big deal? The rules to the games he played with her were constantly changing. This particular mood may be new, but it was another entry in the power struggle they had been having their whole lives. Whichever she chose might be the wrong answer simply because he wanted her to be miserable.

"I could make you go home. Send you straight back without ever knowing what was announced here tonight. Or I could leave you in the carriage all night waiting for us."

"You could." Jane looked to Sofia, pleading for support, but her sister-in-law looked down as if this wasn't happening in front of her.

"You should thank me." Robert took another pull from his flask.

"What?" She whispered, unable to follow his logic, but knowing her reaction would determine the course of her evening.

"You should thank me for allowing you to come here tonight." He leaned towards her, resting his forearms on his thighs. From this distance, he looked like hell with bloodshot eyes and ruddy cheeks permanently marred from the drink. He was freshly shaved, but it looked uneven, as if he kept moving his head as his valet shaved him.

"Thank you." Her voice shook, but she did her best to sound sincere instead of scared.

"Is that as good as you can do? Perhaps you don't wish to attend after all."

"I do! I do. Thank you, Robert. It's so good of you to bring me here. Thank you." Jane gave him a shaky smile.

If he wanted gratitude, he would get it. Her pride had been eroded by the need to get away. She would avoid him as best she could at the party and pray all the revelry shook this mood out of him.

Robert stared at her for a few uncomfortable moments before breaking out in a big grin. "See, isn't this better? I like this new attitude in you, sister."

Jane kept smiling and nodded. There was no arguing with a man in this state.

Robert opened the door and stumbled out; the force of his exit rocked Jane back into her seat. The air inside was stale, but it was less imposing now that her brother was gone. Sofia followed Robert without a glance at Jane.

Sticking her head out of the open door, she took a deep breath of the cool night air. Clouds covered the stars, providing a thin mist that would dissipate as the evening progressed. A crowd had gathered waiting for entry, and for once, she was grateful for the safety a group of people provided because her brother hated to make a scene.

"Stay close, I don't want to chase after you all night," Robert hissed.

He attempted to pull her from the carriage, but she evaded his grasp. Robert stomped off muttering under his breath when he realized people were looking, dragging Sofia with him.

Jane held back in the carriage. A footman came over and offered his hand to help her down, but she ignored him. She counted to five before exiting the carriage. Robert would forget about her once he entered the party and had other things to focus on. His attention span was blessedly short.

Jane looked around at the stately grounds. They were lush and green with marigold flowers scattered around the lawn, giving the grounds a pop of gold that was almost a preview of the coming autumn. The placement of the flowers was meant to invoke a field of wildflowers, but Jane knew what careful control attempting to imitate natural chaos looked like. Freshly cut topiaries and wrought-iron lanterns lined the driveway, giving the grounds an ethereal feel.

The house was a three-story Baroque-style manor made of light brown stone that was beginning to show its age after decades of battling the elements. The curtains were open on the first-floor windows with candles illuminating the party inside. The windows on the higher floors were dark, except for one window on the third floor that had a faint orange glow. A large shadowed figure stood in the window, looking down on all of the party guests. Briefly, she wondered who it was before continuing into the ball.

CHAPTER 2

"*Y*ou don't have to stay the whole time. Just come down for the presentation, shake a few hands, and then you can return to your brooding," said Tristan.

Will stood before his bedroom window, watching as people below exited their carriages and entered his home. The lamps were dimmed so no one could see him watching the crowds, but he still wore his cloak in case anyone looked up.

"No," Will said, giving his brother his final answer, but he could tell by his silence that his brother hadn't accepted it.

Tristan had been planning this ball for weeks, but Will never thought it would actually happen. Last year, Tristan tried to get him to attend a medical conference, but backed off when he thoroughly refused. Will figured the same would happen again, but as he watched people trickle into their home, he accepted the ball was happening.

"You can't stay cooped up here. It isn't healthy."

Will huffed. He didn't *want* to be in his bedroom all night. He would much rather be downstairs mingling or playing cards in the cigar smoke haze of the study. The only people he had spoken to in the last year were his brother, their housekeeper, Mrs. Jones, and Morris, the groundskeeper.

It was a lonely existence, but it wasn't as if he had any other choice.

"I walk the grounds almost every night."

"But only in the dead of night to avoid every other living soul. You need to talk to people, you can't hide in the shadows for the rest of your life."

Will whipped around to face Tristan, fists curled at his side. "You have no right to tell me how to live."

"You're not living, you're hiding." Tristan's cheeks were flushed. "I have done everything I can to help you, but you refuse even to try."

"You don't want a life for me, you only want to parade me around the countryside as your greatest achievement." Will trembled with rage as he stepped forward, and Tristan shrank back. Part of him felt guilty for yelling at his brother, but now that he had started, he felt as if he couldn't stop. "You're the only one who cares if this presentation happens; surely your guests won't mind. Nothing you've done has been out of concern for me, but rather for your ego as a scientist."

"I-I didn't do it for the science. You're my brother. I couldn't..." Tristan's big brown eyes were glassy with unshed tears.

Guilt and shame flooded Will because upsetting Tristan was like kicking a dog. He thought telling his brother how he felt would help, but he felt just as empty as he had before.

"All I wanted was to have my brother back," Tristan continued. "I know you're miserable, and no matter how hard I try, I can't seem to fix you. I thought moving here would help because you loved the summers we spent here as children, but you're just as miserable here as you were in Munich. Tell me how to help you, and I'll do it."

His request was on the tip of his tongue, but he couldn't speak it aloud because his desire felt too dark. Loneliness had bonded to him so deeply that he was unsure if it would ever leave him. What he craved more than anything was a companion, someone who could understand the plight of his new life.

"I know you care, and it's not that I'm ungrateful," Will lied, but

11

he couldn't bear to see the hurt in his brother's eyes. "I can't go down there. I can't stand on a stage and face their questions. This is your achievement, but it's my life." He hit his fist against his chest, flinching when he realized which hand he used.

Tristan's eyes softened, and Will knew he couldn't remain angry with his brother. Not only was he a brilliant doctor and scientist, but he also had the biggest heart of anyone he had ever known. Even though Tristan's actions were misguided, they had come from a pure place.

"We don't have to do the presentation. You can come downstairs and enjoy the party."

"I can't." Will's shoulders slumped, a wave of sorrow hitting him so hard he almost bowed over. "I don't think it will ever be as it was again. Not with how I look or what's happened."

"We don't have to introduce you as my brother. You can even wear the cloak."

"No." Will turned back to the window. "I don't belong down there anymore."

"Come down if you change your mind. You'll always be welcome."

Will felt Tristan waiting for Will to tell him he changed his mind, but after a long silence, he heard the click of the door behind him, leaving him alone again.

Coming to their childhood summer home had helped at first, but the house was filled with the ghosts of their youth. Memories of his palms clumsily perched atop his mother's elegant hands as she taught him to play the piano in the ballroom and the dull thud of wooden swords as he and Tristan played pirates with their father. Their parents had died in a shipwreck over a decade ago, but being there had reopened those old wounds.

His great-grandfather built the estate after securing a royal shipping contract, but the grounds made the place special. The hedge maze, which was the longest in Yorkshire, was the crown jewel of the estate. Made of thousands of English yew trees, it had become an attraction in the area and was undoubtedly the

12

groundskeeper's passion. But the rose garden had always been Will's favorite.

The roses, which had once been plentiful and used in floral displays in the house, were now sparse, so Will had gone to the library to read every book on roses and gardening so he could revive his beloved garden. Rose season was coming to an end, but his beautiful white blooms were hanging on even with the rapidly dropping temperature.

The door to Will's room opened softly, and without turning, he knew it was Mrs. Jones arriving with his dinner. Tristan would have insisted that Will go downstairs to eat, but Mrs. Jones understood he couldn't face anyone down there.

"How does it look out there?" Mrs. Jones asked.

Will turned to see the housekeeper moving dishes from the silver tray to the small birch desk that doubled as his dining table. The woman barely came up to his chest, but she was a force to be reckoned with. Mrs. Jones had been with their family since before he was born, and though her face was now lined and the hair beneath her cap was entirely grey, she still gave Will the same withering glare whenever he tracked dirt into the house.

"Fine." Will shrugged. "It doesn't look to be very interesting."

"It seems to have captured your interest at least."

Will wasn't going to dignify that comment with a response. He was starved for entertainment, and people-watching helped pass the time. Besides, these were guests in his home. No one could blame him for being curious.

"I am on your side," Mrs. Jones continued, "But all of this brooding can't be healthy."

Will snorted. "You don't need to worry about my health."

"Then do it for mine since I'll worry myself to an early grave if you can't find happiness again."

"Don't let Tristan hear you say that or he will interfere." Will stepped away from the window and sat at the table. "Shouldn't you return downstairs? I'm sure you have a lot to do."

"Tristan hired attendants, so I'm where I'm needed."

Will was stuck between being touched that she cared and

annoyed that she thought he needed supervision. However, if Mrs. Jones insisted on babying him, he had an idea how she could be useful.

"You know I am terribly concerned about the roses," Will said as he cut into the roasted aubergine.

"Really, how so?"

"Well, there are so many people here, and the roses are in such great form, I'm worried people will get carried away while admiring them."

"Oh, we wouldn't want anyone to get carried away around the roses."

He did not appreciate the sarcasm in her tone, but he continued undeterred. "Precisely, so if you could go down and make sure the roses are safe, I would appreciate it."

"William, if you want to make sure the roses are being properly admired, you can do so yourself."

Will scowled. "You're sounding awfully like Tristan for someone who is supposed to be on my side."

"My problem is with his method, not the desired result."

"Well, I think you're in cahoots, and it isn't fair." Will took another bite of his dinner. It was difficult to be upset with someone while eating food they've prepared for you.

"I'll leave you to your brooding for now, but I'll watch the bells in case you need anything," Mrs. Jones said before leaving him to his meal.

He really *was* worried about his roses. Images of people trampling them while looking for hints to the hedge maze haunted him as he speared a fingerling potato on his fork. The rose garden wasn't visible on this side of the house, but he should be able to see at least part of the garden from the guest rooms in the opposite wing, so he would know if anyone massacred his roses.

Creeping towards the door, he put his ear against the lacquered wood. Even through the padding of his wool cloak, his hearing was good enough to tell if anyone was in the hall. The stairs were roped off, but he wouldn't put it past nosy people to explore. When there was no noise beyond the distant chatter of the party, he opened the door and slipped into the hall.

Careful to avoid the squeaky floorboards, he kept his steps on the plush carpet to muffle any sound. At this point, he was less concerned about a wandering guest than he was about Tristan or Mrs. Jones catching him. It reminded him of his childhood, when he and Tristan would play "espionage," in which they silently moved through the shadows to complete secret missions. He could almost hear his mother's musical laughter as she said she was lucky to be blessed with two boys whose favorite game was to be quiet and out of sight for hours.

The bedroom he chose likely hadn't been used in at least a decade, but it looked pristine with a freshly made bed and crisp white curtains that were tied back so he could see the glow of the outdoor lamps through the windows. Will jumped when he saw a black shadow in the corner, but relaxed when he realized it was his reflection in the mirror. The mirror was a surprise since he thought he had covered all of them with sheets shortly after he arrived.

Avoiding his reflection, Will looked out the window at the garden below. Most of the guests were indoors, but a group of young men stood before the hedge maze, as if daring one another to go inside. A giggling group of women stood not far from them, and he knew their presence would goad at least one young man to brave the maze.

A pair of young lovers walking through his rose garden caught his attention. They moved slowly, completely enraptured with one another as a chaperone trailed far behind. The woman stopped to smell the flowers, careful to keep a respectful distance from the delicate blooms. Will gave her a sharp nod of approval, even though they couldn't see him. She motioned for her beau to smell them as well, and he humored her with a quick sniff before looking around and plucking a rose from its bush.

White-hot rage flashed through him. The flower murderer handed it to his companion, and Will could faintly hear her giggle and exclaim that she couldn't believe he did that. He responded that a beautiful woman deserved a beautiful flower.

Will could almost feel them forgetting about the flower as they walked back to the house. A flower had been killed for a story that would become a footnote in their lives. It could have lived the last few weeks of its life on the bush in dignity, but instead, it was crushed in their hands. Will turned from the window, unwilling to see the rest of the sad scene.

Once, he would have picked the flower to get a pretty girl to smile at him. Now he couldn't stomach it because he knew how the flower felt when he awoke on the cold slab in Tristan's laboratory with borrowed parts and the harsh knowledge that he would never have to fear death ever again. His brother had acted like it was a miracle, but Will knew a plucked flower could never return to the bush.

CHAPTER 3

*S*omehow, the inside of the grand home was even more impressive. A combination of tall candelabras and gas lamp sconces provided soft light in the entry. Never before had she seen such modern lighting in a private home, but it made sense for a man of science. A coachman ushered her into the main hall, and her breath caught at the beauty of the room.

The floor was black-and-white marble that looked like a chessboard. A long banquet table set with food and drinks sat on a platform in the back of the room, where a throne would have stood in an earlier age.

Most of the room was allocated for dancing, but was currently filled with small groups conversing. Musicians played a familiar tune from a stage that also held a podium prepared for the doctor's presentation. Presiding over the entire room was a glass chandelier that shimmered above like an artificial sun.

Scanning the room looking for Robert and Sofia, Jane's shoulders relaxed when she didn't see them. Now she had a chance to enjoy the presentation without being sniped at. Most of the attendees were familiar, but the new faces must have been the visiting scientists.

It thrilled her that there were so many scientists here for her to question, and she hoped to get at least one introduction. She wasn't the type of woman who wished to be asked to dance, but she did wish someone would ask about her dissection methods.

"Jane Montgomery, is that you?"

Jane turned to see none other than Eleanor Campbell, the younger sister of one of Robert's friends. They were playmates as children because they shared a deep love of reading, but they had lost touch over the years.

"Eleanor, how nice to see you."

Eleanor grabbed her in a tight embrace, and Jane stiffened in surprise. She couldn't remember the last time she had been embraced.

"I haven't seen you in so long that I'm surprised anything could pull you away from your library."

"It's not by choice." Jane frowned as she realized it had been more than a year since she had seen Eleanor. "Although, if you had such a library, you wouldn't want to leave it either," Jane said, thinking longingly of the library her father had built for her in one of their guest rooms. Robert had always been jealous of how their father doted on her, and he still resented the existence of her library. "I am eager for the scientific presentation, so this evening won't be a complete waste of time."

"You picked a good one to attend, at least. Have you met Dr. Gardner? He's quite handsome and single." Eleanor took Jane's arm, dragging her around the room as she searched for their elusive host.

"It doesn't matter to me if he's handsome or single."

Jane was far past the age of a spinster, but people still wanted to marry her off. Eleanor was the only one who could get away with this because of their storied friendship and because Jane wanted to meet the doctor anyway.

"I do admire you for holding out for a husband for so long. You're too smart to marry just anyone, but I think he would be a good match since you're both so scholarly and tall."

"Height is the most desired trait for marriage after all."

"Good, keep being funny. I think Dr. Gardner would appreciate that in a wife."

Jane ripped her arm from Eleanor's iron grasp. If she were to meet Dr. Gardner, she wanted to do so as an academic rather than a prized broodmare.

"What's wrong?" Eleanor frowned, making Jane pause because it was the first time she had ever seen her make such an expression.

Eleanor was the type of person who thought everyone wanted her version of happiness. She married a sailor in the Royal Navy shortly after she came of age, and they had a single son a few years later. The only bit of Eleanor's life Jane envied was the fact that with her husband being frequently deployed and her son off at boarding school, she was often completely alone in her house, but Jane still didn't think the trade-off of marriage and motherhood was worth it.

"I'm not holding out for a husband, I don't plan on ever marrying."

"Come on, Janie, this would be a great match. He went to Cambridge so you would have the smartest babies. Oh! Maybe he'd let you go to Cambridge."

"What do you mean by 'let me go to Cambridge'?" Jane dodged Eleanor's attempt to get her back in her grasp.

"Ooh, I happen to know something about Cambridge that you don't. I'll cherish the moment."

"Eleanor," Jane said, snapping her fingers to get Eleanor back on track. The woman was so easily distracted there was a chance she would forget what she was going to say in favor of a new conversation.

"Cambridge is opening to women this fall."

"What?" Jane's heart skipped a beat.

For the first time, her lifelong dream of studying at Cambridge was *possible*, and there was nothing she wouldn't do to get there.

"They aren't letting women earn diplomas yet, but they're letting us take classes and use the library at the very least."

A degree would be lovely, but at the end of the day, it was a pretty piece of paper. The knowledge was what truly mattered.

Hell, she mainly wanted to go to Cambridge so she could access that big, beautiful library.

"Do you think Dr. Gardner could help with my admission?" Jane dragged Eleanor around the ballroom, searching for their host in earnest. She didn't know what he looked like, but she would approach every single-looking tall man until she found him.

"I should have led with Cambridge if I knew you would be this excited."

"I won't marry him, but I will use any connections I can to get into that school."

Eleanor stopped and turned toward her. Jane braced for the big speech she felt was coming.

"Janie, I don't want to force you to do this. I only thought you two would be a good match. If you want to go to Cambridge, ask Robert to write a letter for you. He's an alumnus, so I'm sure he has influence."

Hypothetically, it could be that easy, but chances were that her brother would say no to spite her.

"I won't marry anyone, but since I do wish to attend Cambridge, the more references I have, the better my chances." Jane gave her a soft smile that widened when Eleanor beamed at her in return. They had been estranged for so long that it was nice Eleanor had thought of her. "Thank you for bringing this to my attention."

The sentiment felt awkward, but she felt like she had to say something.

"We'll get you his reference. And if you happen to fall in love along the way, it only makes for a better story!"

It was a testament to how much she wanted to go to Cambridge that Jane held her tongue and let Eleanor lead her to the stage when a tall man with dark hair walked onto it, signaling for the band to stop. A hush fell over the crowd as everyone turned to watch the man take his place at the podium.

"Good evening, and thank you all for coming. Some of you have traveled a long way, while others are local, but I appreciate your presence all the same." The man paused to clear his throat, and even without an introduction, she knew this must be Dr. Gardner.

Jane could see why Eleanor was so desperate to marry her off to him. He was tall, with curly brown hair that fell over his forehead despite how much he tried to push it back. He had big brown eyes and alabaster skin that spoke to how much time he spent indoors. His voice was sure, but soft. He was the type of man most women would love to be courted by, but Jane could tell that only a few harsh words from her would make him cry, so he held no interest for her.

"I know you were expecting a presentation on a scientific discovery I've recently made, but unfortunately, there has been a setback and the presentation will not be happening this evening. This is a disappointment, but setbacks are common in the pursuit of knowledge. I will continue working on this difficult yet important endeavor, and I hope to have you all back here when I am finally ready to share my findings. In the meantime, please enjoy the food, and we'll get the dancing started. There's no reason why the party cannot continue."

Dr. Gardner's speech was met with polite applause as he left the stage, while the musicians returned to play a waltz that would be good for dancing.

Jane sighed. While she had been looking forward to the presentation, it wasn't difficult for her to put her disappointment aside since she had only learned of it a short time ago. Anyway, Cambridge was her focus now.

"It's a shame the experiment wasn't ready after all. I heard some researchers from London had traveled here for it," said Eleanor.

"He's a victim of hubris. Can you imagine not being sure before throwing a whole ball announcing a discovery?"

Jane would certainly never do such a thing if she had a discovery to share.

Eleanor laughed. "I would expect nothing less than total certainty from you."

Eleanor led them through the crowd until they reached Dr. Gardner, who was speaking to an older man in a top hat and monocle.

"You always were too excited to show off your results, my boy.

You can't bend the laws of nature to your whim," the man laughed. He patted Dr. Gardner on the back before moving on.

Eleanor practically threw Jane at the embarrassed man. Jane wanted the recommendation more than anything, but she wasn't sure if standing there while he was being scolded like a child was the best way to get it.

"Dr. Gardner, I'm so sorry we won't get to see your presentation today. I'm sure it would have been fantastic," Eleanor said.

"Thank you, Mrs. Campbell. I was hoping for a last-minute miracle, but science always moves at its own pace." He dipped his head in acknowledgment.

"You know, my dear friend *Miss* Montgomery recently said the very same thing. She's a fellow scientist."

Jane's face heated at the shamelessness of Eleanor's introduction, praying the poor doctor wouldn't get the wrong idea about what she wanted. Dr. Gardner turned toward her, bowed, and offered a polite smile.

"Miss Montgomery, it's always a pleasure to meet a fellow scientist. I'm sorry to disappoint you, but I'm sure you understand better than most."

"Of course, but it's a shame you went through all this trouble without anything to show for it."

It was a daring thing to say to someone before asking for a favor, but she couldn't help herself. It wasn't as if she was going to start watching what she said now. Luckily, Dr. Gardner laughed.

"You're right. I should have been sure, but I was too excited to share. I have had many successes and valuable lessons, but now I stand before you having learned to be less arrogant with my success."

"The important thing is that we have the opportunity to return. This is such a big house to be holed up in all alone," Eleanor said.

Jane squeezed her hand in warning, but Eleanor didn't wince.

Dr. Gardner, on the other hand, wore a look of pure panic, with wide, searching eyes darting between the two of them. She recognized his expression as one she frequently had at parties like these.

Never before had she considered the struggles of unmarried men, but she expected they faced similar issues.

Though she didn't have too much sympathy for him because the marriage he wanted to avoid would be a good deal for him, but a prison for her. Still, she recognized his panicked look, so she threw out the life preserver no one ever sent her.

"Mrs. Campbell told me you attended Cambridge. It's always been my dream to study there."

"Yes, that was the first university I attended," he said, flashing her a grateful look. "No matter where I go, Cambridge will always feel like home."

"They recently announced they will be accepting women as students," Eleanor said, patting Jane on the arm. "Miss Montgomery is the most intelligent person I've ever met, and I can't imagine anyone who deserves to study there more. I know you must have some influence as such a distinguished alumnus."

Jane's cheeks burned red. No one had ever been so effusive with praise for her, and she didn't know how to take it. Part of her wanted to deny it, as she had been taught that was the modest thing to do, but even though it was embarrassing, she didn't disagree with Eleanor.

"If you could write me a recommendation, I would be forever in your debt." Asking for something so plainly was beyond bold, but if Eleanor believed in her, then she could believe in herself.

As Dr. Gardner looked between the two women with hesitation, Jane's heart sank. Of course, this was when he refused her because there was no reason for him to help her. They were strangers, and she didn't even know if he supported a woman's right to education. At any moment, he would double over in laughter before calling his friends over so they could share in the joke as well. She was a fool to have hoped this would work for even a moment.

Dr. Gardner's brow creased. "I would be more than happy to write a recommendation, but a letter of support from your family is what you would need most if you're unmarried."

"Of course." Jane pasted a smile on her face even as her stomach sank because the true challenge would be getting Robert to agree.

"But once I secure my family's permission, will you write one? I know you don't know me or my work, so I can send over some of my dissection notes if you'd like."

"You perform dissections?" The way the doctor looked at her—not the way she was used to men looking at her, but with genuine interest in her work—thrilled her.

"Not as many as I would like, but mainly foxes and badgers. I'm not picky about my subjects since it's dependent on what dead creatures I can find around the property." Jane's cheeks heated when she realized the man before her had likely never needed to hunt outside for his subjects. "I'm sure it sounds silly to you to source subjects in such a way, but even though it's inconsistent, I've still managed plenty."

"Ah, Miss Montgomery, you'll find that no matter what scale you work on, the sourcing of the bodies is always the most difficult part."

"Which is such a waste. It would be an honor to donate my body to science."

"Your brother told you not to run off for a reason. I've been trying to chase you all over."

Jane stiffened when she heard the familiar voice behind her and turned to see Sofia with an impatient look.

"Your brother wants to see you in the study," Sofia continued.

"Mrs. Montgomery, it's so nice to see you again," Eleanor said politely, but Jane could see the tension in her form. "I had the pleasure of introducing Miss Montgomery to our gracious host, Dr. Gardner."

"I'm pleased to make your acquaintance, Mrs. Montgomery. I'm so happy your family was able to attend my party," the doctor said with another slight bow.

Sofia nodded, but didn't look away from Jane. "You've kept your brother waiting long enough. Come along now."

"I'm still speaking with Dr. Gardner and Mrs. Campbell," Jane said through gritted teeth. She wasn't a dog who would come when called.

Sofia huffed. "You can find them later, but it's rude to keep your family waiting for so long." She grabbed Jane's arm and led her away before she even had a chance to say goodbye.

"That was rude," Jane hissed.

"We told you not to wander. Why can't you ever listen?" Sofia squeezed Jane's bicep, and she fought hard to hide the wince because she didn't want to give Sofia a reaction.

Jane was about to throw out another retort when she stopped herself. She needed something from Robert, and if she upset Sofia, he was sure to say no when she asked about Cambridge.

Sofia dragged her into the study where her brother sat in an oversized brown armchair speaking with a man she had never seen before. The putrid aroma of their cigars swirled around them as Robert threw his head back in a booming laugh that drew sharp glares from other men in the room.

The women stopped just before the men's chairs and waited until Robert finally stopped laughing and looked up at Jane with an inscrutable gleam in his eye.

"I see the ladies have finally found us," the unknown man said, breaking the silence.

Even seated, the man looked to be shorter than her. His light brown hair was carefully tousled in a rakish style, but Jane thought it was a pathetic attempt to cling to youth when paired with the harsh lines of his face and curls that were both greying and thinning. His pinched face had a small nose and a weak chin, but his icy blue eyes were his most striking feature, despite their lack of emotion.

"I was told you summoned me," Jane said, unable to fully play nice with her brother when it was clear he had a plan for her brewing.

"I told you she was tenacious," Robert said, dipping his gaze from her.

Coward.

"I like it better when they're spirited," the man responded as if she weren't there. "Our deal can move forward, Montgomery."

Jane's stomach roiled at the man's tone and leering gaze as he ran those cold eyes down her body, stopping on both her bosom

25

and hips for too long. *This* was how men usually looked at her, which was why it was so refreshing to have Dr. Gardner look at her as if her mind mattered. She fought the urge to stomp on his foot and tell him the only type of man she liked was a dead one because they didn't leer, but that would give Robert an aneurysm, and he couldn't give her permission to attend Cambridge if he was dead.

"Can you hurry up and let me know what you want from me?"

"Careful, dear sister, you don't want to lose your temper with Lord Percy here. That wouldn't be a very good first impression." Robert smirked, taking a generous swig from his brandy snifter. As always, her misery was nothing more than a game to him.

"I can tell by the gleam in her eye that my presence would do nothing to dissuade her, so I will do us all the favor of removing myself so we can both make a better impression later." Percy stood before her, grabbing her hand and placing a wet kiss on her knuckles that she already itched to wipe away. "It was a pleasure briefly meeting you, Miss Montgomery. I'm sure we'll have our proper introduction sometime soon." He sauntered off as she wiped her wet hand on the silk brocade of her dress.

"You won't embarrass me like that in front of him again, are we clear?" Robert was so red she worried he might have a stroke after all.

"Why should I care about what one of your titled friends thinks about me?"

Heart pounding in her chest, she balled her hands into fists to keep them from trembling.

"I can't think of any reason in particular, but you never know what the future holds."

"I'll take that under advisement." She would not. "I was in the middle of an important conversation when your wife dragged me away. What do you want?"

Robert frowned. "What kind of conversation?"

"It was about my future."

"Is there a cause for concern?" Robert asked with a raised brow, turning to Sofia.

"No, I watched her for a bit, and Mrs. Campbell was with her the whole time. They spoke with Dr. Gardner, but he didn't appear interested in her."

Robert relaxed and took another drink. "Then please enlighten me on what kind of conversation you had about your future."

Jane took a deep breath and steeled her spine. "Cambridge is admitting women to study this year, and I wish to attend. Dr. Gardner was helping me with some questions I had about admissions."

"You wish to attend Cambridge?"

"Yes, and I just need your permission." Her voice was frenzied, but she couldn't hide her desperation. "This would be perfect—I could study and be out of your hair for most of the year. We could all get what we want."

"What do you think I want?"

Her brow furrowed. "You want me out of the house."

"You're so confident that I don't want you around."

Of course she was. Everything she did annoyed him. "Are you saying I'm wrong?"

"No," he snorted. "But I'm not convinced Cambridge is the answer to our prayers."

His answer wasn't a surprise, but hope still deflated from her as disappointment sank in. This was when Robert would expect her to roll over, but she wouldn't this time.

"Why isn't Cambridge the answer? What's so wrong with me going to school?"

"Besides the fact that you would be across the country getting up to God only knows what, my other question is, why do you even need a degree?"

"Well, it wouldn't be for a degree, just attending classes."

"So what is the purpose of attending? You can read books at home."

"Because there is still a lot of value in attending lectures, socratic discussions, and being amongst like-minded people."

"What an optimistic vision of university life. I cannot imagine why you would want to waste your time there when you won't have anything to show for it."

"The degree doesn't mean anything to me." It did bother her that she wouldn't be allowed to sit for exams or earn a degree, but she wouldn't waste an opportunity to get a foot in the door. "The pursuit of knowledge is what matters to me."

"My answer is still no."

"Why?" She was careful to keep her temper under control, even as her frustration rose because making a scene would ensure Robert never changed his mind.

"I don't think it's a good idea to have you so far from home all alone."

"Then hire a companion to go with me."

"It's still not appropriate," Sofia said. "Think of your niece. It would be a blight upon her reputation to have an aunt with that kind of education."

"Please, she isn't even three. By the time her reputation is important, it could very well be celebrated for women to be educated."

In the nearly thirty years of Jane's life, she had seen the attitude towards women's education change drastically. As a girl, she had a governess to tutor her while Robert went to school, but her niece would go to a schoolhouse.

"My answer is still no."

"But—"

"No," Robert interrupted. "I don't care about a single argument you have. I don't care if it makes perfect sense, and I agree with it. Even if God himself threatened to strike me down, I still wouldn't let you go to Cambridge."

Her lower lip trembled as tears gathered in her eyes, not from sorrow or fear, but from pure, unadulterated anger. Never before had she felt such rage flowing through her. Her hands shook with the urge to hit him, but the tears were coming as they always did when she was angry. She had to get out of there before the tears started to fall because she wouldn't give Robert the satisfaction of watching her cry.

Jane barreled out of the study at just beneath a run because running would draw unwanted attention. Briskly making her way across the dance floor, she deftly dodged a pair of lovesick fools too consumed with gazing into one another's eyes to watch where they danced. The music's strings turned shrill, making her head throb. The people and the music were too much when she needed somewhere quiet to regroup, but she was in a strange place and didn't know where to go.

On the other side of the ballroom, she saw a dark hallway with a rope in front of it. Since it seemed to be off-limits, she headed straight for it, not caring that she had to push through the crowd to get there. Some of the people she pushed tried to rebuke her rudeness, but she ignored them as she fought back the tears that burned like acid.

The dark hallway was only lit by the residual light from the ballroom, but it didn't matter since she could barely see through her tears. She grabbed the handle of the first door-shaped blob she saw, and was relieved when it wasn't locked.

A sob escaped her as soon as the heavy door clicked shut behind her and she was finally, blessedly alone. Her eyes adjusted to the darker environment, but a lit candle on a desk by the fireplace provided enough light for her to realize where she was and let out a brief, humorless laugh. Of course, in the hour of her greatest need, the universe would steer her towards a library. No matter what happened to her, a library would bring her what she needed most.

CHAPTER 4

*T*he faint echo of strings floated up to the perch on the third floor where Will still stood vigil over his garden like a stone gargoyle ravaged by the elements. He had pulled up a chair to the window where he rested his folded arms on the windowsill. The thick hood of his cloak blocked his vision, so he pulled it back until it rested on his hairline. His forehead rested on the cool glass as he watched the figures below, humming along to the familiar tune.

He missed going to the symphony. Once, he had box seats in London, but that was another lifetime, one that now felt like the remnants of a dream. If Tristan had truly wanted to draw him down to the ball, he should have led with the offer of music. A program of his favorite songs was far more tempting than being poked and prodded for the enjoyment of scientists, but luckily for him, his brother could think of nothing more rewarding than the pursuit of science.

If Mrs. Jones or Tristan asked, he would deny it, but watching over his garden was boring. Very few people wandered over to look at the roses, which annoyed him because it was a feat to have so many blooms this late in the season.

If the attendees hadn't gone outside, then they likely weren't wandering through the house either. It would be an act of sheer lunacy for him to join the party downstairs, but he could get a little closer to hear the music better. Watching the musicians play held little interest for him, but he couldn't feel the emotion of the piece from such a distance.

This house had once been a vague childhood memory, but over the last few months, he had catalogued every inch of this place. He knew all the hidden passageways and servant entrances, so he could pass through the halls undetected. It would only be for a few songs until he returned to the comfortable safety of his room, but that would be more than enough.

As he moved through the guest room, he caught sight of himself in the mirror, but this time with his hood pushed back, seeing his face for the first time in months. His appearance was just as wretched as the last time he had looked, but sick fascination drew him towards the mirror.

It was peculiar to look at your face, but feel like a stranger was looking back. The shape of his big head remained the same, with his square jaw, high cheekbones, and broad forehead. Death had carved away the baby fat that had clung to Will even into his thirties, so now his features looked severe. Tristan had rebuilt his nose from memory, and while he had done a pretty good job, it was a little too straight, too perfect to belong on his face.

Scars marred his face—and the rest of his body—in places where Tristan had given him skin from another cadaver. He never asked how many bodies Tristan had taken from, but he feared it was at least a dozen based on his different parts and scars. His right ear was a stranger's with a smaller lobe and a sharper tip than his left, but most annoyingly, Tristan had sewn the ear on a little too low, so his ears were mismatched in a few ways. His left hand was another's, and he wasn't quite sure which toes were his, since he couldn't remember whether his second toe had always been longer than his big toe.

Worst of all, his light brown eyes—which a former lover once said reminded her of toffee—were now an unnatural yellow that seemed to glow in the dark as though warning others of his wrongness. He had begged Tristan to fix them, but no matter what his brother tried, he couldn't seem to return his eyes to their natural color.

His reflection was a reminder of how he no longer belonged amongst the people below, but he drew his hood to hide his face away and began his journey downstairs to soak in the music for a few minutes of normalcy.

Moving aside a crudely constructed tapestry of Richard the Lionheart's coronation, he opened an old door and descended the hidden staircase. His gloved hand guided him along the wall as he walked down the old, uneven stone steps. Several such staircases were scattered throughout the house, which had proved to be quite valuable when he wanted to move through the house undetected.

The staircase ended at the library, where another door was hidden behind a tapestry of a cherry orchard. It was his favorite because the embroidered birds looked like apples with twigs sticking out of their sides, instead of any bird he had ever seen.

While the garden was his favorite place, the library was a close second. With its high ceilings, rows of dark cherry bookcases, and plush green velvet armchairs in front of the fireplace, it was the perfect place to read on a rainy day.

Walking to his liquor cabinet, he was grateful the good brandy hadn't been commandeered for the ball, so he gave himself a heavy pour before settling into his favorite chair. The room's acoustics muffled the music, but it was a marked improvement over the third floor. Closing his eyes, he imagined what it would be like if he were attending the ball.

As a host, he would be obligated to mingle with the guests to make sure everyone was having a good time, whether they were dancing or gambling away their annuities at the card table. Once he would have resented being forced to dance with single young women to appease their overeager mothers, but now he ached for the chance to have a woman in his arms again.

It felt crude to admit, but he missed women. As a tall man in possession of a good fortune, he had never wanted for company, though he had been careful to ensure his companions didn't expect much from him because he wasn't built for commitment. He missed the stolen kisses, the caress of soft skin, and the feeling of silken tresses as he removed the pins from a woman's hair.

The amber liquid sloshed around the glass as he gently swayed in time with the Viennese waltz that played. The drink was mainly for show as his body metabolized the alcohol too quickly for him to get drunk, but he still liked the burn of the brandy.

He supposed it was lucky he had never fallen in love because he never would have wanted to condemn someone to see what he had become. Not only had he been brought back with the visage of a monster, but he was cursed to remain like this *forever*. Experimentation proved that his new form was immune to disease and could heal itself from any injury, including the normal ravaging of time. Even worse would be having to watch someone he loved wither and die as he remained the same.

You wouldn't have to watch her die if she were already dead. Like you.

He banished that cruel thought from his head almost as soon as it reared its ugly voice again. The idea first crossed his mind months ago, and while it horrified him, it wouldn't leave him. He was ashamed at how close he had been to mentioning it to Tristan tonight. The one saving grace from his twisted desire was that Tristan didn't have the fortitude for murder, but he didn't want to tempt fate. Will certainly had too much respect for life to create death.

The heavy door rattled, shaking him from his spiraling thoughts. He had meant to check that the door was locked when he came in, but was distracted by his self-pity.

His eyes darted around the room, looking for a place to hide. There wasn't enough time for him to get back to the stairs, so he settled for hiding behind a bookcase, crouching behind the books like they were a shield. He prayed it was a harmless snoop who would move on when they saw it was an ordinary library.

The door clicked shut, and his body stiffened when he heard someone move through the room, but relaxed when he heard the rustle of skirts and a feminine sob. Likely, the poor young woman had been rebuffed by a suitor and needed a quiet place to cry for a moment.

The woman let out a heart-wrenching sob that caused him to rub his own chest. He had felt a similar grief after he woke up in his brother's laboratory. Peering around the corner of the bookcase, he wanted to see the woman if only to give a face to the pain.

Her back was to him, and even with her shoulders hunched, he could tell she was tall with chestnut brown hair that had been curled and shaped in such a way that his head hurt in sympathy. Her green silk dress had gold detailing that glittered in the candlelight.

The woman made a sharp sound between a laugh and a sob, and guilt gnawed at him. This room may be off-limits to the party, but she clearly needed a moment to herself. Will had gotten to listen to some music, so now he would be a gentleman and give her the privacy she needed. Though it was a shame his brandy was collateral damage to his chivalry.

Getting to the tapestry was risky, but he could make it as long as she didn't turn. The hidden door was quiet, having been built for discretion. With a final glance at the crying woman, he slowly unfurled from his crouched position, grateful his knees no longer clicked.

Fate had never been kind to him, and he didn't know why he had expected it to start now. A dull thunk sounded throughout the room after his damned cloak unfurled, hitting the edge of the bookcase. Will flinched, reflexively grabbing his cloak even though it was too late.

"Who's there?" She called out with a scratchy voice, but he could hear the strong thread of anger.

Will knew his only option was to make a mad dash for the hidden staircase. His long legs could get him there in a few strides, and even if the woman saw him go through the door, chances were slim that she would follow him, as she was the one trespassing. Heart pounding, he remained frozen even though his mind yelled for him to run.

"Make yourself known, or I will scream that I've been attacked."

Of course, she wasn't going to let this go. Will ground his teeth. *He* wasn't trespassing.

"I was alone until a few moments ago, so it appears I am the one who was disturbed." His hands shook, but his voice was steady as he spoke to his first stranger in well over a year.

"A gentleman would have made himself known the moment a lady entered the room."

"A lady wouldn't have gone into a restricted room."

"How was I supposed to know this was off-limits?"

"Perhaps the rope you jumped had been a clue."

An angry huff sounded from the other side of the bookcase. He couldn't believe the gall of this woman.

"Fine. We'll keep each other's indiscretions a secret then," she said haughtily.

Will's lips twitched; he couldn't help but be charmed by his adversary. It was a shame he didn't know what she looked like. The low light meant she wouldn't be able to see much, but it was more than enough for him to be able to see her. Taking a deep breath, he stepped away from the bookshelf into the aisle.

The woman turned towards him, her shoulders drawing back until she was at her full height. He had been correct that she was tall, yet not quite as tall as he was. His breath caught as he took in her appearance. Her luminous skin shone like moonlight, and tear tracks shimmered over rosy cheeks before ending at her delicate pink mouth. A fierce scowl stitched her brows together, creating a shade over her eyes so he couldn't tell their color in the low light.

"The way I see it," he said, stepping forward. "Is that I have not committed any indiscretions because I am allowed to be here while you are not."

"No one could have expected that flimsy rope to really keep anyone out." Her jaw set in a hard line as her brow arched. "Besides, the door was unlocked, and everyone knows an unlocked door is as good as an invitation."

A retort was on the tip of his tongue when she sniffed, proof her tears hadn't been entirely vanquished. On instinct, he grabbed the handkerchief in his pocket and stepped forward before he could think about it.

Fear flashed in her eyes as she staggered back. "Don't come any closer."

Will froze with the handkerchief in his outstretched hand. While she couldn't see his face, he was a large, cloaked figure lurking in a dark room, so it wasn't a surprise that he made her nervous.

Slinking back felt cowardly, but since she could still use the handkerchief, he balled it up and tossed it to her. Cotton wasn't meant for flight, so it didn't get very far before it floated to the floor between them.

"For your tears." He gave her an exaggerated bow to break the tension. Her scowl deepened before she scurried forward to pick up the handkerchief, careful to keep her eyes on him the whole time.

"Why are you hiding in the dark? It's quite unsettling," she said as she dabbed at her eyes.

"I'm not one for parties, but I wanted to enjoy the music for a few minutes."

"Dressed like a shadow?"

"It's comfortable."

"How do I know you're not a thief and I wasn't the one to catch you instead?"

Her tears had been wiped away, but she kept the handkerchief, folding it carefully as she spoke.

"There's not much in here besides some dusty, old books."

The brandy was likely the most expensive item in the room, but he wasn't about to give her any ideas.

"I've found books to be amongst the most valuable things in the world."

"You haven't had a chance to explore the collection. There are at least three books on barley."

"I'm not sure three books are enough for such an elusive grass."

"I have a rare bookseller in London searching for a fourth, but he's come up empty so far."

36

The woman snorted, shaking her head, but he could see she was fighting a smile, and it warmed something inside of him. He had forgotten how good it felt to just *be* with someone.

"I'll believe you're not a book thief, so why are you hidden away in here?"

His first reaction was to snap that it wasn't her business, but he recognized she had already been vulnerable, so he swallowed his pride. "I'm not comfortable in crowds."

It was an incomplete truth, but it was the truth nonetheless.

"Perhaps if you dressed friendlier, you would have an easier time."

"I'll take that under advisement." Even before he died, he detested talking about himself, but she was a mystery he wanted to unravel. "You still haven't told me what brought you back here."

Shrugging, she turned her attention to the books, tilting her head as she read the titles on the spines.

"Typically, I'm not a fan of crowds either, but my brother forced me to attend. We had a bit of a fight." She sighed before turning her head so he could no longer see her face. "That must sound silly, but I just needed a moment."

A shot of anger flickered through him as he imagined the cruelty that inspired such tears. "He didn't hurt you, did he?"

Will would make an appearance at the ball after all if her brother had laid a finger on her.

"No, it was nothing like that. He made it clear that my attendance wasn't optional, and I didn't want to have to hear about it for weeks. He even made his heavily pregnant wife come tonight."

"He made her break her seclusion for this?" Will frowned. It was highly unusual for pregnant women to be out socially. Many took the time to rest at home, and he had never heard of a husband forcing his pregnant wife to attend a social event. "Is he a doctor or scientist?"

She snorted before turning back to him. "Certainly not. I think he wanted an excuse to make us all miserable, which is why I'm here. It was only my own good fortune that it was a library and not an armory."

"An armory may have been more useful for dealing with your brother."

"Perhaps, but I've yet to find a problem a library couldn't solve."

"Well, I'm not sure if the barley can help, but it certainly couldn't hurt if you would like to borrow a volume."

"I'm not quite that desperate yet, but I'll let you know when I am." She took a few steps over to the chairs, sitting down in his armchair with her dress fanned around her like a silk throne. "I've answered your questions, so now I think you should answer one of mine."

"Should I?" He kept his tone casual, but he knew what she wanted to ask. Careful to keep some distance between them, he walked down the aisle so he wouldn't have to crane his neck to look at her. "How about this? If you answer my next question, then I'll answer whatever you wish to ask."

Next to the candle, he could finally see that her eyes were a strong grey that looked like they could weather any storm. Those sparkling eyes sized him up until she gave him a brusque nod. "Deal."

"What's your name?"

His need to know her was so desperate that he would take any kernel she would give him.

She tilted her head as if considering the question. "You may call me Miss Montgomery. And yourself?"

"Mr. Gardner."

The smart play would have been to lie, but no one had ever accused him of being smart. Besides, neither her face nor last name was familiar to him, so she likely didn't know that he should be dead. However, he would never give her his first name.

"Gardner? Are you related to the doctor?"

"Vaguely."

"Care to elaborate?"

"Not particularly."

"Well, it's a pleasure to make your acquaintance, Mr. Gardner," she said, picking up his glass of brandy and swirling it before taking a sip.

38

"Don't you think it's risky to pick up an unfamiliar drink?"

"I'm familiar with the smell of brandy, so I knew exactly what it was." Her eyes were on him as she took another sip. This time, her pink tongue darted from her mouth to lick her lips. "Was this yours?"

"Yes."

"You have good taste." She sat back in the chair, looking at him like a cat trying to decide how she wanted to toy with her dinner.

"Don't you want to ask your question?"

"Why are you dressed like that?"

Will stood silently, weighing his options. This time, the truth wasn't amongst them.

"I'm shy."

"You're also kind of hard to miss, even more so when you're dressed as Death himself."

Will couldn't help but flinch at the comparison, but he held his tongue so she wouldn't know how close to the truth she was.

"I had an accident, and it's... easier for me to go around like this." He braced himself for ridicule, but she only nodded.

"Did you dislike balls before the accident, or did your aversion begin afterwards?"

"After, although they were never one of my favorite activities. Usually, they don't come with such stimulating conversation."

"I've always hated balls, or parties of any kind." Tipping back the glass, she emptied the remainder of the amber liquid. The pale column of her throat moved as she swallowed, and nothing could have taken his gaze from her. She held the empty glass towards him. "I'll take some more if you're offering."

"I haven't offered."

"But you really should," she said, shaking the empty glass.

Wordlessly, he walked to the liquor cabinet and picked up the crystal brandy decanter. A light pop sounded when he lifted the crystal stopper on his way to the armchair. Grateful for his long reach, he stood at a safe distance so she wouldn't be able to see anything but shadows beneath his hood as he poured.

"Is there anything about parties you like?" He took another step back to put some more distance between them. He wanted to take a drink directly from the decanter, but he would have to move his hood to do so.

"No." She frowned. "Although when I heard there was a presentation tonight, I was looking forward to that, so it's a shame it was cancelled. Do you know what it was about?"

His heart pounded as his palms grew slick with sweat in his gloves. "No, I'm sorry to disappoint you."

"It's no matter." She shrugged, settling back in the seat. "I hoped since you were also a Gardner, you might have some insider information."

"No, the way you're not interested in balls, I'm not interested in Dr. Gardner's projects. Anything he tells me goes in one ear and out the other." Earlier, he couldn't help but tell the truth, but now the lies came to him as naturally as breathing. "Are you a scientist then?"

An emotion he couldn't read flashed over her face before she schooled her expression again.

"I'm more of an academic," she said. "Self-taught, but this night wasn't a waste because I learned Cambridge has started allowing women to attend classes. It's always been my dream to study there." Her expression turned fierce, as if she were waiting for him to scoff at her dream.

"I'm glad to hear that archaic institution is finally progressing." He believed anyone who wanted an education should be able to get one, but he knew not many men did. "So if you found out such good news, why the tears?"

Her face relaxed, and he knew he passed an important test. "My brother is the impediment to my dream. He refuses to allow me to study there out of spite."

"That doesn't sound very nice."

"He's not very nice," she said with a humorless laugh. "Which is why I'm in here drinking with you while I try to calm down so I don't hit him with a chair."

"Please try to refrain from smashing any furniture. Most are heirlooms."

This time, she gave him a real laugh, and it made him proud that he could provoke such a reaction from her.

"I'll be sure to have our confrontation elsewhere to save your heirlooms, don't worry."

"You know, my—Dr. Gardner went to Cambridge. Maybe he could provide a recommendation."

"I already spoke to him, and he told me they mainly cared about permission from my family. Heaven forbid an adult woman be in charge of her own destiny."

"He would still help you any way he could." Tristan was a good man who would do anything for anyone who asked. "I'll make sure he inquires for you at least."

"Thank you, I appreciate your assistance," Miss Montgomery said, her eyes darting down as her cheeks pinked.

They fell into companionable silence, and Will's mind rushed to find a new topic of conversation because he didn't want their chance encounter to end.

"How does my library compare to yours?" He finally blurted out. It was far from the most elegant question he had ever asked, but it wasn't the worst based on the glimmer in her eye.

Her shrewd eyes canvassed the room, her head slowly turning as she took in every corner. He desperately hoped his library was up to her standards.

"Yours is bigger, but I think mine has more books."

Once again, he was grateful his cloak covered his face so she couldn't see him blush.

"I think if you were to take a closer look, you'd find the quality of the books to be quite good."

"Do you impress many women with your library?"

"I haven't had any complaints."

She laughed again, and it set off another little spark inside of him. God, he couldn't believe he was actually flirting with her. He hadn't been sure he even remembered how.

Miss Montgomery set the half-full glass of brandy on the table next to the candle before she stood up and made her way to the door. Reflexively, he shrank back into the aisle.

"As pleasant as this has been, I should return to the ball before anyone discovers I'm missing," she said without looking back.

Will stiffened at the reminder of normal life. It would be disastrous under normal circumstances if they were found in a room together, but he couldn't fathom how much worse it would be now.

"Maybe we should compare book lists sometime," he said before he could stop himself. This couldn't go anywhere, but he wouldn't let this be their last interaction.

She stopped, slowly turning to face him with suspicion heavy in her eyes.

"Just to talk about books. I don't have any other machinations," he clarified.

She was silent for a few beats before giving a quick shake of her head. "You can write to me, but you'll have to figure out my address on your own. In the meantime, try not to lurk about. Someone might get the wrong idea." She left the room without another word.

Will had never met another woman like her, and he felt that he never would. Miss Montgomery was one of a kind.

He flipped the lock on the door to ensure no one else would disturb him, and then sat in the chair she vacated. The abandoned brandy snifter was on the table beside him. Despite knowing he was alone, he still looked around to make sure no one had snuck in to catch him in the act before he picked up the glass. Swirled smudges of her fingertips surrounded the glass, as well as a mark her plush lips had left behind. He put his lips where hers had been and drank the rest of the brandy.

Speaking with Miss Montgomery felt like shaking the cobwebs from his old personality, reminding him that he was more than the self-pity he had marinated in for so long. For the first time since he came back to life, he felt alive.

* * *

THE NEXT MORNING, Will's heart thumped as he walked into the dining room to see Tristan sitting at the head of the table. His untouched breakfast lay before him as he scrawled furiously in his notebook. A full breakfast buffet was set up, despite the table only being set for Tristan.

"Good morning."

Tristan's head snapped up. "Good morning! I wasn't expecting you. Let me ring for Mrs. Jones to set you a place."

"There's no need to bother her." Will grabbed his own plate from the cabinet. He scooped himself fruit and eggs before sitting next to his brother. "How was the ball?"

"It was quite enjoyable. It was nice seeing some of my old school friends and professors."

"I'm glad you enjoyed yourself. If anyone deserves it, it's you." Will paused as he chewed. Subtlety had never been one of his skills, so he figured bluntness would serve him best. "Did you happen to meet a Miss Montgomery last night?"

Tristan narrowed his eyes. "Why do you ask?"

"That's not an answer."

"I'm aware. Yes, I was introduced to her last night. How did you know she was here?"

Will focused his attention on the eggs on his plate. He felt guilty for going downstairs but refusing to take part in the presentation. Talking to Tristan proved his desire to speak with Miss Montgomery again was too great. His brother was right; he was profoundly lonely.

When Tristan was silent for too long, Will looked up to see Tristan smiling. He scowled in return. "What?"

"Did you come down to the party last night?"

Will shrugged. "I went to the library so I could listen to the music. She wandered in looking for a quiet place, and we talked."

"You... talked?" Tristan was taking way too much joy in this, which annoyed Will. He never would have said anything if he didn't need Miss Montgomery's address.

"We just talked. Or sniped at one another if you want to be specific."

"You two were alone in the library? For how long?"

"You cannot be suggesting anything inappropriate happened."

43

He was offended that his brother would even suggest such a thing. He may be a monster, but he was still a gentleman.

"I'm not, I only wanted to make sure I understood the situation. I didn't expect this conversation when I woke up today."

"Try to look less smug. We were a dozen feet apart the entire time, and I was wearing my cloak. She didn't even see my face." Tristan frowned, causing Will to roll his eyes. "Stop looking at me like that and eat your breakfast before it gets cold."

"You should have taken your hood down. You probably scared her," Tristan said between bites.

"This face would have scared her more. It was a good conversation, and she wasn't scared. She's not the swooning type anyway."

He imagined her face contorted with disgust as he lowered his hood, and the thought was almost enough to put him off his breakfast.

"Then what type is she?"

"She's driven and ambitious. She's witty and loves to read. She admired the size of our library." Will finished his breakfast and set his silverware down. "I wanted to discuss something with you. She wants to go to Cambridge. Can you pull some strings for her?"

"I'm more than happy to write her a recommendation, but—as I told her last night—what she really needs is permission from her family. A new college has been created, but it's mainly lectures and some library time. Women aren't allowed to get degrees or sit for examinations. She'll need a chaperone as well."

Will frowned. It seemed like a lot of work for very few benefits, but he didn't know what it was like to be barred entirely from an institution.

"I'm not unwilling," Tristan continued. "It's just not as easy as it should be."

"Agreed, it's ludicrous. Women are just as capable." Will cleared his throat. "I should write her to make sure she knows the requirements. She said you would know where I could send a letter."

"How selfless of you. I'm sure you have no ulterior motive in writing her, I'm sure." Tristan raised an eyebrow.

"Are you going to help me or not?" Will asked. Brothers could be so annoying.

"Of course. It's fun to needle you, though. I'll make sure the letter gets to the right place."

All things considered, Tristan was a good brother. It had been a long time since they were able to joke like this, and when Will looked at his brother, he saw him realize that as well.

"Thank you. I'll get you the letter today."

"I see you're not wasting any time."

Will desperately wanted to wipe the smirk off his brother's face.

"The new term isn't far off, so she will need to move quickly if she wants to make it in time."

"What a convenient excuse. Try not to overthink it. I imagine she would appreciate something direct."

Will stood up. It felt good to have a new objective. He was halfway across the room when he paused. "Do you happen to know her first name?"

"You're planning to send her love poems, and you don't know her name? You do have it bad."

"Never mind." Will turned to leave the room. He didn't have to suffer through such indignities. Tristan laughed.

"Her name is Jane!" his brother shouted after him.

CHAPTER 5

*A*lcohol fumes burned Jane's eyes, but she blinked through the tears as she snapped the bones from the fox's ribcage. With the proper tools, disassembling the skeleton would be a simple task, but she made do with the rudimentary tools available to her, mainly her hands and any whiskey she could swipe from her brother's collection.

Like all of her specimens, she found this fox's body on one of her nature walks. The stage of decomposition had been advanced, so it hadn't taken long for her to strip the bones, soaking them in a whiskey solution of her own creation that also sanitized them. The process wasn't difficult, but it was a challenge to keep her specimen from being discovered and thrown out by the servants.

The snap of bones made an eerie sound. Jane wasn't sure if it was due to the fox's lower bone density or if her bones would make that same dull sound.

"Damn." Her grip slipped as she snapped the next rib, damaging the delicate spinal column she wanted to sketch for her admissions letter to Cambridge. There was no requirement, but she wanted to stand out, so they had no choice but to admit her.

Asking Robert's permission to go to Cambridge had been a mistake she should have anticipated. In the three days since the ball, she had come up with a new plan she felt confident would succeed.

Jane's plan began to fall into place the day after the ball when she received a letter from Mr. Gardner. Dr. Gardner had sent an effusive letter of recommendation back with one of the professors who traveled for the presentation. Since it seemed that family permission was unavoidable, she decided to forge a letter from Robert to be included among the samples of her work. Once Cambridge accepted her, she would secure Robert's permission.

Discarding the broken spinal column, Jane sifted through the rest of the skeleton to find a new piece that would show off her technical skill. Grey bones rattled in the box until she decided on a femur she bisected. A femur wasn't particularly exciting, but she would be sure to detail how she did the bisection herself.

A sharp rap sounded at the door, but she ignored it as the sharp tip of the graphite pencil moved around the page, bringing the femur to life. This library was *hers*, and she alone decided who entered. Currently, she was too far behind to allow any visitors.

The pencil lines darkened as she detailed the bone's bulbous head. Drawing lessons were forced on her by her governess after she quit embroidery and the pianoforte, but Jane had stuck with drawing when she realized she could draw whatever she wanted rather than just the pretty little scenes from her lessons.

Another knock rasped, this one loud enough that she felt it reverberate through her skull. The handle rattled as the intruder attempted to enter, though Jane was unconcerned as she had the only key to the room.

"Miss Montgomery," the butler said, his sharp tone muffled by the thick door.

"Not now, Smythe," she snapped, rotating the femur to get the correct angle for her diagram. "The fireplace ashes were emptied yesterday, and any cleaning can be done later."

"Miss Mary needs to dress you for dinner."

Jane frowned. Typically, she dined alone, taking a tray either in her library or bedroom. Sunday dinner was the sole meal the Montgomerys ate together, but it was only Tuesday.

"Tell Mary I'll take my dinner in here. Leave the tray outside the door."

"I'm afraid your attendance at tonight's dinner is mandatory, but I can get Mr. Montgomery if you wish to discuss the matter with him."

Jane's jaw clenched. It seemed much was required of her these days. Dropping her graphite pencil, she rubbed her temples. Already, she could feel a headache brewing.

"Give me twenty minutes," she sighed. It would give her barely enough time to finish her sketch, which wouldn't put her terribly behind schedule if she started early tomorrow.

"Very well, Miss. I'll let your brother know."

Silence told her the butler left. Even though Smythe hadn't been in the room with her, she felt like her space had been violated. Her library wasn't just where she worked, but it was an extension of herself. It was the one place in the world where everything made sense, and she was too selfish to share it with anyone.

Picking up the pencil, she continued to shade in the cross-section of bone until it was a perfect likeness. *This* was how she would earn her place at Cambridge, by proving she was already producing work worthy of the storied institution.

Satisfied with her drawing, she carefully put it in the pile of papers she had prepared for her admissions letter. The white pages provided a stark contrast against the darker shades of her graphite drawings and the black ink of her essay samples. Her eyes caught on the cream colored letter delivered that morning.

Cowardice had led her to shove the letter out of sight when she recognized Mr. Gardner's tidy script. Jane had yet to respond to his previous letter about the recommendation, so it both confused and excited her that he had written her again. For all the bravery she had in cutting up dead creatures and sending her essays into academic journals, she couldn't seem to muster the courage to open the letter.

The bronze clock ticked away from its place on the fireplace mantel. Each loud tick added to her growing unease about why her brother required her at this evening's meal.

Her work was finished, but she still had a few precious moments until Mary expected her, and she wouldn't waste a single moment while in her favorite place in the world. Even the musty smell of books twined with mahogany and aged leather calmed her. It was built as her consolation prize when Robert was sent off to boarding school, and she had to stay home. At the time, she would have rather gone to school, but now she wouldn't trade her library for anything.

Since it was a converted bedroom, the room was small, but she felt like it made it cozier. Three of the walls had built-in mahogany bookcases that extended from the floor to the ceiling, with a rickety ladder that squeaked with every movement. The fourth wall had large windows meant to provide natural light, but mostly gave her a view of the mist crawling across the heath-covered moors.

As the minute hand ticked closer to her deadline, she sighed before getting up, stretching her stiff muscles from sitting for so long. She was leaving a minute or so early, but it was better to lose that time than to have Smythe or Mary come knocking. The cream envelope stared up at her, and she snatched it, putting it into her pocket before going to her bedroom.

* * *

WHEN JANE LOOKED in the mirror, she almost didn't recognize the woman who stared back. The woman in the mirror was beautiful in her satin navy gown, her hair piled into loose curls that added inches to her already considerable height, but there was a deep sadness in her eyes. The spark that was usually there had been dimmed. Inside, she was filled with fear at what this evening meant for her.

"Mr. Montgomery has requested you meet him and Mrs. Montgomery in the parlor for a drink before dinner," Mary said as she fluffed Jane's skirt until it looked perfect.

Jane's mouth was too dry to respond verbally, so she nodded

before leaving the room. As she walked through the house, she felt separate from her body, as if it were a play rather than her life. Steeling herself, she walked through the doorway of the parlor to three pairs of eyes staring back at her.

A stranger stood in the parlor laughing with her brother and sister-in-law. Well, not exactly a stranger, but the man she had briefly met at the ball. Robert had told her the man's name, but it escaped her at the moment.

"Sister, how nice of you to finally join us," Robert said before taking a generous gulp of whiskey from the crystal glass in his hand, amber droplets dripped from his mouth onto his freshly pressed cravat. Bloodshot eyes sent her a warning glare as he stalked across the room to her, fingers digging into her bicep as he escorted her to Sofia and the stranger. "Let me introduce you to Lord George Percy, the 4th Baron Percy. Lord Percy, please meet Miss Jane Montgomery, my beloved sister."

Jane murmured her greeting and curtseyed, her heart pounding so hard it was the only sound she heard. Robert gave a sharp nod of approval as if she were a dog who had mastered a new trick. It made her want to scream.

Lord Percy bowed, his wet lips smacking against her hand in another unpleasant kiss. "I'm pleased to make your acquaintance, Miss Montgomery. This time, I think we can both give our best impressions. You are just as your brother described."

She suppressed a snort as she couldn't imagine that Robert's description of her was flattering. "You seem to have the advantage here because my brother has never mentioned you."

Robert's grasp on her arm tightened until she worried he would leave a bruise.

"I wouldn't expect anything else. If I had a sister, I wouldn't want to get her hopes up either. A lord's attention can be intoxicating," Lord Percy said with a smirk that had likely worked thousands of times over the years, but now that deep lines etched his ruddy face and permanent dark circles settled beneath his eyes, it looked more ominous than alluring.

"You'll find I'm quite sober." The disgust and fear inside of her was now boiling into anger. Not even the threat of her brother's rage could make her hold her tongue.

Percy laughed. "You didn't tell me your sister was witty, Montgomery."

"It can be trained out of her," Robert said through gritted teeth.

"Don't worry, I still think it's a fair deal. The challenge only makes it more interesting."

Jane curled her hands into fists. She couldn't believe he was talking around her like she was a piece of furniture. Sofia stood there with a bland expression. If this talk bothered her, she didn't show it at all. Jane wasn't sure if she was jealous or not.

"What type of challenge are you referring to, Lord Percy?"

Dread curled inside of her as her suspicion grew, but she was going to make either her brother or this Baron say it out loud. Squaring her shoulders, she elongated her spine so Lord Percy had to look up at her, and the hard glint in his icy stare told her he did not appreciate it.

"Dinner is served," Smythe said, breaking the tension in the room.

Lord Percy's charismatic mask slid back into place as he turned to Sofia to ask if he could escort her into the dining room. Robert held Jane back as the other two walked from the room.

"I don't know what your aim is, but you will not embarrass me tonight," Robert hissed, his whiskey-soaked breath making her gag.

"Why am I here tonight? I could be upstairs minding my own business. You're the one who wanted me here."

"And you best remember that everything you have is because of me, so you're going to go in there, paste a smile on your face, and charm the Baron." Bloodshot eyes looked at her with a depth of hatred that stilled her.

"What do you have planned?"

Robert's hand tightened until she was sure she would bruise. "That doesn't look like a smile."

Tears gathered in her eyes, but she didn't dare let them fall because she refused to give him the satisfaction of thinking he broke her. No one could.

She bit down on the inside of her cheek until she was able to eke out the semblance of a smile; the taste of copper filled her mouth as her cheek bled. Something in her expression must have appeased him because he grunted in approval, loosening his grip as he escorted her to the dining room.

Robert dumped her in the seat across from Lord Percy. Once she and Robert were seated, servants plated the first course.

"Do you spend all year out here or do you spend time in London as well, Miss Montgomery?" Percy asked.

"This is the only place I've ever lived." Jane picked up the spoon, keeping her eyes on her soup.

"How quaint. Are you not interested in travel?"

"I've been to Manchester, but I've never had much of a reason to leave home."

Their father became a recluse after the death of his beloved wife in childbirth, and after he had died, Jane never had the opportunity to go anywhere else. Even if she wanted to leave, she didn't know where she would go or how she would get there. It was difficult to leave the only home she had ever known.

"She prefers to stay home and read. It's nearly impossible to tear her away from a book," Robert added, his silver spoon clanking against the white china bowl.

"Do you like poetry or prose?"

Jane huffed at his presumption. "Neither, I'm an academic. Currently, I'm studying anatomy, and I'm mainly interested in how muscles and ligaments work."

Lord Percy shot a look at her brother, whose gaze was fixed on his empty bowl. Apparently, their discussions hadn't included *every* detail about her.

The bowls were cleared, and oysters were placed before them. Jane frowned. She hated oysters. They had the consistency of mucus and somehow smelled even worse.

Lord Percy attacked his with enthusiasm, slurping down the grey meat and smacking his lips together. Jane swirled the tiny silver fork in her oyster to give the illusion she was eating, even as her stomach turned in time with her fork.

"I suppose single women have to fill their days somehow," Lord Percy sighed, oyster meat flopping over his already very wet lips. "Especially since there's not much to do this far north. I expect our marriage will cure you of such interests."

The oyster fell from Jane's hand, the meat falling on the white lace tablecloth with a dull, wet thud. It felt as if the world had turned upside down at the confirmation of her worst fear. Her chest heaved with shallow breaths, her corset suddenly much too tight.

"What?" Her voice was barely audible, but the room was so quiet she knew everyone heard her.

Lord Percy looked at her as if she were slow to catch on to what was happening. Sofia's expression was politely bland as she ate her oysters. Robert smirked at her, a whiskey tumbler in hand, ready to toast to her misery. The look made her want to launch herself over the table to scratch his eyes out, but she was frozen in place.

"I know it wasn't the most romantic proposal, but I figured at your age, practical was better than romantic."

"I would argue it wasn't a proposal since nothing was asked of me."

"Semantics," Percy said, smacking his lips before shooting back another oyster.

"Accepting a marriage proposal is more than semantics. It is, in fact, one of the main requirements."

Lord Percy stared at her, slack-jawed. Robert's face was a deeper crimson than she had ever seen before.

"Would you not like to be a Baroness?" Sofia asked, delicately placing her oyster fork on the white china plate. "You would finally be able to run your own house. It would give you a purpose."

"I already have a purpose," Jane hissed. "Some of us dream of being more than someone's wife or mother."

"It is not simply a choice to marry or be a mother, but a sacred duty," Sofia said, her face hardening into a mask of disdain. "It is your responsibility as a woman."

"So I'm supposed to relish being whisked away from the only home I've ever known at the whim of a man I've never met?" Her voice rose, rediscovering her strength in anger. "Do I leave for London tonight?"

Percy snorted. "You won't go with me to London. You will stay at my home in Suffolk to raise the children. I'll return every few weeks to check on you, but you could send for me in an emergency."

"And what happens to me if I can't get with child?" she asked, voice shaking with rage. She would drink as much pennyroyal tea as possible to ensure Percy never received his heir.

"You assured me she was still fertile despite her age." Percy ignored her, looking to Robert instead.

Her hands shook as she grabbed her glass of wine, but gulping down the pale liquid did little to quell her fury. Lord Percy saw her as a walking, talking womb, and now she was at risk of being *trapped* with him.

"There's no need for concern. Her maid told me her cycle is still quite regular."

The wine glass shattered when it hit the table, pale liquid spilling on the white tablecloth. A servant came by to mop up the wine and replace the broken glass.

"Please, this isn't an appropriate conversation for the dinner table," Sofia said. Percy and Robert both apologized to Sofia while Jane sat in shocked silence.

Mortification as she had never felt before ran through her. How long had Mary been tracking her cycle on her brother's behalf? Never in even her darkest hours had she thought she would be betrayed in such an intimate way. Was there anything in her life that belonged only to her?

They expected her to sit there with a bland expression and accept everything that happened. Well, they could go to hell for all she cared. This was war.

"You said this had been dealt with already, Montgomery," Percy said with all the arrogance of a lord.

"Don't worry, she'll agree," Robert said, swirling the whiskey in his glass as he looked at her with neither mercy nor remorse.

Jane gripped her fork so hard her knuckles were white. "I'm sitting right here," she said through clenched teeth.

"Are you ready to discuss this rationally, or are you going to act like a feral child?" He spoke slowly, enunciating each word as if she had a problem understanding him.

"I'm being perfectly rational for a person who has been ambushed."

An inferno raged inside of her, but she was careful to keep it on lockdown because if she started yelling or throwing things, they wouldn't take her seriously. Her anger was a weapon to be used wisely.

Robert flicked his gaze to her hand clutching the fork and raised an eyebrow. Taking a deep breath, she opened her fist, the fork landing on the table with a dull clatter. He gave her a small, satisfied smile that made her regret not throwing the fork at him instead.

"This is the most advantageous marriage possible for you. You would be elevated to a Baroness. We wouldn't get to see your shining face at Sunday dinner, but that's a trade-off I'm willing to make." Robert turned towards Lord Percy. "What's your library like, my lord? I'm sure it's grand."

"We have the best collection in the area. My family has been curating it for generations." Percy's annoyance had faded as he returned to polite disinterest. Years of Baron training had likely led to his apathy. She couldn't imagine being trapped in such a life.

"See, there'll be a library so you can live happily ever after," Robert said, downing more whiskey.

"You think a library is enough to make me want to marry? You have absolutely no understanding of what I want. If you really wanted to convince me, you would bring something I want to the table."

There was no way trading her life away in marriage for her dream to go to Cambridge was a fair deal, but anger had loosened her tongue. However, if she was going to be forced into marriage, she might as well try to get a single benefit out of it.

"And what is it that you actually want, Miss Montgomery?"

Percy's icy stare landed on her again, and she saw exactly what type of man he was. He wasn't there to play games because he was a man who always got exactly what he wanted. This was a man who did not negotiate.

Jane swallowed. She was out of her depth, but she wouldn't back down. "Cambridge is admitting women starting this fall, and I wish to become a student."

Lord Percy looked at her before turning towards Robert, his gaze bouncing between the siblings for a few long moments. Jane didn't dare to feel any hope, but the longer the silence lasted, the more she couldn't help but wonder if maybe it would work out after all.

Finally, Percy threw back his head and laughed. It was the type of hearty belly laugh she didn't think was possible from a lord of his stature.

Jane had played her hand and lost. Tears gathered as she clenched her hands into tight fists, fingernails digging into her palm in an attempt to stave off her tears.

Percy removed his handkerchief from his breast pocket and dabbed his eyes. "You want to attend Cambridge? That's truly the best joke I have ever heard."

"I assure you it's not a joke." Jane's nostrils flared, her even voice masking the turmoil inside.

"Rest assured, I had absolutely no intention of allowing her to pursue it," Robert said.

The next course of a venison pasty was placed in front of them, and Jane had to suppress an eyeroll at the choice. Sofia was obsessed with them after reading about how popular they were in London this past season. The small brown pasty steamed, and the strong smell of venison made her stomach churn.

"Good, I have no interest in an educated wife." Percy cut into the pasty as he spoke. He took a bite, and the juice from the meat dribbled down his chin. "It wouldn't be good for the children."

"I think you would find *A Vindication of the Rights of Woman* an enlightening read, Lord Percy," said Jane.

"I think you'll find Miss Montgomery's current level of education to be an advantage when she's raising the next Baron. It's never too early to start preparing children for literacy," said Sofia.

"An excellent point, Mrs. Montgomery. Your perspective on this is very valuable as a mother yourself." Percy's tone was beyond condescending, but Sofia beamed at the attention.

"That is almost the exact thesis of *A Vindication of the Rights of Woman*," Jane huffed.

If she were to raise the next Baron Percy, she would only teach it curse words and about the occult.

"The marriage contract is in my study. If you're satisfied, we can sign it after dinner," Robert said.

She stared at her untouched pasty dancing on her plate through her unshed tears. "I won't agree to it. There is nothing any of you can do to get me to agree to this." Looking at all three of them with the promise of vengeance, Robert laughed at her, and she felt the threat of violence rising in her.

"You're always so dramatic." Robert turned to Percy and continued, "You should know she's all bluster and no bite. She can be loud, but if you know how to control her, you can quickly bring her to heel."

Jane glared at Percy. "I promise you that I bite hard."

"How do you control her?"

"You just have to find what she loves most in this world." Robert picked up something from the chair beside him and held it up. "And threaten it. Do you recognize this, my dear sister?"

Her brother held her research journal, waving it in front of her like a matador brandishing a red cape before a bull. Her heart stopped as she lunged for it, but Robert pulled it out of her reach.

"Give that back to me. You had no right to enter my library or touch my belongings."

"I didn't enter your precious library, don't worry. Smythe retrieved this for me while Mary was doing your hair." Robert opened her journal, carelessly flipping through the pages and smudging the ink with his greasy hands. He stopped on a page, and Jane flinched as he ripped it out. "I think you'll find this one interesting, it's a drawing of a hand—without skin, of course, and the bones have been labeled. It's ghastly, but the technique is promising."

He held it out to Percy, but when he showed no interest, her brother ripped the paper into small pieces and threw them into the air like confetti.

She choked out a sob as the tears she had fought to hold back started to fall. "You've made your point, now give it back." Her hand shook as she held it out for the safe return of her journal.

"I don't think I've made my point clear yet."

Robert flipped to a later page and ripped it out. "This page is less visually interesting, but I think you might find this one to be important. This is about the decomposition rate of a frog." Robert grimaced, his eyes flicking to her. "You didn't do this experiment in my house, did you?"

He balled the paper and threw it in his wine glass. It bobbed on top for a few moments before sinking to the bottom of the glass as the wine consumed it. Two weeks of research were gone in a moment.

"Is that the best you can do? A few idle threats and ripped papers?"

Robert held her life in his hands, but she wouldn't back down. She couldn't. Her tears were the closest thing to a surrender he would get.

"You seem to be under the impression I'm playing a game, but I assure you I am not." Robert stood up with her journal and walked over to the fireplace. With one careless flick of the wrist, he threw her journal inside. "There, now you don't have to worry about my idle threats."

Jane screamed, pushing herself up from the table so quickly her chair crashed to the floor behind her. She watched as the flames engulfed her work. An entire year of her research, notes, theories, and experiments all turned to ash.

Nothing about this evening felt real. From the moment Smythe knocked on her door, it all felt like a bad dream. The only thing that felt real was the anger that raged through her. Her blood sang as Robert walked back to the table with that stupid smirk on his face.

She had to do something. There was no way he could get away with this. Percy and Sofia looked on, but they wouldn't do anything to stop it. No one would come and save her from this hell. It was up to her to find a way out.

Robert deserved to hurt, even if it was only a fraction of the pain she felt. Before she could think through her plan, she grabbed the pasty from her plate. It was hot and greasy with considerable heft, which made it perfect. Throwing her arm back, she chucked it at Robert.

The steaming pasty hit his face with a satisfying wet slap. It exploded on impact, the meat and onions sliding down his face as his eyes widened in pure shock. The right side of his face was deep red, both from anger and from the food. A glob of fat was caught in his hair. His eyes were wide, and his mouth was agape. She laughed.

"That is what I'm capable of," she said to Percy as she pointed at Robert's red face as the fat dripped down. "And I promise you that is only the beginning. I don't know what he promised you, but I guarantee it won't be worth it."

Percy neatly placed his silverware on the table and cleaned his mouth with a napkin. Once he was done, he folded it and put it neatly beside his plate. When Percy looked at her, his face was a perfect mask of calm. "Miss Montgomery, I understand you and your brother have a contentious relationship. Normally, I wouldn't care if you two destroyed each other, but regrettably, you are an integral part of the deal I have with your brother."

Lord Percy walked over to her. He looked her dead in the eye and grabbed the hand that had thrown the pasty, grimacing at her greasy fingers. He took out his handkerchief and wiped her hand clean. "My promise to you is, when you become my wife, I won't steal your belongings or throw your books into the fire." His voice lowered as he lifted her hand to his mouth, kissing her fingers right beneath the knuckle. "I promise you, if you ever act like this in my home, I will have you locked away in a sanatorium, and they will throw away the key." Lord George Percy, the 4th Baron Percy, bowed to her and Sofia before leaving the room.

Ice flooded her veins, dousing the anger that had empowered her to make such a move against her brother. Confinement was her worst fear. It was the one thing she knew beyond a shadow of a doubt she couldn't handle. Any other punishment could become bearable, but a life without her books, her research, and knowledge, without even a walk in the garden, wasn't a life worth living for her. Robert laughed, snapping her from her trance.

"You impetuous little bitch. The look of fear on your face is almost worth getting hit in the head with a meat pie. Almost, but not quite." Ringing the service bell, Robert wiped his face with a crumpled handkerchief. Smythe entered the room. "Take her to her room and make sure she can't leave until I say so."

"You can't do this! You can't lock me away. I'm a person. I'm your sister!" She screamed while moving her arms erratically, accidentally catching the edge of her plate, flipping it to the floor, where it shattered on impact.

When Smythe grabbed her arm, she tried to shake him off, but he wouldn't let go. His grip was firm as she thrashed. Her fingernails tore at his arms, and she tried to kick out his legs, but he continued undeterred.

Sofia went to Robert with a fresh handkerchief to clean his face. She cooed and coddled him as she worked. Jane shouted for both of them—either of them—to help, but neither even glanced at her as she was dragged from the room.

Smythe led her upstairs and into her bedroom as she cried. She begged him to let her go, to stop, but he didn't listen to a word she said.

Smythe didn't let go of her until she was in her bedroom, and even then, he pushed her towards the middle of the room before finally letting go. Her legs gave out, causing her to collapse into a heap on the floor. She tried to crawl behind him to beat him to the door, but she wasn't fast enough. As she hurled her body against the door, the lock clicked into place. The shrieks that came from her sounded inhuman as she pounded on the door until exhaustion took over and she was freed of all conscious thought.

CHAPTER 6

*J*ane awoke curled in a ball in front of her bedroom
door. Discarded hairpins littered the surrounding
floor; some were flattened from her attempts to pick
the lock, while others were a casualty of her distress. Dried blood
caked her fingers from scratching at the now-scarred mahogany
door from trying to dig herself free. Her back ached from a night
spent on the floor, and her head throbbed from screaming and
crying. A metallic taste from her bleeding, cracked lips filled her
mouth. She tried to wet her lips with her tongue, but her tongue
was dry. She was a husk.

Knees shaking as she stood, she staggered through her room in
search of water. Mary filled a pitcher for her each morning and
evening, and Jane prayed she hadn't removed it.

She let out a sound of relief when the pitcher was in its usual
spot on her bathroom counter. The heavy pitcher shook as she
lifted it to her mouth, careful to make sure none spilled. The porcelain spout was cool against her lips, so she didn't mind the stale
taste of the lukewarm water. Her body was desperate for liquid, but
she was careful not to drink too much since she didn't know when
she would be freed. Rationing water now could help save her later.

Once her thirst was partially sated, she poured a small amount onto a handkerchief to clean her fingers. The cuts stung as she rubbed the blood away, careful not to reopen any cuts.

Glancing at the mirror on her vanity, the haggard face that stared back surprised her. She had swollen, bloodshot eyes and broken capillaries on her cheeks. Her carefully sculpted hair had turned into a massive, knotted nest. Most shocking were the pink lines running down her face, neck, and chest from where she had clawed at her own skin. Some scratches were an angry pink, while others had scabbed over where she had drawn her own blood.

Stumbling back, she remembered the golden rope of the service bell dangling by her bed. Hope surged within her as she rushed over, pulling the golden rope with as much force as she could muster. Praying to a God she didn't believe in, that someone, anyone would come and save her.

The rope burned against her lacerated fingers, but she didn't dare let go. She pulled that rope ten, twenty times, but no one ever answered. A sob wracked her body at the cruel realization that no one would come for her. Not until Robert allowed it.

Dejected, she flopped down on her bed, not caring that her legs dangled off the edge. Her back hurt, her hips hurt, her fingers hurt, so much pain radiated through her body, she would do anything for it to stop.

She grabbed her pillow, frowning when a letter dropped onto the bed. In the previous evening's chaos, she had forgotten about Mr. Gardner's letter. The letter was as good a distraction from this purgatory as any, so she broke the red wax seal.

Once again, she was struck by his neat handwriting and the even glide of the ink. It felt silly, but she found good penmanship attractive because it demonstrated deliberate thought. It wasn't a trait she had, but she found it to be admirable, especially in a man.

Their encounter at the ball had been unexpected, but not unwelcome, which surprised her because she thought she was beyond such things. The concept of marriage had always horrified her, but she had never been tempted since her singular experience with courtship had been with a man she could never respect, let alone like. Henry had been blandly attractive, but he had never inspired any feelings in her.

Michael, on the other hand, had inspired *some* feelings in her. Their brief affair had been for the pragmatic reason of ruining herself, but she had found pleasure in their trysts. She chose Michael because he was her height, but she also appreciated his wicked smile and calloused hands that knew precisely how to touch her.

However, he had never been a true option for her, because even if he wasn't a footman, he was disqualified because of having no interest in reading or medicine. Every time she tried to talk to him about either subject, he grew bored and begged her to speak of something else. The few jokes he told fell flat, which was a poor combination with his thin ego. It had been a fun diversion, but she didn't enjoy talking to him, so it wasn't much of a loss when Robert fired him.

While her conversation with Mr. Gardner had been brief, she had enjoyed it immensely. More than any other conversation she had in ages. His cloaked figure should have scared her, but it only made her more intrigued. He was witty and well-read, but had also shown her kindness when she had needed it most. What he looked like didn't matter to her.

Well, it mattered a little, but she couldn't imagine anyone with a voice that smooth to be unattractive.

The letter was brief. He asked how she was acclimating to the change in weather as autumn approached. He lamented this change, wishing his roses had a few more weeks until they retired for the colder months. The letter finished with him asking about her library, if her books had missed her while she had been gone.

Crumpling the letter to her chest, her tears returned. They weren't the body-wrecking sobs from before, but the quiet tears hurt just as much. Those closest to her had threatened her with marriage, institutionalization, and confinement, while a man who was a stranger was the only one who cared about her feelings and what she had to say.

Of course, she had nothing to write in response. Her life had so quickly devolved into a messy, embarrassing horror that she didn't want to explain. Besides, she couldn't imagine Robert's reaction if he found out she had been writing with a man. She couldn't risk his further wrath, let alone put Mr. Gardner at risk. This letter had to be the end of their contact, which caused her to cry even harder.

* * *

THE GREY LIGHT of day had gradually faded to night, and now the shadows cast across her room meant it was daytime again. The faint scent of a fire floated in from outside, but she couldn't see the source from her window.

It had been hours since she had moved from her bed, spending the bulk of her time drifting in and out of sleep. Her water reserves were perilously low, but the last time she drank, it sloshed uncomfortably in her stomach, so she wasn't eager to repeat the experience. Periodically, she heard footsteps in the hall, but no one had even hesitated outside her door.

Both anger and despair had left her. Ringing the bell had done nothing, nor had screaming, crying, or pleading. Since action hadn't worked, she settled on doing nothing. It wasn't satisfying, but at least it didn't expend any energy.

Her brother's heavy footsteps sounded in the hallway. She braced herself to see him, but the footsteps stopped right outside her door.

Moments passed in silence before she sat up. Perhaps she had become so desperate for contact that she had hallucinated the sound, but the shadow in the doorway proved it wasn't her imagination.

"Hello," she called out, clearing her throat.

Silence greeted her.

"Robert, I know you're there." The shadow's stance let her know it was him. Besides, none of the servants would linger like that.

Still, he said nothing.

An ember of the anger she thought her tears extinguished

returned. He was *toying* with her. No longer would she cower at his feet and beg for mercy.

Standing up, her legs wobbled so badly she used the bed for balance until she could stabilize herself and walk over to the heavy wooden door.

"Robert, open the door."

Steeling herself, she rammed her shoulder into the door. Pain radiated down her arm as she repeated the action, but she couldn't stop.

Backing up, she ran at the door before slamming into it, hoping it would break down and fall on him. Momentum caused her to hit the door hard, but it didn't even splinter. Instead, the force caused her to lose her balance as she bounced back, skidding across the floor on her hip.

A click sounded, and the door slowly opened. Robert kept a hand on the brass doorknob as he smirked at the sight of her on the floor.

"You do know the door opens the wrong way for you to try to use yourself as a battering ram?"

"It got you to open the door," she said through gritted teeth. It wasn't until the door had opened that she realized the folly of her plan. She blamed the oversight on her frenzied state.

Robert slowly scanned the room, his eyes passing over the deep plum curtains, the matching bedspread, and the same dark furniture that matched the rest of the house. "It's been many years since I've been in here, but it hasn't changed."

Their mother had decorated the room many years ago, and Jane had never cared enough to change it. "That's because you're not invited."

"Am I invited now?" Amusement glinted in his eyes that made her wish she had another pasty to chuck at him.

"I don't have a choice, do I?" He was too smug, but once she saw the red welt on his cheek, she couldn't suppress her smile. "Your face is looking a little burnt."

He glowered at her. "And here I was about to let you out

because I thought you might have learned your lesson." He turned, and she crawled after him, prepared to use her body to block the door so she wouldn't be trapped again.

"Fine." Keeping her dignity would have been nice, but her freedom mattered more.

"Good, I'm glad to see we're nearly in accord." He walked around her room, looking at her belongings in a way that made her nervous. "I was rather troubled by your display the other night. I didn't expect you to be charming, but you were even more disagreeable than usual."

"You can't be surprised since you were the one who backed me into that corner."

Robert sighed. "I know you don't think so, but you will marry Lord Percy."

"Really? Because I haven't said yes."

"Your mistake, as always, is that you think you have power, but you have none." He stopped in front of her vanity, leaning against it with crossed arms as he lectured her.

"I still have to say 'I do'." No matter how precarious her position was, she couldn't find it within herself to bend.

"You have a lot of confidence for someone who's been locked in a room."

"Yet here you are." He might think she doesn't have power, but he was there because he needed her.

He laughed. "Indeed, here I am." He shook his head and sighed as if she were an unruly child. Not one of his though, as he rarely spoke to his children. "Lord Percy will formally propose tomorrow, and you will accept. The banns will be read beginning on Sunday, and you will be married in three weeks. After which, you'll be the baron's problem. I suggest you treat him better because he won't be as charitable as I am."

"Is starving me your idea of being charitable?"

Robert snorted. "Please, it would take far longer to starve you." Standing up straight, he motioned for her. "Follow me."

A full-body tremor hit as she picked herself up while Robert looked down on her. She wasn't sure whether it was hunger or fear, but it took her a few tries to get up and follow her brother. Robert's heavy footsteps echoed through the hall as she quietly limped behind him. Her empty stomach lurched once she realized where they were going.

Robert stopped in front of her library, and bile collected in her mouth.

"Are you ready?" Her brother asked with a wicked glint in his eye.

Jane glared, but he laughed before he continued. "On second thought, how about you do the honor?"

Jane took a deep breath and opened the door to her library—her only safe place in the entire world—and froze.

It was empty.

Every book she purchased with Robert's money, the books her father gave her, and the books she had pilfered from the family library were gone. The dusty imprints they left behind were the only proof her books had been there at all. Even the curtains she had sewn from her father's old bedspread were gone.

Knees buckling, she fought to keep herself upright as she scrambled for the rickety ladder that had likely been spared only because it was attached to the wall. The corner bookcase had a secret hatch built in the top where she stored her research journals. The clanging of the ladder against the track echoed through the otherwise silent room as she climbed.

Adrenaline kept her going when all she wanted was to curl up and cry. The cuts on her fingers reopened as she blindly groped for the seam in the unfinished wood. The latch popped open, and her hand fell onto nothing. Empty. Robert had been quite thorough.

Heart pounding, she slowly climbed down the ladder. It was all gone. Her desk was the only piece of furniture still in the room. Not even her chair had survived the purge. As she opened her desk drawers, she felt numb when they were empty as well. All of her journals, notebooks, and papers were gone. Her fountain pens and personalized stationery were also gone. Her entire life's work had been in there. It was the only evidence she had done *something* with her life, and now she had nothing.

Her knees buckled, and this time she let herself fall, a sob wailing as she hit the floor.

This was her punishment for striking Robert. He had only locked her away for the opportunity to destroy the only thing she loved. Grief was all that remained.

"Do you still think you have power?" Robert asked as he stepped into the room, eyes gleaming.

"What did you do with my books?"

"You know I've fantasized about doing this for a very long time." He walked until he stood above her, sneering at her as she cried. "Then the other night as the scalding meat dripped down my face, I knew I finally had my excuse."

"Tell me what you did with my books right now."

Crying at her brother's feet was beyond pathetic, but the last of her dignity had left. She would do anything to get her books back.

"This is where I'm worried that I got a little ahead of myself," he sighed. "Smythe loaded them into a cart and built a bonfire in the front garden."

Robert looked at her with such glee that it made her want to hit him until he felt the same pain she felt. Horror spread as she realized the smell of fire she had dismissed earlier was her *books*.

Finding her strength in anger, Jane took off like a shot. Her bare feet slapped against the polished floors as she ran through the house in her ripped dress, with the knotted remnants of her hairstyle flopping with each step.

Bursting out of the house, she saw the orange glow of the flames. Smythe stood dispassionately by the fire, prodding it with a cast-iron poker to make sure not a single page remained unburned.

Part of her wanted to jump into the flames to salvage anything she could, but she stopped herself, both because the pain would be unimaginable and because there was no point. Leather book covers had curled in on themselves as ash filled the air. A page fragment was spit from the flames, floating through the air until it reached

Jane. The smoldering bit of paper landed in her palm, but turned to ash upon contact. All of her books were gone.

"I'm glad I made the correct choice after all," Robert said as he stepped beside her. "It's far more satisfying to see your reaction."

"You had no right to touch my belongings," she said, wiping her tears away.

"I like to think of them as my belongings, seeing as how I paid for them. Think of them as a loan, and now that loan is up."

Jane never needed a reminder that her life belonged to Robert. She was incredibly aware that she had no money or home of her own. Nothing about her life was fair, but it wasn't as if Robert had ever cared. The deck had always been stacked in his favor.

"However," he said, gesturing towards Smythe, who handed Robert a parcel wrapped in brown paper. "I have a wedding present for you."

"You're insane if you think I'm going along with your idiotic plan. There's nothing you can hold over me anymore."

He shook the parcel in her direction. "I think you'll want this."

Jane snatched and ripped open the brown paper. It was *Gray's Anatomy*, her favorite book in her collection.

"You expect me to sell my freedom for a single book?" Maybe she would consider if he also had her research, but her pride cost more than he thought.

"It's not just *any* book, but your favorite. If you're not interested, I can take it back. The fire needs more kindling anyway." He reached for her book, but she snatched it away. "I'll let you keep your precious book as long as you marry Lord Percy."

Her body shook. "I hate you."

Robert put his hand over his heart and smiled softly at her. "Oh, my dear sister. I hate you too."

Jane stepped directly in front of him, looking him directly in the eye. He always hated that they were the same height, so he couldn't lord over her physically as well.

"You've never been able to outthink me, so I don't think you will now."

His jaw ticked. "We'll just have to see, won't we?"

Robert turned on his heel and walked back into the house.

Jane clenched the book to her chest. No one would take it from her now. Her heart was broken, but the pain fueled her. Escaping this house was imperative, but she'd be damned if she had to marry to do so.

CHAPTER 7

*T*he last time Jane had picked a lock was when she was fifteen, but muscle memory had her in the room with a few moves of her flattened hairpin. It helped that this was the same door on which she had learned to pick locks. Back then, it had been their father's office, and she had needed to liberate a confiscated sketchbook. Now, it was Robert's office, and she needed to use his stationery and seal to forge a letter for her admission to Cambridge.

Looking at the room, it was a punch to the gut to see both what Robert had changed and what had remained the same. The gaps in the shelves she created when she had raided the book collection weren't filled in. The writing desk was their father's, but the hideous puce armchair by the bar cart was new. A colorful rug from Sofia's parents was now beneath the desk, and the drapes were a powder blue that didn't match the room, but screamed to be in Sofia's taste.

What remained the same was the bearskin rug in front of the fireplace with a groove on the top of the head from so many years of propping up her books. Her fondest childhood memories were reading on that rug in front of the crackling fire while her father worked. When he was finished, he would tap his knee, and she would run over and tell him about what she had learned.

She ached to tell her father that Cambridge was opening to women. His only condition would have been that she tell him everything she learned. Her father had been gone for so long that the grief was no longer an open wound, but being in here made the old wound throb.

While the office had once been her sanctuary, it was now her enemy's domain. The heavy smell of Robert's cigars replaced the lighter smell of her father's pipe. Messy piles of papers replaced the orderly filing system. The familiar Waterford brandy decanter was in the same spot, but many bottles of whiskey and scotch now surrounded it. A vase of fresh-cut flowers was amongst the bottles, but it did little to disguise the strong smell.

She wiped away her tears before closing the door behind her. She didn't have time for sentimentality since her brother and Sofia could return from their picnic luncheon at any time. Sitting behind the desk, she stared at the disarray before her. Watermarked ringed ledgers balanced between towering paper piles and stacks of letters that were wrinkled and torn. A tumbler lay on its side, the amber liquid it once held had turned into a congealed, sticky mess that stained a letter asking how many shovels were needed at the mine. Dear lord. She bemoaned her lot in life, but she was grateful not to have to answer letters about shovels.

Jane opened the top drawer looking for fresh stationery, but crinkled papers shot out like a spring. She prayed there wasn't an organizational system as she slipped beneath the desk to collect them.

As her fingers closed around the final paper, she heard footsteps in the hallway and froze. The footsteps stopped, but she couldn't tell if it was outside of this room or the dining room across the hall. Slowly, she drew her legs up until she was hugging her knees in an effort to make herself as small as possible. She was still plenty visible, but she hoped to escape detection by virtue of how unexpected it was for her to be folded beneath the desk.

The clock ticked on the fireplace mantle as she held her breath, waiting for the door to open.

Her heart pounded, and her palms sweat as she heard the muffled footsteps move around. They weren't heavy enough to be Robert, but they sounded like Smythe, and it would be almost as bad if he caught her.

Footsteps faded until the hallway was quiet again, and her body relaxed. Her knees ached from being crammed against her chest, and she shifted her hips in an effort to unfold herself. Now that she was out of imminent danger, it was clear that all six feet of her did not belong under there.

Slowly, she rotated until she knelt, banging her head against the bottom of the desk in the process. Pain radiated as she winced at the booming sound. She checked her head to make sure it wasn't serious, her knuckles brushing the smooth wood she had hit. A small knot might form later, but for the moment, it was only sore. Lowering her hand, her knuckles caught on a rough patch of wood that made her frown. This desk had been in their family for generations and should have been sanded to perfection.

She kicked her legs out so she had room to twist around, and she saw that a thin slip of wood had been added to the desk.

A hidden compartment.

The thin wood was so poorly attached that she easily pried it away with her fingers. A few loose papers floated down.

These papers had been neatly filed, free of the torn edges and watermarks that decorated the other documents. She crumpled the edge of the papers as she crawled from beneath the desk.

She picked up the papers with a shaky hand. Her stomach dropped. It was her father's will.

Jane hadn't gone to the will-reading. Their father had fallen ill so quickly that Robert had barely returned from school in time to be with him before he passed. After her father took his final rattled breath, she ran from his deathbed, unable to face a world without the only parent she had ever known. Instead of dealing with the aftermath, she locked herself in her library for days.

Vaguely, she remembered the family lawyer coming to the

house, but she hadn't met with him. When she finally emerged, Robert told her their father had left her their mother's jewelry and that he swore to him on his deathbed that he would always take care of Jane. It wasn't a question of what would happen with the business since Robert had trained his entire life to take over the five Montgomery coal mines.

However, this document told a different story. The will written in her father's steady hand said that Jane got two of the mines. He wrote that he wanted her to have the funds to choose the life she wanted.

The words blurred as her eyes filled with tears. In all of their time together, her father had never bothered to discuss his will, let alone that she would have a substantial inheritance. She flipped to the final page, which was dated the year before he had died, right after she and Robert had turned eighteen.

"You know, I thought you would have found that years ago."

Robert stood in the doorway holding a wrinkled black jacket. His bloodshot eyes looked tired, and though the stench of alcohol wafted from him, he didn't seem to be foxed at the moment.

"Is this real?" The documents shook in her hands.

Robert shrugged as he walked to his liquor cabinet. He gave himself a generous pour of whiskey before downing it in a single gulp. His shoulders relaxed before he turned to her again.

"You're supposed to be the smart one. What do you think?"

Fire shot through Jane's veins. He had been caught with fraud, but he didn't care. Instead of looking guilty, Robert smirked at her as his whiskey tumbler dangled from his hand. She wanted nothing more than to wipe that smug fucking look from his face.

"Why would you do this?"

"Everything was supposed to be *mine*." His eyes flared, and she saw just how deep his hatred ran. "I was the one who worked for this for years. I made all the sacrifices. I wasn't about to give almost half of it away, especially not to *you*."

"Did you keep me from the will-reading on purpose?"

"No, that was a beautiful piece of luck. At worst, I thought he would leave you a paltry sum to keep you going as a spinster. Hell, I

75

even wished for it to happen since that would mean you wouldn't be my problem, but then the solicitor told me that you were to inherit two of the mines." Robert's face flushed a deep red, as if he was living the humiliation all over again. "My entire life, you've been breathing down my neck with your hand out, ready to take a piece of what was rightfully mine."

"You still got almost everything!" she snarled. "You got the house, your education, and your freedom. This would have left you with three mines and more money than even you could manage to piss away."

"I shouldn't have had to give up anything! You could never do any wrong in Father's eyes, while nothing I did was ever good enough. This wasn't about giving something to you, but taking something from me."

Robert picked up the decanter, whiskey spilling as his shaking hand poured another generous shot into his glass. Rage rolled off of him as he knocked back that drink before pouring himself another.

"I'll go to Mr. Anderson and tell him what you stole from me."

Robert laughed. "Do you know what he says every time he sees me? He tells me I'm such a good brother for taking care of you. He would never believe you."

"You could have thrown me some money so we would never have to see each other again." Jane clenched her jaw so hard she feared a tooth would crack.

"I thought about it, but I couldn't risk letting you out of my sight. Not when you could get wrapped up in a love affair and elope without first consulting me, effectively stealing what was meant to be mine for whatever useless man who wanted you."

"But you tried to arrange a marriage for me." She had blown up her entire life to get rid of Henry, and a rage as she had never felt filled her when she realized what he'd done. "You set me up with Henry on purpose with the intention for him to leave me, didn't you?" She had always been suspicious of how quickly he moved on after he had declared how much he loved her, but she assumed it was because she had destroyed his thin male ego.

"Look at that, you are smart after all."

Robert walked around her and sat down, his chair groaned as he leaned back and propped his scuffed Hessians on the desk. She sat on the floor in front of him in a twisted echo of how she used to sit with her father.

"Ruining yourself was the most considerate thing you've ever done," Robert continued. "As long as I'm divulging my secrets, I know I said I would keep your indiscretion quiet, but I made sure everyone in town knew."

It took every ounce of her willpower to keep from shaking him. All of her desperate grabs for independence had played directly into what her brother had wanted at every turn.

"I suppose Percy has something you want since now you're so desperate for me to marry him. So, what are you getting from him?"

"Does it matter? You're finally useful to me. A titled Lord was so desperate for any sliver of our family money that he made a deal with the devil."

Somehow, this was beyond anything she ever thought her brother was capable of. She didn't care about his plans or Lord Percy's—the only person who had ever cared enough to look after her died ten years ago. Not only was she completely and utterly alone, but she was defenseless against the machinations of men who had never cared for her.

"You can't get away with this. You've stolen, lied, and cheated. God only knows what other crimes you've committed."

"But I've already won. Checkmate. There's nothing you can do to stop me." He smiled, maybe the one genuine smile he had ever given her, now that he had ruined her life beyond repair. "I've mapped out exactly how the rest of your life is going to go. You'll marry Percy, produce an heir, and do as you're told. The only thing up to you is if he puts you in a sanitarium directly after your marriage, or if you endear yourself to him so he wants to keep you around. There isn't a single thing you can do to change your destiny."

Bile gathered in Jane's mouth. Pushing herself up from the floor, she barreled out of the room. There was nothing more to say to her brother.

She had no money, freedom, or options. If she went to Mr. Anderson, he would want to speak with her brother before helping her. Then, Robert would charm him, and her punishment would be even worse. He was the charming one, and she was the difficult one. They played their roles well.

Robert had finally backed her into a corner. There was no way for her to have anything close to a life she could live with. She longed run for her library, but that was no longer an option.

All hope seemed lost when an idea popped into her head that stopped her short. Robert had won this round, but she couldn't let him win everything. There was one final move she could make, and she wasn't afraid since her life was forfeit anyway. This way, both her brother and Lord Percy would be fools in *her* game.

* * *

LATE AFTERNOON SUNSHINE filtered through the trees and caressed her face with its warmth. Foxes chattered in the brush, and a bird took flight, but that was the only sound besides the twigs that snapped beneath her feet. It was peaceful, as if she were the only person in the world.

Her feet ached, and sweat poured down her back, but the exertion felt good. Her heavy wool coat was too warm for the late summer day, but it was necessary for her plan. She had walked from her home into town to meet with Mr. Anderson, the family solicitor.

The secretary had been nervous when she didn't have an appointment. He had been eating lunch in his office, but still managed to greet her warmly.

"Miss Montgomery, what a lovely surprise," he had said while wiping the crumbs from his desk. "To what do I owe this pleasure?"

"I wanted to create a will." She had created an elaborate backstory as to why she suddenly needed a will, but he never asked.

Instead, he complimented her good sense in getting a will in place while she was young.

Robert may have been ahead of her at every turn, but *this* was how she would reclaim her power. She left the mines to the local orphanage. Mr. Anderson had commended her generosity, but she wasn't doing it for the children. Her sole motivation was to keep the money from Robert. Even if he wanted to fight her will in court, the optics of suing an orphanage were awful.

Mr. Anderson asked about her other assets, but there was nothing else. The only belonging she had left in the world was her copy of *Gray's Anatomy*, which she decided to leave to Eleanor. Her will was filed with Mr. Anderson's secretary as a witness, and that was her final task.

The only thing she had left to do was die.

Jane walked towards the river. Ideally, she would have gone to the coast, but that journey would take days, and she didn't have that kind of time. Before she left, she had snuck into the family library to look at the map they had of Yorkshire. The map was at least twenty years out of date, but the shape of the land hadn't changed.

When she hit the river, she turned to follow it upstream. The bridge on the map hadn't looked to be too far, but she hoped no one had built anything along the path in the years since the map's creation. Roaring water overpowered every other sound of the forest, hypnotizing her as she walked beside it. Water had flowed through this land for thousands of years and would do so for thousands more.

The world was a marvel. Humanity discovered something new every day. Recently, she read about a doctor who had performed a successful blood transfusion on a woman who bled out while giving birth. It was a dangerous procedure, but the woman would have died without it, just like Jane's mother. The procedure was still in its infancy, but it had the potential to save many lives. There was still so much to learn.

She arrived at the stone bridge she had found on the map. This path was seldom used since better roads had been built, and what had once been the main road into town was now lost to time.

Weeds grew between the stones, and vines crawled up the sides. Loose rocks were strewn about the walkway, and she knelt to shovel as many as she could into her cloak pockets.

The bridge was built for form over function. The thin ledge barely reached her hips, so it didn't take much effort to hoist herself up. She lost her balance for a moment before righting herself. Technically, it didn't matter if she fell, but she wanted to do it right.

The yellow rays of the sun had deepened to orange, and the light blue sky began its transition to a darker slate blue as twilight approached. Even through the trees, she was glad to have a view of the wide open sky. The river beneath her was an inky black. The current was so fast that the more she stared at it, the dizzier she became. She was grateful she never learned to swim.

Jane thought about the feeling of sunshine on her face. The smell of her library. The weight of books in her arms. Yorkshire roses. Lemon tarts. Her father's smile as she told him about her day. She imagined what it would feel like to be held in her mother's arms.

She stepped forward and dropped into the river below.

CHAPTER 8

*W*ill let out a deep breath as he bent over, extending his body until his fingertips brushed his boots. He pushed down on the leather until he felt his toes. Triumph flared at the accomplishment he had been chasing for months. When this training regimen began, he had barely been able to reach his knees without pain radiating through his legs. Stretching had never been a priority when he was alive, so Tristan was unsure if it was a side effect of death or if that was his natural baseline.

He felt the stretch through the back of his thighs and his calves, but there wasn't any pain. Toes were an accomplishment, but the floor was his goal, and he felt like he could make it today. Exhaling again, Will bore down, stretching himself to his very limits.

"Don't strain yourself. This is a good milestone," Tristan warned.

"I'm not," he replied through gritted teeth.

His hamstrings began to strain, but it wasn't dangerous. Even if he tore a muscle, he would heal in minutes. With a bit of momentum, his fingertips grazed the floor. He was almost there.

A gentle push to his backside destabilized him, causing him to fall forward. Luckily, his reflexes caught him before his face hit the floor. Pain reverberated through his wrists from the force of impact, but it dissipated as he turned to his brother.

"Looks like the strain caused you to lose your balance."

"I was doing just fine without your interference."

Tristan held out his hand to help him up, but Will ignored it in favor of pushing himself up.

"Your face was bright red, and you looked moments away from tearing a muscle."

"I would have healed in less than ten minutes."

Tristan rolled his eyes. "That doesn't mean you need to injure yourself."

His only goal was to see how far he could push himself. Tristan tested his strength, flexibility, coordination, reflexes, aerobic activity, and memory every other day. Life as a test subject was dehumanizing, but he enjoyed the satisfaction of achieving a new personal record.

"Are we done yet?"

Will rolled his shoulders. The pleasant burn in his hamstrings had faded, but he wanted to see if he could chase that feeling away from judgmental eyes.

Tristan scribbled in his journal. A few months ago, Will had peeked inside to see what his brother wrote about him. He didn't know if he was relieved or disappointed to find it was statistics without editorializing. Occasionally, a question was posed in the margins or an extrapolation based on the data, but it was always impersonal.

"How has your cognition been?" Tristan asked without looking up.

"I keep forgetting my name. Do you think that's a problem?"

"Be serious," Tristan said, shooting him a glare.

"It's been fine."

Everything was always fine these days. He slept fine, ate fine, walked fine, talked fine, felt *fine*. Nothing felt bad, but it wasn't great either.

"Have you experienced any brain fog? Any confusion or trouble reading?"

"No." Will went rigid because Tristan typically didn't ask any follow-up questions. "Have you noticed anything wrong with me?"

"No, I only asked because you'll notice before I will."

Tristan returned to his scribbling, and Will relaxed. Tristan wouldn't be afraid to voice any concerns if he had them.

"Are we finished for the day?"

"That's enough for now. I need to compare these results to last month." Closing the notebook, Tristan looked at him and smiled, switching from doctor to brother. "Do you have any plans for the remainder of your day?"

"No."

He had wanted to plant some camellias to get his winter garden started, but Tristan had summoned him for tests before luncheon, and now it was well after sunset.

"Well, thank you for your assistance. I won't keep you any longer," Tristan took a deep breath. "This research could prove to be very valuable for medicine and understanding how the human body works. I know I don't say it often, but I do appreciate you doing this."

Will sighed. It was difficult to be annoyed when his brother was being reasonable. As much as he detested being a test subject, he couldn't be selfish and deny his brother's scientific progress after everything Tristan had done for him.

"It's not a problem," Will said before he turned on his heel and left the laboratory.

Bounding down the stairs, his cloak billowed behind him. Wearing the cloak indoors wasn't necessary since everyone there knew his dark secret, but it had become a source of comfort.

"Ah, Mrs. Jones," he said once he reached the final step. The housekeeper was hunched over as she scrubbed the black and white checkered floor. "There you are."

"I've been here all day, William."

Mrs. Jones stood up, leaning the mop against her, as she massaged her hands.

"All day?" Will frowned at the aging housekeeper. The bags beneath her eyes were heavier than he remembered when he last saw her. Instinctively, he reached for the mop, but she moved it before he could grab it.

"It's a big room, but I can handle it. Are you and Tristan ready for dinner? It shouldn't take me long to throw something together."

"No." The last thing he wanted was to give her more work. He and Tristan were more than capable of handling their own meal. "I was wondering if any letters arrived today."

He tried to keep a neutral expression even as his heart thumped so hard he was convinced she could hear it. If his brother were there, he would have ordered many tests to study this abnormality.

"A letter... for you?" She asked with a raised brow.

"Yes."

The housekeeper stayed silent, but Will did not elaborate. He wasn't ready to answer any questions about Miss Montgomery, mainly because he wasn't sure if she would ever write him back.

"No letters for you, but I'll let you know as soon as you receive one. Is there a specific name I should be looking for?"

"No," Will snapped. "You used to be much better at digging for information."

"Forgive me, but it's been quite some time since you've had anything worth digging."

"Do you need help mopping the floor?"

Changing the topic was his safest bet to retain the small amount of dignity he had left.

"From you? No."

Will wanted to argue that he could help because mopping couldn't be terribly difficult, but he knew by her glare that Mrs. Jones saw the fact that he had never mopped as a detriment.

"Who would you accept help from?"

"I can handle it, stop worrying about me."

"Really?" It was Will's turn to look at her with a raised brow. "Because you look like you could use some assistance."

"It's not as if I can bring any real help into the house, can I?"

Will bristled. He had pressured Tristan to fire the other staff because he didn't want people to see him. To know what he was. Now, Mrs. Jones had to do everything herself.

"I suppose not," he said before walking out into the night.

* * *

THE MOON WAS SO bright that he didn't need any additional light to guide him through the forest. Tristan thought he only went out at night to hide, but the truth was that he liked the peace that came with a quiet forest.

His walks were never short strolls through the garden, but rather long walks through the forest until the sun rose over the horizon. Dawn was his favorite time because it felt like the land was taking a deep breath before the new day. Watching the sun rise wasn't a new activity for him, but when he was alive, he only saw dawn as he was stumbling home from a night of revelry.

Remembering who he used to be felt like listening to someone else's dream. Work filled his days, but his nights were spent drinking, partying, or doing his best to ensure he wasn't alone. Solitude made him ruminate, and there was nothing he had disliked more than thinking about his life.

The life of an eldest son was one of duty. The Gardners weren't nobility, but they were knights until their business received a Royal Warrant, which led them from chivalry to commerce. At least his father had been the first Gardner in generations not to be knighted, so Will didn't have to own that familial embarrassment.

The inky-black sky lightened to lavender as the forest slowly began to wake. Baby birds chirped as they waited for their morning meal. He would watch the sunrise over the river before returning home.

Approaching the riverbank, he saw a wad of fabric amongst the rocks. Annoyance bubbled in him at the people who used the river as their personal dumping grounds. The river was dirty enough without the extra debris. He didn't know where he would put them, but he didn't want to leave them on the riverbank until a duck choked on the rotting fabric.

As he approached the trash, he tilted his head. A flash of white was buried in the black fabric, but it took him a moment to realize what it was.

A hand lay nestled in the old clothes. His approach was slow as he waited for whoever it was to shoot up and continue their walk along the river. His boots made a loud squelching noise as he walked, but the figure stayed so very still. Up close, the mass of fabric was a thick black coat with its hem dancing in the current.

Heart pounding in his ears, he looked down at the pale face that stared vacantly at the early morning sky. Horror bloomed in him when he realized he recognized the face. It was Miss Montgomery.

She looked like herself, but also... different, like something was missing. Her face was paler than moonlight, algae tangled in her dark hair that he carefully picked away with his gloved hands. Blood stained her temple from where her head had been crushed, but the wound had long stopped bleeding.

"Miss Montgomery, are you all right?" The raspy question didn't sound like it was his voice, but the vibration in his throat meant it was his.

Shaky fingers searched her throat for a pulse. Tristan had done this to him thousands of times, but Will couldn't seem to find the right spot.

She was going to be fine. He couldn't find her pulse in her neck, but it was much easier to hear a heartbeat than to feel one. Murmuring an apology for being forward, he lowered his head to her chest to listen for her heartbeat.

The world around him was too loud; he needed the pre-dawn silence to return. Frogs croaked, the river wouldn't dampen its roar, and a fox chittered in the distance. Clearly, Miss Montgomery wasn't *well*, but her heartbeat had to be there.

"You must wake up." The command was a whisper, but deep down, he knew the words were only for his benefit.

The only heartbeat he heard was his own, which mocked him with every beat. It had been minutes, but she hadn't taken a single breath. Pushing himself up with shaky arms, he sat beside her in the muck.

Miss Montgomery was dead.

It had only been a few days since he last saw her, and she had been so *alive*. So excited for the opportunity to study at Cambridge. Tristan had kept his word and given her a recommendation. She had been on the precipice of a new life.

The world felt like it was spinning off its axis, so he closed his eyes and propped himself up against his arms so he didn't fall in the mud. The rushing water sounded like a freight train, but it helped to quiet his mind. After a few shaky breaths, he opened his eyes to look at the body beside him.

Will had very little experience with dead bodies—outside of being one—but it didn't look like she had been dead for very long. He didn't know what happened, but thought she may have been on a walk when she fell into the river, hitting her head either on rocks on the way down or in the river itself. Between the strong current and her heavy coat, she didn't stand a chance once she hit the water. A ten-second tumble had stolen her future.

It wasn't fair that he was cursed to walk the Earth forever while she only got a few paltry decades. There was no doubt she would have made a better use of her time.

Will's stomach turned as he realized there was an option after all. Tristan could help her the same way he had helped Will. Her death didn't have to be final.

Her head wound looked superficial, and she didn't have any other visible damage. Good. It would make the process easier this time. Will was glad he had already gone through all of the trial and error, so her procedure could be seamless.

Sunlight filtered through the trees as daylight strengthened. He needed to get her home. This part of the forest was technically on his property, but he didn't want to risk someone getting lost and catching him. Lifting her was awkward as she was a bit stiff, but he barely registered her weight as he walked with her in his arms.

His walk home filled him with purpose. Once Miss Montgomery was brought back, he would help her adjust, be there for her in the way he wished someone had been there for him. She would never know the same soul-crushing loneliness that had permeated him. There hadn't been time to get to know one another while she had been alive, but now they had all the time in the world.

The thinning trees signaled he was almost home. As soon as the house came into view, he sprinted towards it. He ran up the back steps two at a time, only slowing down once he hit the checkered floor Mrs. Jones had spent the previous day cleaning.

Rounding the corner, Mrs. Jones exited the dining room. The housekeeper stopped short, her eyes growing wide as she took in the scene before her.

"What have you done?" Mrs. Jones asked in a quiet voice.

"It's not as bad as it looks."

"I would certainly hope not because it looks like you have an unconscious woman in your arms."

Oh. "Then it's worse than it looks because she's dead." Mrs. Jones looked as if she would faint, so he quickly continued. "I found her like this, washed up on the riverbank."

"You didn't kill her?" Mrs. Jones looked skeptical, but the color was returning to her face.

"No." Will knew this looked suspicious, but he was still annoyed that she assumed he had murdered a woman. "I'm taking her to Tristan to see if he can help her."

Her shoulders relaxed. "Your brother's in his lab. Get her up there before Morris sees."

Even if Morris had walked in at that moment, the man likely wouldn't have asked a single question. When Tristan had tried to explain Will's situation, the groundskeeper held up a hand to stop him, saying it was safer if he didn't know the details. It was why Will got along with him, but he didn't want to put him in the situation of having to ignore the body in Will's arms.

Will bounded up the stairs, adjusting Miss Montgomery in his arms as he reached for the doorknob that didn't budge. The locked door wasn't a surprise, but it was annoying that he had to knock.

"I'm busy," Tristan shouted. He hated being disturbed, but Will didn't care.

"It's an emergency."

Tristan was silent for so long that Will prepared to knock again when the door opened.

"Will," he said as he stared at Miss Montgomery in his arms. "Why are you carrying an unconscious woman?"

"She's dead."

Tristan's eyes snapped to his. "That's much worse," he hissed. "How did this happen?"

"I didn't do it," he snapped.

Being accused of murder for the second time in as many minutes had soured his mood.

"That doesn't answer my question. Don't pretend you wouldn't be concerned if our situations were flipped."

Will let out a deep breath. Tristan was correct, of course. Their suspicion didn't feel good, but it was fair.

"I think she drowned, but I don't know precisely what happened because I found her like this. You have to fix her." Will wasn't above begging.

"If she's dead, then she has no use for medicine."

"You asked me what I wanted, you said you would do anything for me. I want you to fix her, as you did with me."

His heart pounded as his request hung limply in the air. Tristan looked conflicted, which set something off inside him. Where was this hesitation when Will was the one in the ground?

Tristan turned his attention back to the woman in his arms. Will saw recognition flash. "Oh, Miss Montgomery," Tristan murmured. Will felt a glimmer of hope at his brother's grief. "How, exactly, did you find her?"

"I was taking my nightly walk—"

Tristan cut him off, "I don't care about that. How did you come across the body?"

Will swallowed. It felt callous to think of her as a body. "On the riverbank. She was wrapped in a thick wool coat with her head in the water. The head wound was out of the water, but wasn't bleeding. I tried to find her pulse, but I couldn't. I'm not sure how long she was there."

Tristan nodded. "Put her on the examination table."

The metal examination table was in the middle of the room. Will wanted to lay a sheet on the table because he remembered how unpleasantly cold it was, but there wasn't one nearby.

Gingerly, he placed Miss Montgomery on the slab. Tristan placed his black medical bag on the table beside her, pulling out tools and chemicals Will didn't recognize. Tristan probed her head wound, cleaning it with a damp handkerchief so he could see the depth of the wound.

"Can you help her?" Will asked as Tristan pulled out a stethoscope and continued his examination.

"That's what I'm trying to figure out."

It felt like an eternity had passed before Tristan finished the exam and finally looked back up at him. Will didn't like the trepidation he saw in his eyes.

"Do you really want me to bring her back?"

"Obviously."

Will didn't think he could make his intentions any clearer. He hadn't carried her here for fun.

"She's dead, Will."

"I know, but so was I, and now I'm not, so I want you to do for her what you did for me."

"I want to make sure you know what you're asking. You've been so miserable that I never thought you'd ever ask me to do this." Tristan's voice was gentle, which only made Will angrier. He didn't need a lecture about what this choice meant.

"You didn't have this conscience when you brought me back, and you don't need it now." Tristan's face reddened as he opened his mouth, but Will silenced him with a harsh look. "Fix. Her."

Tristan tensed like he wanted to fight, but Will kept his glare. "Please." He said in a softer voice, watching his brother's resolve crumble.

"I'll do it," he whispered, looking down.

Will closed his eyes, letting out a breath. "Thank you. She deserves this chance."

Tristan nodded. "Let me prepare. I'm going to need your assistance."

Will nodded. He would help in any way he could. Tristan left to gather his instruments.

Will's chest ached as he looked at her lying on that table. This shouldn't have been how he saw her again. She should be warm and tucked away in her library with a cup of tea and her research, rather than being cold and waterlogged in the laboratory. Her arm hung limply off the table after Tristan's examination, and Will carefully picked it up and placed it beside her.

"It's all right, you'll be as good as new soon. It'll be like it never happened." He kept talking to reassure her everything was going to be all right, even though he knew she couldn't hear him.

He was doing the right thing for someone in need, but there was a small part of him deep down that he utterly loathed. It was the part of him that was happy he would no longer be alone. There would be one other person in this world who knew what it was like to die and come back. Someone he could spend the rest of all time with. He wouldn't have to hide from her.

This was the most selfish thing he had ever done, but she would forgive him when he explained he had reversed the accident. His gift to her was time. She would have plenty of time to study and learn everything she could. It would be worth it for her.

"Here, put these on," Tristan handed him a white coat and a pair of goggles. "Get some towels and my suture kit by the sink. Clean her wounds and start sewing them together. Try to keep the stitches small, but don't worry too much because they'll heal well."

Will nodded and got started on his tasks, careful to keep his hand steady as he stitched up her head wound. They'd gotten to her quickly enough that Tristan said they wouldn't need to source any additional parts, which made Will relax. He was thankful she would have an easier transition.

CHAPTER 9

*E*ven before Jane opened her eyes, she knew she had failed because the bed was far too soft to be in purgatory. Of course, she didn't believe in an afterlife, but she also never expected to experience consciousness again, so she was prepared to consider the option.

Her single comfort was that her plan hadn't been a complete failure because the stark white ceiling meant she wasn't at home. However, she had no idea *where* she was. The white walls and bedding evoked the feelings of a hospital, but she had never heard of a hospital with the funds for feather beds and hand-carved armoires.

Memories of her fall were hazy, but she remembered slamming into the water, being whipped around in the strong current, and the burn in her lungs before she lost consciousness. She braced herself for a deluge of pain, but it never came.

Jane frowned because she felt good. Too good. Her fingers and toes wiggled appropriately, her arms rotated, and her spine twisted without an issue. Jane was relieved her pain-free body wasn't the result of a spinal cord injury, but it didn't make any *sense*. If she'd been unconscious long enough to heal, her brain damage would be so severe she wouldn't have woken up.

The door creaked open, and she grabbed a pillow, ready to attack whoever came through the door. A proper weapon would have been nice, but she could use it as a distraction to make her escape.

Dr. Gardner stepped into the room, and she gripped the pillow to her chest. She was grateful neither Robert nor Lord Percy had passed through the door, but Dr. Gardner was too much a stranger to bring her much comfort.

"Good day, Miss Montgomery, I'm glad to see you're finally awake," the doctor said as he walked to the side of her bed, placing a doctor's bag on the bedside table.

"How long have I been out?"

"Not too long."

He still hadn't looked at her directly, but she had the chance to study him as he pulled tools from his bag. Dark circles were beneath his eyes, and his mouth was drawn into a severe line as he pulled a long needle from his bag.

"Have you been bloodletting me?" It was a barbaric practice, one she assumed modern doctors had left behind. She readied to swing the pillow if that needle got any closer.

"No, I'm taking a sample to look at your blood under a micro-scope to make sure your treatment has worked." The doctor pasted on a bland smile that was probably meant to comfort her as he prepared the needle.

A knot formed in her stomach because his expression wasn't quite right. His eyes darted everywhere but her, and sweat beaded at his temples.

"What treatment did you give me?"

"It's an experimental procedure I developed while in Munich."

Her eyes narrowed. "Why do you need to confirm it worked with a blood sample? Did you not pull me from a river?"

"Yes." Dr. Gardner paused, wiping the sweat from his face. "The water severely damaged your lungs, so I gave you some medicine to accelerate the healing process."

"What kind of medicine?"

"I can explain it later, but I would like to take your blood sample now."

Jane shrank back. "You can't get my blood until you explain exactly why you need it."

"I want to compare it to the previous sample I took to make sure you're healing. I know it's a bit unorthodox, but since it's such a new treatment, I want to make sure it went as planned."

Her jaw was set in a hard line, and she could see the exasperation in his eyes when she made it clear she would not bend.

The doctor sighed. "I'll let you look at both of the samples once I'm done."

"Fine."

The offer was made reluctantly, but his instinct to let her inspect the samples was correct. She had never seen a microscope before, but even the idea of using one made her giddy. Besides, if she had been unconscious, he had already had ample opportunities to hurt her.

Scooting towards the doctor, she placed the pillow on her lap and lay her forearm on it. After he cleaned her arm with alcohol, she turned her head before he pierced her with the needle.

Despite her interest in medicine, she hated needles. The pain was intense for a few moments before melting away, which was strange because usually she felt every moment the needle was in her. It spoke to his skill as a doctor that he could do it so painlessly.

"Dr. Gardner," she said with her head still fixed to the opposite wall in case the bloody needle was still visible. "I'm grateful for your assistance, but how did I get here?"

The doctor was silent as she heard him fiddling with his tools. Something was going on, but she didn't have the faintest idea of what it could be.

"You were found with a head wound on the riverbank, which may be why you're experiencing some brain fog. I do have a question for you as well, if you don't mind."

"What would you like to know?" She asked, turning to him as her heart rate climbed.

The needle had been put away, but a vial of her crimson blood remained on the table. It was a bigger vial than she had expected from such a painless procedure. Looking at her arm, she frowned because she couldn't see a mark where the needle went in.

"How did you get in the river?" He asked before quickly wiping the crook of her arm with a handkerchief.

"Oh, I'm not sure. I was on a walk. Knowing me, I likely tripped, but it's a little hazy."

If he was going to lie, then she would do the same.

"Are you usually clumsy?"

"Sometimes," she shrugged. "Will you take me to the microscope now? I'm feeling quite well."

"Um, let me review your new sample first, and then I'll retrieve you if it looks good."

"Why can't I go now?"

"I think it's for the best if you get some rest for now."

"I don't need to rest. In fact, I think it would be best if I moved around some."

Sweat dotted the doctor's brow, and his eyes avoided her again. "Your injuries were extensive, so it will take you some time to heal."

"But I feel fine. My muscles aren't even stiff from being in bed. If my injuries were so extensive, then why can't I feel them?"

Dr. Gardner scrubbed his face before looking behind her. "What do you want me to say?"

Her blood chilled as she realized they weren't alone. Her heart thumped as she turned to see a cloaked figure haunting the doorway.

"I think you were doing well until the end. Is she all right?" The cloaked figure rumbled, and she recognized both the cloak and the deep, brooding voice as belonging to Mr. Gardner.

"*She* would like you to stop talking about her as if she isn't here."

"My—he was the one who found you," Dr. Gardner said, shooting a glare at the lurking figure before he continued. "I can ask him to leave if you wish."

"Oh." Jane threw another glance at Mr. Gardner. "He can stay if at least one of you starts answering my questions. What were my injuries?"

Dr. Gardner shot another look into the hall. She frowned because he seemed to be consulting the non-doctor too often. "You don't have to worry about them because I was able to heal you."

The pasted-on smile returned, and her unease grew because there was no reason for him to be so evasive. If her injuries were slight, then why couldn't he tell her?

"When was I found?"

"It's been nearly a week," he sighed. "You really should rest. We can discuss this later."

"No, I can't have been unconscious for that long." She ran her fingers around her scalp, checking for contusions, but she couldn't find a tender spot. "That timeframe suggests a serious injury, but I don't even have a scratch."

Dr. Gardner shifted. "You were out because of a sedative I gave you rather than your injuries. It made it easier for your body to heal," he said, his eyes darting back to the hallway.

"For nearly a week?" She screeched. She might not have all of his fancy degrees, but she wasn't an *idiot*. "I know you're up to something—both of you. Your story doesn't make any sense. I know I was in the water, and I know I should be injured."

If not worse.

"I told you this was a bad idea," Dr. Gardner said.

She held the pillow to her chest to act as a shield against her captors. "You're going to let me go now," she hissed. "When my brother finds out you've kidnapped me, you will be in a world of pain."

It was a hell of a bluff since the last thing she wanted was for Robert to get involved, but she needed them scared enough to let her go.

Mr. Gardner finally walked into the room, holding up his gloved hands in an attempt to look less threatening. It did not work. "I understand you're scared, but we aren't going to hurt you."

"Which is exactly what a murderer would say." She glanced at the bedside table. The only projectile was a half-burned candle, but it would work in a pinch. "You're dressed like a prowler, yet you expect me to trust that you mean me no harm?"

He stopped several feet from her. "I wouldn't have taken you here so my brother could heal you if I meant you harm."

"Brother? But Dr. Gardner's brother is..." she trailed off, eyes bouncing between the two men. It was ludicrous to give voice to her suspicions, but she could feel the panic pouring from them. Picking up the surprisingly hefty candle, she considered which one to throw it at. It would depend on whoever annoyed her more. "You're going to tell me what's going on right now."

"You need to calm down—" She threw the candle at Mr. Gardner before he finished his misguided sentence. The candle bounced off his shoulder instead of his head, but he was doubled over, so it wasn't a complete failure.

With one Gardner down, she threw off the blankets and tossed them at the doctor to block his vision so she could bolt to the door.

It was the fastest she ever ran, but with one foot in the hallway, a pair of hands grabbed her, hauling her back inside the room. His gloved hands held her like iron, but she thrashed in an attempt to escape. He may have caught her, but she wouldn't be an easy victim.

Kicking back, she aimed for his kneecap to make his leg fold beneath the pressure, but she misjudged her angle and caught him in the shin. He winced, but didn't let go.

Her head tipped back to meet where his eyes should be when she realized just how tall he was. It was rare for her to have to look up at someone, so it annoyed her that she had to now. No one had any business being six and a half feet tall.

Most of his face was still covered by that ridiculous hood, but she could see his strong jaw and plush lips that twisted into a grimace when he realized she was looking up his hood. Embarrassment heated her cheeks at being caught staring, so she scowled and tried to shove him away, but his hold was still too strong.

"Let me go or... else." He was too big to intimidate physically, but she would never stop trying.

"Or else what? You don't have anything left to throw," he said. She could feel his warm breath against her ear, and she fought the shiver the sensation caused.

"Please, Miss. Montgomery, we aren't holding you hostage.

You're free to go as soon as I explain your situation." The man behind her started to voice his disagreement, but the doctor shut him down with a glare. "Please, sit down, and I'll explain."

Dr. Gardner gave her a meek smile. His willowy limbs looked easy to snap, so she was willing to pause while he answered her questions. Jane picked the candle back up in case either of them tried something she didn't like.

"Miss Montgomery. When you were found on the riverbank, your injuries were extensive. Your left leg was shattered, you had seven broken ribs, a punctured lung, a snapped collar bone, and a fractured skull. I'm not sure how long you were in the water, but it was at least a few hours, and your lungs were completely waterlogged."

"No." Jane's brow furrowed. The doctor wasn't making any sense. "Those are fatal injuries."

"Yes." Dr. Gardner finally looked at her.

Jane's heart pounded as she waited for him to continue. Surely he would add that it was a miracle she got to him in time, and she would have been dead if she arrived even a moment later, but the addendum never came. Biting the inside of her cheek, the brief flare of pain told her she was awake.

"How am I alive?"

"I'm a medical doctor, but I don't see many patients in favor of focusing on research." He paced around the room as he spoke. "My focus has always been on the study of life. How it is created, even the end of life, and what that process means. I spent years experimenting with the generation of life, regeneration specifically. So when your body was brought to me, I knew I could bring you back."

"I was dead, and you brought me back to life."

"Yes."

It was the most ridiculous thing she had ever heard, but he looked so serious she didn't know what to think.

"Was that your first time?"

Dr. Gardner paused before shaking his head. "No."

Laughter bubbled from her. She slapped a hand over her mouth in an attempt to quiet herself, but it didn't work.

"I'm sorry, it's not very funny, but I can't seem to help it."

"It's quite all right," Dr. Gardner responded. His composure had returned at the very least. She could feel the other one at her back, but he hadn't said a word. "Allow me to introduce you to my brother, Mr. Will Gardner."

His *dead* brother, she had heard people whisper about it at the ball after her brother had told her in the carriage. She waited for the other Gardner to say something, anything to refute what the doctor said, but he remained silent.

Turning, she looked at him to see if there were any clues that he was dead, but he was still covered from head to toe. Well, being perpetually covered might be a clue that whatever was beneath the cloak was horrific. Her skin didn't feel like it was rotting away when she examined herself, but maybe it would look different. Jane had never been vain, but she didn't want to look like a corpse.

"What's wrong with you?" She internally flinched as soon as the words left her mouth. She meant to ask why he was wearing the cloak. Which was still impolite, but with slightly more tact.

"Nothing more than what's wrong with you."

"No." It felt like the wind was knocked out of her. The rejection was a reflex, but deep inside, she knew he was telling the truth.

Raising his arms, she could see the tremor in his hands as he lowered the hood so she could see his face for the first time. He didn't look at all like she expected. She thought he would be decomposing with maggots falling from holes in his face, but he looked relatively normal. Handsome, even.

His face was scarred, some were thick like the one that bisected his left eyebrow, while others were thin like the one that ran over his chin or the faint line where his hairline had been stitched together. Some of the work was neat, but much of it was messy, with jagged, uneven lines. His skin was so pale it seemed as if he hadn't seen sunlight in ages, but there were competing undertones which piqued her curiosity. His most traditionally handsome feature was his jaw, which looked as if it had been carved from marble. His yellow eyes seemed to glow in the gas lamps' light. He wasn't exactly pretty, but he was compelling, which was better because his face was one you would never forget. They were both dead. Or had been at the very least.

Her suicide was successful; she had been freed from Robert and his machinations, but only for a few moments before she had been snapped back into the web of life by a different pair of men. Jane had thought there was nothing else she could lose, but she didn't even have autonomy over her death. She felt so hopeless and helpless, and didn't know how to fix it. The sole idea she had failed horrifically, so she did the only thing she could think of to relieve the growing pressure inside of her. She screamed.

CHAPTER 10

*M*iss Montgomery's scream felt like a stab to the gut. Will's hands shook as he lifted his hood back into place. He knew he wasn't pleasing to look at, but he didn't think he was quite so monstrous to evoke this response. His presence was a curse even amongst the formerly dead.

"It'll be all right," Tristan said as he inched his way toward the devastated woman. When he didn't get pelted with another projectile, he pat her on the shoulder. "There's no reason to be frightened."

"I'm not frightened," Miss Montgomery snarled, her hands gripped the pillow so tight her knuckles were white. "I'm furious. Who gave you the right to bring me back to life?"

Eyes wide, Tristan took a step back. He stammered, unable to come up with a response when all he had to do was blame it on Will. If anyone deserved her ire, it was him.

"He brought you back because I asked him to." He took a step forward, ready for whatever punishment she deemed appropriate.

"Fine, why did you make him bring me back?"

Because I was so profoundly lonely, you looked like my salvation washed up on the shore.

However, it was a shamefully poor excuse, so instead he squared his shoulders in preparation to take accountability. "I don't want anything in return, if that's what you're worried about. I saved you so you could be free to live your life however you wish."

In his most selfish moments, he had dreamed of finding a companion in her, but he had let go of that naive dream.

Miss Montgomery was silent for a long moment before throwing her head back in a sharp bark of laughter that sounded more like madness than humor. Tristan looked at him, imploring him to step in and do something, but Will was frozen.

"You didn't save me, you condemned me."

No," he said hoarsely. Will would never do that. He *helped* people. Tristan helped people. "You fell in the river, and I saved you."

"Do you really think I wore my heaviest cloak and stuffed rocks in my pockets and accidentally fell? No, I jumped. I wanted to die."

Will stumbled back, feeling as if he couldn't breathe. He knew better after spending so long cursing his existence, but he still damned another to this existence. There was nothing he could do to rectify this.

"Oh, no," Tristan said softly. "I know it's not enough, but I'm so sorry." He heard the catch in his brother's throat. That was Will's fault too.

An apology was where he needed to start, but the words turned to ash on his tongue. His palms sweat, and his heart pounded so hard it was all he heard. Both she and Tristan were silent, as if they were waiting for him to say something, but he couldn't. This was yet another entry on his long list of failures.

In an act of cowardice he already hated himself for, he ran from the room without another word. Pounding footsteps echoed through the halls as he dashed down the stairs. His chest heaved as he made it to the final step, but it still felt like he couldn't breathe.

Passing by the library, he considered ducking in to lose himself amongst the books, but being indoors felt too constricting. Running through the ballroom, he threw open the glass doors and ran outside.

It was well after midnight, but the moon was hidden behind

clouds as he stumbled across the lawn. Fumbling with the silver clasp at his throat, he finally managed to unhook the cloak, and the garment floated to the ground behind him.

Finally unencumbered, he took big gulps of the cool night air. The panic receded some, but it wasn't enough. His heart raced, and he felt like he was on the edge of a cliff, but he wasn't ready to see what waited for him at the bottom.

Without realizing it, he had made it out to his rose garden. He wanted to laugh. Of course, he would come out here, to the one place where he truly felt at peace. The fragrance of the flowers surrounded him, loosening more of the anxiety that choked him.

The bushes were largely bare, but he had noticed a new bloom yesterday. The white rose was visible even with the starless night sky, and he was pleased to see it was still hanging on. Carefully, he ran his gloved finger over the petals, imagining their velvety soft feel. It had been ages since he had directly touched a flower.

Kneeling in the dirt, he cleared some of the dead leaves, and his heartbeat stabilized as he worked. His trousers would be a mess after this, but he would apologize to Mrs. Jones for the additional laundry later. There wasn't much he could do without light or his tools, but it felt good to bring order to something as he cleared away the dead growth.

Now that his body had calmed, the heavy guilt finally had the chance to settle in. He hadn't meant to hurt Miss Montgomery. Intentions weren't as important as actions, but there was also no way he could have known how she ended up on that shore. However, that also meant he couldn't have known if this life was what she would want. *He* had been the one who wanted her to live.

Will lay down on the grass already damp with pre-morning dew, lamenting that the stars were hidden behind the clouds. He loved the stars. Tristan once told him the stars had been there for thousands of years and would be there for thousands more, just like him. And now Miss Montgomery.

God, she didn't even know all of the details of her new reality.

"I thought I'd find you here."

Will turned to see Tristan walking towards him with a lantern.

"I want to be alone," he said, turning his head back to the sky. He would be useful later, but right now he just wanted to brood.

"I don't care." Tristan stopped directly above him, the lantern giving him an ominous glow. "We need to talk."

"We can talk later." Will closed his eyes, hoping he would take the hint and leave.

Tristan was silent for a few long moments, but Will should have known he wouldn't give up that easily.

"You shouldn't have left like that."

"I know." He already had enough guilt without any more being piled on.

"She had a lot of questions, and it would have been nice if you had been there to help answer them."

Will snorted. "I wouldn't have been much help. I was just your first subject."

"She still wanted to hear from you, and I think she deserved to. There were some questions I couldn't answer."

Will's eyes popped open. "What could I possibly answer that you couldn't?"

"I don't know what it's like to live in a body like yours. Besides, she keeps asking what's going to happen to her, and I'm not sure what to tell her."

"And you assume that I do?"

"I thought you had some kind of plan when you brought her to me."

"I didn't plan this," Will huffed. Everything had gotten so out of control. This past week, waiting for her to wake up had been so stressful that the relief he felt when he saw she was awake and coherent nearly floored him. "There's no plan except for her to live however she wants."

"I don't think she'll appreciate that answer, so you should think of something else before you see her again."

"Of course, this is all left up to me," Will said, squeezing his eyes shut. He knew he should quit while he was ahead, but he couldn't stop himself now. "The fun part is over, so now you don't give a damn about what happens to either of us."

"I don't think continuing this conversation is productive at this time," his brother said coolly. "We can continue this tomorrow after you speak with Miss Montgomery."

Tristan's footsteps gradually faded as he walked away, but he didn't open his eyes again until the world around him was silent again.

Will needed to find a way to fix what he had done. If she hated him forever, that was fine, but he would make sure Miss Montgomery was all right somehow. Every problem could be solved with enough time, and luckily, time was one thing he had plenty of.

CHAPTER 11

*J*ane stared at the wall until dawn broke, and golden sunlight crept up into the room. Her brain just kept repeating last night's conversation.

From a purely scientific perspective, what Dr. Gardner had achieved was incredible. Beyond incredible, it was a true act of God, and he was doing *nothing* with it. His grand plan had been to unveil it at a ball full of townsfolk who would never appreciate the magnitude of what he had achieved.

Balls were for gossip and matchmaking, not science. The town had only turned out so they could see how the house was decorated and judge Dr. Gardner if he served cheap brandy. The crowd would have sooner turned on him than celebrate the accomplishment.

If this were Jane's discovery, she would have partnered with a major university and invited academics from every continent. After the presentation, an article with her findings would be sent to newspapers and medical journals. Meanwhile, this man had the worst plan, and it wouldn't hurt a single one of his opportunities.

Unfolding her legs, Jane stretched them out before her. Usually, sitting cross-legged for too long hurt her back, but she felt no pain. All of her minor aches and pains that had been part of her for so long were gone. The pain had never been severe, but she never realized how much it had always been in the background.

Stretching herself as far as she could, her fingers brushed her ankles before she felt the strain in her hamstrings.

Interesting.

She tried again, pushing herself to her very limits as she touched her fingertips to the top of her toes. Her muscles strained as she held the position. Pain radiated down her legs as her muscles were pushed to their limits, but she gritted her teeth and held on. She had an experiment to run.

The pain hit a crescendo that nearly made her cry out when the pain dissipated like a candle that had been blown out. One... Two... Three. She counted three glorious seconds until the strain returned. When she relaxed, the strain was immediately gone.

It was eerie to have your body behave so differently. Dr. Gardner's story of reanimation had been outlandish, but she felt too strange to discredit him. Not necessarily bad, but definitely strange.

Memories of drowning resurfacing during the night vanquished the last of her doubts.

It was no use to dwell on such memories, so she got up to shake the unpleasant thoughts from her mind. It was time for her to move forward and focus on what she could change.

Her life had changed dramatically, but her situation was, regrettably, the same. She was still completely reliant on the men around her. She had no money, no prospects, and no idea what she should do.

Never returning home was non-negotiable; she would sooner slit her own throat than return to her brother's home. However, that was no longer an option according to Dr. Gardner. She considered testing that theory as well, but it would be a shame to go through all the trouble of dying just to come back. Again.

Before Dr. Gardner left, she asked him for a mirror, and he had left it on the bureau for her. It was silly, but she still hadn't gathered the strength to look at it. Vanity wouldn't serve her, but she hoped she would still be recognizable. Steeling herself, she picked up the silver hand mirror before she lost her nerve.

Relief nearly floored her when her reflection was the same as ever. The only difference was a thin, angular scar that extended from her temple to her hairline, but she barely noticed it.

With one fear vanquished, it was time to conquer the next. Tightening the belt on her borrowed dressing gown, she slipped on the house shoes left out for her and made her way into the hall.

Part of her expected Mr. Gardner to be waiting in the shadows outside her room, but she was strangely disappointed to find an empty hallway instead. It shouldn't have been a surprise since she hadn't heard any movement all night, but she wasn't sure if that was a comfort. Loneliness wasn't unfamiliar, but she had seldom been *alone*. Usually, she could hear servants or the squealing children in the nursery, but here the silence made her feel truly alone.

Luckily, her room was by the stairs. As much as she was tempted to explore, the growl of her stomach told her breakfast was the more pressing concern.

As she descended the staircase, she was struck by how different the home looked when there wasn't a ball. Luxe Persian rugs covered the checkered floor, and oil paintings of local landscapes had been replaced on the walls. The dim illumination from the few sconces cast dark shadows across the massive room.

Her footsteps echoed through the grand room as she tried to determine where to go. The only rooms she knew were the study where Robert crushed her dreams, and the library where she met Mr. Gardner.

"Hello?" Her voice echoed to no answer.

Fear shot through her. What if they had packed up in the night and left her here all alone? They went through an awful lot of trouble to bring her back, but she didn't wake up grateful. Instead, she had raged at them. If they hadn't liked her reaction, then perhaps there wasn't an incentive to stay.

Her hands trembled as her heart raced. No, she couldn't afford to think like that. Leaving her behind would be unspeakably cruel, and even though she barely knew them, she couldn't imagine either man being so cruel. Anyway, the gas lamp sconces were lit, which no one would do before abandoning a home.

As much as she was loath to admit it, she wanted to see Mr. Gardner again. He was an arse for storming out, but she could recognize the night hadn't gone as he had planned. Likely, he expected her to be a shrinking violet who would fawn over him for being her knight in shining armor. She didn't *want* to care about his feelings, but what Mr. Gardner did was technically the nicest thing anyone had ever done for her.

Figuring she might as well go with what she knew, she began her search in the library. The fireplace was lit, but the room was empty. The depth of her disappointment surprised her.

Where the common areas were impersonal, this room was lived in. The accessories were chosen for comfort rather than fashion, if the ugly patchwork quilt draped over the armchair was any indication. The table beside it held a small stack of books about the Roman Empire. Jane picked one up and flipped through the pages. It was the type of book she found painfully dull, but it had been well-loved with underlined passages and folded corners.

Following the curve of the room, she looked for a hidden door. There was no doubt that there was another way into the room since she didn't imagine he would have chanced getting close to the party.

Another armchair back was tucked amongst the bookcases in the back of the room, next to a window overlooking a rose garden. This chair had an indent in the cushion, and a battered ottoman toppled on its side with a copy of *Bleak House* that had been carelessly set down open with the spine facing up and a cup of tea balanced on the windowsill.

Jane placed her hand around the china cup, narrowing her eyes when it was still warm. Someone had recently been there, and she was sure it was Mr. Gardner.

The coward probably heard her enter and ran off rather than face her. Jane picked up the book and slammed it shut, not just saving the poor book's spine, but making sure he lost his place.

She had *questions* for him. Important ones, like whether she was immortal or also invulnerable? Was she going to age? She was currently both hungry and thirsty, so those functions stayed the same, but would she need to eat more or less? And most importantly, what was she supposed to do with her life now?

She could milk her recovery for a few more days, but house guests always wore out their welcome. Once Mr. Gardner got over his savior complex, he would grow bored with her, then, once again, her existence would depend upon the mercy of men. She could ask for a settlement, but even if they gave her money, she didn't know how to hire a coach or find a place to live. She had never even stayed at an inn before. The only purchases she had ever made were at businesses where her family had an account. She couldn't even remember the last time she held money.

After leaving the library, it took her four doors before she finally found the dining room. The long table had twelve chairs, but only one place was set at the head of the table.

Jane stared at the empty seat, unsure if it was for her or not. No one had told her about breakfast, but they had to feed her at some point. Starving your guests was impolite.

Her growling stomach decided eating was more important than social cues. Though it did feel strange sitting at the head of the table. She considered moving to her preferred spot on the left side of the table, but worried that rearranging the table was rude.

Her hands were politely folded on the table as she waited for a servant. A bowl of cut fruit and a few silver cloche-covered dishes mocked her growling stomach as they sat before her. She was fully capable of serving herself, but didn't know the unspoken service rules of this house. Smythe would have made a snide remark about her appetite if he had entered to see her scooping her own eggs.

Minutes ticked away as she waited for someone to notice she was in the dining room. Robert believed good servants worked without being seen, but this was extreme. A house this size should have a substantial staff, but it seemed like no one worked there.

Looking around the empty dining room, she wasn't sure what to do when she saw a discreet service bell next to the empty buffet table. Jane walked over to pull it before sitting back down.

She waited long enough that she considered ringing the bell

again or giving up and returning upstairs, when the door flew open and an older woman rushed into the room.

"My apologies, Miss Montgomery, I was unaware you were up," the frantic woman said with a curtsey. "I'm Mrs. Jones, the housekeeper."

Mrs. Jones uncovered the dishes, revealing a bowl of porridge, sausage, and steaming bread.

"That's quite all right, I was able to find the dining room eventually. I didn't realize you had such a small staff."

"Yes, Dr. and Mr. Gardner prefer it that way, so you'll have to forgive me if you wait a while for service." The housekeeper gave her a tight-lipped smile, but Jane could see the deep bags under her eyes.

"So I suppose asking for a lady's maid is out of the question."

Mrs. Jones's eyes tightened as Jane's attempt at humor fell flat.

"There's no one to spare to be a full-time lady's maid, but I can help you dress for dinner if needed."

"Is Mr. Gardner in residence? I haven't seen him. Or Dr. Gardner." Jane's cheeks pinkened as her eyes flitted to her porridge.

"Of course," Mrs. Jones said, frowning. "They're always around. Would you like me to fetch one for you?"

"No," Jane said quickly. "I just wanted to make sure they were around. Thank you for the information. I do have one final question: would you be able to procure some clothing for me?"

She wasn't sure whether she was considered a prisoner, but there was no way she could go to the modiste without alerting her brother.

"Yes, the dress you arrived in has been washed and mended and is waiting for you in the bureau. I was able to find a few more frocks as well as a dress for the evening, bedclothes, and undergarments. If they aren't up to your standards, I can attempt to source others, but it could take a few days."

"Thank you, Mrs. Jones. I'm sure your choices are more than adequate." Fashion had never been much of a concern for her. As long as the clothes were clean, they would be fine.

Jane picked up her spoon and started eating as a silent dismissal to the housekeeper. She didn't need to put her foot in her mouth any more than she already had.

Unfortunately, Mrs. Jones did not take the hint that had always worked on Mary. Jane tried ignoring her, but the woman's stare burned a hole through her. "I don't require anything further."

"As long as you don't require anything else." Mrs. Jones curtseyed before leaving the room.

Jane's cheeks heated. She was very familiar with a sarcastic curtsy; however, she was typically the one who doled them out.

The porridge was simple, but it tasted so good that part of her wanted to call Mrs. Jones back just to compliment the food, hoping to get on the woman's good side.

The scrape of the spoon against the porcelain bowl echoed through the room. Jane felt better knowing she wasn't all alone in this big house, but annoyance flared at the idea that Mr. Gardner was trying to ignore her.

No one ignored Jane Montgomery.

* * *

As JANE WANDERED the halls of the manor, she discovered three important things. First, Mrs. Jones was the only servant, which was why she stayed in her dressing gown rather than chasing down the poor woman to help her dress. The second was that the library collection truly was impressive. There weren't nearly enough books on science for her liking, but there were a remarkable number of first editions. The third was that Mr. Gardner was better at hiding than a chameleon.

Instead of her elusive cloaked savior, she found a conservatory, parlor, morning room, many bedrooms, a few bathrooms, and a damp cellar with an underwhelming wine collection. There were so many empty rooms that she no longer worried about being kicked out. If they tried, she would pick an empty wing and never be found.

Jane gave up on her mission and trudged back to her room. She stopped short at the hooded figure outside her door.

112

"I don't know why I'm surprised this is where I finally find you," she said, her heart racing even as her voice remained steady.

"I wasn't trying to lurk."

"So it just comes naturally then."

"I've been trying to think of what to say."

"And how has that been going?"

"Not well," Mr. Gardner sighed.

Jane crossed her arms, suddenly self-conscious of her borrowed, ill-fitting dressing gown and hair that had been to hell and back. It felt silly to want to primp when he had already seen her at her worst.

"Well, what do you want to say? Perhaps I can help."

"I want to apologize, but it feels less sincere if you help me with that."

Jane stiffened. "I only want to know why you brought me here."

He was silent for so long that she was almost sure he was going to run away again before he finally answered. "I thought I was helping, but I only made it worse. You were so full of life the last time I saw you that I thought you deserved a second chance. I'm so sorry, Miss Montgomery."

Never before had a man apologized to her, and as much as she hated to admit it, his words softened the inferno of anger inside her.

"Now that's been settled, what do you plan on doing with me?"

"What do you mean?"

"Please tell me you had some sort of plan before you dragged me back to your lair?"

His letters had made it clear he liked her in some way, but she just wasn't sure if he had kidnapped her because it was *her* or if his loneliness had broken him so profoundly that he would have taken *anyone* to have a companion.

"You can go back to the life you had before."

"No," Jane said quickly. "You haven't contacted my brother, have you?"

"No, we were waiting to make sure you came back all right before we contacted him."

"Good." She let out a relieved breath. The one thing worse than an uncertain future would be returning to Robert. "I've decided something since the last time I saw you."

The decision had only come to her moments before, but he didn't need to know that.

"And what's that?"

"Since you decided I was worth immortality, I've decided I'm your problem now."

"What?"

"You can't get rid of me because you're bored or I annoy you. You're going to be in charge of housing me, my food, and paying for my lifestyle."

What Jane needed above all else was security. It chafed that she needed to be dependent on yet another man, but this time she would do it on her own terms while she worked to secure her future.

"It seems like you've got this all planned out."

Jane shrugged. She'd let him think she had some grand plan while she figured things out."I figured someone around here should."

"Are you going to let me know what your plan is?"

She stepped forward to open the door, and he jumped back as if she had attacked him.

"You'll figure it out at some point," she said, closing the door behind her without looking back.

CHAPTER 12

*D*irt kicked up into the air as Will dropped a crate on the floor of the garden shed as he looked for his missing shears. He could have sworn he put them back on their hook, but the hook was empty, as was the bench, and all of the storage boxes.

He had asked Morris if he had borrowed them, and the groundskeeper grumbled that he had no use for Will's inferior tools. However, he wasn't convinced Morris hadn't misplaced them. The man had no respect for the organizational methods he was trying to implement. Will explained that the new system would make it easier to find things in the crowded shed, but Morris insisted he already had a system.

The last box on the shelf only had a few broken pieces of pottery, and Will huffed. So much for Morris' organizational methods. Sighing, Will sat on the workbench as he mentally retraced his steps from the previous day. It wasn't as if shears could vanish into thin air.

There were dozens of better things for him to do than search for his missing tool. Several days had passed since he had last seen Miss Montgomery, which had given ample time for more guilt to settle in.

Technically, he wasn't avoiding her, not after that first day when he had slipped through the servant's passage after she entered the library. Since then, he had made himself scarce around the house, but he always knew where she was, so he made sure their paths didn't cross. It was easier than he expected, especially since Tristan hadn't summoned him to the lab since he had a new scientist playmate.

Spending time in the garden was a risk since there wasn't a way to escape beneath the open sky, but the lab overlooked the front of the house, so he was willing to take the chance.

Will swung on the black cloak, clicking shut the metal clasp at the hollow of his throat. Long summer days grew shorter as the morning fog stuck around longer and the evening clouds rolled in earlier. Soon, the unmistakable chill of autumn would be in the air, and he couldn't wait. Even though summers in York were mild, it was still too warm to wear a wool cloak every day.

Latching the door behind him, he walked back to his garden, ready to get to work. Pruning may be out of the question, but weeding didn't require tools. As he rounded the corner, he stopped short when he saw who was waiting for him in the garden.

"Are you looking for these?" Miss Montgomery asked as she dangled the missing shears by one handle, the blades bouncing in the air.

He hadn't put his hood on when he left the shed, and his fingers itched to do so, but it wasn't as she didn't know the truth of both who and what he was.

"Be careful! I just sharpened those."

"After you ran out on me the other night," she said, glaring. "Your brother let me know I don't have to worry about injuries or illness anymore. Should I try? I haven't tested this yet."

She adjusted her grip on the shears and brought the blade to her wrist.

"Don't!"

Will staggered forward to snatch the shears from Miss Montgomery's grasp, but her hand pivoted so he couldn't get a grip on the shears. His left hand reached for her wrist to hold it still so he could safely wrestle them from her. Her pulse thrummed beneath his grasp for a moment before he recoiled at the realization of which hand he had touched her with.

He had been too distracted by the possibility of her spilled blood to remember which of the limbs wasn't his.

"Why not? Unless you're lying, and that's why you've been avoiding me."

"Of course not," he snapped. "It's common sense that you shouldn't cut yourself open. You'll heal quickly, but it will still hurt."

His mind flashed to her waterlogged body in his arms when she was too cold and too pale. He shoved the memory from his mind. She was in front of him now with rosy cheeks, scowling, and alive.

"I'm not scared of a little pain."

"Being stabbed hurts more than a little."

"I drowned. I think I can handle a little scratch."

"It's not a competition. Give me the shears." He held out his right hand, hoping common sense would prevail.

If you had bothered spending any time with me, you would know I hate being told what to do."

Miss Montgomery pushed the shining blade into her wrist, and dark red rivulets marred her creamy white skin. As she slowly moved the blade from her wrist to her elbow, a river of deep red followed. Will wanted to reach for the blade, but he worried she would drive the blade deeper into her arm.

Looking at her blood was too much for his churning stomach, so his gaze landed on her face since he couldn't look away from her entirely. A fallen lock of chestnut hair caught by the afternoon light looked almost red. Her eyes were tight, but she didn't otherwise telegraph any pain. When her eyes widened, he knew her healing had begun.

He had watched his own wounds heal themself so many times that now it was commonplace, but he saw the novelty in it again as she gazed at her arm in wonder.

"See, I told you it would be fine," she said, holding up her forearm that still dripped with blood, but had no wound.

"Clean up before you bleed all over my roses."

He held out his freshly pressed handkerchief to Miss Montgomery. It floated limply in the air between them for a few moments before her delicate fingers plucked it from his grasp.

"Tristan warned that you weren't any fun, but I thought you could handle some blood."

"I'm sorry that my idea of fun doesn't include bleeding all over the place. I'm of the crazy notion that blood should stay in your body."

"Blood's gone! You don't have to worry about fainting anymore."

Miss Montgomery held up her arm, and it looked like nothing had even happened. Blue veins were visible beneath her pale skin, but the pink tinge meant blood pumped through her circulatory system without a problem. Her chest expanded and contracted with every breath, which made his own pounding heart relax.

Not that he was staring at her chest, he only cared because it was an essential biological function. Besides, her dowdy black dress didn't show anything interesting. It was an ill-fitting garment that buttoned up to her throat with tight sleeves that barely reached her elbows. Upon further inspection, the dress might not be awful since it was so tight across her chest that he could see the curve of her breast.

Clearing his throat, he shook himself from his lurid thoughts. As she looked at him with a raised brow, his cheeks flooded with color when he realized she must have said something while he was staring at her ugly dress. He wasn't prepared to have this conversation today, but ever since she had told him he was now responsible for her, he had been thinking of what they should do next.

"Miss Montgomery—"

"Jane. You've seen my dead body, so you can use my Christian name," she interrupted.

"Oh." He already knew her pretty first name, but it felt different to have permission to use it. "My name is Will."

"It's nice to formally meet you. Our faces are visible, and we're both conscious. Isn't this nice?"

"Maybe you should try being cloaked before we decide."

"Do you have another prowler's cloak on hand? I think it loses its impact if we share one."

"I'm afraid I only have one."

"Then I suppose we will have to settle for conversing like normal people."

Will's retort died on his tongue when he remembered that they weren't normal. Will wasn't sure if they qualified as people anymore, but that was more of a philosophical question.

"Now you can proceed with whatever excuse you have for avoiding me."

"What makes you think I'm avoiding you?"

Jane raised an eyebrow. "You haven't been to the lab in days. Tristan said you're normally there every day."

"Don't flatter yourself, I would do anything to avoid being my brother's test subject. I figured he didn't need me since he now has a willing subject."

"What a convenient excuse." She placed a hand on her hip, and he thought it was a shame that the dress wasn't tight all over. "Do you want to know what I think?"

"Please enlighten me."

"I think you fell apart once your white knight fantasy was shattered, and now you're trying to avoid everything in the hope it will all magically go away."

He stilled. She wasn't terribly off base, and he wasn't sure how he could be so transparent. He never thought of himself as a mystery, but he wasn't sure when he had become so pedestrian.

"Well?" Her eyes held the expectation that he would agree with her assessment and continue with his tail between his legs. Which was precisely how he had behaved since he woke up in Tristan's lab.

Will didn't want to be predictable.

"And what do you think my fantasy was?"

Her eyes narrowed. "I think you wanted your brother to build you a bride so you wouldn't have to be lonely anymore."

Jane lightly blushed as she tripped over the word 'bride,' and the corner of his mouth tipped up.

"A bride? What an interesting choice of words you've chosen for a companion."

"Because a companion is too benign a word for what you're looking for. I feel bride better represents the role you imagined for me."

"Yes, because I'm the one who killed you. This was all a conspiracy to get you to me, which is why I've spent so much time with you since you've woken up."

"Please, I don't think I'm all that important in the grand scheme of your plan," Jane snorted. "You would have done the same for anyone you found in that condition."

No, I wouldn't have.

"Well, I suppose we'll never know since you were the one on the riverbank and now you're my problem."

Jane's eyes hardened, and Will knew he had chosen the wrong word. *Shit.*

"And what do you want to do with your problem?"

As much as he wanted to, he couldn't say she wasn't a problem because she wouldn't believe him. Partly because of his careless words, but he also imagined her scars ran deeper.

"I don't suppose you've changed your mind about wanting to go home?"

"No," she said flatly.

"I'm sure they miss you. We can craft a story that will protect your reputation if that's what you're worried about. People will believe almost anything for someone they love."

As Jane's eyes tightened, he knew he was pushing his luck with her, but he needed to know if she was only worried about returning home or if home was dangerous for her. Something drove her to suicide, after all.

"If you even *try* to take me home, I will tell Robert everything, and you won't be allowed to hide anymore." She snipped the shears in the air to punctuate her point, but he saw the fear in her eyes.

"Why don't you want to go back?"

"That's personal," she snapped. "I want your word you won't involve my brother."

"I'll give you my word if you tell me why."

He was bluffing, but she didn't need to know that. Her nostrils flared, and he could see her anger grow, but he preferred anger to fear.

"Fine," she said through clenched teeth. "I told you I went into the river on purpose, but more specifically, it was to escape the fate my brother was trying to force on me. He wanted to marry me off in a business deal against my will. He stole my inheritance and threatened me with institutionalization if I didn't comply."

"What?"

Anger surged within him with such force it surprised him. He wasn't a violent man by nature, but he would deck her brother if he ever got the chance. He couldn't understand threatening anyone like that, let alone someone you were supposed to love. He and Tristan may have their issues, but they both knew they loved each other at their core.

"Don't look at me like that," she said while waving the shears again. They weren't close to him, but he leaned back anyway.

"What look?"

"The look that says you're desperate to be my knight in shining armor."

"I don't think you need to be saved. Though I wouldn't mind the chance to avenge you."

"Don't worry, I got my revenge on the way out."

"Good, but know you only have to say the word if you want me to take a pound of flesh from him as well."

"I'll keep that in mind, but you should know that I am neither your wife nor your captive. I can take care of myself."

"I'm sure you can," he agreed. "Although I will say that I find it to be interesting that you keep returning to the idea of being my wife."

A storm brewed in her grey eyes. It was too easy to rile her up. Her hand with the shears remained still, so he knew he wasn't in danger.

"I only used that as shorthand because it's the polite way to say what you want from me."

Will laughed, which made her eyes narrow to slits.

Leaning in close, he invaded her space while leaving a bit of room between them. Her eyes widened, but she didn't step back.

"Are you sure?" he asked, pitching his voice down in the way he knew women liked. "You aren't a little curious about what it would be like?"

Her breath hitched before her scowl returned. He didn't even attempt to suppress his smirk. It was nice to see he could affect her just as much as she affected him.

"I wouldn't get ahead of myself if I were you. I'm not even convinced everything still works. You did die, after all."

"What do you think doesn't work?" He played the fool on purpose to hear her say it.

"You know exactly what I mean." Her cheeks flushed pink as she looked pointedly at his trousers.

"Ah, that," he said, leaning down so she could feel his breath against the shell of her ear. "I can assure you *everything* still works quite well."

Will plucked the shears from her hand before Jane stiffly turned and walked back to the house without another word. Shocking her to silence was a better reward than any retort.

CHAPTER 13

 ane slammed the door to Tristan's laboratory behind
her so hard the test tubes rattled on their stands.
Tristan looked up from the microscope he was
hunched over, and she murmured an apology for disturbing him.

Grumbling, she took her dingy apron off the hook and tied it
over her borrowed dress.

"I take it you found my brother?"

Jane glared as she sat on the stool next to him. The first time she
wandered into the lab, Tristan had been surprised she wanted to
watch him work after he checked her vitals, but now he had a place
ready for her.

"I don't understand why you even bothered bringing him back."

She pulled the journal over so she could see what he was
working on. He was comparing blood samples, his versus hers.

"He grows on you." Tristan adjusted the microscope's magnification and looked at the sample again before he stood up and slid
the journal back. "You can take a look if you'd like."

Her heart thumped with a burst of excitement. This was the
first microscope she had ever seen, but she had read about how to
use one. Stepping towards the device, she lowered her head and

attempted to project nonchalance as if this was a regular occurrence.

"Don't rest your head against the lens or you'll bump the sample."

"Thank you," she murmured, cheeks heating as she lifted her head. She expected him to be standing over her, ready to chastise her like a child, but he just scrawled in his notebook unconcerned.

She brought her head back down to the microscope, but this time her head hovered just above the lens. Dozens of little red circles moved around the glass slide, bouncing off one another. "They're blood cells."

"Correct."

She frowned as she watched how fast the little cells bounced around the slide. This was the first time she had ever seen anything beneath a microscope, but from what she knew about blood cells, this didn't look right.

"Here," Tristan said, replacing that slide with another. Jane lifted her head while he made the switch, and he checked the sample to make sure the magnification was correct. "Look at this one and tell me what differences you see."

She swallowed as she leaned back down to examine the new sample. It seemed like an easy enough test, but she was worried it would look the same to her untrained eye, and her career as a research assistant would be over before it had even begun.

"I see," she hesitated. This sample *was* different. "There are fewer red blood cells, and they're hardly moving."

"Precisely."

She lifted her head. "Do you know why?"

"No, but I'm forming some theories. Do you know whose samples these are?" She shook her head. "They're ours. Do you know which is which?"

Furrowing her brow, her attention returned to the sample. The cells didn't look unhealthy, just lethargic in comparison to the first. Because the other one had been first, she thought that had been the control, but maybe it wasn't. "I think the slow one is yours, and the quick one is mine."

"Correct again! I appreciate your willingness to provide me with a sample. Will has refused to give any blood samples, so I haven't been able to study the differences until now."

Jane shook her head. Of course, he wouldn't agree to such a simple request. "I don't know how you put up with him. It would take hardly any of his time to give you the sample, and it's so valuable for your research."

"I know, but he's stubborn." He shot her a look. "I don't suppose you have much experience with stubborn people."

"I would *never* obstruct medical research."

"Good, then we'll stay in the lab while he stays in his garden. That way we all win."

"Well, as I told your brother, I am now your responsibility, so I will be here until you forcibly remove me."

Tristan's hand paused on the page before he looked at her. "And what did Will have to say about that?"

"Not much, but he did look at me in horror. Although that could have been because of the blood running down my arm."

Tristan raised an eyebrow. "And where did the blood come from?"

"I had to test my healing capabilities, of course."

"Of course. How did you choose to test it outside of the laboratory?"

"I stole Will's shears, and it made him so nervous I thought it was best I remind him there isn't a cause for concern if I wave sharp objects around."

The idea of testing her healing had occurred to her the other day, but she had been too nervous to check, on the off-chance this had been an elaborate hoax. Relief mixed with amazement as she watched her skin stitch together.

"Did you make any observations?"

"Nothing of interest, it was a pretty shallow cut. If you wanted to do some exploratory surgery, I would be open to that as long as I had something for the pain."

"You want me to perform surgery on you?" Tristan furrowed his brow. "For what reason, fun?"

"It would be for science, but having fun would be a side effect as long as you didn't give me too much anesthesia. We'll have to practice to make sure we have the correct dose. Do you think my ability to metabolize drugs has changed?"

"I'm not doing surgery on you at all, let alone when you're awake."

"Why not?"

"To begin with, Will would kill me, and unlike you, I would not come back."

Jane frowned. "Why would it matter to him?"

She had never been fragile, but she especially wasn't now. Pain was inconvenient, but temporary.

Tristan looked like he was about to speak before he sighed and scrubbed a hand over his face. "The Gardners were a chivalric order going back hundreds of years. My brother may not have the title of a knight, but he does have the soul of one. It's difficult for him to watch anything suffer."

"Once we figure out the correct dosage, I shouldn't suffer."

"Which brings us to the second point, where I do not want to do exploratory surgery on an awake patient."

"It'll be fine. I'm sure you've done riskier operations."

Tristan crossed his arms as he leaned back. His glasses were perched on the end of his nose as he considered her. "What type of surgery do you want?"

She shrugged. "You can cut me open and poke around." The only thing she cared about was witnessing surgery.

"If you want to poke around some insides, we can arrange to get a corpse instead."

"Are you sure you can be trusted with a corpse, or do you think you'll want to bring them back too?"

"Between you and my brother, I have my hands full, so you don't have to worry about me adding to the collection of people who did not wish to be saved."

Jane cleared her throat. "Then I suppose we'll have to figure out another way to further science. I promise to earn my keep somehow."

"There's no need for you to earn anything. We are more than happy to have you here without any conditions." He took a deep breath and shuffled in place uncomfortably before he continued. "However, if you would like to work as my research assistant, I would appreciate it."

Her heart soared, and she couldn't keep the smile from her face. She would be working as a *real* research assistant. No one had ever believed in her like this before, and it touched her deep in her soul. "I would like that very much."

"It won't be very glamorous. I'll need you to clean slides and parse through my notes, so they make sense."

"I've already looked at two samples under a microscope. I assure you, this job is more interesting than anything else I have ever done."

"Good, then let me get you last week's notes, and you can see if you can put them back in order. Mrs. Jones knocked them over, and it's been chaos ever since."

* * *

JANE BOUNDED DOWN THE STAIRS, amazed that her knees felt fine on the stone staircase. One day, she would get used to the new marvels of her body, but it wouldn't be today. Weeks ago, if someone had asked if she thought she was in good condition, she would have said she was. She wasn't even thirty, and while aches and pains were normal, she would have insisted hers weren't bad.

Now her back pain was gone, her hand no longer cramped when she wrote, and she only had to sleep a few hours. It freed up her brain for other activities, which was how she finished all of her work before dinner. She had gotten through the stack of notes so efficiently that she didn't even have time to engineer an excuse as to why she needed to take dinner in her room.

"What were you doing in the lab all day?"

Jane jumped, turning to see Will silently following her down the stairs. It was jarring to see him again so soon after she spent several days unable to find him around the house.

"Why do you care?"

"Is he running experiments on you?"

"What?"

His sudden concern baffled her. This wasn't the first day she spent with Tristan in the lab, and Will knew that.

"Has he been making you do calisthenics or trying to take some of your blood? Is that why you look so tired?"

"If you're trying to charm a woman, you shouldn't tell her she looks tired."

"I want to make sure he isn't taking advantage of you."

She snorted. "How do you think he's taking advantage of me? By answering my questions or teaching me what I want to learn?"

"You don't need to be poked or prodded any further. You've been through enough."

"Once again, you are assuming you know what I want," she huffed. He seemed dedicated to making her regret wanting him around.

"What do you mean?"

"You," she said, jabbing his chest with her finger. "Assume I'm not interested in being part of Tristan's scientific research, but that's only because you're not interested."

He shrank from her touch, and she ignored the brief sting of rejection. "You can't possibly be okay with him taking your blood for his use."

"What do you think he's doing with it?"

"I'm not sure, but whatever it is, he doesn't need to be doing it with *your* blood."

"He's not doing anything with the blood! You don't understand science."

"And you do?" He practically growled.

Anger flashed through her; this man didn't understand her at all.

"I helped him compile his research, but don't worry, I didn't let him take my blood." Will's shoulders dropped as she smirked. "He taught me how to take a sample, so I did it myself."

"My apologies that I was trying to save you from an existence of being a pincushion. You know it's never going to stop, there's always going to be something else he wants to study."

She could see the fire in his yellow eyes, and she didn't know if she wanted to step closer or away from this infuriating man.

"As he should. What he's done is incredible and should be studied. There is so much to be learned about the human body, but you're too selfish to partake in the testing." She jabbed his chest again, and this time she felt his muscles tense beneath her touch.

"I have subjected myself to an endless amount of tests. I do calisthenics and let him check me for injuries and test my muscles and reflexes. I track what I eat and how I sleep. I do all of that, yet he won't be happy until I bleed for him." He took a step closer so she had to tilt her head back to keep eye contact. "I didn't ask to be brought back, and I certainly wouldn't have agreed if I had known it would have led to an eternity of being experimented on."

"I didn't ask to be brought back either! I *wanted* to die, but you decided to bring me back. You don't get to decide how I spend my time."

Will's square jaw set in a hard line as he stared at her. Her own breath was ragged as she stared daggers right back at him.

A heavy knock at the door broke their tension as they both turned towards the bottom of the stairs. At first, she wasn't sure if she had heard a knock or if it was a hallucination caused by her frustration at Will. When all color drained from Will's face, she knew it wasn't in her head.

The knock sounded again. In her home, Smythe would have already answered the door, but there was a marked lack of servants in this house. Mrs. Jones was likely stuck in the kitchen cooking dinner and hadn't even heard the door. Even if she had, the woman deserved some help, so Jane continued down the stairs. Answering the door couldn't be terribly difficult.

As she stepped off the final stair, a hand grabbed her. His grasp didn't hurt, but it was too firm to shake away.

"What are you doing?" Will hissed.

"Answering the door. Even I can manage that."

His eyes widened until she worried they would pop out of his head. "You can't answer the door, you're supposed to be *dead*."

"Please, the only people who know I'm dead are in this house. I look normal, so they won't suspect a thing."

He flinched, and inwardly she cringed at her word choice.

"They'll know you aren't supposed to be here. Don't you think there will be questions about what you're doing here with a bachelor scientist who is in this big house all alone? Your family knows you're missing by now. This would cause a massive scandal."

Even though she had no care for her own reputation, she didn't want to ruin Tristan's life. Obviously, Will had to hide since he was known to be dead, but even if he wasn't, she could admit that his appearance could cause a few questions.

Another knock sounded, this time it was louder and lasted longer. Her heart raced. Now she didn't know what to do as the person on the other side of the door grew agitated. She looked up at Will, wanting him to decide what they should do.

Quick footsteps sounded in the hall, and a red-faced Mrs. Jones burst through the doors at a slow run towards the front door.

Will pulled her to a thin door in the entry, throwing it open and shoving her inside before closing the door behind them.

Instead of the room she expected, it was a small closet, luckily devoid of outerwear because the space was already too small. Arms and legs pushed against each other as they struggled in the pitch black darkness before they settled in a semi-comfortable position with Jane smashed against the door and Will hunched behind her, contorting himself so their bodies weren't pressed together. However, he was still close enough for her to feel the heat radiating from his body.

The hinges creaked as the front door opened.

"Good evening, I'm sorry for keeping you waiting. How can I be of assistance?" Mrs. Jones said between gasping breaths.

"I'm here to speak with Dr. Gardner."

Jane felt like the breath had been knocked out of her, and her knees buckled. The only reason she didn't fall in a heap to the floor was because Will caught her, his strong arm bracketing her around her waist.

Robert had found her.

CHAPTER 14

"*May* I ask who is calling, sir?"

"You can tell him Mr. Robert Montgomery is here to speak with him. Now."

Jane closed her eyes. The last time she heard her brother's cruel voice was only a few days ago, but it felt like another lifetime. Technically, it was another lifetime.

Will sucked in a breath. She tensed, worried the sound was too loud, before she remembered their hearing was enhanced.

"Let me see if Dr. Gardner is home. He may be away. Please wait here, Mr. Montgomery."

"In the entry?"

"I'll only be a moment," Mrs. Jones replied as her voice faded away with her footsteps pounding up the stairs.

Slowly, Will's arm moved until she was pressed against his body. His heart raced, but he was otherwise solid. He leaned down until she felt his hot, steady breath on the shell of her ear.

"Be quiet, all will be well," he whispered so quietly she was the only one who heard. She repressed a shudder at the sensation.

As Robert's heavy footsteps sounded on the other side of the door, her body tensed even though she knew he wasn't going anywhere. Her brother hated standing still, so she was used to his frequent pacing. However, she never expected it to elicit a fear response.

Jane let her full weight collapse onto Will. There was a time to stand alone in her strength, but it wasn't when her biggest enemy was only steps away.

Her lungs were on fire as she could only manage shallow breaths. Her fists were clenched so tight her nails dug into the meat of her palms, her teeth clenched the soft skin of her mouth until she tasted the tang of her own blood, but nothing would stop the panic that urged her to run as far from Robert as possible.

Behind her, Will's broad chest expanded and contracted with each of his steady breaths. His hand flexed on her waist. Their intimate position would be uncomfortable in any other circumstance, but she found comfort in their connection.

Soon, her own breaths deepened, and her chest rose and fell in time with his. Her hands fell open at her side.

"Mr. Montgomery, what an unexpected pleasure."

Tristan was so loud she cringed, but it wasn't so bad that it would rouse Robert's suspicion. Probably.

"Dr. Gardner, you're a difficult man to get a hold of. It's unfortunate we only had the chance for a quick hello at your ball."

"The downside of hosting is that you never get enough time with your guests. What can I do for you this evening?"

"I sent you a letter that went unanswered, and I figured it would be better to follow up in person to ensure you received the message."

"My apologies, I currently have a stack of unopened letters on my desk. I've been so busy with my work, my personal correspondence has suffered."

"Is this work related to the failure you announced at your ball? I thought it was quite brave of you to do so in front of a crowd."

Jane cringed at her brother's biting words.

"Success in science is never linear, so I'm not embarrassed. Every failure is proof I never stopped trying." Tristan's voice was hard in a way she hadn't heard before. Hints of the kind, soft-spoken man she had come to know remained, but it was clear he wouldn't let Robert push him around. "What is it you need from me?"

"I'm surprised you haven't heard, but my dear sister, Miss Jane Montgomery, has gone missing. We've been searching for her, but we haven't even found the hint of a trail."

Jane tensed. Robert searching for her wasn't a surprise, but she never expected it would have brought him to the Gardner home.

She gasped when she remembered Sofia had found her while she had been speaking with Dr. Gardner. It was a flimsy connection, but it was the only one she could think of.

Will squeezed her in warning of the noise she made, as if she wasn't fully aware of exactly how important it was for them to stay quiet.

"I'm so sorry to hear that. Unfortunately, I've been shut away here so I haven't heard anything, but I won't hesitate to contact you if I do. Do you think she's run off, or are you worried something worse happened?"

Will's thumb rubbed her stomach. It was a comforting action, but each swipe of his thumb stoked something inside of her. All around her, she could feel Will. Not just her body pressed against him or his breath on her neck, but his scent of leather, flowers, and dirt surrounded her like a cocoon. His scent was of life itself, and for the first time in years, she felt totally and completely safe.

"I think the foolish chit ran off because she didn't like the husband I secured for her."

Anger burned through Jane, but she focused on the slow swipes of Will's thumb on her waist instead, as confronting her brother wasn't an option. No matter how desperately she wanted to after he called her a *chit*.

"Ah, well, I only had a chance to speak with her for a moment, but she seemed to be a bright, pleasant young woman."

Robert snorted. "Perhaps you did only spend a moment with her." He paused, and Jane heard the echo of his heavy steps. "We are at a loss on where she could have gone since no one saw her hire a coach or walk around town. She had no money or really any sense, so I thought maybe she didn't run off after all. Then, her maid told me something interesting."

Jane knew that tone; Robert was snaring a trap for Tristan to fall into. She wished there was some way to warn him, but she could only listen helplessly while it happened.

"And what did she say?"

"She told me that in the days leading up to my dear sister's disappearance, she received two letters from a Mr. Gardner."

Before she could even think to gasp, Will clasped his hand over her mouth. Part of her wanted to bite through his thick leather gloves, but his hand had muffled an indignant sound that slipped from her, so he wasn't necessarily wrong.

"I am *Dr.* Gardner, and I assure you I sign all of my letters with that name."

Jane was proud of how hard Tristan's tone was against her brother's accusations.

"I do find it interesting that she goes missing less than a week after being in this house. And writing to someone with your name."

"I would ask you to speak plainly because I don't respond to insinuations in my own home."

"I'm not insinuating anything. Think of it as musing over some curious coincidences. I do think the detectives in town would find these musings quite interesting, so if you have anything to refute them, I would tell me now."

"Where are the letters you claim are from me?"

"I don't have them," Robert sighed. "I turned over her room, but couldn't find them. Her maid says she remembered the name because it was so rare for my sister to receive letters."

Will's hand tightened as Jane huffed. Robert was making her sound pathetic. She was glad she had the foresight to take both letters with her. They were in her cloak pocket when she went into the river and were currently hidden in her bureau upstairs.

"Then I would appreciate it if you left. I am quite busy, and I don't have any news for you. I will be sure to write you if I find anything, but I would appreciate it if you didn't show up at my home unannounced again."

"Careful now, you sound like you have something to hide."

Will's hand stroked up her stomach, covering her ribs. His hand was perilously close to the lower swell of her breasts. When she took a full breath, his scent flooded her lungs. Their breathing was perfectly aligned, and she had to imagine he also felt the tension between them. The way he overwhelmed her with his size. The prickly stubble on his jaw scratched her temple. It had been so long since she had been held that she hadn't even realized what she'd been missing.

"I have nothing to hide, but I know if you had any compelling evidence, you would have already gone to the authorities rather than trying to scare me. Have a good evening, Mr. Montgomery."

The hinges creaked again, and she heard the unmistakable sound of Robert's footsteps leaving. She was surprised he left without getting the last word, but it was also clear Tristan wouldn't be pushed around, and there was nothing Robert hated more than losing a fight.

Only when the iron lock clicked did she let out a sigh of relief. Robert had suspicions of where she was, but nothing concrete. Still, she didn't move on the off-chance it was a trap, but also because she wanted to stay in Will's grasp.

The closet door opened to reveal Tristan's furrowed brow, his eyes swimming with concern.

"Are you all right?"

Will's gloved hand remained over her mouth. Her face heated in embarrassment, so she snapped her teeth, and he quickly dropped his hand.

Jane nodded, clearing her throat. "I'm fine."

"I didn't know your brother was coming," Tristan snorted before rubbing his face. "I mean, I didn't know he sent a letter or was looking for you. I would have warned you if I knew."

"Of course." Her voice was raw. Will was still rubbing her stomach, and she stumbled forward, embarrassed to be caught in such a position. "I should have thought it was a possibility, but I didn't think he would care this much."

"We'll just have to be more careful," Will said as he calmly walked from the closet.

"How do you suggest we do that? It's not as if we go anywhere."

"Luckily, I'm very good at hiding," Will said, his attempt at humor falling flat, before he continued. "He was only here to bluster. If he truly suspected Tristan, he would have played it differently. He came by to see if he could scare information out of him, but now that he knows Tristan doesn't scare easily, I don't think he'll be back."

Jane blinked at Will. She didn't know what to say to him. It was sweet of him to want to comfort her, but he didn't know Robert. If he suspected Tristan, no force on this planet could stop him.

"But what if he does come back? He won't stop. That's why I jumped into the river. I knew it would drive him to madness when my body wasn't found."

Will's face went blank, and she could see the raw sympathy in Tristan's gaze that made her wish she had remained quiet. She needed to evade Robert, but she also wanted to make sure the Gardners didn't get caught up in it because neither deserved Robert's ire.

"We'll figure it out. You don't need to worry about him. I've dealt with many men like your brother before," Tristan said.

"I promise, you'll never have to worry about him again," Will said with such purpose it felt like a vow.

Jane smiled and thanked them, behaving exactly as she should. As any woman would when she was being saved, but she couldn't leave this to them. Robert was a problem she would take care of herself.

* * *

WALKING DOWN THE GRAND STAIRCASE, her stomach did a little flip when she thought about Will joining her for breakfast. It had been a few days since Robert had shown up at the house, and she had finally relaxed. Robert was still a problem, but she trusted that he wouldn't come back and break down the door.

The one positive consequence of her brother's impromptu visit was that Will had started coming down for meals. It had been pleasant. Perhaps even enjoyable. Last night, he made her laugh harder than she had in recent memory.

Her hand paused on the brass doorknob when she heard the murmur of voices inside. The polite thing would be to make herself known, to clear her throat as she opened the door, or to make her footsteps heavy. Eavesdropping was rude, but she couldn't help that her hearing had improved so much.

"Do you know when she will be down?" The gravelly low tone of Will's voice caused her stomach to flutter again. It was a silly reaction, but she couldn't help how much she liked his voice.

"No, she dresses herself in the morning," Mrs. Jones replied. Jane could hear metal clang against wood as the housekeeper served the morning meal. "It's still a bit early for her to be down."

Bile formed in her mouth as the bitter feeling of overhearing a conversation about yourself settled over her. She needed to announce her presence, but sick fascination kept her still. It was difficult for her to read Will, and she wanted—needed—to know what he thought about her.

"I suppose I'd better wait for her to come down. I don't think it would go over well if I knocked on her door."

"Probably not," the housekeeper said with a snort of laughter. "Are you sure you want to go through with this? Once you bring it up, you won't be able to take it back."

"I know," he sighed. "Unfortunately, I am quite sure about what I'm going to do. Even if she doesn't initially agree, I'll fight with her until she does."

She swallowed, careful to make sure the slight tremor in her hand didn't cause the door to rattle. There were a great deal of things she could fight with him about, but her biggest fear was that he wanted her to leave. She thought her work with Tristan would be enough to keep her in good favor, but maybe it hadn't been enough. Once, he had promised he would never throw her out, but that was before her brother had come looking for her. If it were a choice between her and Tristan, she knew who Will would choose every time.

"Hopefully, there isn't a fight at all."

"I don't think she'll fight me. I know she can be difficult, but I think she'll see the sense in this."

Difficult.

She couldn't hear the rest of the conversation through her heart pounding in her ears.

It certainly wasn't the first time she had been called *that*, but it was different to hear it from a voice other than her brother's. Will thought she was difficult. Mrs. Jones thought she was difficult. Tristan also probably thought she was difficult. All the while, she had been on her best behavior.

It didn't matter how hard she tried or where she went, all anyone would ever see her as was *difficult*. What use was there in trying to be better when people would only ever think of you one way?

She closed her eyes and took a deep breath, focusing on the expansion and contraction of her lungs until her peace returned. None of them really knew her, but if they thought she was being difficult now, she would show them precisely how difficult Jane Montgomery could be.

The hinges squeaked when she opened the door with more force than necessary. It wasn't on purpose, but both of their heads whipped towards her, and she was pleased to make such an entrance.

"Good morning, everyone's up early today," she said with feigned cheeriness.

"Yes, well, I have something I wanted to speak with you about, so I wanted to make sure I didn't miss you." Will kept his voice cordial, but she could see the suspicion in his eyes, as if he could see right through her cheery façade.

"In that case, I hope I didn't keep you waiting for too long."

She took the seat to his right instead of her usual spot at the other end of the table. If he were kicking her out, she would make him look her directly in the eye as he did it.

Mrs. Jones moved her breakfast from Jane's usual spot to the place in front of her. "Thank you, Mrs. Jones. Good morning to you as well."

Tension was thick in the air as she waited for the proverbial sword to fall.

"You wanted to speak with me?"

Jane picked up her delicate bone china teacup to keep her hands busy. The sweet liquid tasted sour, but she still forced herself to swallow.

"Yes," he said, clearing his throat. "We don't have to get right into it, though. You should enjoy your breakfast, and we can talk afterwards."

His eyes flicked to his plate as if he couldn't stand to look at her. She wanted to scream.

"So the moment I don't measure up to the fantasy version you had of me, you want to throw me away?"

His head snapped up. "Pardon?"

She ignored him. If he was going to be surprised by her audacity, then she would really dig in. "You're stuck with me until *I* decide it's time for me to leave."

"You think I want to send you away?"

Will's eyebrows stitched together, but Jane continued undeterred.

"I understand you think I'm being difficult now, but I have not even begun to be *difficult*."

"I think there's been a misunderstanding," he started before she cut him off.

"The misunderstanding is that I will go easily. If we really are to live forever, then I plan to be a thorn in your side for all eternity."

The corners of his mouth twitched, which made her want to chuck her teacup. Even now, he refused to take her seriously. She opened her mouth to continue her tirade, but he put a hand up to stop her.

"Don't you want to know what I'm going to do with you? Because I finally have an answer."

His smirk boiled her blood until she didn't know if she wanted to slap or kiss it off.

"I don't care what you do as long as you beg for my mercy," she said, leaning in close for her declaration of war.

"I'm taking you to Cambridge," he said, amusement sparking in his honey colored eyes.

Jane's brain sputtered to a stop. For the first time in her life, she was struck speechless. Will looked entirely too pleased with himself as he took in her stunned expression. Usually, that would have annoyed her, but she was too stunned to process anything else.

"To... visit?" She refused to get her hopes up in case this was him just wanting to take her on a field trip to placate her. It would work, of course, but she wouldn't reveal her hand this early.

Will shrugged. "We could visit, but I thought you would like to study there more."

CHAPTER 15

*W*ill fought as hard as he could to keep a neutral expression as he watched shock radiate over Jane's face. Days had been spent planning this surprise, but her brother's showing up accelerated his timeline. Her reaction was gratifying, proof he wasn't only capable of doing the wrong thing.

Then she shot up from the chair, the forgotten teacup falling to the table on its side as she paced around the room.

"Why?" She asked, eyes narrowing. "What do you get out of this?"

This line of questioning didn't surprise him, but it did wound something in him to see her so distrustful of kindness.

"I told you I'd help you get into Cambridge, and the offer didn't expire because you did." He flashed what he hoped was a supportive smile, but dropped it when her frown deepened. "Also, your brother may return, and it's best if we aren't here when he does."

"But why Cambridge? We could go anywhere in the world."

"Why not Cambridge? It's somewhere in the world, after all. That is, if you are still interested in attending."

Clearing his throat, he internally kicked himself for not considering the possibility that she was no longer interested in attending school. Things had changed for her, which he should have taken into consideration. He would hate to be forced into a dream he had outgrown.

"Oh," she finally said after a long silence. "Yes, I'd still like to go."

"Good."

Musical laughter bubbled from her. She tried to put a hand over her mouth to quiet it, but nothing could contain her joy. He couldn't help his own smile from bursting forth as well. There were many details for them to go through, but he couldn't bring himself to break the moment.

Her laughter gradually faded until her expression fell into another frown. "Don't I need permission from family to go? I don't know if we should forge a letter from Robert on the off-chance someone asks him about it."

Will cleared his throat. "That's been taken care of." His eyes fell to the table as uncertainty bloomed inside of him. This was where he worried the yelling would begin. Bracing himself, he continued. "I told them we're married so that I can give permission, and I'll double as your chaperone."

The room was so quiet he only heard his own ragged breaths. He wasn't sure if her silence was the calm before the storm or if she was processing the information. It was a lot for him to process, and he was the one who came up with the idea.

Looking up, he was relieved to see she didn't seem to be angry. Instead, her face was blank.

"This cannot possibly be your best idea."

"We don't need to actually get married since the documents are easy enough to forge, but chances are no one will even ask for proof." He leaned back in his chair to project a casual attitude, as if this was no big deal to him and didn't make his heart race.

"But marriage," she sputtered. "Cannot possibly be our best option. If documents are so easy to forge, then make some from my father, or you can pretend to be my brother."

There was no world in which he would ever pose as her *brother*.

"But then you would be a single woman in a school filled with single men. Men will always notice a single woman, but they ignore a married one."

Jane's fists curled as her face turned deep red. He wasn't sure if she was upset with him or the world at large, but he knew enough to stay silent.

"I suppose men will only ever respect the ownership displayed by another man," she spat out the words as if they were poison. "But why do I have to pretend to be married to *you*?"

What little pride he had left deflated as her words echoed through his head. He itched with the desire to pull up his hood and hide, but he remained frozen.

"I know I'm not exactly a prize," he said, annoyance melting away his shame and embarrassment. He was doing this for her. It wasn't as if he was actually proposing. "But I am your only option since Tristan is too busy to go to school with you, and we can't risk anyone else finding out your truth. Unfortunately, you'll have to suffer looking at my face every day."

Jane huffed. "Please, don't do me the indignity of pretending you are some hideous creature cursed to limp through eternity."

"Do you not see this?" Will frowned, pointing at his wretched face. "My brother prowled burial notices for weeks to put this together. I am monstrous."

"You have scars and... other parts, but that doesn't detract from anything. The bones and general shape of your face are pleasing," she said, stumbling over her words as her face turned a deep crimson. "If anything, the scars enhance your attractiveness by making you unique."

Will snorted. Never before had he heard such forced compliments in his life. "I'm sure you find me very attractive, that's why you screamed the first time you saw my face."

He never held her reaction against her, but neither could he forget her scream of terror.

"I didn't scream because of your appearance. It was my reaction to my general frustration at being reanimated. I wasn't scared of you, I've never been scared of you. Not even when you were dressed as a prowler in the library the night we met."

It was Will's turn to be stupefied, his mouth opening and closing a few times as he tried and failed to find the words.

"But you looked so scared," he rasped, finally finding the words as the memory of that night flashed through his head.

"I was scared." Jane sat in the chair next to him. "I woke up in a strange place with two strange men who told me I had died. It would have been concerning if I hadn't been scared. If you had stuck around, you would have seen it. I calmed down once Tristan started answering my questions."

"I suppose that does make sense," he said slowly.

Truly, he had never considered another perspective on her feelings. He had been too wrapped up in his own self-hatred to notice.

"In fact, I would say it is rather egotistical of you to assume my reaction had anything to do with you at all."

"Yes, I have gathered that now," he said, embarrassment threatening to boil him from the inside. "Does that mean you will take me as your pretend husband after all?"

Jane sighed, but the corners of her mouth twitched. "I'm not sure how I feel about to have and to hold."

"No holding necessary. At least we already have for better or worse covered."

Jane laughed, and Will couldn't help but puff out his chest a bit. Making her laugh was a precious accomplishment.

"*If* we are to do this, I do think there should be some ground rules."

"Of course, I fully expected you would have some demands," he said, prompting her to continue.

"We need to have two separate rooms."

"What are people going to say when they see a newlywed couple staying in separate rooms?"

He had already reserved two rooms at the hotel, but he enjoyed arguing with her. He loved the cute lines that gathered between her brows when she scowled.

"I'll tell them you snore."

"Fair enough. Any other conditions?"

She paused, chewing on her lip as she thought. Will found it to be incredibly distracting as he could not take his eyes away from her plush pink mouth.

"No terms of endearment."

"But I was so looking forward to calling you my little bunny rabbit."

Shooting him a glare, Jane continued, "No matter how much you want to help, I don't need your unsolicited advice or you trying to fix any problems for me."

"I'll try my best." He would try, but he wasn't making promises. Surely, she didn't expect him to stand by while someone harassed her.

"I need you to teach me how to navigate the world. I want to learn how to make travel arrangements, find reputable inns, and how to handle money in support of my independence."

Will frowned. Those were skills he didn't even remember learning. A woman's education was different, but he didn't know why she wouldn't know at least some of those things.

"What do you need to learn about handling money? It's fairly intuitive."

Jane stiffened, her jaw set in a hard line, and her face became curiously blank. Yet again, Will had said the wrong thing. It was practically a gift.

"I've never had money of my own, but I don't owe you an explanation on my terms."

"Of course, I will teach you whatever you want. Your terms are all quite reasonable."

"Do you have any terms?"

"No."

His terms were pretending to be married, but he didn't want to chance kicking the hornet's nest again by bringing that up. There was nothing else he wanted.

"Good," she said with a satisfied nod. "Do we need to sign a contract?"

"If you trust me, we can settle this with a handshake."

Jane held out her hand without a moment of hesitation. She

trusted him, and he wouldn't do anything to jeopardize that. He took her hand to shake on the deal.

"Are you always going to wear those gloves?"

Will looked down to see his black leather gloves as he grasped her pale hand. Tristan gave them to him for Christmas years ago, but now they were practically a second skin.

"Yes."

"What if I said one of my demands was for you to take the gloves off?"

"You missed your chance since we already shook on it." The only reason he felt comfortable touching her was because of the gloves.

"Maybe I'll add it when we renegotiate."

There was nothing she could offer to get him to change her mind, but that wasn't a fight they needed to have at that moment.

"When do we leave?"

"First thing tomorrow morning. We'll take the carriage to Wakefield and then travel the rest of the way to Cambridge by train."

"Then I suppose I'd better pack," Jane said, rising from her chair before turning on her heel to leave the room.

Most of his packing was already done as he had been preparing for days. He would have told Jane sooner, but the final confirmation hadn't arrived until the previous evening. He hadn't wanted to get her hopes up in case there were any issues.

The door opened again, and Mrs. Jones returned to the room.

"I'm glad that went well. I only heard one dish clatter."

"And it didn't even break. Everything went better than I could have imagined."

The housekeeper smiled as she cleared the plates, but it didn't quite reach her eyes.

"Tell me your concern," Will sighed.

"It's not really a concern," Mrs. Jones said. "I only want you to be careful. You have a big heart, and I don't want to see you get hurt."

"Do you think Jane would hurt me?"

"No, she's a nice girl. I don't want you to see things that aren't there and hurt yourself."

"Ah." He would have loved to say he didn't know what she meant, but his heart raced as he thought of spending so much uninterrupted time with her. The excitement he felt when she agreed to pretend to be his wife told him his heart was at risk, but that was his responsibility. "I'll be careful."

He hated lying to Mrs. Jones, but he didn't want the woman to worry about him while he was gone. Will suspected it was already too late to guard his heart from Jane Montgomery.

CHAPTER 16

*J*ane stood before the carriage holding her packed bag. Everything she had in the world had been packed ten minutes after she had left the dining room. She had a few dresses, a few notebooks and pens Tristan had given her, a comb from Mrs. Jones, night clothes, and the cloak she arrived in. The benefit of starting her life over was that she could carry every- thing in one hand.

"When you weren't in your room, I was worried you absconded in the night."

Turning, she saw Will walking towards her with his hood pulled down over his face. There weren't any bags in his gloved hands, which caused her to frown.

"Some of us spent our time getting ready. Am I going to have to wait for you to pack?" She asked with an arched eyebrow. Already she had waited long enough to go to Cambridge.

Will raised his hands. "I'm ready. The coachmen are bringing my trunks down now."

As if on cue, two men carrying trunks came out of the house, followed by Tristan and Mrs. Jones. Embarrassment flooded her as she realized she had been ready to leave without giving either a proper goodbye. She had spoken to them both about the trip yesterday and was ready to leave it at that.

"I'm glad we caught you before you left," Tristan said as he came to a stop before her with his hands clasped behind his back.

"Well, we never could have left without saying goodbye."

Will snorted, and she shot him a glare.

Tristan's eyes gleamed as they bounced between them. "Regardless, we wanted the chance to see you off." He revealed a big brown parcel and handed it to her. "Here's a congratulatory gift to mark the start of your new academic journey."

Taking the heavy parcel from him, she slipped her fingers beneath the wax seal, ripping apart the thick brown paper.

"Oh, this is lovely," she said, tears gathering in her eyes. "I'll cherish it forever, thank you."

He had given her *Gray's Anatomy*. As soon as he handed her the parcel, she knew it was a book, but she never expected it to be *this* book. It was a different edition than the one she had left behind, but this one would be even more precious to her.

"Of course. These are the first steps towards your bright future in medicine."

Before she could think better of it, she threw her arms around him in a tight hug. He hesitated before woodenly patting her on the back.

"I'm glad to have you as a mentor. I appreciate everything you've taught me," she said quietly, so he was the only one who heard.

"It may not always be easy, but I promise you it will be worth it. Don't be afraid to write if you find yourself needing advice."

"Don't worry, you won't get rid of me that easily."

Tristan laughed as they broke apart before he moved on to say his good-bye to Will. The brothers kept their conversation to a low murmur. Jane could have listened with her newly improved listening, but decided to give them privacy.

Mrs. Jones stepped in front of her, her usual mask of professionalism in place. Jane shifted in place, unsure of what to say to the housekeeper. They hadn't spent a lot of time together outside of dressing, but she didn't think the woman liked her very much.

"Make sure you two take care of each other. I don't want to get any letters about you fighting," Mrs. Jones said, her tone was so dry Jane couldn't tell if she was joking or not.

"We'll try our best, but I'm afraid I can't make any promises."

Jane's face grew hot as they stared at one another. Mrs. Jones' lips didn't even twitch. It wasn't a very good joke, but she had hoped for a polite smile at the very least.

The housekeeper surprised her by throwing her arms around her middle and squeezing her so hard it was difficult to breathe.

"Make sure to have a good time and remember that he is all bark and no bite, so don't let him get to you. Don't be afraid to give it back to him either."

Mrs. Jones stepped back, winking at her. The interaction was so unexpected that Jane didn't know how to respond. When Will called her name, she turned to see him holding open the carriage door.

Grasping her bag to her chest, she stepped forward, ready to begin the journey into the next stage of her life.

"Are you going to hold onto that for the entire ride?"

Jane stopped, looking up at Will with a furrowed brow until he gestured to the bag in her hands.

"If I must."

In truth, she only held onto her bag because she didn't know how to affix it to the carriage. It wasn't heavy, so she didn't mind holding it.

Will huffed and held out his hand.

"Really, it's fine. The other bags are already up there, and we need to leave."

He snatched the bag from her and slung it on top of the carriage in one fluid motion. Unhooking one of the straps, he adjusted the luggage so her little bag was nestled between his trunks.

"Thank you."

"It was such an arduous process that I can see why you avoided it."

"I'm glad you said something because I was worried we were at risk of having a nice moment."

Will held out his hand to help her into the carriage, but she ignored it in favor of climbing in on her own.

The interior of the carriage was black, with the seats upholstered with red fabric that was soft beneath her fingers. Matching curtains swayed as Will climbed in behind her. The space was big enough that they were able to sit at opposite corners without touching on the long journey to the train station.

They may not have been close enough to touch, but she was still very aware of him in the small space. He didn't spread out and impose himself on her like Robert, but his presence commanded the space all the same. Somehow, it was even worse because it wasn't like she could physically push his presence away.

Jane kept her eyes in front of her, but even with his face covered, her skin prickled under his heavy stare. "What?"

She didn't mean to snap, but it was difficult to think when his eyes were on her.

"We should come up with our story now so it will be convincing by the time we make it to Cambridge," he said.

"Isn't our story that we're pretending to be married?"

Jane still couldn't believe she had agreed to such a ridiculous ruse. The worst part was that she didn't dislike the idea of the charade. She liked that it gave Will an excuse to keep close to her, even if it made her feel like a traitor to herself.

"Yes, but we need to make sure we have the details correct or else the story will fall apart."

"What kind of story do we need? One day we were single and the next we were married."

Gravel crunched outside as the coachman walked by and settled into the driver's seat. Will knocked on the ceiling twice, and the carriage started their journey.

"How did we meet? You know that will be the first question anyone asks us."

She sighed because he was right. People loved nothing more than to be nosy around newlyweds. "We can say we met at a party.

You were instantly smitten with me, and wore me down until I married you."

"I'm not telling people I had to wear you down to get you to marry me," he snorted, the black hood shaking with the movement.

"Why not?"

"It's humiliating. I do have some standards to uphold."

"We're pretending to be other people. Why do your standards matter?"

"It's the principle. I'm not a desperate man."

"You could have fooled me when you wrote me twice in as many days without a response."

It was a pity Will's face was covered because she could only imagine him gaping like a fish.

"That wasn't desperation, it was tenacity."

"Ah."

"What does that mean?"

"I wasn't aware tenacity was what they were calling desperation these days."

Will huffed. "How about mutual love at first sight?"

"Hmm," Jane mused, tapping her chin with her index finger as she pretended to think. "I'm not sure if my character is the type to fall in love at first sight."

"You're that sure of your character already?"

"Of course. I assume you already created names for us since you had to enroll me in Cambridge."

"I did. We are William and Jane Byrne."

"Will and Jane? My, how ever did you come up with names like that?"

"It took a few hours of hard work, but I figured hiding in plain sight would be easiest."

Once again, his idea seemed foolish at first, but there was sound logic behind it.

"I probably would forget to answer to another other name. Where did Byrne come from? I hope you don't expect me to fake an Irish accent."

"It was my mother's maiden name. I figured it made it easier to say Tristan and I were cousins if we had a background that could at least be partially verified. The accent is optional, but do keep in mind that you may need to keep it up for multiple years."

Years.

The idea that she could be a student at Cambridge for years filled her with a type of glee she couldn't even name. It was made all the sweeter by the fact that Robert couldn't taint it now.

"I think I'll stay away from an accent then. I'm sure my Yorkshire accent will cause enough confusion."

"It will be seen as quite exotic."

Silence unfolded between them, but it wasn't awkward. Typically, conversations left her anxious about what to say or how to react, but she didn't have those concerns with Will. Even when she said the wrong thing, he never made her feel bad about it. It was a new experience, and she found she quite liked it.

"What would cause you to want to marry someone?" Will asked, cutting into their comfortable silence.

It was her turn to snort. "It's unlikely I will ever marry, seeing as the last time it was suggested, I killed myself to get out of it."

Will stilled, and she heard a sharp intake of breath.

"I don't suppose we've reached the point where those types of jokes can be funny, " she continued.

"No."

The silence stretched between them, and this time it was less companionable.

"Fine," she said in a put-upon tone, crossing her arms over her chest. "We can tell everyone it was mutual love at first sight."

She felt transparent in her attempt to lighten the mood, but the little tension dissipated just as quickly. She only wished she could see his face so she could read him better.

"So, when you're my chaperone, is this the way you'll be dressed? Because if it is, you certainly will be the talk of the school, but not because you're such a good husband."

"It's better this way. The way I look is too distracting, and there would be too many questions about us if I were to walk around uncovered." His voice was vulnerable in a way she had never heard from him before, and she realized it was more than just vanity.

"I understand your desire for discretion," she said carefully. Comfort wasn't one of her strengths; she was far more likely to offend than to help. "But this is far more unsettling than if you went without the hood. Dressed like this, people will notice you because you look like you have something to hide. If your hood is down, they'll notice you, but it won't be long until you fade into the background."

"If you refuse to be seen with me like this, then we can hire another companion."

That compromise made the most sense, but as she thought about it, she found she didn't want another companion. When she imagined going to class, she imagined Will at her side.

"No, you are the perfect companion, but you would make everyone more comfortable if you kept your hood down."

"Are you not worried about what people say about you when you show up with your husband looking like this?"

"They'll think we are well-suited since we're both tall."

"Is height what matters most in marriage?"

"Of course. First, it's height, then it's money."

"I do have a lot of money."

"Then you're already the perfect husband."

"Are you sure people won't take one look at me and know that something's wrong?"

"I'm not going to say that no one will notice you, but they're just going to think you had an accident and then move on with their days. No one will even come close to being correct because it would be lunacy to accuse someone of being reanimated."

"I suppose the chance of anyone correctly guessing what happened is rather slim."

Even though she couldn't see him, she heard the smile in his voice and relaxed.

"Precisely. Anyway, they will be too busy marveling over how good you are at carrying my books to worry about your appearance."

"Is that what I'm to do all day while you go to class, follow you around carrying your books?"

"At last, you're good for something," she said primly.

Will laughed, the sound a beautiful baritone that cinched itself around her heart. She turned her gaze out the window to hide her blush.

The world speeding by on the other side of the glass was still familiar, but soon she would see a brand new part of the country. She couldn't wait.

CHAPTER 17

$\mathcal{W}$ ill leaned down, exhaling as his fingers grazed the rough wooden floor of the inn they had stopped in for the night. The bed was so bad that his lower back ached when he woke up. The slight discomfort would heal itself momentarily, but he liked stretching when no one was recording the results.

The carriage ride had been easy. Most of the ride had been silent as Jane looked out the window, while he looked at her. By the end of the day, he was eager to get out and stretch his legs. He had been about to ask Jane to join him for dinner when she said she wished to retire to her room for the night. Will ordered dinner and a bath to be brought to their separate rooms.

A delicate chime from the mantle clock told him it was time to leave if he wished to remain on schedule. Pulling on his leather gloves, he scanned the room to make sure nothing was left behind before going to Jane's room.

Luckily, the walk to Jane's door only took moments as she had the room next door.

"Are you ready?" he asked, knocking on the door.

"I'll be right out!"

The door opened, and Jane slipped out, her half-full bag slung over her shoulder. They had been apart for less than twelve hours, but seeing her again settled something in his chest. He had missed her.

Reaching out to take her bag from her, he got a good look at her and frowned. "What are you wearing?"

She looked down at her outfit and then raised her head, furrowing her brow. "My dress?"

"Yes, but why are you wearing *that* dress?" He glared at her because she knew exactly what he meant since the last time he saw this dress was when she was on the metal slab in Tristan's lab.

Her eyebrows shot up. "It's freshly laundered, and it actually fits me. It's a few seasons out of style, but nothing else is wrong with it."

"It's the dress you *died* in."

She blinked as if his reason for disliking her dress surprised her before her scowl returned.

"It's not as if I have many other options."

Oh. Mrs. Jones had been tasked to pick up a wardrobe for her, but there hadn't been much time to prepare. It must have been quite the adjustment for a woman of Jane's station. "You can wear it today, but I'll get you a proper wardrobe so you never have to wear that again."

He would burn the dress so neither of them ever had to look at it again.

"Is that so?" She challenged as she pushed past him. "I happen to like this dress, and I will wear it as much as I want."

Following her, he watched her messily pinned curls bounce as she rushed down the stairs. Annoyance flashed through him at her long stride, since it was usually much easier for him to catch up to someone.

"You know it's macabre. The only reason why you're wearing it is to make some point to me," he hissed, careful to keep his voice low so the other patrons couldn't overhear, but heads still turned as they rushed through the lobby. "I don't know why Mrs. Jones didn't throw it out when she had the chance."

"Maybe because she knew I wanted to keep something of mine."

He snorted. "Right, the dress you killed yourself in is the kind of memory you want to save."

Once they exited the inn, she whirled around. A storm surged in her grey eyes as she jabbed his chest with her index finger. "Don't think our arrangement gives you the right to have a say in anything I do, anywhere I go, or anything I wear."

"The last time I saw you in that dress, it was waterlogged, and your skin was nearly the same color as the collar. You *died* in that dress." Taking a ragged breath, he pushed away the image of her head lolled against his shoulder as he lifted her from the riverbed. Looking at her flushed face and furrowed brow, it was irrefutable evidence that she was alive. "You don't have many options, but this is something I can easily take care of for you."

The bright morning sun beat down on them, and he squinted. It felt like it was too early for the sun to be this bright.

The sun hadn't been this bright in a while, and he stilled once he realized why. His hood was down. Yesterday, his hood was down while he was in the carriage, but he was careful to raise it the moment the carriage stopped. This morning, he had been too occupied fighting with Jane to notice he hadn't put up his hood.

No one screamed, cried, or jeered. The few people who stared could have been staring because they were fighting in public rather than because of his appearance. Jane was utterly infuriating, but in this, she had been correct. He had hidden himself from the world out of fear. It was easier to reject the world before it rejected him.

"I'll make a deal with you," he said, regaining his composure. "I won't wear my hood up anymore if you promise you won't wear that dress."

"Why do you even care?"

Because her death haunted him. Not just the image of her dead body in the water and in his arms, but the idea that it would have been just as likely that he would have missed her. She could have washed up elsewhere on the river, or he could have stayed in, or one million other things could have made it so he never knew her.

"Because you shouldn't wear something with such horrid memories. You should be able to put it all behind you."

"Why?" Jane sighed. "I'm not trying to be difficult. I don't have a problem with what happened in this dress. I died, then I was brought back. It's just another part of my story."

"Was this your favorite dress?"

"No, I only picked it because wool soaks up the most water."

Will's jaw set in a hard line. "I have no problem sitting with my hood up while I'm next to you in class."

Her eyes narrowed. She was waiting for him to break, but she was going to learn she wasn't the only stubborn one.

"Fine, but you're taking me to a modiste. I want clothes that actually fit me."

"Your dresses have been fine." He was rather fond of the dress that popped a button at dinner the other night, giving him a flash of the creamy skin underneath. "Fine, I'll take you to the modiste. You can get whatever you want, and I won't complain about the price."

"That's how you end up paying for a wardrobe made entirely of silk."

"Then I suppose I'll have the prettiest wife at Cambridge."

She snorted. "You'll have the only wife at Cambridge."

"Then you win either way."

Will successfully maneuvered her bag from her grasp as he guided her to the carriage. Opening the door, he held his gloved hand out to help her inside. She grabbed his hand for balance as she stepped inside. For the first time, he regretted wearing the gloves because he longed to know how her bare skin felt against his.

"YOU DO KNOW you're supposed to get on the train, don't you?" Will asked Jane dryly.

He received a scathing glare in return.

They had arrived at the train station at least fifteen minutes previously, but still hadn't made it to the platform. Instead, they stood in the doorway of the train station. Close enough to see the train roll into the station while receiving plenty of glares for blocking the door.

Travel was such a regular part of his life that he hadn't thought about how magical it was in many years.

Jane surveyed the scene before her as if she wished to remember this moment forever. Her face was a perfect mask of restraint, but he could see the awe in his eyes. It was a privilege to see her experience such things for the first time, but it also made him want to smack her brother for keeping her so sheltered.

Smoke billowing from the train's chimney created a moody scene for the tearful goodbyes happening on the platform. The sharp train whistle cut through the air, and both he and Jane flinched at the sharp sound while those around them continued as usual.

"Let's find our compartment before they leave us behind."

Holding his arm out, she looped her arm through his. Her grip was loose, but he could feel her body heat radiate through their many layers of clothing. Unlike most of the women he had escorted through the years, she was tall enough that he didn't have to hunch. They fit together quite nicely.

Their private compartment was dark with faded green upholstery that had seen better days. It was a bigger space than the carriage they had shared, but the low ceiling made it feel intimate.

Jane slid onto the bench opposite him without taking her eyes off the window as the train slowly started again. He wanted to ask her what she thought of their surroundings, but he didn't want to distract her from her enjoyment.

Once the train had pulled out of the station, she looked away from the window and towards him.

"Will we reach Cambridge tonight?"

"Yes."

"Where are we staying?"

"At a hotel Tristan recommended. One of his mentors lives there during the year and assisted with getting us accommodation."

"You don't have a house there? I thought Tristan went to school there?"

"He lived in the dormitories back then and hasn't visited the school for more than a day or so since he graduated."

"I don't suppose the dormitories were an option then," Jane said, lips twitching.

"No, but I can assure you that you aren't missing anything by skipping that experience."

"And when we get there, we're pretending to be married."

Jane's facial expression was carefully blank, but he could see the tension in her hands clasped on her lap.

"Technically, we already are pretending to be married, as I registered our train tickets under Mr. and Mrs. William Byrne." Will frowned as from then on she would be referred to as Mrs. Byrne. Her identity would be enveloped in his, and it didn't seem fair. "I'm sorry you're stuck with another man's name."

"What do you mean?" She asked, cocking her head.

"Well, everyone will be calling you Mrs. Byrne instead of your name. You'll be going to school, but not as *you*."

If they were properly married, then his name would become hers. Suddenly, that didn't feel fair either, as there was no choice for her in the matter.

"I'm still going as Jane, the surname is the only difference."

"And that doesn't bother you?"

"No, I'm not attached to my family name. It was my father's, but he's been dead a long time, and he was the only other person I knew with the name that I liked. Really, I'm trading one man's name for another."

Will could recite the Gardner line going back ten generations, but barely knew anything about the Byrnes. He had met his grandparents a few times, but the memories were fuzzy because he was quite young. The information was likely in a family Bible, but there was also a good chance it had been lost to time. Half of his history had been wiped away because it belonged to his mother.

"Do you know why my parents named me Jane?"

Will's head turned to her. Her hands remained on her lap, but the tension was gone.

"Of course, you don't know *why*," she chuckled. "I meant more to ask if you wanted to hear the story behind it?"

"Of course."

"Robert and I are twins, but our parents had difficulty conceiving. They were married for many years before my mother fell pregnant. Naturally, they were ecstatic. My mother kept a diary, and she was convinced she was having a boy. They chose the name Robert on their honeymoon, and she wrote so many messages to their little Robert during her pregnancy. Even as she grew bigger and there was a flurry of activity inside her, she thought he was growing bigger and stronger."

Jane drew in a ragged breath, and Will was stiff on the seat. He wanted to throw his arms around her and give her the comfort she deserved, but he knew she needed to get through this.

"When I came out, my father said it was quite the shock. My mother held me, surprised that she had been so wrong when the labor pains returned. She passed me off while she birthed Robert, their boy. Things went bad so quickly that she didn't even get to hold Robert before she passed. My father was left with two children and no wife."

"They never discussed names for a girl. They decided that if they were to have only one child, they wanted a boy to have their male heir. After I was born, the doctors assumed he would name me after her, but he didn't want to give me a legacy to live up to before I was even an hour old. Truthfully, I think he didn't want to say her name all the time. Jane came to him because it was the name of my mother's childhood doll."

"It's lovely he included her in your story." He would have said he was sorry, except he was reasonably sure it would chafe at her because she didn't see the sadness in the story.

"The point of the story is that it's just a name. I had to be called something, and Jane Montgomery was as good a choice as any. So naming me Jane Byrne won't make me any different."

"I still am rather fond of Jane." His cheeks pinkened at what he revealed, but it felt important that he bare his soul for a moment.

"Me too," she said with a soft, curving smile before she returned her attention to the window.

CHAPTER 18

*T*he moon glowed from its place in the sky by the time they rolled up to their hotel in Cambridge. Their new residence was a white building with dark green shutters in the middle of the city square. The front garden was neat, with a few tightly manicured spiral-cut topiaries that rolled into the public gardens, which also had a football pitch and a small lake on the grounds.

Will jumped out of the carriage before a coachman could help him out the door. Holding out his hand, he helped Jane disembark. Once she was on solid ground, he leaned in to her.

"Remember, we're married, Mrs. Byrne," he murmured in her ear, and she shuddered.

In a bold move, he brushed his thumb against her knuckles. He wanted to lean down to kiss the back of her hand, but he wasn't sure how forward she would allow him to be.

He was there to be her chaperone, her protector. Maybe even her friend, but if he squandered her trust, then he would be nothing to her.

Her hand slipped to the crook of his elbow, their arms positioned as if it were a move they had done a thousand times.

They walked into the hotel arm in arm until Jane broke away

TIL DEATH DO WE START

once they reached the desk. He mourned the loss of her body against his, but was thankful for the space so he could breathe.

"Good evening, sir. How may I assist you?" The desk clerk asked.

"I have two rooms for the term reserved for William Byrne."

The clerk looked at his reservation book and frowned. Will's stomach dropped as the man flipped through the book for a long time. Too long.

"I'm sorry, sir, but we don't have a reservation under Byrne. Might it be under a different name?"

"What about under Harris? He had the arrangements made for us to stay here."

Sweat formed on the back of Will's neck as he panicked that he may have placed the reservation under his actual name. He took a deep breath, willing himself to relax as panicking wouldn't help.

"I don't think it would be under a different name," Will said. He spelled the last name for the clerk just to be sure.

The clerk looked back down at his book as Jane wandered over.

"Is there a problem?" She asked.

"I'm sure it will be fine." He gave her a tight-lipped smile, and she arched an eyebrow at him. He had done so much work to get them there, and he prayed they wouldn't have to go around town begging for rooms.

"Ah, yes. I see what the confusion was. The name was inverted, so it was saved under Byrne William instead." The clerk frowned. "Though it looks like only one room was reserved."

Will's relief was short-lived. "Are we able to add a room? Preferably next to each other, but we will be fine with any two rooms you have. We must have two rooms. There isn't another option."

"For you and your wife?"

Will's mouth went dry as his brain searched for any worthwhile excuse. This was their first trial in their pretend marriage, and he was already floundering.

"My husband snores, while I am a very light sleeper. I'm here to attend the University and will need my rest. I'm afraid even two rooms won't be enough to separate me from the sound, but we don't like to be far from each other since we've only recently wed. I'm sure you understand." She smiled at him softly and attempted to flutter her eyes. It looked like she had something in her eye, but Will still found it charming.

The man's face softened towards Jane. "I greatly apologize for the oversight, Mrs. Byrne, but we don't have any additional rooms."

Jane turned to him expectantly. This was the moment where they were supposed to speak without words. A few well-timed facial expressions would be all they needed to get their points across to each other if they were truly married. His parents had many such moments, and he had even managed to do it with Tristan a few times.

Jane set her steely eyes on him, and he blinked dumbly in return. He didn't have the slightest idea what she could be thinking. Sighing, Jane turned back to the clerk with a radiant smile.

"My husband and I will take the one room."

Sputtering, he tried to undo her agreement, saying they could find other arrangements, but she elbowed him in the ribs. Hard.

Somehow, he managed his way through the rest of the transaction even though his face burned so hot he must have looked like a tomato. Beside him, Jane was the perfect mask of calm as she answered the man's questions, sprinkling in some polite small talk. At one point, she looked up at his extremely red face and asked him if he was all right, gingerly placing her hand on his forearm. He cleared his throat and said he was fine, then brusquely took the key and the file with Jane's school information, left for them, and headed to their room.

Jane had asked him to teach her how to navigate the world, but so far she was doing a far better job than he was.

The polished oak staircase creaked as they climbed to their third-floor room. The dimly lit hallway flickered with gas lamps turned onto their lowest setting. The thick brown carpet muffled their footsteps. Their room was close to the stairs, which was less than ideal due to the traffic that would pass by their door, but even with his improved hearing, he only heard some muffled snoring.

Their room was bigger than he expected, with a generously

sized sitting area, and the bedroom was in a separate room with a door. There were certainly worse rooms for them to share, but he would have loved some extra space so he could have somewhere to go where he wouldn't feel the echo of her presence.

Two olive colored velvet armchairs with ornately carved wooden armrests with spindly legs were placed before the fireplace. The brown rug matched the one in the hallway, but this one was less worn. The wallpaper was cream with brown designs that looked like vines crawling up the walls. A writing desk faced one of the tall windows that would provide ample light during the day. Leaning down, he turned on the gas lamp on the table between the two armchairs.

Jane slumped against the heavy door, her hand hovering over the handle as if she were ready to escape.

"I'm so—" he started to say before she stopped him with an abrupt cut of her hand through the air before putting a finger to her lips to indicate he should be quiet.

Indignation burned through him at being quieted in such a way. She had every right to be angry, but he wasn't going to be dismissed like that.

A loud knock sounded, and Jane opened the door.

"Yes," she responded. A lanky teenage boy was in the doorway. His black uniform was clean, but rumpled as if he had been roused from sleep.

"'Scuse me, sir, madam," he said, giving them a little bow. "I have your luggage. Where would you like me to put it?"

Will was more than happy to drag their belongings inside himself and send the porter on his way, but Jane responded before he could send the kid back to bed. "You can place them in the bedroom, thank you."

The boy nodded and scrambled to place their luggage into the bedroom. Despite his lanky build, he lifted the trunks with ease.

"Thank you, sorry to have bothered you so late," Will said as he fished some coins from his pocket and handed them to the boy.

"It's no problem, sir. Be sure to ring if you need anything else. Have a good night, sir. Ma'am." He nodded at them before scrambling out the door. Will hoped he would be allowed at least a few hours of sleep.

Jane slumped her shoulders after the porter left. She looked haggard after a long day of travel, and he was sure he didn't look any better.

"Apologies if I snapped, I knew he was coming and thought it was best if we didn't have this conversation in front of him."

He nodded. The last thing they needed was someone hearing them bicker about their fake marriage. "You did the right thing. Your hearing must be incredible if you heard him approach."

"The man at the desk said he would send the porter up with our belongings."

"Ah." His cheeks heated. He hadn't paid attention to the conversation after all.

"I do apologize for putting you in this situation." He hadn't meant to put her honor into question with this journey.

"These things happen." Jane shrugged. "We have to keep up the ruse anyway, and this will make it easier."

"Yes, people would likely get suspicious over why I never spent the night with my pretty bride." He didn't know why he said it, but his sense of self-preservation seemed to fly out the window when he was around her.

"They'll be talking about us enough that we shouldn't be giving gossips any additional ammunition anyway," Jane said, smoothing her palms over her coarse wool skirt. "It's been a long day, I suppose I should go to bed."

"Of course, we both probably should. Tomorrow is a big day."

Jane went to the bedroom while he went over to the chairs. He could face them toward each other and dangle his body across like a hammock. It wouldn't be his most comfortable night of sleep, but it wouldn't be the worst.

When she got to the bedroom door, Jane turned and frowned at him. "What are you doing?"

"I'm getting ready for bed."

"Do you often sleep standing in the middle of rooms?"

"Of course not." He motioned to the chairs. "I'm going to sleep there."

She frowned. "You can't sleep in an armchair."

"Of course I can, I've slept in worse places before."

The one comfort he had was that any back pain would be very temporary. The most significant upside to being reanimated was that he no longer lived with back pain.

"Maybe for one night, but we are going to be here for *months*."

"I'll move to a new room as soon as one opens, so this will be temporary."

"Who knows when or if another room will become available. Just sleep in the bedroom."

"I can't. I won't compromise you further." He had done enough wrong by her that he was determined for this to be the one thing he got right.

Jane rolled her eyes. "I want you to sit in that chair and tell me if it's comfortable."

The armchair would have been a little small even if he weren't as tall as he was. It looked better suited to a dollhouse than as a usable piece of furniture. Looking back at her, it was clear she was convinced she was about to win their spat, which only steeled his resolve. He would sleep in this blasted chair even if it splintered beneath him. Holding her stare, Will lowered himself into the olive chair.

The chair was even closer to the ground than it had looked, and he sank forever before he made contact with the unforgiving cushion. The chair's width exactly matched his hips, locking him in place. His knees were folded into his chest, the wood groaning as it adjusted to his weight.

"It's very comfortable," he said while trying to shift so the wooden bar that poked him through the upholstery didn't dig into his spinal cord. "I'll be asleep before you even shut the door."

"You look like you're being eaten by a snake," she said, crossing her arms.

Jane expected him to fold, but this was the hill he was willing to die on.

He needed her to go to the bedroom so he could free himself from this infernal contraption. He would stand all night if he had to, but this chair certainly wasn't a viable option. "It's a perfect fit. Like we were made for each other."

Walking over to the corded bell pull, she gave it a few healthy yanks while grumbling about how stubborn he was under her breath.

"Why are you calling the porter? The poor boy probably just got settled."

"I wouldn't have had to call him if you had gone into the bedroom."

His jaw hardened as he stared at her. "There's no need to call him if *you* had gone into the bedroom."

They continued their staring contest until there was a knock at the door, when Jane broke to let in the porter.

"I'm so sorry to bother you, but I was wondering if you could get us some extra pillows?"

The porter nodded, running off to fulfill her request. Will glowered, but she refused to back down.

The porter returned a short time later with a stack of pillows so high it obstructed his vision. "Your pillows, ma'am."

Jane took the pillows from him while Will struggled to reach his pocket to produce some coins for the poor porter who had now been dragged from his bed twice to deal with their nonsense.

The chair groaned and squeaked as he flailed as he tried to reach his pocket. Jane buried her face in the mountain of pillows to hide her laughter. The tableau was so beyond absurd that Will didn't even have it in himself to be embarrassed. He knew the porter would have a phenomenal story that would spread to the other employees by dawn.

"Excuse me, what is your name?" Will asked the young man, attempting to keep as much dignity as he could muster, but he could feel the sweat drip from his brow. Will was impressed that Jane was the only one laughing.

"It's Oliver, sir," he said, shifting in place. Personal introductions were likely frowned upon by his superiors.

"Oliver, it's nice to meet you. Would you please help me up from this chair?"

Jane's muffled laughter got louder as her eyes peeked up above the stack so she could watch. Oliver came over, grasping both of Will's hands in an attempt to pull him up. The boy was strong, but the chair had such a firm grip that the effort only pinched his hips.

"Sir, try bracing your feet on the ground and wiggle your hips as I pull."

"Wiggle?" Will raised an eyebrow, and Oliver nodded seriously in return. Will sighed. It wasn't as though he had any dignity left, so he might as well wiggle.

Bracing his feet on the floor, he moved—he was a grown man, he did not *wiggle*—his hips as Oliver pulled. After a few moments of hopeless, embarrassing movement, he popped out of the chair like a cork out of a champagne bottle.

"You might be onto something with wiggling Oliver." He patted the porter on the back as he dug into his pocket with his other hand and handed him a heavy handful of coins. The young man had certainly earned the riches.

"Thank you, sir. Our pig used to get stuck around the barn a lot, but I never thought that would ever be good practice for something."

Jane's muffled laughter turned to a coughing fit. Will couldn't help the twitch of his own lips.

"Well, this certainly amused my wife, so I suppose it was worth it." Jane's laughter died, and her eyebrows shot up. Will walked Oliver to the door. "Have a good night, we'll let you rest now."

"Oh, it's not a problem, sir," Oliver said as Will shut the door behind him. He turned back to face Jane, but all he saw was her back as she scampered into the other room with her pile of pillows. Taking a deep breath, he followed her into the bedroom.

CHAPTER 19

*J*ane placed the pillows on the floor as she stripped the bed. Going over to the closet, she pulled out the only extra quilt. It was made from the same green fabric that covered the rest of the room, but was soft to the touch.

She turned around, stiffening as she noticed Will holding the stack of pillows she had set down. "What are you doing?"

"I was going to build a nest for myself in the other room. Thank you for thinking of this. It will be far more comfortable."

"Put the pillows on the bed," she snapped, inwardly cringing at her harsh tone. The connection between her brain and mouth was tenuous in the best of times, let alone after a long day.

Will opened his mouth as if to argue with her, but thought better of it when she shot him a withering glare and dropped the pillows onto the bed without further commentary.

She considered the bed for a moment and then put the quilt down on the left side. The bedspread that had been on the bed was placed on the right. They were both adults more than capable of sharing a bed without anything untoward happening.

The bed was surprisingly large, and since she slept on her side, there wasn't a worry of them touching in the night. Still, she arranged the pillows as a wall between them just in case.

"See, you don't need to build a nest. We can share the bed." She held her arm out as if she were a child presenting an art project. Will frowned, his eyes bouncing between her and the bed.

"You mean for us to share the bed?" He looked so thoroughly confused that she took pity on him and bit back her snappy retort.

"Yes."

Dumbfounded, he stared at her for a few long moments. "Are you mad?"

Her smile fell into a scowl. She was being very thoughtful and nice, yet he couldn't be gracious enough to accept. "The bed is big enough for two, there's no reason why we can't share it. I've built a wall, you keep to your side, and I will keep to mine."

"It's not proper, if anyone was to find out—"

She cut him off, "I think my being dead is a far bigger issue than whether I have my virtue or not."

He met her scowl with one of his own. "You know what I mean, if anyone finds out we aren't married, then you'll be ruined. I'm only trying to think about your future."

She wanted to scream, of course, everything in her life came back to how it would affect the hypothetical man she didn't even *want*. The comfort of a fake man would always be more important than the pain being caused to a very real woman.

"But you're assuming that's the life I want at all. I didn't dream of marrying as a little girl, let alone now. I'm not some wallflower who never had the opportunity." She stepped closer to him, louder than she probably should be, with her hands balled into fists at her side. "Maybe you're the one desperately trying to protect your virtue, because I don't have anything left to protect."

She hadn't planned to reveal that to him, but now she felt it necessary because she needed to know if he thought less of her because of it. She wouldn't even waste friendship on someone like that.

His nostrils flared as she steeled herself for disappointment. "Oh, please," he said. "It's not the logistics of virginity that matters, just your reputation. You completely refuse to recognize the reality of the world we live in."

Her shoulders relaxed because this was a fight she could win. "Why do we still have to play by their rules when we don't really live in that world anymore? If anyone finds out we are pretending to be married, that lie is far worse than the reality that I've been alone with a man."

He tensed, and she knew she had backed him into a corner. "We can't pick and choose what rules we follow."

She shrugged. "Then why are we even here? We lied to get me here, and most people in society would disagree with my studying here. Hell, the university barely wants women here. We're here for progress that won't be seen for years, and what is that if not choosing our own type of society to follow?" His shoulders slumped, and she could see the determination in his eyes waver. She went in for the winning blow. "Do you even want to live in a society that would ruin either of us for being alone in a room?"

Sighing, he sat on the left side of the bed. "I suppose you are right. We'll see a lot of new worlds. We might as well get used to it."

She tried to keep her face as neutral as she could as she took mental congratulations from herself for winning the argument when he glared at her.

"You don't need to gloat," he snapped.

Jane let it go because sometimes it's important to be gracious. However, she wasn't gracious enough to apologize.

They stood silently staring at one another. She didn't know what to say. Sharing the bed had been her idea, but she couldn't just get in bed, no matter how tired she was.

"You can use the dressing room first to get ready for bed," Will finally said, breaking the silence.

"Thank you," she said, her shoulders slumping in relief. The past few days of travel had taken a lot out of her. "I promise not to take long."

She grabbed her bag and rushed to the dressing room before he could say anything else.

* * *

JANE SAT at the small vanity, looking at her reflection as her long brown hair dripped onto the rug. Her hair was tangled beyond belief, so she thought to wet it, but she only made a bigger mess. She ran the comb through her sopping wet hair and winced as she felt the water soak through the collar of her dressing gown. In her haste to get dressed, she had forgotten the towel for her hair.

Not only was her tangled hair sopping wet, but she had also dressed herself in the most clothing she had ever worn. She wore her stockings, two shifts, a nightgown, and her dressing gown. Her arm could barely bend, which only made combing more difficult. However, the clothes felt necessary for sharing the bed.

Even though sharing the bed was her idea, she was suddenly quite nervous. She had never slept beside a man before. Well, she had never shared a bed with anyone else before. It hadn't felt intimate when she had been arguing with Will, but once she was undressed in the next room, she felt vulnerable, so she put on all of her layers to act as armor.

Yanking the comb through her hair, she winced when it got caught on a knot. She could wrap her hair up and deal with it in the morning, but it would be far worse once she woke up tomorrow.

The door opened, and she saw Will enter through the mirror's reflection. He was rumpled in a way she had never seen before. His white shirt was untucked and hung around his thick thighs. His cravat was missing, and the top of his shirt was open so she could see the dark hair peeking through. She had never paid attention to men's physiques before, but he was *very* well-formed.

She looked at him for so long that it went from staring to gawking as her eyes traveled over his body. His chest heaved with a ragged breath, and his throat bobbed. When she finally got to his face, his eyes were dark with desire. She flushed deep red at being caught staring, but was glad she wasn't the only one suffering from attraction.

Their eyes caught together in the mirror as if they were under a spell. His yellow eyes were always intense, but this was the first time she felt the full weight of his gaze. His eyes dipped to her body, and she saw the disappointment laced with relief across his face when he saw how clothed she was. It was for the best.

She returned to combing her hair. Her new goal was to finish as quickly as she could so she could get in bed and sleep through the awkwardness.

"What did your hair ever do to deserve such a punishment?"

Her eyes moved back to the mirror to see that Will was behind her, close enough to almost feel his touch on her shoulder. Part of her wanted to close the distance between them, but that was an awful idea if she wanted to sleep next to him. Platonically. "I'm not punishing it."

"You're scowling at your hair as if it owes you money." He held his gloved hand out, palm up over her shoulder. "Give me your comb, and I'll help."

She turned to him as confusion swarmed her face. "What do you want?"

"The comb. I can do your hair."

"Why?" Her face heated as she imagined how good his hands would feel in her hair.

"It's painful watching you struggle. It's incredible how little coordination you have." He sighed when she remained silent while she mentally scrambled for a comeback. "Mrs. Jones warned me that you may need some assistance."

She stiffened, turning back to the mirror. "I can do my own hair." His offer no longer tempted her if it came from a place of pity.

He snorted. "I wouldn't be too sure about that."

She scowled and went back on the offensive against the knot she was fighting. "Did my maid use to do this for me? Yes, but that doesn't mean I can't figure it out. It's *my* hair."

"Is that why you had the worst hairstyle I've ever seen today?" Will asked with a raised brow.

With a huff, she slapped the comb on his palm. The wooden comb made a dull thud on the leather. "If you think you can do better, you're more than welcome to try."

He ran his hand through the section of hair she had been

working on so gingerly she suppressed a shudder. She wasn't about to let him know how good it felt.

"You're dripping wet," he said in a low voice that resonated within her. "I'll be right back."

Her face burned, and her tongue froze as Will went to the other room, returning with her forgotten towel. Slowly, he worked through her long hair section by section, gently removing the excess moisture. It took a long time since she had so much hair, but he gave it the same concentration he usually reserved for his garden.

Once he was satisfied with her hair's moisture, he picked the comb back up and worked through her hair in the same sections in which he had dried them. He combed her hair from the ends up. She was loath to admit it, but he was much better at this than she was. Even though he was able to work through her knots with minimal yanking, he still murmured an apology every time she winced.

"How did you get to be so good at doing a woman's hair?" She tried to keep her voice light, but she couldn't help the husky tone in her voice.

"I had lots of time to practice on my best girl." He diligently worked on what she hoped was her last knot. His brow furrowed in concentration, and where she would have worked faster, his strokes slowed down to become even more deliberate.

"I suppose this is the move you use on all the girls." She tried to sound teasing despite the surprising tendril of jealousy that snaked through her.

"No, not *all* the girls. I've only ever done this for one girl," he sighed. "I met her when I was ten. Her name was Apples, and my father said I could only keep her if I learned to take care of her on my own."

"You learned to do hair for your horse." Her lips twitched as the jealousy turned to amusement.

"Of course, I had to make sure her mane was taken care of." He finished with the knot and then gave the rest of her hair one last comb through. The comb easily slid through her hair, and she was amazed at how well he tended to her hair. He could give Mary a run for her money. "Her hair was thick and dark like yours, but yours is much softer."

"How are you so sure it's soft through the gloves?"

It felt like a petty gripe to bring up when his hands felt so good, but a tiny, bitter part of her wanted his bare hands in her hair. She wanted to feel his skin against hers.

"I can tell by how easily it slides through my fingers. How easily the comb slides through it. I can tell it would feel like silk on my bare hands. It's too fine for my rough hands to handle."

Jane wanted to argue that point, but she didn't want him to stop threading his hand through his hair. Gooseflesh ran down her back following the journey of his hand.

"Well, I'm glad to win something against Apples. Is she one of the horses in the stables?"

He sectioned her hair evenly into two sections and began his plait on the right side of her head. Brow furrowed, his pink tongue peeked through his lips as he worked. He took his job so seriously that it sparked amusement inside of her.

"No, she was older when I got her. It's part of what made her such a good horse for me to learn on. When I was twenty-three, her vision had become so poor I stopped riding her and would walk her around our favorite trails."

He finished one plait, and it was long and neat, much better than any she had ever achieved. She handed him a piece of cord to tie off the end.

"One day, she was in the meadow and broke her leg tripping over a gopher hole. Luckily, I was home when it happened. I gave her a couple of apples and made sure she would never be in pain again." His voice had gotten quiet, and his eyes were distant.

"I'm so sorry." It didn't feel significant enough to say in the face of his loss, but she didn't have any other words. Her heart ached for him.

He kept the end of her plait in his hand, absentmindedly rubbing the curled ends. She brought up her hand and gently brushed her knuckles against his. The contact was slight, but he flinched as if she had burned him, dropping her braid in the process.

"I'm glad for all of the good years we had together."

He ran his hands through the unbraided side of her hair; his gloved hand got caught in her tresses, and it pulled her hair, and she shivered. "Sorry."

She was too embarrassed to admit her reaction was born out of pleasure rather than pain. Her hair had been in someone else's care thousands of times, but she had never reacted like this before. If his hands felt this good on her head, she couldn't even imagine how good they would feel elsewhere.

"Did you not have a horse you could use to practice braiding?"

"No, I found I belonged in the library early. My father did teach me how to ride, though. I complained the entire time, but I am a certified rider."

"Certified? How did you manage that?"

"I refused to get on the horse the first few times he tried, but I agreed when he told me I would be a certified rider once I finished five rides."

The certificate was still in the desk drawer in her room. Well, maybe it was still there. Sofia had likely cleared out her room.

"Did your father typically create certificates to trick you into doing things?"

"Not nearly as often as he should have, but I do have a certificate in embroidery and drawing. I tried to get one in penmanship, but I never passed the final exam. Too many ink splotches."

"I didn't realize I was in the company of such an accomplished woman."

"You would have gotten the penmanship certificate."

"Oh?" He asked, his hands stilling.

Her eyes slid to her hands, feeling foolish to bring such a thing up now.

"You have very nice handwriting."

"I wasn't sure if you had received my letters," Will said, continuing his plait.

"I did." She didn't mention that they were both in her bag next to the bed. "I didn't know how to respond. Things went bad rather quickly."

"There, now you have two even and neat braids." He put her plait down, and it curled onto her chest. His eyes briefly followed it, but he looked away.

She admired her hair in the mirror. "Apples was a lucky girl, you have deft hands."

He laughed. "I'm glad to see my work flourish. It's a lot easier to braid when I don't have to be worried about being kicked."

"There's still time for me to kick you." Her lips twitched, causing him to laugh again. They locked eyes in the mirror, his intense gaze heating her from the inside. His hand flexed as if he wanted to reach out and touch her, but he cleared his throat and walked away.

The spell between them broke, and she blew out the candle and scrambled into bed before she could embarrass herself further. She lay on the very edge of the mattress facing the wall. Her heart raced as she braced herself, waiting for Will to join her in bed.

CHAPTER 20

*V*olunteering to braid Jane's hair had been reckless when his control around her was already so precarious. Every moment around her only made him want her more. He had longed to run his hands through her hair, but even though his hands were gloved, it was still worth every moment.

The act had started friendly enough, but as her eyes grew hooded, he knew she enjoyed it as much as he had. It had been easier to handle when he thought the attraction was one-sided, but he wasn't sure how strong he could be when she looked at him with such desire. If she had issued an invitation, he wasn't sure he had the strength to decline.

However, she had stayed silent, so he stood at the window trying to will his body to relax instead of lying beside her in bed.

The sheets rustled behind him, and he took a shaky breath as he imagined Jane between them. She was wearing maybe the most clothes he had ever seen on a person. He had meant to tease her, but all words left him when he saw how lovely she was with her long, unbound hair flowing around her. Asking to plait her hair had been an act of selfishness because he had longed to get his hands on her chestnut tresses since the moment he laid eyes on her. Stifling a groan, he imagined her hair wrapped around his fist.

His cock ached at the image. There was no private place for him to go where he could relieve himself. Even the idea of going to the next room to do so while she tried to sleep made him feel vile. So, he discreetly shifted himself in a bid to alleviate some of his discomfort as he tried to will the issue away.

The best he could do was stand at the window thinking about croquet. It was an asinine game he hated to play since the mallets were comically short for someone his height.

Thoughts of croquet were working to tamp his desire before the image of Jane hunched over a croquet mallet flashed in his mind. Bent over with her heavy breasts straining against her bodice, desperate to break free.

He stifled a groan. Croquet wasn't working anymore. He scrambled for anything else. Taxes. Roman battle strategy. The happy sound Jane made when he ran his hands through her silky hair.

Not helpful.

"What are you doing?"

Startled, he turned his head to see Jane peeking over the pillow barrier at him.

"Thinking," he said, wincing as it was one of the most profoundly stupid things he had ever said.

"Well, think in bed. Your hovering is making me nervous."

She disappeared behind the pillows again, and he frowned. There was no way to deny her request without coming clean about his current predicament, and that information couldn't be tortured out of him.

Despite his best intentions, he was doomed to live with his arousal, so he might as well suffer horizontally. He situated himself on the edge of the bed. Somehow it was less comfortable than standing, but he could always get up again once Jane was asleep.

"Are you asleep?" Jane murmured so quietly he thought he had imagined it for a moment.

"No," he replied at full volume.

"Is it kind of silly that I'm nervous about tomorrow?"

"I don't think so." He was nervous too, but she didn't need to know that. He worried about being around so many people, but he was primarily nervous over how Jane would be received.

"Going to school was the only thing I ever wanted, but now that it's here, I'm so scared of failing that I don't know if I can go through with it."

"Nerves are normal. I would be worried if you weren't nervous, but you've prepared for this moment all your life. The only way you could fail would be if you didn't go."

He swallowed, hoping his words were a comfort. He was better with emotion than his brother, but neither of them had been raised to do much more than brood.

"I'm worried the fantasy will be better than the reality, and I won't enjoy my time here. That everything I have worked for will be for nothing." Her voice was barely above a whisper, as if she worried speaking the words would make them come true.

He turned to face their pillow wall. He would do whatever he could to help her because she deserved to face tomorrow steady and confident in her place at Cambridge.

"It's going to be different from what you've dreamt of, but that's unavoidable. It might not feel right in the beginning because it's so different from how you thought it would be, but it will be better than anything you've ever dreamed of because it's real. An imperfect reality beats imagined perfection every time."

"But what if I don't like the reality of it? What if I don't like school and *everything* in my life has been a waste?"

"Then you don't like it." He wanted to tear down the wall between them, but he also knew she was only able to be this honest because they couldn't see each other. "The beautiful thing about life is you're allowed to change your mind. Even if it isn't permanent, that doesn't mean it wasn't an important part of your story. However, I think you're going to like attending school. How did you feel working with Tristan in the lab?"

"It felt like I found a part of myself that had been missing."

He smiled at the resignation in her voice. Jitters were normal, but she needed the confidence that he felt for her.

"I think you'll feel that way about school as well. It may take some time, but you'll find your place. And if you don't, then at least you gave it your all and won't spend your life wondering what could have been."

"It's almost annoying how good you are at talking me down."

"I'm very familiar with panic." Self-doubt was a subject he was quite familiar with, but he had never been so successful in vanquishing it for himself.

"Have you lost a dream like that?" The pillow moved slightly, as if she had moved closer.

"Not exactly," he sighed. It was a difficult question because he wasn't even sure if he knew the answer himself. "My life wasn't particularly great, but losing it was indescribable. I spent my life dedicated to my family's trade business, but I also resented the responsibility."

"Ah, the perils of the eldest son," Jane teased. After a comfortable silence, she continued, "What happened to your parents?"

"They were traveling through Europe on business and sightseeing. On their way home, their ship hit rough waters and sank."

"I'm so sorry."

The pillow between them shifted again, but this time a pale hand snaked over the top. He went to take it, to accept the comfort she offered, when he saw his own pale, scarred hand. He had removed his gloves for the night because they were uncomfortable to sleep in, and he already had to sleep in his trousers.

He could ignore her hand, and nothing would change between them, except he was sure she would never reach for him again. With his less cursed right hand, he grazed his fingers against hers. The touch was slight, but he still felt a jolt between them when their bare skin touched. Her fingers were soft and warm, a reminder that they were both alive.

"Thank you. It was a blessing they went together. They never spent more than a night apart in twenty years."

"It still must have been difficult to lose them both at once."

Their fingers were barely touching, but neither made a move to withdraw.

"I don't think there's a good way to lose your parents."

His parents had been gone for so long that the pain was no longer raw, but it would always be there. Their memories were a comfort rather than pain.

"No." She was quiet for so long he thought she had fallen asleep. He considered moving his hand, but hers was still there, and he wouldn't be the one to move first. "Is that why Tristan studied reanimation?"

"Yes." Tristan would be annoyed at him for saying this, but his psyche was fairly easy to figure out. "He got his first doctorate right before their journey. He didn't want to have a funeral for them because he was sure they weren't really gone. He insisted they had washed up on some beach and were fighting to come home. His research changed, and he became obsessed with the mechanics of life and death. I had no clue about the ramifications of what he was doing."

"So when you woke up, you didn't know it was an option?"

"No," he laughed. Those first days were filled with such anger and confusion. If someone had told him back then that he would eventually be in bed with a woman he genuinely liked, he would have laughed in their face. "It was a difficult few days before I came to terms with my condition."

His breath stilled. He still hadn't truly come to terms with his condition, had he? Even with Jane, the single person equipped to understand his plight, he still felt separate from her. When he looked at her, he didn't see a monster, but that was how he felt every day.

"I think my adjustment took much longer, actually. It might still be happening."

Jane's thumb rubbed over his knuckles. It wasn't until she arrived that he felt alive again.

"Why are you so scared to face the world?"

Part of him wanted to brush her off. Feign sleep and then pretend the conversation never happened when they woke up, but he couldn't stop the confession pouring from him.

"It feels like everyone will take one look at me and know I'm an undead aberration. I don't blend in, and it feels like the more someone looks at me, the more they will be able to tell there's something *wrong* with me," he said with a ragged breath.

"We're different, but there is nothing inherently *wrong* with us. We don't have to be sequestered from the rest of society."

"It's not just that we were once dead, but we are now physically different. We heal at a different rate, our senses are sharper, and you even said our blood looks different now. We died once, but we won't again. We'll live longer than every single person in this town. We aren't the same anymore."

He sat up and looked down at her, breaking their unspoken rule of the night. She looked up and frowned, her braids sprawled across the pillow.

"Do you plan on being a danger to anyone? Of exploiting their vulnerabilities and ruling over them?"

"No." There was nothing he could think of that would be less appealing than appearing to humanity as an undying savior.

"Do you think I'm going to do so?"

"Of course not," Will scoffed.

"Then we don't need to lock ourselves away, waiting for an angry mob that will never come after us." She sat up, looking into his eyes with a ferocity that both worried and excited him. "You're correct that we aren't part of their society anymore. Right now, we are still chronologically young, but we won't always be. We'll see Queens and Kings come and go, and whatever may one day replace them. We will experience eras we cannot even comprehend. We don't need to conform to their norms. We can create our own society for the two of us."

She leaned forward and pressed her lips to his. Shock froze him, and she pulled back before he had the chance to kiss her back.

She lay down on her side facing the wall. Her two neat braids looked up at him like a smile that curled around the back of her head. "Good night, Will."

He lay down on his side facing the opposite direction, completely bewildered. His fingertips felt his lips where the ghost of her touch remained. He could hardly believe she had reached for him at all. If she wanted to recreate society with only the two of them, he wouldn't complain. From the moment he saw her in his library, he wanted her. He had thought the dreams he had spun of the life they could have together were killed the moment she realized what he had done to her, but now there was a new chance for them—a future where they could be together.

CHAPTER 21

*W*hen Jane woke up the following morning, she was pleased to see the wall of pillows had made it through the night. She had been half-afraid she would wake up to find she had thrown the pillows off the bed and spread herself over Will like jam on toast. When she peeked over the wall, the other side of the bed was empty. She was both grateful to have a bit of a break from Will and disappointed that he wasn't there.

Last night had been a revelation. She still couldn't believe she kissed him. It only lasted a few seconds, but it left her wanting more. Attraction had simmered between them since they met, but last night had been something more. Being vulnerable had always scared her, but it ended up feeling nice. They had comforted one another, and she wasn't worried about him using her insecurities as a weapon against her in the future. It was a minor miracle she had managed to get any sleep since she had been swimming with nerves, both about him and the upcoming day.

Today was her first-ever day of school. She had a governess and tutors as a child, but her instruction was always individual. There was no homework, tests, or lectures. Nerves churned in her stomach, but she wasn't sure if they were out of excitement or fear.

"Ah, you're up," Will said, entering the room carrying a white box.

"Good morning."

"I hope you slept well."

Will placed the package next to her on the bed.

"What's this?"

The box was too big to be books, but she wasn't sure what else he could procure for her so early in the morning.

"Oh, it's not much," Will said, cheeks flushing slightly pink. She found his embarrassment rather cute. "I just wanted to get you something for your first day of school."

It was her turn to blush, and she ducked her head while she opened the box. She liked presents. It wasn't a revolutionary stance to have, but her only hesitancy was the fact that he had already been so generous with her. The gifts she was used to had hidden costs.

She opened the box, and her heart stuttered. Inside was a dark blue muslin dress with a high neck. Lifting it from the box, it was a simple dress. No embellishments or lace, but it was fashionably cut in a quality fabric.

"This is lovely, thank you so much." It was the exact dress she would have chosen for herself.

"I thought you deserved something nice for your big day."

"You just want to make sure I don't wear my grey dress anymore," she teased.

"I would do anything to get you out of that dress."

"I promise you don't have to work that hard to get me out of my dress."

"Ah, but how much clothing do you have on underneath the dress?"

"I'm sure I can find another layer if I try hard enough."

"I'll wait downstairs while you get ready," Will said before leaving the room.

He wore the cloak, but the hood was down, and that was a good enough compromise for her. The gloves were back, but she had felt his bare skin last night. When she had passed her hand over the wall of pillows, she had fully expected to be met with his gloved hand. Truthfully, she wouldn't have been surprised if he had slept in them.

Though he had touched her with reverence and spent so long reassuring her against her fears, a kernel of doubt burrowed itself deep inside of her. It felt too good to be true that this man would whisk her away from her nightmare into the life of her dreams. Cambridge alone was a gift beyond measure, but he respected her intelligence and dreams as well. If there was anything her life had taught her, it was that something awful loomed around the corner.

She *liked* Will. More than she ever thought was possible. He liked her too, but was it lasting? They were going to live forever. It was an amount of time she couldn't even comprehend. What would happen to her if he got bored in one year? Or ten years. What would happen if *she* got bored?

In some ways, she was free, but in others, she was just as trapped as she was with her brother. She cared for Will, and she would continue to do so while they figured out whatever was blooming between them, but she needed to take care of herself and her future.

* * *

"YOU WERE RIGHT, this is quite different from what I expected," she grumbled as she surveyed the courtyard filled with boisterous young men.

Not only were her fellow students loud, but they were also rude. Never before had she been so gawked at in her life. None of the looks were lurid, but were instead the kind of stares reserved for a dog walking on its hind legs.

Will laughed. "Were you expecting a bunch of kind and quiet bookworms?"

She had, in fact, expected them to be kind and quiet bookworms hurrying from class to class with towering stacks of books in their hands. However, she didn't mention that out of concern for being laughed at.

"You must remember the vast majority of undergraduate students are young men, and as a rule, they are all feral."

The boy walking in front of them had his books knocked out of his hands by one of his friends, as if punctuating Will's point. "I knew they were wild, but I didn't think they were this bad."

"Only female attention can get boys this age to behave."

Of course, it always came down to that. The world was full of unfortunate cliches. "Well, someone should tell them that women are now attending so they can behave."

"Don't worry, they'll figure out you're here soon enough," Will said, smiling while Jane glared.

She didn't particularly want her male classmates to notice her, but she wouldn't complain if her presence shamed them into behaving. The only thing she wanted was for them to respect her intelligence, but she wasn't holding her breath on that either.

They stopped outside the lecture hall. Class didn't start for a few minutes, but she was glad they were early so they could get good seats.

"Excuse me." Jane turned to see a small blonde woman smiling up at her, who looked to be around the age of the male students. "I'm so sorry to bother you, but are you a student here as well? Or are you accompanying one?" Her eyes darted to Will for a moment before quickly returning to Jane.

"I'm the student, he's accompanying me. I'm Miss—er, Mrs. Byrne. Mrs. Jane Byrne. This is my husband. Mr. Byrne." She patted Will on the arm in the hope it was enough to save the fumbled introduction.

The young woman's eyes widened. "You're here with *your* husband?"

"Yes," she snapped. It was unkind, but she didn't like the incredulity over her being married.

She could be married if she wanted. Well, as far as this young woman knew, she *was* married.

The blonde woman turned a deep red. "My apologies, that was incredibly rude. I was surprised to see a married couple here. Most of the men I know would never allow their wives to attend school, let alone accompany them."

"Oh." The wind was immediately knocked out of the sails of her anger." `1Yes, well, he's very supportive of my endeavors."

Jane also didn't know any men who would unabashedly support their wives' endeavors, especially not in education. Maybe Eleanor's husband, but since he was largely absent, Jane wasn't sure if it was support or if he pretended not to know what his wife got up to in his absence. Will truly was unique. Even though they weren't really married.

"It's not difficult to be supportive when my wife is brilliant."

Jane turned deep crimson at the compliment. She knew she was brilliant, but it felt different that he did as well.

"You both must think I'm frighteningly rude. I'm so sorry. My name is Miss Amelia Thornton." She gave a slight curtsey and then gestured to the white-haired woman standing behind her that Jane hadn't noticed, as she was somehow even smaller than Miss Thornton. "This is my companion, Mrs. Talbot. She's my former governess and now a dear friend."

Will bowed to both women. "I am pleased to make both of your acquaintances on this fine morning."

"It's nice to make your acquaintance, Miss Thornton and Mrs. Talbot," Jane said as she gave a wooden curtsey. It had been a long time since she had done a proper curtsey, but she wasn't going to be shown up by her fake husband.

"I'm so glad to meet you as well. I was worried I would be the only woman in this lecture. There aren't many of us."

"I've heard there are only four."

"Which is all the more reason for us to stick together," Miss Thornton said as she glared at the men staring at them as they crowded outside the classroom. The young woman leaned close to Jane before continuing softly. "Do you think the low enrollment is because the university is trying to keep us out or because families won't let their daughters attend?"

"I only found out women were allowed to enroll just before term, so I'm sure many of our finest students don't yet know it's an option, but it's up to us to be here so they will one day have the same opportunity," Jane said. Any lack of female students was due to a lack of opportunity, not interest.

The lecture hall door opened, a gangly boy darting from the room to prop open the door so they could enter. "Come on, I got a tip that we should sit in the front. Let's show them we can't be intimidated," Jane said as she beckoned for Miss Thornton to follow, and the young woman beamed up at her.

"The term has barely begun, and you already have a devoted follower," Will said to her under his breath.

"Shush, don't make fun."

Miss Thornton was barely out of childhood, but her enthusiasm made Jane wistful for her own teenage years when her soul was lighter. Jane hoped she could stay that way for as long as possible.

"I'm not. I think it's genuinely nice of you to take her under your wing." He deposited her at a seat where she could sit next to Miss Thornton before taking the seat on her other side.

"I would want someone to be nice to me, too," she said with her eyes downcast as she settled herself in her seat.

"I think you underestimate the pull you have as a leader," he said to her as he handed over her school bag that he had insisted on carrying for her.

She blushed as she pulled out her notebook and pens. She didn't think she was much of a leader, but this wasn't the time or place to start an argument.

The professor walked into the room and prepared for his lecture at the podium. She traveled halfway across the country and walked the storied campus, but it wasn't until this moment that it sank in that she was truly a student. It was the most exciting moment of her life.

CHAPTER 22

*W*ill had forgotten how boring school was. After more than a year of brooding and tending his garden, he thought he would be immune to boredom, but today had proven him wrong. So very wrong.

The first lecture had lasted somewhere between two hours and eighty years. It had been about musculature, and he had no clue how there had been more to talk about, but when Dr. Harris said he would continue the lecture at the next class meeting, a chill ran down his spine. Heaven help him if he had to endure weeks of lectures on muscles.

He was cursed with sitting in the front, so he couldn't even sleep since he was so visible. No one else had joined them in the front row, as if they were avoiding the women. He wasn't wild about the idea of a bunch of male underclassmen trying to get close to Jane, but he detested the idea of her being left out. She was just as much a student as they were.

The second lecture of the day was only slightly more tolerable. It was a general anatomy class. After working with Tristan, he understood most of it, but sitting next to Jane had been the best part.

For much of the day, she had been the picture of concentration.

Her jaw had been firmly set, and the only movement she made—besides her hand moving quickly over the page as she took notes—was the occasional nod she would give to show she was paying attention.

All day, he had been looking forward to one thing. That morning, he had met Dr. Harris in the lobby, and they spoke while Jane got ready. During their conversation, the professor told him the library schedule.

It floored Will to learn that women weren't given free rein of the library, but he shouldn't have been surprised. Today was one of their approved days in the library, and he couldn't wait to take Jane.

"Are you going to sit here all day?"

Will snapped out of his thoughts, looking up to see Jane standing before him with her school bag slung over her shoulder. The other students were filing out of the room. He had missed the end of class.

"Sorry, I was trying to absorb the lecture."

"Ah, I see. And what did you learn?"

"I learned that going into business was the best choice for me. It took far less time to get to the heart of that subject."

"Buy low, sell high?"

"I see you are already familiar with the most important tenet," Will said, grabbing her school bag from her. "Come along, I have a surprise for you."

"What kind of surprise?" Jane's eyes narrowed. "I'm not fond of surprises."

"Then we really got off on the wrong foot, didn't we? Don't worry, you'll like this one."

Will led Jane through the courtyard until he found the right stone building. The outside was unassuming, so he had the pleasure of seeing Jane's face light up when they went inside, and it was the library.

"Oh," she softly exclaimed as she looked around the room with glittering eyes.

The library was two levels with floor-to-ceiling bookshelves that curved throughout the room. It carried the typical old library smell of must, dust, rotted wood, and worn leather that tickled his nose, but Jane took a deep breath and smiled.

"Is this a good surprise?"

"The best," she responded with a smile that made him want to give her the world.

"And how does this library stack up to your expectations?"

"Well, it's much bigger than yours."

"Just what every man longs to hear."

"Well, you know what they say. It's not the size of the collection, but the contents."

"I'll let you in on a secret, we all wish to win on size and collection."

"I'm afraid some renovations are in order if you're trying to catch up to this."

"How do you think Tristan and Mrs. Jones would feel if I knocked down a few walls and extended the library into the main hall?"

"Tristan probably wouldn't notice, but I think Mrs. Jones may riot at having more to dust."

"Well, we can't have that. I suppose the expansion will have to be put on hold."

A stern-looking man turned from the nearest table and loudly shushed them before returning to his work.

"Come along then," Jane said, leading him outside. "Let's leave before we get banned from my new favorite place."

"We can stay here, your approved library time runs for the next few hours."

"We can go back to the hotel. It's been a long day, and I want to organize my notes and put together my reading list. We can do a proper library visit tomorrow."

"Your next library time isn't until Wednesday morning."

"Then I suppose that's when we'll go to the library," Jane said with a tight smile. This one didn't radiate pure joy.

Once again, he was struck by how unfair the plight of women was at this school. He didn't bother voicing those thoughts to Jane because she didn't need the reminder.

Will led them to where he could hire a carriage to take them back to the hotel, when Jane tugged on his arm.

"Do you think we could walk back? I need to expend some energy."

"Of course." The late afternoon light was beginning to fade, but their walk wasn't terribly far, and the light grey clouds didn't look like rain. "How was your first day of school? Did it live up to your expectations?"

"Somehow it did. The lectures were engaging, and I managed to learn a few things," Jane said, but her eyebrows pulled together.

"But?"

She shot him a sheepish smile. "I don't see the point in spending so much time on the names of each vertebra when you can easily learn that information from a textbook."

"Not everyone can be such an exemplary student."

"Still, this is *Cambridge*. You would think they would hold the students to a higher standard."

"Of course." He recognized his role in this conversation was to agree with her.

"I'm sorry, my blathering must be boring you."

"I love listening to you blather."

It was the truth, but she rolled her eyes at him as if it were sarcasm.

"Did you enjoy the lectures?"

He paused. "I found them to be enlightening." He was stuck between lying to her and dimming her joy and wasn't sure which was the correct choice.

"Enlightening? I've never heard that as a synonym for boring before."

"It's not that I found them *boring*," he paused, and her eyebrow cocked. "All right, I found them to be so unbelievably dull I wished to claw my eyes out."

"Unbelievably dull? And that was just the first day. Imagine how boring you'll find it in a month."

He shuddered at the thought of such horrors. "I suppose if they get worse, I'll have to pray for a meteor to strike Earth to free me from the tedium."

Jane laughed. He adored her soft, musical laugh that was at odds with her usual demeanor. Her laughter didn't come easy, so it was a gift each time he coaxed it from her.

"Hopefully, the professors find some way to engage you before you wish a disaster on us."

"I'll survive," he sighed. "You don't need to worry about me."

"I'm not worried about you, but I am concerned that your boredom's dark energy will somehow bleed into me. I can only handle so many pensive sighs in one day."

"I didn't sigh once."

"Not out loud, but I felt it in your soul."

"Have you always been psychic, or is this a new side effect we should tell Tristan?" He teased as they walked down the road. This stretch of road was unpaved, and he was glad no carriages rolled past to kick up dirt onto them.

"I tried to transmit the information to him psychically, but he's yet to pick it up. In the meantime, I do think we should find you a hobby. Mrs. Talbot worked on her needlepoint during the lecture. Perhaps she could teach you?"

"I'm not sure if you could tell," he said, gesturing to his face. "But needles and I don't exactly get along."

Jane laughed. "We'll take embroidery off the list. How about reading? I know you enjoy that."

He shook his head. "I can't read in there. The memories of being whacked with a ruler for not paying attention in class are too strong. I could never focus."

"Luckily, I didn't see Dr. Harris with a ruler, but even if he had one, I'm confident you could best him in combat."

"Spoken like someone who's never had their knuckles rasped with a ruler."

"My governess wasn't the corporal punishment type. If I ever misbehaved, she made me practice the piano."

"That doesn't sound like much of a punishment."

"Ah, but you haven't heard me play." She was quiet for a few moments before she continued. "What kind of hobbies do gentlemen have?"

"Who knows? I'm not one anymore."

"Please, you haven't been dead for so long that you wouldn't know."

He considered the question as they turned into the city, their footsteps echoing on the stone street. "Mainly drinking, gambling, and shooting."

A gentleman may deny it every time, but debauchery was their true passion. He knew from experience.

"I'm not sure if they'll let you gamble during class. Oh!" She exclaimed, stopping short as she looked up at him. "Your hobby's gardening!"

"I'm not sure if they'll let me prune in the middle of the lecture hall."

"Obviously, but you could plan your garden for the spring."

"How?" Truthfully, he had a bit of a plan already. There was a list of seeds he wanted to acquire, but he didn't see how list-making could keep him occupied for more than a few minutes.

"You could draw how you want it to look, and then you can figure out how to achieve that from there. I think it would be easier to visualize that way anyway."

"I'm not much of an artist."

Grand images had always lived in his head, but he wasn't sure he would be able to translate them into anything worth looking at.

"You don't need to send them to the National Gallery. I can give you some tips if you so wish."

"Are you an artist as well as a scientist?"

"I wouldn't say I'm an artist, but I know how to draw. It was the only feminine hobby I took to."

"So there's no embroidery in your future either?"

"No, but I can do sutures at least."

They arrived at the hotel far too soon. He was content to just *be* around her for hours, but her mind was a treat. She was so much more than he had ever dreamed she would be.

"Do you want to walk around the garden? We can judge it against yours."

He smiled. "And if there's anything good, we can be sure to steal it."

They walked around the hotel to the garden in the back. Though their room looked down at the garden, he hadn't had a chance to look at it since they arrived so late.

However, he hadn't missed much because it wasn't an impressive space. The land was mainly grass with a few trees whose thin branches would likely splinter at a strong gust of wind. Overgrown bushes spilled over the dead flower beds that were planted so close together he doubted they would bloom come spring. A wrought iron bench sat beneath a trellis that should have been crawling with vines, but they had withered, not even a foot from the ground.

"Is it just me, or does this look awful?" Jane asked with a grimace that he felt deep in his soul.

"No, whatever they are paying their gardener is far too much."

The garden was abysmal for any business, especially when the public garden out front looked so lovely.

"Would you like to sit beneath the saddest trellis I've ever seen?" Will asked.

"Yes."

The best thing he could say about this garden was that the black wrought iron bench was quite nice. The tall backrest was intricately carved with black flowers and gold-leaf detailing that looked freshly painted.

Jane's head tipped back to look at the trellis. The late afternoon light highlighted the profile of her face. The delicate swoop of her nose acted as an arrow to her plush, pink lips. From this distance, he could see she didn't have any laugh lines, which was a shame because her smile was stunning.

"I think this would be pretty with some greenery," Jane said, gesturing to the naked trellis.

"It's not entirely hopeless." The potential was there, but the land needed a fair amount of work and a lot of patience. "The flower beds are a little crowded, but the shrubs are in decent condition, and the trees would provide good shade in the summer if they weren't so aggressively pruned."

"See, you're a gardener after all," she teased, brushing her shoulder against his.

Even that small amount of contact left him wanting more. If they were really married, he would take her hand and kiss her in the open air where anyone could see. Last night they shared a quick kiss, but he wasn't sure if the same would be all right under the cold light of day.

Her grey eyes looked up at him in expectation. With just one finger, he gently tilted her chin upwards to better access her mouth.

"May I kiss you?"

Tension burned between them while he waited for her response. In those few moments, he felt eternity flow between them. He would have waited any amount of time for her, but, blessedly, she nodded, and he closed the gap between them.

The first brush of their lips was light as they tested each other. Growing bolder, he pressed a little harder until she kissed him back. He groaned as Jane leaned into him, her breasts pressing against his chest as she clung to his shoulders. Nipping at her bottom lip, she finally opened up for him. There was no way he could ever get enough of her intoxicating taste.

Gravel crunched behind them, and they broke apart. Will looked back to see a young couple deep in conversation walking around the garden. They were too engrossed in their conversation to notice Will and Jane, but the moment had been broken all the same.

"I should go study."

"Of course," he said as she got up. He thought about joining her, but she needed to work, and he couldn't spend all of his time waiting for her. He hadn't yet sunk to that level of pathetic. "I'll stay out here and soak up the charms of the garden."

Jane left him to his thoughts, which drifted back to the garden. It would never be the main draw for the hotel, but the potential was there for it to be so much more with a bit of care.

A shadow fell over him, and he looked up to see Oliver standing over him.

"Hello, Oliver."

"Good Afternoon, sir. I'm sorry if I disturbed you."

"You're not a bother at all." Will admired his endless enthusiasm. "Actually, there is something you can help me with. Who is in charge of the garden?"

"The gardener quit at the beginning of summer, and no one has replaced him. A few people have been assigned maintenance, but no one likes to do it."

Will sighed. That explained the sorry state of affairs. "Will you take me to see your boss? I have an offer for him."

CHAPTER 23

*J*ane wasn't sure if she was more surprised or disappointed when Will didn't join her upstairs. Their kiss had been good. Great, even. Her departure wasn't intended as an invitation for escalation, but she wouldn't have said no to more kissing. It had been years since she had been so thoroughly kissed, and she had nearly forgotten how good it could be.

Focusing on her book had proved to be a difficult task. At first, her eyes turned towards the door at every little sound, but once she accepted he wasn't coming, it was easier to learn about musculature. The world beyond academics melted away until she became one with the text.

When the door finally opened, she was surprised to find the room was pitch black, save for the gas lamp that glowed on the table beside her. Time had slipped away from her as she read.

"You've been gone for a while."

Even to Jane's ears, it sounded like the nagging a wife would do. What he was doing shouldn't matter.

"My apologies, but I had an idea, and I wouldn't be able to rest until I saw it through."

He ran a hand through his sweaty hair. His usually tidy cravat hung loose around his neck. Carefully, he removed his mud-caked boots, leaving them by the door.

"Were you working in the garden?"

"Yes," Will said, shooting her a crooked smile that was almost criminal as he mopped his brow with his cravat. "I persuaded the manager to let me overhaul the garden until they can hire a new gardener come spring."

"Did it take a lot to convince him?"

"Not once he realized I wasn't asking for a paycheck."

Jane was sure the offer had confused the man, but only a fool declined free labor.

"I'm going to clean up. I'm too tired to go to the dining room, so I ordered dinner to be served up here tonight. That way you can keep working as well."

As if on cue, the door opened, and Oliver entered with a massive pail.

"Good evening, Mrs. Byrne," he said as he struggled through the door. Will held the bedroom door open for him.

"Good evening, Oliver. How are you today?"

"I'm quite well, ma'am," Oliver shouted from the next room over the slosh of water hitting the bathtub. "I was helping Mr. Byrne in the garden."

"Are you a gardener as well?"

"No, but I hope to learn," he said as he walked back into the main room. "Today was the first time I ever worked in a garden, but I liked digging. Mr. Byrne said I could help him tomorrow as well."

"I'm glad you've found a new interest."

"Me too. I'm going to get more water, and your dinner should be here shortly."

The boy was off like a shot before Jane could thank him. The door to the bedroom was shut, no doubt so Will could bathe. Since Oliver would be returning shortly, he would still be dressed, but soon he would be naked with only a flimsy door between them. It was far too tempting.

Picking up her book, she was ready to dive back into the world of musculature. The subject matter was easy enough for her to understand, but instead of dry professional imagery, she thought of Will's wet washcloth passing over each muscle group she read about. She closed the book, jumping up to stand before the window.

She couldn't see the garden below, but she pretended it was quite interesting as Oliver delivered the final pail of water, and then she heard the soft splashes of Will bathing.

If she were truly bold, she would walk in there and take the washcloth from him under the guise of an anatomy lesson. When they kissed earlier, she felt how strong his upper trapezius muscle was, and knew the rest of him would be just as powerful.

But she wasn't brave because she just stood in front of the window with her hands clenching her skirt.

Dinner was delivered, and she sat at the table waiting for Will. After what felt like an eternity, the bedroom door opened. Turning, she hoped he was still unclothed, but was disappointed to see he was dressed.

Will's dark, damp hair was messily pushed back from his face. It was the most unkempt she had ever seen him, so naturally, it was her new favorite look. A droplet of water ran from the bottom of his jaw, down his neck, and settled into the hollow of his throat as her eyes followed its journey. She imagined licking it away. A light smattering of chest hair peeked through the wide-open collar of his shirt, and she wanted to take her tongue and move it down—

"Are you all right?" He asked, snapping her out of her lascivious fantasy.

"I'm fine," she squeaked. "I read a lot and am a bit tired."

"It's understandable, you've had an eventful few days."

"I have."

Her world had grown in thousands of ways that made her head spin if she thought about them too hard. Losing her library had been devastating, but she had gained more than she had ever thought possible because of the man before her.

"What are you thinking about?"

"Nothing, why?"

"You're blushing, and I wanted to know why."

"I'm not blushing." She felt her cheeks heat even more at the lie, and the corner of his mouth turned up. "Sometimes I'm a little red."

"Well, that explains it," he said, sitting across from her.

She scowled. Really, it wasn't fair that he was attractive to the point of distraction, but there was no way she could ever live down telling him that.

"I was thinking about the musculature reading I was doing before you got here."

"Was it difficult to understand?"

"It's not difficult, but it was thought-provoking. There aren't any illustrations in the book, which is a missed opportunity."

"Ah, so you're a visual learner."

"Yes, I can get a lot out of words, but pictures always help. That's part of why I draw so much, it helps me make sense of it."

"If there's any way I can be of assistance, please let me know. I'd love to help."

Jane's eyes fell to her plate as she thought about her earlier desire to catalogue his muscles. Looking up, she watched him across the table. The top of his pectoral muscles flexed as he speared macaroni with his fork. She wasn't brave enough to ask him to remove his shirt, but that didn't mean she couldn't find another way to touch him.

"Actually, I do think you can help me. I've been having trouble with hands because there are so many tiny bones and muscles. If I were to examine yours, it would help a lot."

Will stiffened as a torrent of emotions crossed his face until he landed on resignation.

"I don't feel great about you skinning my hand, but if it will help your studies, I'll do it once. We'll need to find some strong pain medicine. I'll metabolize it quicker than I'd like, but it would take the edge off at least."

Jane's jaw went slack. "You think I want to *skin* you?" She was horrified that he thought she would ask such a thing, but was even more horrified that he was going to let her.

"How else were you going to study my hand?"

"With the skin on! I was only going to touch your hand and move your fingers around." As soon as she said her plan aloud, it sounded ridiculous that she even brought it up.

"Oh," he said, looking at the gloved hand that clutched his fork. "Which hand did you want to look at?"

"I'm not attached to one, so I guess it's up to you."

"You can study my right hand. Just my right, though."

"Okay." Curiosity prickled at his request, but she would hold her questions because she didn't want to lose her chance to touch him. "Would you like to move to the couch?"

"All right." Will stood up, then walked woodenly to the couch that had been delivered while they were in class.

Jane followed, carefully folding her skirts as she sat down. The green couch was big enough for them to sit at either end without touching, but that was antithetical to her mission. Next to Will's stiff form, she slid in, facing him. One leg was folded on the couch, and her other remained on the floor to stabilize her.

Slowly, she took his right hand from its stiff position on his thigh and placed it on her lap. His left hand had a death grip on the armrest.

"I can't learn much while your gloves are on," she teased, in an attempt to help him relax.

"Oh, yes. My mistake."

He lifted his hand, but she caught it before he could escape.

"Allow me."

His black gloves were clean despite his earlier gardening. She thought of him washing in the bath with them on and had to bite back her smile. While she didn't have much experience with men, she did know they typically didn't enjoy being laughed at, especially not at such a vulnerable moment.

Gently, she tugged the fingers until she got a good grip on the soft leather and pulled it off in one fluid motion. Due to his extreme secrecy, she expected his hand to be grotesque with missing chunks and gnarled fingers. Instead, she was confronted with a normal hand.

Will's hand was pale with thick fingers and clean, trimmed nails.

The back of his hand had a few scars, but nothing unusual, especially in comparison to his face. Turning his hand, she examined his palm, which was soft and callus-free despite all of the time he spent working in the garden. Though the gloves protected his hands, she imagined this was another side effect of their improved healing.

"What do you need me to do?" Will's low voice startled her out of her admiration.

"Um, try making a fist and then squeeze."

Will obeyed, his knuckles white as they pressed against his skin. Her fingers stroked the tendons stretched tight over the back of his hand. Truthfully, there wasn't much for her to learn, both because she already knew the musculature of the hand and because he was correct that it wasn't particularly useful without being able to see the muscles.

There was no world in which she would be skinning his hand. Even the thought of putting him through that much pain made her stomach turn.

"Is this helping your studies?"

This close, the deep timbre of his voice resonated within her. She loved his voice and would listen to him say anything. She had half a mind to ask him to read her textbook to her, but she knew she wouldn't be able to pay attention to the words.

"Quite," she murmured, unfurling his fingers before turning his hand again.

This was little more than a ruse to touch him, but her academic interest could never be contained. She pushed his fingers back, impressed at their range of motion. Her other hand slipped down to his wrist to feel his tendons stretch.

Her thumb settled over his pounding pulse. Scooting closer, she molded her shin to the side of his thigh, and she felt his pulse race. Moving both hands to his palm, she massaged little circles into the meat of his hand.

A groan rumbled from him. Her eyes flicked up to look at him through her eyelashes. His yellow eyes smoldered like swirled honey.

"It feels nice."

"Good," she said, turning back to the soft warmth of his hand.

"Jane, come closer."

"I don't think there's any way I could get closer."

"I think you can."

Will's left arm moved towards her, but he quickly jerked it away. Instead, he wrestled his right hand from her grasp and herded her onto his lap. She straddled him—because that was the least awkward position—and twined her hands over his shoulders. From this position, she was taller, and it was a novelty to look down at him.

"Can I ask you a question?"

"Always."

"Why won't you touch me with your left hand?"

Will froze, but she didn't regret her question. Earlier, she was willing to let it go, but now it was clear there was something about his left hand that truly bothered him.

"Can we enjoy our evening and discuss it later?"

Her conviction wavered momentarily when Will's eyes implored her to drop her line of questioning, but she needed to push through, or else she feared they would remain stuck in place.

"Please just tell me."

Her fingers brushed against his jaw. Sections were rough with the stubble. A raised scar ran along his jaw from his ear to the apple of his cheek. Another scar bisected the eyebrow on the other side of his face. His forehead had been sloppily stitched together beneath his hairline, and there was a jagged scar in the divot between his lower lip and chin. Without them, he would be blandly handsome, but the scars gave his face character.

"I was dead far longer than you were, which came with its own challenges for Tristan. Not all of my parts are original." Will lifted his left hand, and Jane leaned back in his lap so she could see. "This hand isn't mine, that's why I don't want it touching you."

"Whose is it?" It was the least important of the thousand questions she had, but it was the only one she could think of that he could maybe answer.

"I don't know, I never asked. Although chances are Tristan

never bothered to learn. Ethics weren't a priority when he was grave robbing."

"That does sound like him." She grabbed his forearm to keep him from snatching his arm away. "Can I see it?"

"Are you going to pester me until I bend to your demand?"

"Yes."

Will kept still as Jane removed the glove from this hand the same way as she did the other, but this time she threw the glove behind her, not caring where it landed.

Will's left hand looked even more normal than his right. The most interesting discovery was that this hand wasn't scarred. She assumed it was because the corpse it had been harvested from was newer, but she tucked that question away for the next time she saw Tristan. His fingernails were as trimmed and clean, but the fingers were slimmer. The palm felt a little thicker as well. She wanted to compare the two hands directly, but that would have to wait.

Her thumb moved down his hand until it hit the small raised scar that circled his wrist. The scar was clean, and the difference in the skin was slight, but visible.

"I think I know whose hand this is."

"Whose is it?"

"Yours." She pressed a kiss to the middle of his palm.

Emotion was thick in Will's eyes, but he remained still beneath her. Being perched on Will's thighs suddenly felt too intimate. Too close.

"I'm going to get ready for bed." She kissed his palm again before going to the bedroom.

Her night had been quite successful since she touched Will, even if it only made her desire for him burn brighter. As she changed into her nightclothes, her eyes kept flicking to the door, hoping Will would come in, but he never did.

The crackling fire burned hotter tonight. Already, sweat dotted her brow from all of her layers. Sitting at the vanity, Jane started pulling out the hairpins until her long hair tumbled free. This morning, she had settled on a low bun that sat at the nape of her neck because it was one of two hairstyles she could reliably do.

"Can I braid your hair again?"

Jane turned to see Will hovering in the doorway. She nodded, her mouth too dry to even attempt to speak.

Will walked to the vanity and picked up her comb before going to work, but this time he wasn't wearing his gloves. She didn't bother suppressing her shudder when his fingernails scratched her scalp.

"Your hair is even softer than I imagined."

"I imagine most things are better when you can actually touch them."

His fingers moved deftly through her hair in a way that hypnotized her. It was truly impressive how good he was with her hair. If they ever went to a ball, she would have to see how he was with curling tongs.

Before she was ready for it to be over, he tied the end of her braid. This time, he only did one plait.

He leaned down, placing a quick kiss on her jaw. "Good night," he said, before walking quickly to their bed. He didn't lie down, but sat stiffly on his side of the bed.

"Are you going to sleep like that?" She blurted out as she stared at the thick expanse of his chest from his clavicle to his sternum that was exposed by his open shirt. She had no qualms about the shirt, but he looked uncomfortable in his belt and trousers.

He looked down at what he was wearing, frowning before looking back at her. "Yes," he paused to look at her, her body heating as he looked over her. "Are you going to sleep in that? You look a little warm."

"I'm fine. In fact, I may be chilly." A bead of sweat ran from her temple, but she rubbed her arms to sell the lie.

"If you're cold, I can grab my cloak. The wool will keep you warm."

"Are you sure you don't need it because the top of your chest is very exposed. You might catch a chill."

He grimaced. "If my level of undress distresses you, I'll go—"

"No!" She waved her hands and took a step forward to cut him off. "What you're wearing is fine. You could even be wearing... less."

"You want me in less clothing?" His low voice sent another bolt of heat through her. "And what about you? What would you say if I told you I'd like to see you in less clothing?"

Words failed her, so action would have to take its place. Her fingers loosened the knot of her belt before she shrugged off her dressing gown, the heavy fabric making a dull thump when it hit the floor.

"What about you?"

Will raised an eyebrow. "You're still completely covered, while I only have my shirt and trousers. It doesn't seem very fair."

"Maybe if you impress me, I'll remove another layer."

Her nightgown, shift, and stockings were still on, so she had plenty to tease him with if he was willing to play.

Their eyes were locked as he slowly stood up. She didn't take her eyes from him as his hands moved to undo his buttons.

His trousers fell to the floor. His shirt went to his mid-thigh, so what she really wanted to see was still covered, but his legs were well-shaped. Thick thighs led to the curve of muscular calves with dark hair on his legs. "Is this enough?"

No, but she nodded because he deserved a reward. Her nightgown was a dowdy thing that buttoned all the way up to her throat, with long sleeves and a hem that grazed the floor. It was perfect for the dead of winter, but too much for warmer nights.

Starting at her throat, she undid buttons until the nightgown fell from her shoulders and floated to the floor. Will sucked in a breath as she stood in her chemise. Closing her eyes, she felt the relief of the cool air against her skin, her nipples pebbling against the thin fabric as she lifted her arms above her head. It felt nice to stretch, but the added benefit was that the angle made her breasts look fantastic.

"Good night," she said, sauntering to her side of the bed. She lay down and propped her head up with her hand.

"Aren't you going to join me?" The sleeve of her chemise slipped off her shoulder. Will's eyes hungrily roamed over the newly exposed skin.

Will's cheeks turned a rosy pink as his eyes darted around the room, and he failed to stammer a response. His hand dropped to his front, but it bounced back quickly to run it through his hair. Her eyes looked down to see what the issue was. Oh. *Oh.*

"I just need a moment," he said through gritted teeth, pacing with his back turned to her.

"You can take care of yourself, if you wish." She tried to sound casual, but her voice came out breathy.

Will grunted before he extinguished the candles and stiffly lay down on his side of the bed. She imagined him on the other side of the barrier, achingly hard and desperate for relief. Her own core pulsed at the thought. It would be so easy to slide her hand down her body, touching herself over her shift in an effort to be discreet.

"Do you need to take care of yourself as well?" He finally asked after a long silence.

"Yes." Her answer was quiet, but Jane knew he heard because he sucked in a breath.

"Then you can take care of yourself as well. If you so wish."

She nodded, but realized he couldn't see her. "Okay."

Movement sounded across the barrier, and Will's breath hitched. Her own breath stuttered as she imagined his hand around his cock. His body was so big she imagined his cock was proportionate.

"I don't hear anything over there."

She debated giving a biting remark, but decided to surprise him by complying. Running her hands over her breasts, she gave a sharp tug on one of her nipples, gasping as she imagined Will's hands instead.

The bed shook as she shimmied her shift to her waist and spread her legs. Her core was exposed to the cool night air. Even though Will couldn't see her, it was strange to be exposed when he was so close to her. The same way she imagined him, he was imagining her. Instead of feeling self-conscious, she felt powerful as her hand moved down her body. She teased herself before dipping a finger inside to gather some wetness before circling her clitoris. She didn't even bother trying to be quiet.

Will's rhythm stuttered as he groaned next to her. She sped up to match his rhythm, imagining his big body over hers. Her legs would need to be splayed wide to accommodate him. One of the pillows moved as she rolled her hips, and her knee hit Will's thigh.

"Jane," he groaned. "I've thought about you like this so many times."

"With your hand on your cock?"

"Yes," Will whimpered.

The heady feeling of how much she affected him shot through her. "I'm imagining your hands on me right now."

He groaned again, and it was the most erotic sound she had ever heard. "Grab your breast for me."

Her other hand floated to her chest, kneading her breast through her chemise before thrumming her nipple until it peaked under her touch.

"Let me hear you," he growled.

Will's strokes slowed like he was trying to draw out his pleasure. She wanted to drive him wild, to make him lose control. Before she could overthink it, she removed her shift and dropped it over on Will's side.

Touching herself wasn't unfamiliar, but having an audience amplified her arousal in ways she never expected. She plucked her nipple again, the feeling echoing in her core as she let out another breathy moan.

"Does that feel good?"

"Yes, but I know what would feel even better." Slipping a finger inside of herself, she kept the heel of her hand against her clitoris. Her hips rocked to meet her strokes, and the additional friction was what she needed.

Will grunted, and she imagined his—hopefully—thick cock pumping away in his hand, the beginnings of his seed beading at the tip. She imagined leaning over him to lick it away. It wasn't anything she would have done with her previous lover, but she whimpered at the thought of doing so for Will.

The pleasure within her mounted, climbing further and further until it plateaued. She felt so good, but she couldn't get over the edge of her orgasm.

"What do you need, love?" He asked, the pillow by her head lifted, and she turned to face him. It was too dark to see much, but she could see the subtle glow from his yellow eyes.

Occasionally, she ran into this problem, so she knew what she needed. Sitting up, she grabbed the pillow from Will, bunching it between her thighs and adjusting it until it was in the perfect spot.

Will was sprawled out on his side of the bed as he watched her. She wasn't sure how well he could see her, but she would put on a show for him all the same.

She plumped her breasts as she rolled her hips. The pillowcase's added texture made her breath stutter. Will's hand shuttled up and down, synchronizing to her rhythm.

"You're like something out of a dream."

Between the new stimulation and his praise, she felt herself nearing her peak again. Her hands dropped to support her knees as she rode the pillow.

"May I touch you?"

"Please."

His hand traveled up her body, exploring her through touch. When his hand finally found her breast, he pulled on her nipple harder than she would. The slight shock of pain intensified the pleasure, making her grind her hips harder.

"There you go, love, you're almost there."

It never felt like anything even close to this with her previous lover. Part of her worried over the implications of that, but the intense pleasure made it easy to shove any concerns away.

Will switched his attention to her neglected breast, rolling her nipple between his fingers. He groaned, and she knew he was close as well.

One of her hands joined the pillow's attention to her clitoris while the other snapped to Will's wrist, both to keep his hand where it was and to give her some support. He cried out one final time, and that pushed her over the edge as well.

With a cry of Will's name, the tension finally snapped inside of her, and wave after wave of pure pleasure pulsed through her. She looked down to see Will's hand still on her breast, supporting her weight. Her hand was still around his arm, her nails digging into his forearm so hard she worried she would break skin.

"Sorry," she said as she unhanded him. Little half-moon indents were left behind on his arm.

"It's fine, I heal quickly," he said with the voice of a man who had been thoroughly sated.

Turning towards Will, she nestled under the blanket. The wall of pillows lay broken between them, but there was no point in rebuilding the wall between them.

"Good night," she murmured. Will hummed in response, sleep already claiming him.

CHAPTER 24

"The biggest problem, of course, is sourcing the bodies for an autopsy. Only recently have people been willing to sign their corpses over to science," Dr. Harris droned from his podium.

Talk of corpses always drew Will's attention back to the lecture. It was macabre, but at least it was more interesting than naming ligaments.

Dr. Harris nodded at a student with a raised hand. "What about unclaimed bodies? Is there a time limit for someone to claim them before a body could be automatically donated?"

The professor removed a handkerchief from his pocket and used it to clean his glasses as he contemplated the question. "Unclaimed bodies are difficult. Typically, you would like to identify the body quickly, but locating the family usually takes several days. During that time, the body begins its decay, and the organs will rot. Once that happens, the body isn't as useful, but there can still be plenty to learn about the human body even if the organs are off the table."

Will suppressed a shudder. He doubted he would ever get used to the professors speaking so flippantly about death. Autopsies were particularly grim, especially with the attitudes most medical professionals had about the dead. He hadn't had an autopsy because the knife in his gut made his cause of death apparent. He wondered if there was a French doctor out there who was still bitter he wasn't able to harvest the organs of the murdered Englishman.

"But what is there to learn," another student asked in a nasally voice. "If you don't have the organs? You won't be able to ascertain the cause of death or anything useful."

Will saw Jane roll her eyes beside him, and he bit the inside of his cheek to keep from laughing. After class, they loved to discuss the asinine things her classmates said. Already, he was looking forward to today's ride home.

"Cause of death isn't the only useful thing to learn," Dr. Harris said, leaning against the podium. "We can learn about the effects of different lifestyle decisions. See how the bones healed and whether there are any abnormalities. How do you think we discovered various muscles and ligaments? There's so much about healing in the body that we don't know."

Dr. Harris's eyes gleamed in the same way that Tristan's always did when he talked about medical advancements. His brother had the same arguments about the importance of science, but Will had learned to tune him out. Scientific advancement had never felt like a good enough reason to be poked and prodded, but perhaps it was.

Jane gathered her belongings, and he knew class had been dismissed while he was brooding. The boys in the class discussed weekend plans, but because Miss Thornton wasn't in this class, there was no one for Jane to speak with. One day, he asked her if being ignored by her male classmates bothered her, and she looked at him as if he had two heads. It bothered Will.

She took her notebook to the podium to speak with Dr. Harris. These were the moments when he wasn't sure what he should do. He wanted to allow her the opportunity to navigate school independently, but he was still her chaperone. Jane and the professor stood several feet apart as they conversed. Everything appeared to be proper, but Will was supposed to be her *husband* in addition to her chaperone.

He had no idea how a husband would react. Would he allow her to take the lead, to trust her to make her own decisions, or would he lurk behind her at every turn, personally guaranteeing that nothing happened without his knowledge? Will knew the type of husband he would be, but he wasn't sure if society would support it.

In a compromise that was the worst of both options, he hovered a few feet away while holding her belongings. Close enough that he could hear their conversation, but far enough to give the illusion of privacy.

He felt a clap on his back and was surprised when he turned to see the young man with the nasally voice behind him.

"We heard you married her," he said, motioning his head towards Jane, "and took her here as a wedding gift."

"Yes." He was wary of any attention Jane got after being ignored for so long. He didn't trust this boy to have pure intentions.

The young man clapped him on the back again. "I'm sure it was a tough go, but good on you for making the best of a bad situation."

"What do you mean?" Will knew exactly what this little twerp was getting at, but he was going to make him say it.

"I'm sure you didn't have many options, but I admire you for making it work with the last pick of the season. No one wants a wife who's a know-it-all, but it's always better when they're thankful."

Will seethed, balling his hands into fists at his side. He fantasized about hitting this prat in the face, but Jane would rain hell down upon him for fighting in the lecture hall, so he took a moment to get ahold of himself.

"I recognize you're barely more than a child," he said, stepping towards him. Will was more than a head taller, and he took great joy in how far back the boy had to crane his head to keep eye contact. "But you don't ever, *ever* talk about my wife like that, do you understand me?"

His eyes widened, and he took a step back as he raised his hands, "Listen mate, I'm—"

"No," Will interrupted. "We are not friends. We don't know each other, and I have no interest in knowing you. Do you understand what I'm saying?"

The boy's face was ashen with eyes as wide as saucers, but he nodded.

"Have a nice day." Will patted him on the back so hard the boy rattled. It was more force than necessary, but he had a point to make. The cowardly boy scampered off, likely to tell his friends that Will was insane, but he didn't mind as long as they got the message not to hassle Jane.

"What was that about?" Jane asked.

"Nothing," he smiled, praying he looked casual as he turned to face her. "He thought he was funny, but I assured him he was not."

She snorted. "When Robert was sent off to school, I cried for a week because I couldn't go. My father would have been spared several headaches if he had set me in a room with a few teenage boys for an hour."

"As someone who survived it, trust me, you're better off without that experience." She laughed as he picked up her books from the table. "Are you ready to go? I thought it would be nice to take a walk through town."

Oliver told him about a bookstore in town that specialized in medical textbooks and journals. He couldn't wait to watch her face light up when she saw it.

"Actually, I thought it might be nice if I went to town alone." Jane pulled them to the side so they could look at one another. "I like spending time with you, but I have so little experience with the world that I want the chance to explore on my own."

"I see," he said, trying hard to stamp out the ejection he felt. This wasn't about him, but feelings weren't rational. "How long do you think you'll be?"

"Enough time to find a few shops and maybe buy something. I've never handled money before, so I'd like to try that."

Hope sparkled in her eyes, but there was also the bitter expectation that he would say no. It made his chest ache that she was convinced her simple ask would be met with rejection. In that moment, he realized he would never be able to deny her anything.

"Of course, it sounds like it will be quite the adventure." He removed his wallet from his breast pocket and handed it to her. "I trust you to use this well."

"I only need a few coins. I won't make any large purchases."

"The first rule of exploration is to prepare for the unexpected. I'll be back at the hotel, so you don't have to worry about whether I'll need it."

Jane put the wallet in her pocket. It made him feel better to know that she would be out there with all available resources.

"Don't worry, you'll barely have time to miss me before I return."

Will laughed at her obvious joke, but he missed her already.

WILL FELT pathetic as he waited for Jane to return. He tried to tend to the garden, but gave up when he went inside to check the time four times in fifteen minutes. Since then, he had settled on the couch with a book. He hadn't managed to read a word, but it was better than staring at the door.

They had only been at Cambridge for a short time, but the axis of his life had already changed. The loneliness that had defined him was gone. His days were spent sitting next to Jane as she went to class, his afternoons were spent in the garden where he only had to look up to see her hunched over her desk in the window, and he slept beside her every night. They hadn't gone further than touching themselves, but the pillow wall hadn't been rebuilt either.

Already, he was addicted to her.

The door opened, and he perked up when Jane walked through the door.

"How was your exploration?" He asked, closing the book.

"Good, there are some quaint shops. I didn't go many places because I only needed a few supplies, but I got you something." Jane handed him a parcel before she put her other bags down. Carefully unwrapping the brown paper packaging, he revealed a sketchbook. "I know we didn't settle on a hobby for you, but I can feel you crawling out of your skin during lectures, so I figured drawing was a good place to start."

The sketchbook had a brown leather cover with thick pages suitable for pencil or ink. "I feel like this will be wasted on me. I'm not an artist." In his youth, he had been a prolific doodler, but it had been many years since he had even attempted to draw.

She shrugged. "You don't need to feel pressured if you're not interested. I thought it would be nice after our conversation the other day." She avoided his eyes, but he knew he had hurt her feelings.

"Thank you, this will be especially useful as I try to avoid the more gruesome parts of the lecture."

"You mean to tell me you don't enjoy hearing about the best way to empty the intestines during an autopsy?"

His stomach lurched. "I'm pretty sure the memory of that lecture will be with me for the rest of my long, long life. Did you get anything for yourself?"

"Nothing major, but I got some new pencils."

"Did you find exploration to be everything you dreamed it to be?"

"It was good, it helped to put my mind at ease. I had a little trouble counting out the money, but the shopkeeper was helpful. I had more than enough money, but I would like to try again with a more modest budget to help prepare me."

"I'll never send you out without more than you'll ever need." His anxiety at her being on her own was bad enough without him having to worry if she was also stranded because she ran out of money.

"Well, I won't stay with you forever. At some point, I'll want to go out on my own and explore the world. Currently, I'm ill-equipped to do so, so I thought it would be best for me to get some worldly experience while I still have you to fall back on."

The words felled him like a blow. He wanted to tell her that she could stay with him forever, that he longed to spend years, decades, centuries at her side. Instead, he nodded and willed the bile to travel back down his throat. "Of course, I'll help you however you wish."

"Thank you, I really appreciate everything you've done in helping me secure my freedom. I know it must be boring having to follow me around, but I do appreciate it. I know you probably want to get back to your life and garden."

"At some point," he said, feeling the gulf between them widen. "I am at your disposal for as long as you want me."

"I'll try not to keep you tied up for too long. I may not be able to earn a degree, but I'm hoping the experience I gain will be enough to get a paid research assistant position. Dr. Harris mentioned there may be some opportunities for me."

"When did he say that?" His voice burned with jealousy.

"After class today. I asked him about a paper he recently published. He said it was an astute observation and mentioned he might have some work for me."

Suspicion rose in Will because while Jane was remarkably bright and competent, she was still in her first term. However, he wasn't sure if there was anything behind that feeling other than his own bitterness at her wanting to leave him, so he held his tongue.

"You've given this a lot of thought."

"I always have a plan. You've seen what it's like when I don't have a good plan. I'm going to need a lot of help preparing to make sure I get it right this time. Will you help me?"

"Of course, I'll help you with whatever you need." It would be breaking his own heart, but he was more than willing to do so if it meant her freedom. He would never deny her anything.

CHAPTER 25

*J*ane wasn't too proud to admit she was completely lost in Professor Franklin's lecture. The subject matter wasn't difficult, but she couldn't focus, which aggravated her to no end. Paying attention should be easy, but she still couldn't manage it.

Instead, her eyes shifted to Will for the thousandth time since they sat down. He sat slouched in his seat, doodling in his sketchbook. She strained her eyes trying to see what he drew, but the sketchbook was angled so she couldn't see his work.

Something was wrong, but she couldn't figure out what it was. The lectures had always bored him, but he still sat dutifully beside her every day out without complaint. Now the brooding had returned in full force.

After braiding her hair last night, he wished her a good night and went to bed without even a cursory kiss goodnight. Or anything else, even though she hadn't rebuilt the pillow wall.

Embarrassment churned through her at the memory. She had thought the boundary between them had been ripped down, but perhaps she had misread the situation.

"Are you ready?"

She jumped in her seat and turned towards Will, who stared at her with his sketchbook in hand. Looking around, she saw everyone else had already packed up, while she hadn't even noticed class was over.

"Of course," she said, a touch too loud. Slamming her notebook shut, she shoved her belongings into her bag without any care. Muscle memory had her hand the bag to Will, but she hesitated. Was she too presumptuous? After all, she did say she wanted to be more self-sufficient. Perhaps he expected her to start now.

Will frowned as he took her bag. "Are you all right?"

Her fingers itched to smooth his furrowed brow, but she kept still. "Oh yes, I'm divine," she said, flinching internally at the awkward turn of phrase. "I'm just processing the lecture."

He searched her eyes and must not have found anything suspicious because his brow relaxed. "As long as you promise to let me know if you aren't feeling well."

"Of course."

"Mrs. Byrne?"

She was nearly out the door before she remembered that was her false name and she should probably answer to it.

Suppressing a sigh, she turned, pasting a bland expression on her face as she walked to the podium. She wasn't in the mood to be chastised when all she wanted was to go home and lie down with a cool compress over her eyes.

"Yes, Professor?"

"You've taken to the curriculum quite well. Your work has impressed all of your instructors. There were plenty on staff who didn't think women were capable of higher education, and you're proving them all wrong," he said without a hint of shame.

Will's heavy presence followed closely behind her; the idea that he would hear her castigation made her want to melt into the floor.

"Is that all, sir?"

It took a great deal of effort to keep her face neutral because it wouldn't do her any good to get into a verbal altercation with a professor. She wasn't some parlor trick to entertain small-minded men.

"It will be an interesting experiment to see if your greater intellect will help you rear children better. I'm sure they'll be smarter at the very least. You'll need to stay in contact so we can conduct a study. It could make for an interesting paper."

Rage made her fingers tremble and her breath shake. She wanted to rip his stupid lecture notes to ribbons and topple his podium to show him what a woman really was. She was smarter than every other man in her class. She knew beyond a shadow of a doubt that she worked harder than any of them, but it didn't matter. The only value she had to any of them was as a womb.

"Is there a purpose to this, or are we free to go?" Will asked coldly.

Her face heated as she remembered the audience to her humiliation. She would have preferred Will to hear the professor yell at her for being stupid. At least that was respectable.

"Oh yes, my apologies, sometimes I get distracted. You won't be needed in class next week as the other students will be sitting for exams. I'll see you the following Monday." He finally looked up at her with a smile. Professor Franklin was an older man with deep laugh lines and eyes that crinkled when he smiled. She always thought he looked friendly, but he hid his chauvinism better than most.

"Of course," she said through gritted teeth. "I will see you then."

Turning on her heel, she stomped from the room, not caring if Will followed. Her only goal was to put as much space between her and this room as possible. Part of her prayed someone would say something about her being unchaperoned, if only so she could unload some of her rage.

The courtyard was packed, as per usual. Still, she slipped through groups of rowdy boys, occasionally throwing an elbow when they didn't move quickly enough.

"Jane!" Will called after her, but she didn't turn around. Her height meant she couldn't melt into the crowd, but even without her height, she stuck out as the only woman in a sea of men.

Men whose place was never questioned. Men who were allowed to take tests and earn degrees. They didn't have to be chaperoned or only allowed in the library during certain hours.

At one point, she was stuck behind a group of young men walking five abreast, which was the height of absurdity, as that wasn't even a good way to have a conversation. No matter which way she attempted to go around, they managed to cut her off.

"He's reached the end of his patience with the crude man," a nasally voice drawled. She thought she might recognize it, but she had trouble parsing out individual male voices as they all seemed to speak at the same frequency with the same posh accent. "If it weren't for the fact he told his creditors he had the money, he would have given up long ago."

"Still, he's been made a fool of," shouted a boy at the end. "There should be some sort of punishment."

The first boy snorted. "He was never going to hold to his end of the bargain."

Finally, she found a break in the line and was able to shove through them

She burst from the campus, turning towards the road to their hotel. It was a long walk, but she didn't have any money on her.

Will called after her again, but she prayed he would leave her alone. The only thing she wanted was a few minutes alone. Tears welled behind her eyes, but she was determined to keep them in until she was in the room.

"Jane!" Will was out of breath as he jogged up beside her. She kept her eyes forward as she sped up. "I'm sorry he spoke to you like that, he's—"

"I don't want to talk about it," she said, cutting him off.

"We don't have to, I just wanted to say—"

She whipped around to face him. If he wouldn't leave her alone, then she would give him the conversation he so desperately wanted. "What do you wish to discuss, my being banned from class for a week or the humiliation of being told my best use was as a breeding experiment?"

Taking a step back, Will's eyes widened. "I wanted to tell you that you deserve to be here. You're just as smart as any of your classmates."

"You think I don't know that?" Will didn't deserve her ire, but she was so wrapped up in her anger, embarrassment, and hurt that she was powerless to stop it from spewing from her. "It doesn't matter if I'm as good as them or even better. I will only ever be a woman in their eyes. They don't take me seriously as a student or even as a person. No matter what I do or how hard I work, I will never be good enough."

"It's not fair, and it's not right, but you're so much more than that. You worked so hard to get here and deserve to be here. Let the rest of them catch up to you."

Rubbing her face, she barked out a laugh. Her mental state was cracking. She needed to stop the conversation and go home, but it was as if now that she was in motion, she couldn't stop. "The only reason I'm here is because they think you're my husband, and your brother wrote me a letter. They don't care that *I'm* here. The only thing they cared about was my proximity to a man who would allow it."

Will put a hand on her shoulder, but she shoved him off. Part of her longed to fall into his arms and let him comfort her until her hurt melted away, but she wouldn't let herself become dependent on him. Not when she was planning her freedom. Besides, he said the right words now, but one day he would disappoint her as well. Everyone else did.

The old Jane would have squeezed every opportunity possible out of this, knowing that it could be ripped away at any time. She wouldn't have been distracted by the attention of a handsome man. He had made her weak, and she hated him for it.

"I don't understand what you're going through, but I can help if you let me."

"No," she croaked. "You can't help me because you don't understand."

"I'm here for you. You only have to talk to me."

"Now you wish to speak to me? You've been brooding all day, but now that I've been kicked down, I'm of interest to you again. The only time I'm worth anything to you is when you think I need to be fixed."

This was when she would typically be filled with triumph at winning an argument, but instead, Will looked so stricken that she deflated. Lashing out at Robert had always made her feel better, but doing so to Will only made her feel worse.

"Just let me go back to the room. We can fight about this some other time," Jane sighed.

"No." Hurt was evident on his face, but anger was there as well. "Do you want to know why I was so hurt last night? It's because you said you wanted to *leave* me. You said it as if it was nothing to you, as if *I* was nothing to you."

Last night, she had been busy riding the high of her independence, but he had been in her thoughts the entire time. She picked out his sketchbook before she thought of anything for herself. She thought about how proud he would be of her and couldn't wait to tell him. Oliver procured the paper, but she had wrapped it herself. Will believed her to be careless when she cared far too much.

"Did you really think I would stay with you forever?" Regular people only had to manage decades together at most, while they were looking at centuries, maybe even longer. There was no way she could manage a relationship like that, so it would be for the best if she put it to a stop now before either of them grew too attached. "Do you want to *actually* marry me? To tie me to you for the rest of time to cure your loneliness?"

"I would take you any way I could have you." Anger faded from his expression until only hurt remained.

"You can't have me," she said, proud of the way her voice didn't waver as she broke her own heart. This pain was inevitable, so it didn't matter if it happened now or later. "You are my chaperone, and I am your ward. Perhaps one day we'll be friends."

"As you wish, you won't have to worry about me bringing this up again." His face shuttered, and she saw him close himself off to her. "I trust you can see yourself home?"

She nodded, unable to trust her voice. If there was one thing she could do, it was take care of herself. Will gave a sharp nod before walking in the opposite direction, leaving her standing in the grass

beside the dusty road. Jane watched as he walked away, lifting the
hood of his cloak for the first time since she had asked him to leave
it down.

ill could handle rejection. It wasn't a surprise that she didn't want to be with him; the only problem was his wounded pride. No matter how hard he tried to bat back his pride, it always seemed to rear its ugly head. His evening had been spent pulling apart his feelings as if they were an elaborate knot. He was telling the truth when he said he would never mention his feelings for her again.

The downside of sharing such a small space was that they had nowhere to be alone, so he walked for a while before he sat in the garden until he was sure she had gone to sleep. It was cowardly, but he wasn't ashamed to need some time to lick his wounds.

When he returned to the room, a gas lamp on its lowest setting cast a dull orange glow. The clock on the mantle ticked loudly, but he could hear Jane's steady breaths in the next room.

Slowly, he opened the bedroom door to ensure the hinges didn't squeak. Jane was curled on her side, facing the door with only her head visible beneath the blankets. Sleeping beside her didn't feel right, not because it would confuse his feelings or he would do anything untoward, but he wasn't sure how Jane would feel about sleeping next to him.

The pillows from their broken wall were stacked on the floor, so he took a few and returned to the sitting room. While the couch was bigger, it still wasn't big enough for him to sleep on without his knees being against his chest. So, the floor it was.

Will dropped the pillows on the rug in front of the fire before undressing, deciding to remove his vest and cravat, but he kept his trousers on. It was too undignified to sleep with his bare legs on the floor. Shaking out his thick wool coat, he lay down, pulling the cloak over him like a blanket. Mercifully, sleep came easily.

* * *

When he came to consciousness again, his eyes flew open as something poked his shoulder. An unfamiliar walnut ceiling greeted him. Frowning, he tried to remember where he was, but panic made it difficult to think. The one thing he knew was that it wasn't the sterile interior of his brother's lab or his bedroom.

He took in a ragged breath. The last time this happened, Tristan told him he died. Logically, he knew that wasn't happening again, but terror never listened to logic.

"Are you all right?" Jane asked as her head popped into his field of vision.

"I'm fine," he croaked, relief running through him as he remembered where he slept. "I didn't recognize where I was for a moment."

"Why did you sleep on the floor?"

Rubbing his eyes, he cursed his luck. Of course, the first morning he woke up in a panic in months would be the day after an awkward conversation. "I thought it would be better if I slept out here in case you changed your mind about sharing a bed."

"That's ridiculous. Why would I want you to sleep on the floor? I'm the one who insisted you sleep on the bed since that first night. I didn't even remake the pillow wall."

Maybe *he* hadn't wanted to sleep next to *her*. "You were asleep when I came back, and I didn't want to disturb you."

"I waited up for you as long as I could, and when you weren't in bed this morning, I panicked. I was going to ask the front desk to send out a search party when I saw you in a heap on the floor."

Her hair stuck up like a messy brown halo around her head, and her dressing gown was inside out. Remembering that her fear showed like anger, he relaxed. "I'm sorry I worried you. I wanted to sleep alone last night. I would have done so even if we had a chance to speak last night."

She sighed, her sharp gaze softening. "No, if we had a chance to speak last night, you would have slept in the bed."

"If I want to sleep on the floor, I'll sleep on the floor."

"Is this truly the hill you wish to die on?"

"It could be," he said, setting his jaw in a hard line. She wasn't the only one who could be stubborn.

"Then I suppose I'm sleeping on the floor with you tonight."

"Why?"

"If you're so adamant about sleeping on the floor, then I'm worried there's a problem with the bed."

Silence stretched between them. He knew this fight would end in a stalemate, both of them too stubborn to back down. The sheer ridiculousness of their argument finally broke him.

"Then I suppose I'm sleeping in the bed tonight."

"Good," she said with a satisfied smile that melted the last of his icy mood.

"I tried to wait up for you last night because I wanted a chance to speak with you before things between us had a chance to fester."

"You don't have to, I'll be fine, I promise."

He knew what was coming, but he would rather never speak of yesterday again.

"I spoke to you in anger yesterday, and that wasn't right."

She looked down at him expectantly as she worried her lip between her teeth. He hadn't the faintest clue what she wanted.

"Okay."

"Professor Franklin's words upset me."

"I figured."

The clock on the mantle clicked as they stared at each other. He wanted to get up and use the facilities, but it felt rude of him to move while she stood there.

"You could accept my apology," she cried, throwing up her hands.

"That was an apology?" It took all his effort to keep from smiling as he was in kicking range.

"Yes! I admitted wrongdoing."

"Typically, apologies contain the words either 'I'm sorry' or 'I apologize.'"

"Do I really have to do that?"

He had not expected or even wanted an apology from her before, but now that it was clear she was truly awful at apologies, it was all he wanted. "Yes."

"Fine," she said through gritted teeth. "I'm sorry for what I said to you yesterday. It was cruel, and I didn't mean most of it."

"Thank you for your apology. I accept."

Jane still looked like she had swallowed a handful of nails, but she gave a sharp nod and a grimace that may have been an attempt at a smile. Apologizing was difficult for the best of people, but he was sure this was her first-ever apology, and he was honored.

"Promise me you won't relegate yourself to the floor again, no matter how awful our fight."

"I promise."

"I'm glad that's been settled." She straightened out and took a step back. "You'll be free of being my shadow today."

"Oh?" He sat up, bringing up his knees to rest his forearms on them. The aches would quickly pass, but sleeping on the floor had not been comfortable.

"I'm working on compiling some research for Dr. Harris."

"That sounds like a great opportunity for you," he cleared his throat, unsure of how to phrase his next point in a way to make sure she wouldn't be uncomfortable. "However, I want you to know you don't ever have to worry about money. No matter if you're with me or on your own, I'll ensure you're taken care of no matter what."

Jane took a deep breath. "Thank you, I appreciate your generosity, but I don't want to have to rely on you for the rest of my existence. I want to know I can take care of myself."

It burned at his male pride that she wouldn't let him take care of her, but this wasn't about him. "I understand."

She relaxed. "This doesn't mean I'm waiting to leave and go out on my own right now, either. I like being with you. I just want to feel like I have another option. I don't want to feel like I'm trading my affection for security."

"I understand." It would have devastated him if she were with him because she thought it would guarantee her future. "I like you as well, a great deal. I want you to feel comfortable. I hope at the very least we are friends."

"What if I liked kissing you? And perhaps other things as well?" Jane flushed a deep red as her hands fidgeted with the tie of her dressing gown.

"I would be fine with that." Truly, nothing could be more of an understatement, but he didn't want to scare her off with his eagerness.

"Good." Her hands dropped the tie, and the color of her face evened out. "I do have work to get done today, though," she said before going back to the bedroom.

It was endearing how nervous she was after the intimacies they had already shared, but time would make her more confident. She might not yet believe in him or his promises, but that was fine because he would keep showing up until she did.

* * *

WILL SURVEYED THE GARDEN, hands on his hips as he took in the land he had spent the last several days working on. The warm-weather bushes had been repotted and placed indoors. A few tree saplings had been replanted so they could thrive in the limited sunlight. Dead flowers had been dug up and removed so new ones could grow come spring. He and Oliver had spent the morning pruning the remaining bushes.

"What's next, sir?" Oliver asked, mirroring Will's stance.

"I think we're done." It had taken a lot of hard work, but he was glad they finished before the ground froze.

"Really?" Oliver frowned.

"We'll still prune every week or so until it snows. And then the real work begins once the snow melts."

"I guess I'll have to go back to my regular duties," Oliver sighed.

"Yes, but you'll be thankful to be indoors once it gets cold."

"I like working outside."

Will glanced at Oliver to see the forlorn look on the young man's face. "Since the bulk of the work is already done, how about I leave you in charge of all the pruning until spring. That way, you'll get some time outside, and maybe the new groundskeeper will take you on as an apprentice next spring."

Will had offered to take on responsibility for the garden out of boredom, but he was thrilled to have instilled a love of gardening in Oliver. He would grease whatever hands were necessary, so Oliver got to work where he wanted. "I need to check on Mrs. Byrne. Why don't you clean up your tools, then you can get on with your day."

"Have a good day, sir!"

Oliver took off in the direction of the gardening shed, moving much faster than Will was comfortable with while those garden shears were in hand, but that was just Oliver.

Will returned to their room to find Jane hunched over the desk, her pen hurriedly scratching against the paper as she wrote. He smoothed the gloves in his hands and frowned. Disappointment shot through him. He still wanted to take Jane to the bookstore, but he didn't want to bother her.

He cleared his throat. "I've finished my work in the garden, if you would like to go on a walk. With me."

"Thank you, but I've still got quite the backlog of work, and Dr. Harris sent notice that he would have another stack of papers sent over later," she said, patting the stack beside her without looking at him. The stack had grown considerably since he left, which made him frown.

"Did Dr. Harris stop by to drop them off?"

"No, he had one of the porters bring them up with a note. He said we could meet in the dining room if I had any questions."

Will didn't like that the professor had begun sending work to her while she was at home, but he would have to tread very carefully. If he mishandled this situation, he would lose Jane forever.

"Are you all right with this additional work?"

"Of course, it's my *one* opportunity to do actual work. It's not like I'm allowed to do anything else until next week."

"As long as you don't overwork yourself."

Jane ignored him, but he expected nothing else. The only reason he said anything was to prove he had warned her once he made her stop working later that day. She worked too hard.

Will didn't like how eager Dr. Harris was to use Jane's labor. Will knew how academia worked. There were legions of research assistants and other more senior students to hand this work off to. The one difference he knew between them and Jane was that she was too eager to prove herself to turn down any project. Even if it was better suited to a paid position or to a student who would receive a diploma.

Part of him was proud, but he also worried that she was ripe for taking advantage of.

If Jane wanted to learn how to navigate the world on her own, the first rule of surviving a cruel, indifferent world was that she would have to look out for herself because no one else would. Well, *he* would always look out for her, but she wouldn't like it if he told her that.

He didn't trust Dr. Harris to have her best interest at heart, but he didn't know how to tell her that without sounding like a jealous lover.

When he hit the lobby, he took a detour through the dining room to see if Dr. Harris was there, but the dining room was empty, save for a mother teaching her daughter proper table manners for afternoon tea. Looping back through the lobby, he found Oliver hanging around the main desk. He covertly beckoned to him, and Oliver jogged over.

"What can I help you with, sir?"

"I have a mission for you, but I need you to keep it a secret."

Oliver's eyes sparkled. "Of course, what do you need from me?"

"Could you let me know if Dr. Harris sends any correspondence to our room or meets with Mrs. Byrne. You can find some way to discreetly tell me if anything has happened, Mrs. Byrne isn't to know you're watching out for her."

Jane would be beyond furious if she found out he was meddling, but *someone* had to look out for her.

"Do you suspect any foul play between them?" Oliver lifted an eyebrow conspiratorially.

"No, and I don't want you to even consider that." This had the chance to be good gossip if Oliver truly thought Will was trying to uncover an affair, but he hoped the rapport he had with him would keep it from spreading through the staff. "Mrs. Byrne is doing a lot of work for him, and I want to make sure he treats her fairly."

Oliver's gaze hardened as he gave a sharp nod. "As you should, but I'll keep an eye out as well." His head swiveled as if he expected the professor to jump out from behind a pillar.

"Make sure to be discreet. I only want information. I trust you to make sure this doesn't become gossip."

"This mission will die with me, sir." Oliver was so serious, he half expected the boy to salute.

"I don't think it will come to that, but I appreciate the sentiment," he said before slipping the boy a few coins to buy his silence.

His hand twitched as muscle memory almost took over to raise his hood. It was still strange to be so exposed in public, but he was getting used to it. Sunlight filtered through the massive Beech tree in the front garden, and he decided to keep the hood down. The sun had barely been out the past week, and it would likely be many months before it returned. He was determined to enjoy the sun warming his skin while he could.

The public gardens crawled with people who had the same idea. Families picnicked beneath the shade of trees, and a group of students he recognized from the university played a rowdy game of football. Everyone was enjoying the last sunny day until spring.

Almost everyone, at least, he thought as he looked behind him to see that the curtains to their room were still drawn. It was easy to find their room since every other window was open.

"Watch where you're going!"

Will's head snapped to a man snarling at him as he guided the woman on his arm out of the way. Will jumped to the side to ensure he didn't clip her shoulder. He hadn't realized he had been walking at an angle, but it served him right for walking with his head turned.

"My apologies to you both," Will said with a tilt of his head towards the lady.

She raised her lace parasol so it wouldn't poke him in the face. "No need for apologies, the crisis was averted," she smiled before her male companion pulled her away.

A brown blur hurtled towards his face. Before he had a chance to ponder what it was, it hit him in the face, crunching his nose. Blood poured from his nose as his hands clasped to his face in an attempt to stop the carnage. Leather, however, was a less-than-ideal fabric to mop up blood. Looking down, he saw that the offending object that had hit him was a brown leather football.

"Sorry, mate. Didn't mean to clip you, but you should keep your head up when you're walking," a young man said as he jogged towards him.

The pain was fading, though his nose definitely broke based on the awful crack. He felt the cartilage fix itself together before the man reached him. Even with his accelerated healing, the blood had flowed too quickly to save his white shirt.

"I didn't expect to have to dodge anything on the trail," Will said, narrowing his eyes. He kept his hand over his nose to hide his lack of injury.

"Fair enough," he laughed, holding out a handkerchief that Will snatched. "Although I saw what caught your eye, and I don't blame you."

Will had to stop himself from rolling his eyes.

"Turner," another young man shouted out of breath as he ran up with two more following not far behind. They were all without waistcoats, their untied cravats flapping in the air, and their shirts sticking to them from sweat. "We never should have let you play. You couldn't hit water if you fell out of a rowboat."

The new lad stopped by his friend, the smile slowly dropping from his face as he got a good look at Will. When he pushed his dark brown hair away from his face, Will recognized him as the idiot from Jane's class who had tried to talk to him the other day.

"There's only so much I can do with your shit passes," Turner said, punching his friend in the arm.

"At least you managed to hit the one person here who wouldn't be able to notice the damage," the idiot said with a gleam in his eye.

Will froze. This was the moment for a vicious remark, but he had nothing.

"Oh, back off, Percy," Turner said, his eyes darting to Will. "You don't have to be an arse all the time, you know. Leave the poor man alone."

Will bristled. He didn't care if it was just good-natured ribbing; he didn't deserve this nonsense. "Both of you need to watch it. This isn't your private park."

"This is the bloke who's married to the girl in our class," Percy said to his friend, ignoring Will. "I'd be surprised anyone would tie themselves to this ugly mug, but she's a freak, too. The only saving grace is that they took each other off the market so they wouldn't make anyone else suffer."

Will dropped his hand from his face, curling it into a fist as he took a step towards Percy. He didn't care if that little weasel of a man saw the truth of who he was. That he was a man with injuries no one could have survived. Injuries that came from rotting beneath the Earth for months. That his nose had been broken moments before, but the only evidence left was his blood-soaked shirt.

"I've already warned you once about talking about my wife," he snarled, blood dripping down his face. "I won't give you another chance."

His head tipped back to meet Will's eyes. "And what are you going to do about it?"

This was where Will was supposed to be the bigger man and

leave. There was a flicker of hesitation in Percy's eyes as if he had realized this wasn't a fight he would win. This was Will's cue to tell him to never speak to or about Jane ever again and go on his way. It was what he would have done in his previous life, but that man had been gutted and left for dead in an alley in Paris.

Instead, he pulled back his arm and popped Percy in the face. The man's nose crumbled beneath his fist. A broken nose for a broken nose seemed fair. Turner shouted, moving to help his friend.

"If I *ever* hear you talking about my wife again, I'll come back and hit you harder. Every time."

The football lay forgotten at his feet. He kicked it, not caring where it went as long as it was far from where they were. Will walked away before he could see where it landed.

CHAPTER 27

The muscles in Jane's hand spasmed as her hand moved across the page. A few weeks ago, writing fifty pages in a day would cause her to ice her aching wrist for days. She had become accustomed to pausing every few paragraphs so she could stretch her fingers and wrist before the tingling set in. Now she didn't feel any pain as she wrote.

Periodic spasms were the only indicator that her body was working hard to combat the damage she created. She made a mental note to record this new side effect in the notebook she bought to record her observations for Tristan. In the beginning, she wrote him letters with her new findings and hypotheses, but her rate of discovery was so high that one day she sent him three separate letters, so she found an alternative that wouldn't clog the mail. She would either give it to him the next time she saw him or mail it to him once it was full, whichever happened first.

The heavy door creaked open, and her hand froze. She had wanted to go for a walk with Will, but if she didn't finish her work, she would have spent the whole time feeling guilty instead of enjoying her time with him. The door closed with a thunk, and she heard a familiar deep sigh. "Do I even want to know what you forgot?" She teased as she turned in her seat.

Will was slumped against the door, the hood on his cloak drawn over his head.

"What happened? Are you all right?"

He was silent for a long time before sighing again. "I promise it's not a big deal."

"Well, now you're lying because people only say that when it is a big deal."

"Jane."

It was said in the tone she hated, the one that begged her to be reasonable. Not to lose her temper or overreact in any way. However, that meant something happened that could merit an overreaction.

"We can either fight now and after you tell me, or you can tell me now, and we'll have the one fight."

Will lowered his hood with shaky hands, and she shot out of her chair so fast it toppled to the floor with a loud thud. Two streams of dried blood caked his face that ran from his nose over his lips, and down his chin. There wasn't any bruising around his nose, and it looked as it did when he left, but she was reasonably sure his nose had been broken. "What happened?"

"I'm fine, it healed almost immediately."

"Your face is covered in blood; you cannot possibly be surprised that I want to know how it happened," she replied, crossing her arms.

He might not have been in any real peril, but that didn't mean there hadn't been any danger. They might not be able to die, but they were more than capable of feeling pain as he told her each time she wanted to experiment on herself.

He unclipped his cloak and placed it on the hook by the door. When he turned, she saw that the front of him was covered in blood. The black waistcoat showed no bloodstains, but the white shirt was soaked red.

"Well?" She prompted because she wasn't about to let this go.

"It was an accident." He settled down onto the couch, rolling his neck before continuing. "Some boys accidentally kicked a football at me. I was distracted and didn't see it coming, so it got me good."

She nodded. Noses tended to bleed quickly, so the carnage made sense. "Let me get you cleaned up." She went to the bedroom to get a washcloth and a pitcher of water.

She sat beside him as he turned to face her. Their knees touched, and she felt him tense, but he otherwise remained still. Carefully, she soaked the towel before wiping his face.

His yellow eyes tracked her every movement as she cleaned his face. Up close, his eyes weren't the liquid honey she thought they were. Instead, there were flecks of brown, orange streaks, and the slightest hint of green.

"What?" He asked, snapping her out of her trance.

"Nothing," she said, quickly returning to her work after being caught staring.

He frowned but didn't say anything as she poured a little more water on the towel to help her remove the stubborn bloodstains on his chin.

She couldn't remember if she had touched his face before. She may have placed a hand on his cheek while they kissed, but she wasn't sure. His skin was softer than she thought it would be. Up close, she could see the slight differences in tone and texture between the scars. Their bodies could easily heal any new damage, but Tristan hadn't quite unlocked how to heal their pre-death damage.

When his face was clean, her hands slid down to loosen his cravat.

"Why are you trying to undress me?"

"Don't flatter yourself, I wasn't trying to undress you." Technically, she had been, but not to get him *naked*. She was only going to go as far as his stained cravat. "I wanted to see if I could save your cravat, lord knows your shirt is a lost cause. You might as well throw it in the fire."

Will looked down at his bloodied shirt and then back at her. "Why would I throw it in the fire?"

She gestured to his shirt, the blood having dried to a brownish-red color. "It's ruined! The stains have set."

"So, you think I should burn my shirt," he said slowly. "Instead of laundering it."

"It's ruined!" Her face heated because, based on his reaction, she had a suspicion that burning the shirt wasn't the correct choice, but she was going to hold her position no matter how dire it got.

"Maybe, but a laundress may be able to get the blood out. It's worth a shot at the very least." The muscles of his jaw ticked, and she knew he was trying not to laugh.

"And if it's not able to be saved?"

"Then we could cut the shirt and turn it into cleaning rags or find another way to utilize the fabric. Do you typically burn your clothes when you're through with them?"

Sputtering, she tried to form a logical response when he threw his head back in laughter. His broad chest shook as his abdominal muscles expanded and contracted with each laugh. She had seen him laugh before, but it was always subdued, while this was pure joy. She liked his laugh, even if it was at her expense.

"I'm sorry," he said as his laughter slowed and he wiped tears from his eyes. "I just can't believe your first instinct is to *burn* ruined clothing."

"It's not," she snapped. She wasn't about to tell him that it wasn't just clothing she burned when she wanted to get rid of something. It only now occurred to her that it wasn't normal behavior. "Those boys should have hit you even harder with that ball."

"Trust me, they wish they hit me harder, too."

She stilled. "Why?"

"No reason," he said quickly. "I'll take this down to be laundered. Thank you for trying to save my cravat, but I think it's a job for a professional."

"Don't change the subject. Why would they want to hit you harder?"

"It's not a big deal."

"If it's not a big deal, then you'll have no problem telling me." She smiled, knowing her logic was sound.

He grimaced. "When I was hit with the ball, it was an accident. However, when the lads came over to retrieve their ball, one of them happened to be a classmate of yours, who is a bit of an arse.

He said something rude, so I hit him." He winced and rubbed his jaw.

"Who was it?" She hardly paid any attention to the men in her class, but she wanted to know who was foolish enough to tussle with Will.

"You don't have to worry about him. He'll leave you alone from now on."

None of the male students liked being in class with her, but they all ignored her. She had expected some taunts or sneers, but instead they pretended she wasn't there. It was an arrangement she was incredibly fond of since she had no interest in them either. The only students she spoke with were the other women, but even that was rare since they were typically in different classes.

Jane narrowed her eyes. "I wasn't aware they weren't leaving me alone. No one has said a word to me."

"Good, I don't want you to worry about it. You should be focused on your studies anyway."

"Well, if you won't tell me what happened, I'll talk to them myself." She stood up; she wasn't some wilting flower who had to be kept safe from the world around her.

"No." Will's arm shot out to grab her wrist, his hand easily encircling it. "I don't want to upset you because it's not worth it. They're not worth it."

"Do you think I am new to the cruelty of men? I bet they're not even half as creative as my brother."

"Which is why you don't need to take on this as well." His expression was so earnest it was as if he was prepared to stand between her and the rest of the world as her knight in shining armor. It was both sweet and frustrating.

Part of her wanted to pick a fight with him. To yell at him about how she didn't need anyone to look out for her because she was more than capable of taking care of herself. That she wasn't interested in his misplaced male protective streak, but, unfortunately, she did kind of like it because no one had ever defended her before.

Looking down at him, she raised her eyebrow. Nothing else needed to be said because he knew exactly what she wanted. His jaw was set in a hard line, as if his will was immovable, but he was sorely mistaken if he thought she would back down. No one could match her will.

Finally, he broke. "He doesn't think you should be able to attend school. Then he taunted me about our marriage. Said it was good we had each other, so no one else had to suffer."

"What?"

She didn't care if her classmates thought she should be a student or not. The dean said she could be there, so she didn't care what the other students thought. What she couldn't stomach was anyone saying anything about Will.

"Honestly, it wasn't even creative. He deserved the punch, but there's no need to dwell upon it." He still had a hold of her wrist, and he rubbed the back of her hand with his thumb.

This man was precious, and it enflamed her to think of anyone who found him lacking. Sometimes, he could drive her up the wall, but he had the biggest heart of anyone she had ever met. Slightly less important, he was the most handsome man she'd ever seen with his strong jaw, lush lips, and enchanting eyes. His smile lit up the room better than any gas lamp, and his laughter was her favorite melody. He was beautiful inside and out, and no one should ever make him feel like he was anything else.

"Hopefully, you knocked some sense into him at the very least."

He snorted. "I wouldn't hold my breath on it, but I think he has been dissuaded from saying anything else about you."

"I don't care if he says anything about me, just leave him alone from now on." She didn't like having to look at his blood.

"It's not like they can do any real damage."

If she were brave, she would say the idea of him being hurt was unbearable, but the words caught in her throat. Instead, it was easier to be abrasive. "I never asked you to defend me. The only thing I need from you is to keep pretending to be my husband and chaperone, a *silent* position."

"Do you think I would ever let my *wife*," he said in a voice that was so low it made her stomach swoop as he stood up. "Be talked to in such a way? Especially by men who can't see her worth?"

She didn't know if she wanted to kiss him or rage at him. That was her cue to hit him with a devastatingly clever retort, but she couldn't think with him this close to her. He overwhelmed her senses.

Before she could think better of it, she grabbed him by the collar and crushed her mouth to his. He froze for a moment before he came alive in the kiss. His lips were firm against hers as he held her close. She bit his lip to regain control of the kiss she had meant as a challenge.

He growled, lifting her so he wouldn't have to stoop to kiss her any longer. His hands had an iron hold beneath her arse, her legs wrapping around him as he walked them into the bedroom.

Once in the bedroom, she took to her feet again. Will's hands flew to the buttons at her throat. He successfully opened the first, but fumbled with the second.

"You might have a better chance if you removed your gloves."

"It wouldn't be a problem if these blasted buttons weren't so small," he grumbled, removing his gloves.

She slipped out of her dress and underskirt before he grabbed her again. His hand ran over the front of her corset to find the hooks. When he had trouble with those as well, he flexed, ripping the garment down the middle. The metal clasps chimed as they hit the wooden floor. Her core clenched at the display of brute force. "There's no need to destroy my clothes."

"It was in my way," he said, peeling the ruined garment from her.

"You'll be the one explaining to the seamstress why it needs to be repaired," she said, before stretching up to kiss him.

His big hands gripped her waist tightly before he broke away. "I don't think she'll need an explanation. I highly doubt it will be the first time she's made such a repair."

She opened her mouth to prepare another retort, but he picked her up and tossed her on the bed before she could speak. Flabbergasted, she floated through the air for a moment before sinking into the feather bed. No one had ever *tossed* her before.

"If I had known how effective this would be against you in an argument, I would have thrown you ages ago."

He crawled up the bed, his hungry gaze intent upon her like a predator who finally has his prey in his grasp.

"Only because you'll lose any battle of wits." Her words held no bite in them as she said them between gasps as he ran his hands up her body, purposefully missing her breasts.

"Careful," he said as he dipped down to kiss along her jaw. "If you're not nice to me, then I don't have to be nice to you." He nipped at the skin just below her ear, and it was her turn to growl.

She grabbed him with a desperation to anchor herself to him. Running her hands over the hard planes of his body, she marveled at his strength. Gardening had done his body well. "As if you could ever leave me wanting."

Lifting his head, he looked into her eyes. They were full of desire, but there was a layer of tenderness beneath that made her heart ache. "Never," he said before kissing her with passion that left her breathless.

She sank into his kiss, into him. Knowing that no matter what happened, she was safe with him. He lazily drew a path up and down her torso with his hand, setting sparks through her. Fed up with the teasing, she moved his hand to cover her breast so he would get the hint.

She felt him grin against her before he murmured. "So needy."

"I didn't think you needed this much direction." Pausing, she thought about what else she wanted. "Take your shirt off."

"What's the magic word?"

A dark curl fell into his face as he held himself above her. She moved the silky lock back into place.

"Now."

Will barked a laugh before pushing himself up to his knees. "Bossy too," he said, finally removing his shirt.

The dark hair on his broad expanse of chest gave a contrast between his pale skin and raised scars. The most shocking scar was a thick, jagged line across his gut. His pectoral muscles bounced under her gaze. She was about to tease him about showing off when she saw the trepidation in his gaze.

Pushing herself up, she ran her hands over him, over the harder muscles of his pectorals and the softer plane of his stomach. The scar didn't bother her, but she avoided it all the same because she didn't want to make him self-conscious and ruin the moment.

"I can't believe you've been hiding all of this under your cloak."

"I used to look better," he said, blushing, but he still couldn't meet her eye.

"I think you're beautiful. Do you know why I like the way you look?" She kissed his chest, relishing the feel of his muscles beneath her lips. Her eyes flicked up, and he shook his head. "Your scars are proof you're a scientific marvel. You were the first creation of a new age. These scars should be a point of pride."

Emotion swam in his eyes before he crashed down upon her, flattening her to the bed as he kissed her, showing her how her words made him feel.

His mouth moved ravenously down her body before sucking on her nipple through her thin chemise. Grabbing the back of his head, she slipped her fingers into his hair and held him to her, her body rolling beneath his divine touch. She bit her lip to stifle her moan so hard she thought she might draw blood.

"Let me hear you, I never said I wanted you quiet," he said before moving his mouth to give her other breast the same attention.

"I thought your goal was to shut me up."

He stopped to look at her, and she whimpered at the loss of his touch. "I've never once wanted you quiet, love."

She cupped his face in her hand. His skin was imperfect, but he was soft and warm and *alive*. They had been dragged back to this realm, and while that never bothered her, she knew he had warred with himself over it. Against all odds, they had found each other, been awarded this gift of time together that she didn't want to waste a single moment.

Running her hands over his shoulders, she rolled them over so she could have her way with him. Easing her hand down his body, she cupped his sizable length through his trousers, feeling his cock twitch beneath her grasp. His yellow eyes were wild, his pupils blown out as she stroked him over the fabric.

Slowly, she unbuttoned his trousers like she was unwrapping a gift. He kicked off his trousers, and she finally got to see her present. He was thick, hard, and perfectly formed.

"Quit playing," he grabbed her, flipping them so she was beneath him before she had the chance to react.

"I just wanted to make sure it worked," her tease ended on a gasp as he finally touched between her thighs.

He slid his finger up and down, gathering some of her wetness before circling her clitoris. Rolling her hips, she begged for more. He slipped a finger inside her, pumping in and out before a second finger joined.

"Now who's playing?" She tried to sound wry, but was too lost in pleasure.

He kissed her as he kept his thumb circling her clitoris, his fingers fucking her in a steady rhythm. She tried to move her hips to speed him up since she was right on the edge of her pleasure, but he was immovable. The only thing she could do was take it.

"I don't know why I thought you'd be patient."

"I'll never be patient, not for you." She wanted him too much. All she could think about for days was him fucking her—with his fingers, cock, or any other way she could have him. Now that she knew how he felt, she could never have enough.

Time seemed to stop as her pleasure crested, but Will never did. Her eyes were screwed shut as she moaned and panted through the waves of pleasure that crashed through her. It was completely undignified, but she was beyond caring.

Finally, he ceased his ministrations, and she caught her ragged breath. She opened her eyes to see him hovering over her with the side of his mouth kicked up in a devastating smirk as he removed his fingers from her with a messy sound. Maintaining eye contact, he rumbled in pleasure as he sucked his fingers clean.

"You taste even sweeter than I imagined."

Usually, she would have thrown out a barb to check his ego, but she let him win this round. He deserved it.

CHAPTER 28

*W*ill's cock was harder than it ever had been in his entire life. It was a miracle of biology that he didn't come at his first taste of Jane. The small taste wasn't nearly enough, but he needed to be inside her.

"What are you waiting for?" She asked, her face awashed in a beautiful glow.

Lining himself up with her entrance, he stilled for a moment. "Are you sure you can handle it?"

"Do your worst."

Jane cried out when he entered her in one hard thrust. He paused for a moment so they could get used to each other, but she bucked her hips, urging him on.

Tilting her hips, he took her at a fast pace, but she met his every thrust. She was a vision beneath him, beyond beautiful. From now on, whenever he was bored in a lecture, he would think of her like this. Breasts jiggling, her face contorted in pleasure, and the wicked sounds her body made were burned into his memory for all time.

When she whimpered and braced herself against the headboard, he knew he found the right spot. He poured everything he had into her, his desire, need, and gratitude. They were so different, but they complemented each other so well.

Her nails raked down his back, not nearly hard enough to make him bleed, and he mourned that she would never be able to leave a lasting mark.

His balls tightened; he wasn't sure how much longer he could last, but he wanted to hold out until he felt her come around his cock.

"Are you ready to give me another?"

"Maybe."

"If you don't, then our score will quickly become even." Slipping his hand between them, he felt her inner muscles squeeze him when he rubbed that special place between her thighs.

On a hard thrust, an errant thought hit that immediately stilled his actions as horror bloomed inside of him.

"Why did you stop? I was nearly there." Jane frowned. She rolled her hips in an attempt to spur him on again, but he remained immovable.

"Are you able to become with child?" It wasn't his most eloquent question, but his arms shook, and his heart raced. He sucked in a frantic breath, but he felt like he was suffocating.

"Huh," Jane's brow furrowed as it always did when she was deep in thought. He felt like he was on the verge of cracking while she only looked curious.

They had been so cavalier, getting swept away in a rush of passion. They should have thought about the repercussions. *He* should have thought of them.

"How are you not worried?" The only thing he could think of was impregnating her with some undead monstrosity. Something that wasn't truly alive, but also could not die that would follow them until the end of time. "Wait, you don't want a child, do you?"

"Of course not," she snorted, and he relaxed.

"Then why aren't you worried?" The more his panic ratcheted, the calmer she looked.

"I think you're worried enough for the both of us." She leaned up to kiss the side of his mouth, then moved her lips down to place a lazy kiss on his chin and nipped at his jaw. "If it's any consolation, I don't think you'll have to worry about becoming a father."

"Are you sure?"

"I haven't had a cycle since I was brought back. Previously, I was incredibly regular."

Will withdrew from Jane on a groan and rolled over to stare at the ceiling. "Was this part of your tests with Tristan?"

The last thing he wanted was to invoke *his brother's* name, but he also wanted to make sure they could be together safely.

Jane snorted. "Do you really think he would know more about women's reproductive organs than me?"

"No." He trusted her to know both the science and her own body. If she were sure, he would be as well. "I trust you."

Silence loomed over them as his embarrassment grew. His anxiety had ruined the mood yet again. Ignoring his fears wouldn't have been right, since it was an important discussion, but he should have thought it through beforehand. Now, he didn't know if they would ever be able to capture that magic again.

"I can feel you spiraling." Jane pushed herself up and over him, steadying her hands on his chest as she straddled his stomach. "Tell me your worries."

He sighed. There wasn't enough time in the world to address all his worries. Placing a hand on her hip, he rubbed his fingers over her soft skin, and the knot in his chest loosened. "I feel foolish ruining the mood."

"There's nothing to feel foolish over, especially not a very valid concern. Could you imagine if I did get pregnant?" Jane shivered. "Even if it was a silly concern or if you just didn't wish to continue, that would be fine."

"And that goes for you as well."

"Good," Jane said, lightly scratching his chest. "That means we can continue."

Leaning down, she kissed him hard. Her teeth bit at his lower lip, and then her tongue plundered his mouth. His panic receded with every swipe of her tongue.

He broke off their kiss and looked up at her. She was a living goddess. He ran his fingers up her body, following her curves, watching the goose-flesh follow his path. "You're incredible," he said on an exhale, and she smiled, beaming down on him like the sun.

"In case you wish to confirm my science with further testing, I figured we could explore some other options." She shot him a devilish look as she crawled down his body, taking his length in her hand.

Without breaking eye contact, she licked up his length before swirling her tongue around the head of his cock. Her lips surrounded him, and he had never seen a more delightful view than watching himself disappear into her mouth. His hips jackknifed up when she sucked. Hard. This woman was beyond perfection.

"I'm going to finish in your mouth if you don't stop."

She took him further down her throat instead. He gripped the sheets as he met her rhythm with his own shallow thrusts. Bellowing her name, he spilled into her mouth until he had nothing else to give.

Jane sat up and looked at him with a smug smirk. He sat up to meet her halfway, pulling her mouth to his, and tasting himself in their kiss.

"Lie back and get comfortable. It may be a while until I'm finished." He needed to taste her properly more than he had ever needed anything else.

"I promise you it won't take that long."

"You misunderstand. I plan on feasting on your cunt until *I'm* sated."

Jane's eyes widened as he kissed down a line from her knee, nipping at her inner thigh before tossing her leg over his shoulder. Dipping his head down, he licked a long stripe up her center. She made his mouth water, and he went back for more.

Her hands flew to his head, fingers digging into his scalp, tugging his hair in relation to where his mouth was on her cunt. It didn't take long for him to decipher her communication. If she liked what he was doing, she scratched his scalp. If he had the wrong spot, she tugged his hair until he was where she wanted. When she mewled while pulling on his hair out from the root, he lifted his head for a moment to check in with her, but she squeezed his head between her thighs to keep him in place.

He sucked hard on her clitoris, thrumming the bud with his tongue as he speared her with two fingers. Her cunt fluttered as she whimpered for release. She was a woman who was firmly in control at all times, so having her at his mercy was exhilarating.

Jane arched her back, stilling as she screamed. "Oh God."

"No, you only get to say *my* name when I'm inside you."

This time, when he added a bit more pressure to her clitoris as he moved his fingers within her, she spasmed, crying out his name and ripping at his hair while she rode out the waves of her pleasure. Even as her muscles relaxed, he never slowed his pace and kept his mouth on her. It wasn't long until she clenched around him again, but he still kept his fingers pumping gently inside her until she tapped his shoulders to get him to stop.

Somehow, he found the strength to pull away and settled into his spot on the bed. Jane slotted in next to him, her head resting in the crook of his shoulder as he brought his arm around her. The motion was so fluid that it was as if they had done it thousands of times.

"Can I ask you a question?" Her fingers ran over his chest, tracing over each scar with her light touch.

"You already have."

"Don't ruin the afterglow."

"Go ahead."

"How did you die?"

Her fingers traced the edges of his least favorite scar, the biggest, ugliest scar on his stomach. The muscles beneath her touch tensed, and he also had the urge to bolt to put as much space between him and this conversation as possible.

However, that wasn't fair. In comparison, he knew so much more about her. She trusted him with her secrets, her vulnerabilities. It was time to return the sentiment, no matter how much it hurt.

"I was in Paris on business, but that was a thinly veiled excuse for debauchery. After a long dinner and many drinks with friends, we went to my preferred gambling hall in the city."

He hadn't played a hand of cards since that night. It wasn't as if he had sworn off all vice after his death, but no longer felt the desire to gamble.

"I was having a good night, the kind gamblers dream of. More of the hands went my way than not, and when I did lose, it was on the smaller pots. Most of the men I played against took losing in stride, but one became particularly irate. I had my eye on him and could tell he was desperate, and desperation is dangerous."

Jane kept petting him as he told the story. It was helpful to focus on something physical so his memories didn't drown him. Since he tried his hardest not to remember that night, he thought his memories of that night were fading, but as he spoke, he relived it all again.

"I purposefully threw a hand so he won, and then cashed out my three hundred francs. It was still early, so my friends stayed while I walked back to my hotel, a little drunk and not paying nearly enough attention. I went down an alley for a shortcut, and when I rounded the corner, the man from the game was there. I probably should have stopped or maybe even tried to run. Instead, I walked toward him, and he stabbed me in the gut without a word."

"He stole the money, of course, and left me to bleed out. I stared up at the stars and thought about how stupid I was. I had wasted so much time, and now I was going to die with nothing to show for it. And even worse, Tristan was going to be all alone."

Jane brushed a finger over his jaw, and he looked at her. There was pain and concern in her expression, but none of the judgment he feared. The story had been painful, but not nearly as bad as he thought it would be. Still, he tightened his grip on her. They were both alive. All would be well.

"What happened next?"

"I'm not as clear on that part. You'd get better details from Tristan's journals."

"I would rather hear it from you."

"Something in Tristan broke when he got to Paris, and I had already been buried. He had been teaching in Munich at the time.

They refused to exhume me, so he did it himself and took me back to his laboratory in Germany."

"How did he..." Jane trailed off.

"How did he know he could do it?" He could see the wheels turning in her head. She wanted the emotional part of his story, but she couldn't turn off her inner scientist. "He had been studying the mechanics of life for a few years at that point. He managed to bring a rat back to life a month or so before my death, but he only had one success after hundreds of tries. Mrs. Jones said he was dedicated in a way she had never seen before."

"Did she know what he was trying to do?"

"No, she likely would have put a stop to it. He didn't tell her until he had been successful. Though I think a part of her hoped that's what he was trying to do."

"How long did it take?"

"Almost three months." He heard her sharp intake of breath. "Because it had been so long, he had a lot of me to sew together. He used borrowed skin, and not all of my organs are original. My left hand was crushed when he dug me out of my shoddy grave, so he sourced one from the morgue." He held up the stranger's limb. It flexed when he commanded it to, moving as if it were his own. Maybe it was his now. Jane didn't seem to mind it at the very least. "The final try took two days. I came to with him shaking me and crying out my name, and I was so, so confused."

A lump caught in his throat as he remembered the early days. It had taken him so much work to put himself back together.

"I had a vague memory of who I was, but no clue where I was or how much time had passed. I felt *wrong*. It took a week for me to remember who I was and that my last memory had been dying in an alley in Paris. Tristan then sat me down and told me the full story. I was so angry that I was back. That I was forced to feel again, that my body no longer felt like my own. My brother had brought me back to life, but it felt like he had robbed me of everything I was."

Jane wiped away his escaped tear. Her grey eyes glistened, and he kissed her on the top of her head. He could get through anything because he wasn't alone anymore.

"My rage clouded every other emotion. I had never felt anything close to that when I was alive. Tristan wanted to perform tests, but I wouldn't even see him."

Not even Tristan knew the next part of his story, but if anyone would understand, it would be Jane.

"One night, I snuck into his lab to steal a scalpel and slashed my wrists. As the blood poured from me, I felt hope because I would be free again. Until the wounds slowly closed. I hacked away at my arms for hours, but every single time those wounds closed too." He wiped his thumb across his perfect, smooth wrist. Jane took his hand, twining her fingers with his.

"Do you wish you were still dead?"

"No." It was the question he had wrestled with for over a year. Tristan had never dared to ask because he was petrified of the answer. "It was easier not having to think or feel. Being thrust back into feeling was exhausting. And then to find out my life would go on forever felt like too much to bear."

But now he had Jane, and his suffering had been worth it even if they only ever had these few perfect moments. He didn't dare say it because she still planned to leave, and he would never want her to stay out of obligation. Being alone would be less painful.

"I think it was different for me because I wasn't dead for very long," she said. He stroked her arm, relishing the ability to touch her freely. "I remember the sense of peace as I died, but I wasn't dead long enough for waking up to be jarring. It felt like waking up after a long nap."

Will felt Jane's chest move with her every breath. Her skin was soft and warm against his—nothing like how he found her. The nightmare of her lifeless body wouldn't leave him anytime soon, but every time she smiled, laughed, or even yelled at him, it helped to smooth over those memories.

"I'm glad you didn't suffer as much." He paused, nervous to ask his next question, but he had to know. "Do you wish you were still dead?"

Silence stretched between them in what felt like the longest moments of his life as Jane considered his question.

"No," she finally said. "I don't regret what I did to get away from my brother, but I'm glad to be here with you. This life is unlike anything I could have dreamed of, so I can't find myself regretting anything that happened."

"I have some regrets."

She pinched his side. "Hush. You know this is better."

"It is." The woman he wanted to spend forever with was in his arms. There was no way he could regret anything that had ever happened to him.

CHAPTER 29

*J*t had only been a week, but it felt as if Jane had been away from campus for an eternity. She missed the sound of her footsteps on the stone floor, the creaky chairs, and the groan of the heavy doors as they opened and closed. She even missed the chatter of her classmates. They were still deeply annoying, but integral to the ambiance.

Will ushered her into the lecture hall, where her classmates continued to ignore her, but her place in the front row was open. Will took his customary spot and pulled out her chair. It was one of the many considerate things Will had done for her. Guilt may have propelled him to bring her to school, but it didn't make him braid her hair or carry her books. He did those things for *her*.

"Mrs. Byrne, it's so nice to see you." Jane looked up to see Miss Thornton setting her belongings beside her.

"Good Afternoon, it's nice to see you as well. I hope you had a pleasant time away," Jane said. At first, her response was reflexively polite, but she found she actually did miss speaking with the young woman between classes.

The younger woman grimaced. "It was fine, my aunt and I visited my parents in London."

"I hope you were still able to enjoy the city despite your parents' presence."

Jane had never been to London. It hadn't made sense to even dream of going before, since Robert would never have allowed it. Maybe Will would take her after the term ended.

Miss Thornton waved her off. "Oh, of course, I learned how to slip away when I was 12," she gasped and turned a light pink. "I don't mean that I sneak away to do anything scandalous, I just go to the bookstore or to visit with my friends."

"There are many boring reasons to sneak off, but the scandalous ones are more fun to gossip about."

Jane wouldn't have cared even if she had done something scandalous, but she didn't want to shock the young woman when she was already in distress.

"Of course," the young woman stammered. "I just didn't want you to get the wrong impression about my character."

"Why should it matter what I think?" She couldn't help but laugh. She had never cared about her own propriety, let alone anyone else's.

Miss Thornton's face crumpled, and Jane knew she had the wrong reaction. "Oh, I didn't mean it like that." She went to tap the younger woman's gloved hand—she learned physical touch could be comforting—but she withdrew her hands before Jane could make contact.

"No, you're right. It is silly, I shouldn't have bothered you."

"I don't think it's silly," she said, a heavy ball forming in her stomach. No matter how hard she tried, she seemed to offend everyone around her. "Isn't it a bit ridiculous that we spend so much of our time concerned about propriety. Like, making us attend classes with a chaperone, what could happen in the middle of a crowded classroom?"

It was another way to keep women back in society. Her "marriage" to Will had given her freedom, but only because he was a decent man. Lord Percy would have locked her away in an attic if given the chance.

"Oh, yes." Relief flooded Miss Thornton's face, and it eased some of her guilt. "Between the chaperones and our strict library hours, it feels less like we are students and more like we're captives."

"Ah, but we are captives who let them say they accepted women before Oxford."

Miss Thompson laughed before her chaperone commanded her attention.

"It's all right," Will said, his warm breath against the shell of her ear. "She is still firmly in your society of admirers."

She nudged him with her shoulder. "Please, there isn't any such society." It embarrassed her to think of Miss Thornton holding her in such high regard when she had barely given her a second thought.

He laughed. "She's gunning to be the president of the society, just watch. She'll want to introduce you to her mother next."

"If there is a society for me, are you in it?" She asked, brow raised in mock question. They had spent the past week enjoying one another in and out of bed, but she wasn't sure how that would translate now that they were back to real life.

"Of course," he said, smirking. "Who do you think she has to fight for the presidency?" He winked, and she flushed a deep red.

She focused on her notebook instead. Class was about to begin, and she needed to get a hold of herself. Dr. Harris needed to regard her as a serious academic. Flirting with Will would have to be on her own time.

"Don't worry," he said, his voice dropping to the register that heated her. "I don't plan on letting anyone else win."

It was a miracle she had been able to pay attention to the lecture with how distracting Will was. The worst part was that it wasn't even on purpose. Every time she risked a glance, he had only been sketching his garden. He hadn't once taken the opportunity to shift closer or run his finger against her arm.

Over the past week, he touched her whenever he could. His hands were always running over her body or through her hair. Two weeks ago, she would have said that much physical touch annoyed her, but now she mourned the loss.

Not touching was the professional choice. Even though everyone around them believed they were married, it still wouldn't be appropriate. Still, he could have run a knuckle over the side of her hand or brushed their knees together.

Voices rumbled around her, startling her out of her fantasies of the man beside her. She scrambled to get her notes together. This time, she hadn't missed part of the lecture at least.

"Montgomery."

Jane whipped around to see who said her name, but no one was behind her. The boys were all filing out of the room without even a glance her way, but her hands still trembled.

"Are you all right?" Will frowned, searching her face to detect what could be wrong.

"I'm fine," she said quickly. "I need to give Dr. Harris my notes." Grabbing the stack of research from her bag, she walked to the podium.

"Mrs. Byrne." Dr. Harris greeted her with a smile that relaxed her. "It's so nice to have you in class again. With you back, I know at least one person understands my lecture."

"I'm glad to be back. I didn't realize how much I would miss school." His warmth was contagious, so it was easy to return his smile. The male students always talked about how intimidating he was, but she had never found him to be anything other than welcoming.

"I transcribed your research." She shoved the papers at him before she could get nervous. She took a deep breath as he looked through her work, bracing herself for rejection. "Your trials involving blood typing are fascinating. I worked on something similar while assisting Dr. Gardner. If you ever need an assistant, I would be more than happy to help however I could."

His eyes snapped back to her. "You've used a microscope?"

"Yes." She tried not to let her excitement get ahead of her, but this was a job she could do. "Dr. Gardner taught me."

"I don't know if I've ever met a woman who knew how to use one, color me impressed. I currently have as many assistants as I need, but I'll let you know if I have use for your services. In the meantime," he said, handing her a sizable stack of papers from his bag. "I have more notes for you to work on. Next class will be a practical lab experience, so this should be completed by then."

He gathered his lecture notes in dismissal, and she thanked him before scooting back to Will, who looked on with a slight frown. He opened his mouth, but she shook her head, instead taking his arm to drag him from the room so she could recount the conversation.

"What were you discussing?" He asked as soon as the door shut behind them.

"I told him I was interested in being his research assistant, and he said he would let me know when he had an opening. Hopefully, I'll be working for him by the end of the term."

Will was quiet for so long that it sent unease through her. She hadn't expected effusive praise, but she thought he would have *something* to say. Part of her had even hoped he might be proud of her, but instead his face was carefully blank. "What?" She didn't mean to snap, but he could have at least pretended to be happy for her.

"Did he make any promises about working with you?"

"No, but I'm not a child," she said in a chilly tone. She didn't like what he was insinuating. "He told me he didn't need another assistant right now, but he would let me know when he did."

"Did he say he wanted you as an assistant?"

"If you must know exactly what he said, he told me that he had never known a woman who could use a microscope and that he was currently full up on research assistants, but he would let me know when he had use for me." Will was trying to look out for her, but she would never let him interfere with her career. "Does that satisfy you, or do you have more objections?"

They walked through the courtyard on their way to the library. Women were only allowed in the library for a few hours on Mondays, but her class cut that time in half. She had a lot of work to do, and she didn't feel like fighting with him.

Will sighed, and her hackles raised. It was the sigh she was so incredibly familiar with. It was the Jane-you're-being-so-unreasonable sigh. It meant that she should be thankful he was willing to put up with her at all, and it made her blood pressure spike because Robert gave her that same sigh whenever he felt she was ungrateful.

"It's not that I don't wish to see you succeed." his voice was still careful, but the underlying tone was tender instead of exasperated. "I just don't want you to chase something you'll never catch."

"And why don't you think I'll catch it?" Genuine anger threatened to bleed into her voice, but she tried her best to keep it back because she didn't want the emotions to make her seem weak, even though it hurt that he didn't believe in her. "You don't think I'm just as good as these other fools." She motioned around the courtyard to the groups of men congregating. They never had to question their worth or if they deserved an opportunity. It made her so angry that she could scream.

"Of course not," he snapped. "I think you're better. Not to discount the others, but they're still young and learning discipline. You're not only brilliant, but you also have an incredible work ethic."

They stopped in front of the library doors, as they would be unable to continue the argument inside. The wind had been taken out of the sails of her anger with that simple statement. It wasn't fair of him to say such nice things when she was so mad at him.

"Then why are you so convinced I won't get it?"

He hesitated, as if he was prepared for her wrath. Part of her wanted to give him the offer that she wouldn't get mad at him no matter what he said, but she didn't want to lie.

"I'm not," he sighed. "I know how these academics are with their politics behind the scenes. I don't want you to get excited, and then the job is handed to someone whose uncle donated a lot of money."

Her shoulders dropped. His worries were rather sweet when they weren't related to her abilities.

"You worry too much, Will." She stepped towards him, placing a hand on his shoulder. "I know you're only trying to care for me, but I don't need to be coddled. The world is harsh, and sometimes I will succeed, but othertimes I'll have to fail."

"I know, but it's difficult to see it happen, especially when I can help you avoid such things."

"Telling me that Dr. Harris won't hire me isn't helping me to avoid failure. It's trying to get me to avoid even trying. I would rather he reject me than never know whether he thought I was good enough for a job. You can't protect me from everything, especially if you won't always be there."

Will's eyes shuttered, and she removed her hand, feeling guilty for even mentioning leaving. It had been more than a week since she discussed her desire for freedom.

"So that's it then, I either fall in line with what you want, or you'll leave?"

"No," she scowled. Obviously, Will would be content if she stayed with him forever. That was why he pulled her from the river, after all. "I've told you from the beginning that all I want is freedom. Part of that is learning to stand on my own. Even if I am with you, I still want to be self-sufficient, especially regarding my career."

Truthfully, the more time she spent with Will, the less she wanted to leave him. Perhaps in a few years she would rethink it, but the part of her that wanted to stay grew louder every day.

"You're right, it wasn't fair of me to throw that back in your face. I'm sorry. Our deal remains, I'll still help you learn how to be independent."

"Thank you." She gave him a small smile, and he visibly relaxed. "I'll even let you fuss over me some as long as you don't go off half-cocked trying to defend my honor."

"Don't worry, I won't do anything half-cocked where you're concerned," he said with humor glinting in his eyes.

CHAPTER 30

*L*ying was a state of mind. As long as he didn't believe he was lying, he wasn't. Perhaps there was a level of deceit to what he was doing, but he hadn't graduated to lying. Asking Oliver to keep an eye on Harris wasn't technically interfering with her education. He knew of all the notes passed between them and each time they spoke in the dining room, but he had never once stopped it, so, technically, he wasn't a liar. Yet.

Usually, the library was able to provide some level of distraction, but when he had grabbed a volume of Lord Byron's poetry, a terse young man walked over to demand its return before he even got five pages into the book.

Jane dutifully worked beside him, copying notes from an anatomy textbook with a focus that made him jealous. Leaning over the book, her bosom nearly grazed the edge of the table, and she bit her lip as she digested the information on the page. When Jane was focused on something, her attention was absolute. That incredible focus was placed on him yesterday when she had practically tackled him after he returned from an afternoon stroll.

Discreetly checking the clock, which had been placed passive aggressively in their section, he saw they had less than an hour left. It infuriated him that they were timed down to the minute. At five minutes left, the pimply library assistant would hover over them, clearing his throat for the final minute until they made it through the door. His darkest fantasy was to whack him upside the head with Jane's heaviest textbook as they left.

Jane never seemed to notice the intrusion. Unlike Will, the library assistant's presence never flustered her, but she also never acknowledged him. She would fight with him to her very last breath, but she accepted these parameters without a fight, which made him angrier because her acceptance meant she knew she couldn't win. There was no reason why the women of Cambridge couldn't have full library access.

While he knew it rankled Jane to be chaperoned, it was the one policy he agreed with. The boys currently held no interest in the women in their classes, but he knew that could change in a moment. If they did decide to show an interest, the harassment could easily become unbearable, which no woman deserved. As Jane was seen as a married woman, it made her largely invisible, but that wouldn't necessarily dissuade a particularly bullheaded young man.

Shifting in her seat, Jane drew his attention back to her. Most of their morning was spent distracted, so her hair had been hurriedly pulled back into a bun with such poor structural integrity that most of her hair had fallen from the pins. Tendrils of her dark hair curled against her nape, tempting him to reach out and take a lock between his fingers.

She smelled like the lavender soap they shared and ink. Never before had he even considered the smell of ink, but now it ranked amongst his favorite things.

The graceful curves of her body enticed him as she sat there, utterly unconcerned with his presence beside her. It was incredibly inconvenient that he was half-hard when they still had so much time left before they could go. It was his own fault for not diverting his line of thought to taxes or the watering patterns of gardenias as his arousal built, but he was transfixed by her. He was attuned to her every movement while she ignored him in favor of her work.

It made him want to test how hard it would be to break her concentration.

A large bookshelf blocked their table in the very back of the library, but he discreetly shifted himself to block her in case anybody walked over. No one had walked past them in at least forty minutes, but he wouldn't take a chance for her. Besides, Jane would never forgive him if he got them banned from the library.

Reaching out with his index finger, he caressed the inside of her wrist, watching to gauge her reaction. Her navy dress had long sleeves, but when she didn't react to his touch, he grew bolder. He slid his fingers up her arm, dragging them over the crease of her arm, up her bicep, before settling on the top of her shoulder.

What he did like about this dress was that the collar was relatively low so that he could see the column of her throat, the hollow of her collarbone, and all the way to the top of her bosom. The neckline wasn't as low as he would have liked, but that was easily remedied.

Tugging her sleeve until he could see her shoulder, he leaned in to give a feather-light kiss to the newly exposed skin.

"What are you doing?" She whispered, finally looking at him.

"Distracting you," he murmured as he pressed down another kiss.

"We're in public," she hissed, though he could see the desire in her eyes.

"I don't see anyone," he said, turning his head to prove what he already knew. They were completely alone with no one else even remotely close to their stacks, but he wouldn't pressure her into anything. "Say the word, and I'll stop."

"I have a lot of work to do," she said, biting her lip.

A smile curled on his lips because that certainly wasn't *stop*. "Would you like me to continue?"

Indecision warred on her face. Likely, she was stuck between what she wanted and propriety. Finally, she nodded.

"Is that a yes? I need to hear you say it."

"Yes."

"Then by all means, don't let me distract you." He kissed her arm again while scooting his chair as close as possible to her, his fingers dancing over her skirt.

"You happen to be quite distracting," she said, her muscles tensing as he found her thigh.

Smiling against her skin, he said, "We can make a game out of it. I'll touch you while you try to stay as quiet as you can." The muscle of her thigh jumped beneath his hand as he squeezed.

"If it's a game, then how do we know who has won?"

"I win if I can bring you to pleasure here." Slowly, he raised the hem of her muslin skirt. "And you win, if you're able to stay quiet while you're brought to your climax."

"It seems like either way I win." She sighed as his hand traveled up her leg, going from her stockinged knee to the bare skin of her thigh.

"I see you've caught on."

He pulled her dress down a little further and then leaned forward to kiss the newly uncovered strip of skin beneath her clavicle.

"No," she whispered, pushing his head up. His hand stilled on her thigh. "You can't undress me here. Figure out a way around."

"Your wish is my command," he said, more than willing to take her up on her challenge.

Her expression turned icy as she redirected her attention to her work. He hooked her foot around the chair leg to help open her legs. When her face remained passive, he continued.

His thumb stroked against her inner thigh as he let her get accustomed to his touch. Her breath was even as she flipped through the pages of her book. The trick would be to balance his touch against her studies. Moving his hand up through the separation of her bloomers, he ran a finger over her center. He couldn't feel her wetness beneath his glove, but the easy glide of his hand told him all he needed. Jane let out a small gasp at the contact.

"I'm sorry, did you say something?" He asked, a touch louder than he spoke to her before.

She glared at him. "Take off your glove."

"Why?"

"Because I don't want it inside me."

Will stilled. He no longer cringed at the thought of touching Jane and didn't wear the gloves in their room, but he still wore them whenever he went out. If it were his right hand, he would take it off without question, but of course, it was his left.

"No one will notice," she continued. "If anyone would care, it would be me, and you know I don't."

With a shaky hand, he slipped off his glove. Looking at the hand, he realized it was no longer unfamiliar. Removing his other glove, he looked between his two hands. Minor differences remained, but they weren't as glaring as he once thought. He placed both gloves on the table.

Leaning in, he kissed her jaw as he returned his hand, this time feeling how slick she was with his bare hand. He gathered her wetness before moving his fingers up to circle her clitoris.

While she had been dedicated to her studies, he had been dedicated to studying her. While she bloomed beneath many of his touches, what she liked most was to be teased. To have her fire stoked until she became overcome with need. He teased her with slow circles, careful not to touch her clitoris directly because he wanted to draw this out until she begged him for mercy.

He slipped a finger inside of her while his thumb continued his slow circles. She clenched around him as he slowly moved in and out of her. The only reaction she gave was to shift her hips to allow him better access.

There was something about her seeming so unaffected while also feeling her arousal that made his cock swell so much he wasn't sure how he would walk from the library with dignity.

He kissed a line down her neck, from just beneath her ear to the sensitive spot where her neck met her shoulder—feeling her breath stutter when he nipped at her before laving that place with his tongue. The sole downside to the game was that he couldn't bend her over the table and fuck her as he wished.

Her cunt fluttered as he fucked her with his fingers. Jane let go of the pen, ink spilling onto her notes, the slow-moving black puddle making her work useless. Her eyes were still trained on the page, but he knew from her glassy expression that she wasn't able to read a thing. Smugness settled into his chest. *He* was the one who made her come apart like this.

"Come on, love." She was on the edge, and his words could usually push her over. "Accept your defeat at my hand."

She made a small sound of disagreement. "I don't know what you're talking about," she murmured, turning her head so she could spill the words directly into his ear. Her head bobbed to the side as she bit her lip.

The challenge in her voice spurred him on as he intensified his efforts. His reward was a sharp intake of breath. "It certainly sounds like *something* is happening."

She may have been able to keep her moans contained, but she couldn't keep the rest of her body as quiet. The obscene noise her body made threatened to expose them, but neither was willing to stop.

He was so wrapped up in her that it took a moment for him to register footsteps approaching their corner. Jane went rigid as he slowed the rhythm of his fingers, but still kept them slowly pumping inside of her to keep her on the edge.

She grabbed his wrist. "What are you doing?"

"If I need to explain what's happening, I think we're in trouble." Her grip on his wrist was tight, and he could see her desire and concern warring within her. "If you want me to stop, you only have to nod."

He watched her for the slightest bit of movement. It was only fun if they were both equally invested. Stilling his hand, he waited for her decision, but her head kept perfectly still. Her hips bucked to spur him into motion again.

The footsteps grew louder until the owner stopped in the aisle just before theirs. If they were to look down their aisle, they would see a chaperone sitting very, very close to his chaperoned, but his big body would block their view of anything incriminating. The footsteps stopped, and Will waited as he heard someone remove a book before they finally receded. Will's shoulders relaxed. He may have said he didn't care if they were interrupted, but he in no way wished to be caught.

Once they were alone again, he began a relentless rhythm, having lost all desire to tease her. The death grip she had on his arm and her erratic breathing pattern told him she was close. Sometimes staying quiet was difficult for her, so he tilted her head into his chest so any sounds she made would be muffled by him.

As she squeezed his fingers with her climax, she leaned into him and *bit* his neck. His cock spasmed in an unexpected reaction to being bitten. They would need to explore that later.

Storm grey eyes looked at him, glassy with pleasure as he removed his fingers from her, careful to keep his hand from staining her dress. Her body swayed, and before he could think better of it, he fed his fingers into her mouth, and the fire reignited in her eyes. Her tongue swirled around his fingers before she hollowed her cheeks and sucked. When his fingers had been thoroughly cleaned, he removed them from her mouth.

In a just world, he would bend her over the table and make her his in her favorite place, but that dream would go unrealized as they were dangerously close to the end of their time. The sniveling library assistant would be there any moment to kick them out.

He gathered up her belongings while she took her books to be reshelved. Checking out books was yet another privilege reserved for the male students. The school had truly done the bare minimum to ingratiate women into their student body.

"Are you ready?" She whispered. Her beauty struck him with her flushed cheeks and the dark tendrils of hair that framed her face.

"Yes."

Settling her book bag on his shoulder, he held out his arm, which she took before smiling up at him. For her, he would tamp down his anger at the school, the professors, and the other students. There was nothing he wouldn't do to protect her dream.

They left the library just as the kid at the desk was walking towards them. He stared them down as they went by him, as if he expected them to stop and set up camp in the middle of the walkway. Jane held her head up high, ignoring him and every other man who glared at her simply for being a woman existing in their space.

The courtyard was blessedly free of other students. He didn't care if he saw the pricks from the park again, but he didn't want them hassling him in front of Jane. Although when he had seen them earlier in class, they hadn't even glanced his way.

The dark sky opened in a drizzle as they got into the carriage. It was a shame the rain had come in because he so enjoyed walking with her. He would mourn the loss of her body beside his, but the benefit of the carriage was that he could look at her the entire ride. And it took a fraction of the time, so they would be alone again that much sooner.

"The garden looks nice," she said as he led her from the carriage to the building. "Is this what you and Oliver have been working on?"

"Yes, we cleaned up the bushes and planted some violets, but they won't bloom for another month or so." He wanted to plant primrose, but the local greenhouse was out of seeds, so he had to send for some from London. The flowers wouldn't bloom until the dead of winter, but they were worth the wait.

"It's quite nice how you've taken Oliver under your wing."

"He's a good pupil." He held the door open to usher her inside.

Oliver was at his perch by the front desk. His eyes widened when he saw them enter, and he jumped up. Will's stomach dropped. He knew that look on Oliver's face meant he had something to report, and he prayed the lad was smart enough not to mention their deal around Jane.

"Mr. Byrne, I need to speak with you." Oliver's eyes kept shifting to Jane. The boy was many wonderful things, but subtle wasn't one of them.

Nausea roiled inside him. Jane couldn't find out like this. "Can it wait? We have some things we need to do before dinner."

Guilt gnawed at him for being so short with Oliver, but he would sacrifice anything to get Jane away from the lobby. Jane frowned because this attitude was so far from his usual demeanor.

Oliver took Will's foul mood in stride, which only made him

feel worse. "There's a man here to see you. He says he knows you and Mrs. Byrne. I told him he could wait in the dining room."

Jane's frown deepened, "Who would come to visit?"

"I'm not sure, let's go see."

Anyone coming to see the Byrnes was an issue, but he would take this mystery over revealing his arrangement with Oliver. Byrne was a common enough surname that there was a chance they weren't there for them at all.

Walking into the dining room, Will couldn't believe he had dodged two major bullets in less than a minute.

"Finally, it felt like I waited a lifetime for you two," Tristan said, setting aside the journal he was reading.

CHAPTER 31

"Tristan! What a surprise, I didn't know you were coming!" Jane wanted to throw her arms around him, but didn't want to cause a scene in the public dining room.

"I thought I'd keep it a secret to see your reactions, and it was well worth it. You're pleased, and my *cousin*," he said, leaning in and making far too big a deal about their lie. "Looks nauseous, so my goal has been achieved."

Jane laughed as she sat across from Tristan. Will had been off since they entered the hotel, but if she worried every time he behaved strangely, she wouldn't get anything done. "You know him, change gives him indigestion."

Tristan laughed. "I'm glad you're keeping him in line."

Will woodenly sat at the empty place setting between them. "It's quite normal to dislike surprises."

"Of course, but it's fun to needle you for it," Tristan said with a mischievous glint in his eye.

Jane picked up the white china teapot and poured tea for the three of them. Her old governess would be beside herself to see her do something so domestic after so many years of Jane insisting she never, ever would.

"Must I suffer this from both of you now?" Will sighed.

Jane glanced up, unsure if he was actually upset. His tone was annoyed, but the spark of humor in his expression made her relax. "And it's only going to get worse, so you should stop trying to fight it."

"Precisely," Tristan added with a sharp nod as he picked up his teacup.

Her own cup of tea swirled to a lighter brown as she poured the milk. "What brought you all the way down here?" She took a sip of tea. It was deliciously hot, but a touch too bitter for her. It was less than ideal, but she would persevere.

"I'm here to assist Dr. Harris with his practical lab unit. Every year, he hounds me to meet his students, so I decided to take him up on it."

"And it meant you got an opportunity to spy on us," Will said, frowning as he set his cup of tea back in the saucer. Leaning across the table, he picked up a sugar cube with the silver tongs before dropping it into her cup.

Her face flushed pink as Tristan raised an eyebrow at the undeniable act of intimacy, one that Will would have never even attempted the last time Tristan saw them.

"I wasn't sure if I would find anything worth spying on, but I'm glad to be proven wrong."

"Well, I'm glad Dr. Harris wore you down then," she said, barreling past his attempt to fish for information. She wasn't sure how she wanted to name her relationship with Will to herself, let alone to the outside world. "Do you know what you'll be teaching?"

Tristan shrugged. "Nothing definite, but I know he'll want me to talk about my research strategies. I imagine he'll also want me to teach you all how to use the new microscopes. The ones he had were ancient, and he'll need some time to adjust to the new technology."

"Do you have the updated model?"

He nodded. "I try to keep all of my equipment as current as possible. Progress comes quickly, and I don't want to be left behind."

A smug thrill ran through her that she was ahead of her classmates. They might be able to sit for exams, but *she* knew more about the practical uses of their education.

"Do you think Dr. Harris is stuck in old-fashioned thinking overall?" Will asked.

"I don't know if I would refer to him as old-fashioned. Sometimes he can be rather stubborn, but he will change his mind as long as he has been provided with sufficient evidence."

"Which is the mark of a good scientist."

Will ignored her and continued his line of questioning, "Do you know how he feels about having female students?"

Jane wanted to kick him beneath the table, but she refrained because she didn't want to kick Tristan by accident. She settled on staring daggers at Will instead.

Tristan stilled, his attention flicking between Will and Jane. "Jane," he said. "Has Dr. Harris given you any trouble?"

"No," she snapped. "He never hesitates to call on me or to ask me my thoughts. Even when I'm wrong, he doesn't embarrass me or make snide remarks like some of the other professors. He's been lovely. "

Tristan frowned. "Who tried to embarrass you?"

"Embarrass is a strong word, I suppose," she huffed. It must have been a Gardner family trait to cling to the statement she wanted to discuss the least. "Franklin doesn't think I should be there, but he's managed to be civil in class. Occasionally, someone will comment on being surprised a woman knows something, but it's nothing I can't handle."

"I wouldn't pay too much attention to Franklin. He's been cranky since his research funding was pulled. I imagine he's lashing out at everyone."

"That doesn't make it right," Will said with narrowed eyes.

"Of course not, but it's useful information for Jane to have."

"I'm not concerned about him. I'm only the first in a long line of female students he will have to stomach."

Tristan shifted his attention to his brother. "Why are you suspicious of Dr. Harris?"

"I can't say it's my instincts without you two gaining up on me,"

Will sighed, easing back in his seat. "I don't think he believes Jane to have an inferior intellect."

"Then why are we even going on about this!"

"Because I think he's taking advantage of you," Will hissed.

"How?"

"You do a lot of work for him, but what is he doing for you? You can't get course credit, and he's certainly not paying you. He isn't even trying to advocate for female students to be fully integrated into the university."

"I don't need money or glory. I want to be taken seriously as an academic, and he's doing that."

Reaching across the table, she took his hand. It was sweet of him to be so concerned, but it was also terribly misguided.

"What kind of work are you doing for him?" Tristan asked. His eyes followed their physical contact, but he didn't say anything.

"I'm compiling his research notes right now. It's very similar to the work I did for you."

"How did you start working for him. Did he ask or did you?"

"He gave me alternate work to do since I wasn't able to sit for exams. There wasn't any coercion."

Tristan looked to his brother. "It doesn't sound like anything to be alarmed over. If he were having her record data or do other work in the lab without anything in return, that would be suspicious, but what she's doing is appropriate for undergraduates."

Will's stubborn jaw was set in a hard line, but she could see the defeat in his eyes. "I don't trust him."

"And I'm sure Jane is fully capable of advocating for herself."

"Good." She forced a smile. "Then there is no use in further speculation on any hidden motives Dr. Harris may have."

"Fine," Will said. His eyes caught on something behind her, and his face went blank. "Apologies, but I must excuse myself. I'll see you both later." He stiffly got up from the table and buttoned up his suit jacket.

She turned to watch him leave the dining room and saw Oliver waiting for him.

"Do you know what could have drawn away his attention?"

KATE CROW

"He's befriended a porter here, and I think they have some sort of game going on."

"He's made a friend?" Tristan raised his eyebrows.

She nodded. "Yes, Oliver, he's the boy who was in the doorway. They've spent hours working in the garden together. It's very sweet."

Emotion flickered across Tristan's face as he cleared his throat. "I'm glad he has found someone to spend his time with."

She studied his face. Sibling relationships that weren't built on disdain still confused her. Her initial reaction was that he was jealous, but it looked more complex than that. "Are you worried about their bond?"

He shook his head. "No, I think it's a gift that he's found someone who makes it worth it for him to come out of his shell." He gave her a shaky smile, "Besides you, I mean."

Her eyes dropped to the cream colored tablecloth. "I'm not sure I've done all that much to help him."

"You have. I mean, to even see him showing his face in public is a gift I wasn't sure I would see again."

She snorted and looked back up at him. "That only happened after I yelled and threatened him, not because I healed his soul." She wasn't the type of woman who could heal anyone's soul.

"Which is exactly what he needs. He doesn't need some wilting flower he has to save at every opportunity. He needs someone who will put him in his place."

She shook her head because pushing back felt better than admitting the two of them were good for each other. "You know how deep his chivalry runs. I'm not the type of woman who wants or needs to be saved."

Tristan leaned in. "Which is exactly why you're perfect for him. You won't let him throw himself away."

"He is far too self-sacrificing."

"It must be nice for you to get him out of your hair from time to time as well," Tristan gave her a sly look. "Sometimes a bit of distance is needed when you're spending so much time with a *friend*."

Jane ignored the insinuation because they were friends. She still wanted to go on her own at some point, while he wanted to return to his garden back home.

"At first, I worried he would follow me around the whole term like a lost duckling."

Tristan laughed. "He can be rather single-minded sometimes, but once you've earned his loyalty, it will never waver."

She nodded. That was precisely why she had been so careful with him for so long. Even the idea of breaking his heart made her sick to her stomach. "Yes, and he deserves that same loyalty in return."

He studied her face for a long minute before he finally nodded. "Good, I couldn't accept anything less for him."

Her face heated, even though part of her was thrilled at passing such an important test. Picking up the teapot, she topped up both of their cups.

"I do have something important I would like to ask you now that Will is gone."

"Oh." Her stomach dropped at how serious Tristan's face was. "What do you need to know?"

"Does Harris still do that awful lecture, moaning about how difficult it is to get subjects for autopsies?"

Jane's shoulders dropped. "He does. It bothered Will, but I couldn't help but laugh. I can only imagine how much he spent on bribes to morticians before the laws against it took effect."

"I'm sure he visited quite a few graveyards with a shovel in his day."

They went back and forth, sharing pots of tea and gossiping about the professors. Tristan told her about those who held grudges against each other and other petty arguments that occurred over the years, while she told him about everything that had happened so far that term.

* * *

Several hours and many pots of tea later, she finally shut the door to her and Will's room behind her. Will had never rejoined them, but she was glad to see him now. However, she was surprised to see him at her writing desk.

"Who are you writing to?" She had only ever seen him write to Tristan.

Will turned towards her with a small smile. "I finally figured out the rest of the flowers I want to plant for spring, so I'm writing my seed contact in London in case any are difficult to source."

"I didn't realize one could even have a seed contact."

"It's very different from the contacts I used to have," he said, one corner of his mouth kicking up in a devastatingly handsome smile, "but if there's one thing I know from a life of debauchery, it's that there is a contact for everything."

"And what would your past self think of the fact that now your only contact is for seeds?"

"I think he would be thrilled that my contacts are still *seedy*."

"That was terrible," she said, smiling despite the truly awful joke.

"Yes, but you love me anyway."

Her smile faded. *Love*. It was a word she thought of occasionally regarding him, but she always concluded that she didn't love him. She couldn't. She loved science, school, and her freedom.

Will's eyes widened, as if he was experiencing similar panic. "I didn't mean it like that, obviously."

His words were correct, but she couldn't help but feel a twinge. "Of course."

Will said it with such a reassuring smile that most of her relaxed, even as a smaller part of her curdled at the idea of them being *friends*, even though she had insisted upon the title while talking to Tristan.

"How does one get a seed contact anyway?" She asked, bringing the conversation back to a safer place.

"Really, you can find anything in London. I found mine while looking to trade some of my clippings. I sent Mrs. Jones to different greenhouses with a letter to see if they had what I wanted."

"I'm sure she loved that job."

"Oh yes, it went over about as well as you'd imagine. I was pathetic enough that she said yes. Luckily, at the third greenhouse she tried, a young man was selling some of his plants. He overheard Mrs. Jones' requests and told her that if she gave him three days, he could get her everything on the list."

"Three days sounds impressive."

"Which is why I was further impressed when he did it in two. Now, I write him whenever I want something, and I always receive an envelope of seeds."

"That is quite impressive. It also explains why you're already planning so far ahead as well. We haven't even hit winter, and you're already planning for spring."

Will shrugged. "It sneaks up on you so much quicker than you think. Besides, it might be months before he sends them. He's never failed, but sometimes it takes him some time to locate them."

"When will you start planting?"

"The real work will start in February or March, but it depends on how much frost we get this winter."

"I'll certainly miss you, but I do hope all of your seeds come in." February was still months away, but it also felt far too soon. Already, she knew she would miss him terribly as he planted his garden.

Will frowned. "My days will certainly be full, but you'll still see me. I'll need to sleep sometime."

"Yes, but February is next term. I'll be back here after the winter break, and you'll be in York."

Will's frown instantly disappeared. "I'm planning the hotel garden. Here."

"Oh." Her stomach flipped at the realization, but she was also deeply pleased that he was staying with her. "I thought you were sending for seeds for your garden back in York."

"I've only been working on the hotel garden. It may not be mine, but I've grown to care for it. They'll hire someone around spring, but that likely won't be until after the planting is finished. Morris will take care of my garden back home."

"So, you'll be with me next term as well?

"Yes."

Her cheeks burned from holding the smile at Will's revelation. Love might be too big a word, but she certainly was glad he would continue to be with her. That was enough.

CHAPTER 32

*W*ill stifled an eye roll as Dr. Harris prattled on about his newest research proposal as the carriage bounced down the cobblestone street. Rain had rolled in overnight, leading Tristan and Dr. Harris to hitch a ride with Jane and Will. Jane suggested the arrangement as the four of them waited beneath the hotel awning, saying it was silly to wait for multiple carriages when they were all going to the same place.

Several days had passed since his spat with Jane regarding the professor. Will had made a silent vow to give the man another chance since the two people he cared for most looked up to the professor, but the man seemed desperate to make Will break that promise.

Jane and Tristan, however, were enthralled. They hung on to his every word, even though Will thought the man's idea to study automatic reflex centers sounded like an excuse for him to poke at a dead brain. He didn't understand how his brother could even feign interest in such a banal experiment. Tristan had managed to regenerate *life*, while this charlatan wanted a round of applause for rehashing someone else's discovery.

"What do you hope to accomplish with this research?" If Will were smart, he would have remained quiet, but no one had ever accused him of being smart.

Jane shot him a murderous look while the professor looked surprised that anyone dared to question him. Tristan's eyes danced between the three of them as he waited for the fireworks to start.

The carriage rolled to a stop, saving them from Will's poor impulse control. Jane threw the door open, dragging him out before he could dig himself into a deeper hole. Dr. Harris followed, frowning at Will.

"Thank you for the ride, Mrs. Byrne," Dr. Harris said warmly, before shooting Will a quick glare. "Hopefully, we will have the chance to finish this conversation later."

"Of course," Jane replied warmly. "You're more than welcome to ride back with us as well, even if the rain stops."

"Well, I certainly won't want to miss the ride back," Tristan said, jumping down, careful to miss the puddle on the drive. Will had the strongest urge to push him into that puddle.

Jane inclined her head to say her goodbyes before leading them to the library before her first class.

"I don't understand why you must antagonize him."

"Have you thought perhaps he is the one antagonizing me?"

"No, you decided you don't like him, so now you find fault in everything he does."

He sighed. "I am trying to give him a chance, but he makes it... difficult."

"Well, he's my professor and someone I happen to respect a lot." She pulled him into an alcove off the path. "I understand your concern, but if you really care about me, you'll leave him alone. If I have any concerns, I'll come to you."

Rain pounded on the stone awning as she waited for him to answer. As he looked at the stubbornness in her eyes, he saw the underlying truth of what she was telling him. This was her line in the sand, and if he crossed it, she might want to reevaluate their entire relationship.

"I only wanted to look out for you."

Any remaining tension in her face was replaced with tenderness. "I know." She placed her gloved hand over his. Even through all of the layers that separated them, he could feel the warmth of her touch. "You have a good heart, but I don't need you to try to fix all of my problems. I am more than capable of taking care of myself, and I want you to give me that respect."

His mouth was dry, and his heart pounded, but he nodded. She smiled at him, her head tilted back so she could see him beneath her wet bonnet. It would rip her apart if she ever found out about the deal he had made with Oliver.

"I'll be better for you, I swear."

This time, it was the truth because as soon as they got back to the hotel, he would tell Oliver to stop spying. It was another little fix, but he swore on his very soul it would be the last one for the rest of their lives.

He held his arm so he could deposit her where she belonged at the library. He would get her books, fill her pens with ink, or do anything else he could to support her.

* * *

BY THE AFTERNOON, the heavy rain had faded to a light mist, but they had been thoroughly soaked by then. His waterlogged cloak made a dull slap against the carriage door as he stepped out in front of the hotel. Lifting the heavy garment, he used it as a woolen shield for Jane as she stepped from the carriage. Skirts in hand, she dashed from the carriage to the covered veranda in just a few steps thanks to her long-legged stride.

He followed Jane, leaving his brother and Dr. Harris to navigate their own way.

"I'm going to be damp until spring," Jane said, frowning as water dripped from her cloak.

"I don't think that's likely." He removed his hat and shook it out, careful to make sure the water droplets sprayed opposite to where she stood. "Snow will overtake the rain, so you'll be damp for a few months and then frozen until spring."

"Must you do that here?"

Will turned to see Tristan, sputtering with his hands up to block the water that flew from his hat.

"Sorry," he said with a wry smile as he shook his hat directly at his brother. "But I can't help it if the water loves you."

Tristan glared daggers at him, and a memory of Tristan looking at him the same way after he splashed him while swimming as children flashed to his mind. The memory had only returned when he saw his brother glaring at him like a half-drowned cat.

"Maybe the water loves you too!" Tristan shook his hat wildly, spraying Will with some water, but his aim was so poor that he got Jane wet as well.

"No!" Jane shouted, wiping water from her face. "If you insist on playing in the rain, do it out there!"

Will grinned at his younger brother. "I guess the water doesn't like me after all."

"Oh, the joys of youth," Dr. Harris said, walking up the porch steps. He stopped at the mat to wipe the mud from his shoes. "If you will excuse me, my old bones and I will be holed up by the fire in my room with a hot toddy and the new serial novel I got in the post."

"At least someone around here has the right idea," Jane grumbled as she followed Dr. Harris inside.

Will held out his hand to his brother. "Truce?"

His brother eyed his outstretched hand with suspicion before finally taking it. "Truce."

Will clapped his hand on his brother's shoulder. The younger man's frame shook under the force. His wiry brother had always been the brains to Will's brawn, but while Tristan may have been physically weaker, he had always exacted his revenge in more creative ways.

Walking to the door shoulder to shoulder, Will dropped back to give Tristan the right of way so he could covertly squeeze water from his cloak into his brother's collar.

Tristan yelped as the cold water made contact. Rubbing the back of his neck, he grumbled. "You're a menace. I don't understand why anyone wants to be around you."

Will laughed. It was a strong sound that came right from his belly. He hadn't laughed like this since he died, but even before that, he wasn't sure the last time he felt this light. "I'm sorry to tell you, but you lost your chance to get rid of me."

Tristan froze, which caused Will's smile to waver, unsure if his joke was too far for his brother's sensitive heart.

"Do you want me to take those to dry, sir?" Oliver asked as he bounded over to them.

Will sighed as he handed the wet clothes to the exuberant porter. "What have I told you about calling me sir?"

The heavy, wet fabric slapped against the boy's back as he hefted the waterlogged clothes over his shoulder. "Sorry, Mr. Will, you know habit and all." His eyes shifted to Tristan and narrowed. It was the first time Will had seen him look anything other than happy.

"Have I had the chance to introduce you to my cousin, Dr. Gardner?"

"Mrs. Byrne introduced us when they had tea together the other day," Oliver shot Tristan another deeply distrustful look before leaning into Will, lowering his voice. "*Alone.*"

"Ah." Fighting to stave off his smile, he looked at his brother and saw they shared the same struggle now that the motive behind Oliver's dislike was known. "You can trust him. We're as close as brothers, and I know his friendship with Mrs. Byrne is quite chaste."

"I promise the bond I share with Mrs. Byrne is solely based on science." Tristan placed his hand over his heart.

Oliver's eyes narrowed further. "That's what Dr. Harris claims as well, but we've got our eyes on him."

"You do? Is Mrs. Byrne aware of this?" Tristan raised an eyebrow at Will.

Will's cheeks reddened. "Oliver, I've been thinking about it, and I don't think we need to take such precautions anymore. Mrs. Byrne is an adult who is more than capable of spending her time with whomever she chooses." Will grit his teeth to get that last point out, but it was important for Oliver to hear.

"Is your opinion of Mrs. Byrne so low that you think she can be seduced away?" Tristan asked, turning the psychological power of his eyebrow towards Oliver.

"No, sir, I know Mrs. Byrne is an honorable woman." Oliver steeled his spine, looking back up with a ferocity Will had never before seen from him. "But there's more than one way to take advantage of a woman, and I know I used to see him working in the dining room a lot, but I hardly see him working at all anymore, while Mrs. Byrne works her fingers to the bone for him."

Will gave Oliver a reassuring pat on the shoulder. He was a good kid who would turn into an even better man. "Thank you for all you've done. You don't have to worry about Mrs. Byrne. I'll take it from here."

Oliver nodded, then wished them a good day and took their outerwear somewhere to dry.

The brothers walked to one of the public rooms where Tristan settled into an armchair by the fire while Will poured them both a generous amount of brandy to warm their bones. There was no danger of a chill settling into him, but his brother could, so he needed to look out for him.

Handing Tristan one of the glasses, he then settled into the brown leather chair across from him. The fire crackled as he took a sip of the amber liquid.

"Has the visitor returned since we left?"

Since Will had been spending so much time with Jane, he hadn't had the chance to discuss her brother with Tristan yet. Using his name felt like evoking a demon, so he avoided it, but he knew Tristan understood precisely who he meant.

"Once, a few days after you left. It was only more bluster, but when he realized I couldn't be intimidated, he moved on, and I haven't seen him since."

"Do you know what he's up to?"

"No, I tried poking around for information, but the towns-people weren't forthcoming. What I do know is that there are two distinct sides, one that thinks she's dead and the other that's convinced she ran off."

Will rubbed his temples, bemoaning the mess this situation had become—yet another thing he should have considered before forcing Tristan to reanimate Jane. No part of him regretted that decision, but he still could have thought through a few of the finer points.

"Do you still feel the effects of alcohol?"

Will's head snapped up to see his brother's head tilted to the side. Will could see the wheels turning in his head. It was the look he always gave him when their time spent as brothers warred with his desire to continue his research.

"Sort of," he said, taking another sip. "It's mainly just the burn. If I drank a lot very quickly, I could probably get drunk, but I don't think it would last long."

"Yes, your metabolism has increased, so your body would quickly burn through the alcohol. It may be technically possible to beat it, but it would take a massive amount of liquor to maintain inebriation." Tristan's eyes unfocused as he retreated into his mind. He wasn't really speaking to Will, but processing information aloud.

"Is this how it's going to be now?" He hadn't meant to sound so bitter, but he couldn't help it.

"What do you mean?"

The look of utter confusion on his brother's face only stoked his flames. "Will we never again have a conversation where I'm not your experiment? Can't we just be brothers?"

"But we are brothers." Tristan's brow furrowed.

"It hardly feels that way anymore." In so many ways, his brother was absolutely brilliant, but he always had trouble separating his life from his work. "Every time we have a conversation, I tense because I'm waiting for you to bring it back to your research."

"I'm just trying to help—"

"It makes me feel like nothing more than your experiment. Every time we speak, it feels like you're waiting for me to reveal something you might find interesting. It feels like the only thing I am to you is your creation."

Will's chest heaved. He hadn't meant to have this conversation now, but once he started, he couldn't stop. Tristan's eyes were downcast, and his empty glass of brandy lay forgotten in his lap. Upsetting Tristan had always made Will feel as if he had kicked a puppy, but perhaps he had spent too much time trying to protect him.

"When they told me you died, it felt like my own soul had withered away." his brother's voice was barely louder than a whisper. The fireplace crackled like a gunshot in the silence. "I wasn't even thirty and already, I lost everyone I loved. I was completely alone in the world, save for Mrs. Jones, but she had always liked you best." He wiped at his glassy eyes, giving Will a shaky smile.

"Nonsense," he said, voice thick with emotion. "You know she loves you."

"She does, but you are her favorite. The only reason she's still around is to take care of you."

Will cleared his throat. Talk of favoritism had always made him uncomfortable, since Mrs. Jones had chosen him because their parents chose sweet, precocious Tristan. Will may have been their heir, but Tristan was their light.

"She doesn't need to stick around to take care of me. I'd support her through any retirement she wanted."

"And how has that worked out for you?" Tristan snorted. He stood up from the plush armchair, picking up Will's empty glass to top off both their drinks.

He made her the offer many times over the years, and the housekeeper responded with a scowl each time, saying he wouldn't get rid of her until she was ready, and not a moment before.

"I knew there was such a minuscule chance that bringing you back would work, but I couldn't stop because that would mean accepting you were gone. No one was more surprised than I when it worked."

"I promise you that's not true."

Tristan snorted. "That's fair." Tristan handed him his drink, a far more generous pour than Will had given. "It was difficult for me and Mrs. Jones to see you so adrift. It didn't matter where we moved or what I did, you always locked yourself away."

"I tried," he rasped. It wasn't his fault that he had been consumed by melancholy, but he felt ashamed all the same. "I know it didn't look like it, but I wanted to do more than just survive. I wanted to live."

"I always saw how hard you tried, which was why I was so desperate to help. If I thought you had given up, maybe it would have been different." Tristan flashed him a small smile, and for the first time, he saw the weariness his brother must have carried for years. It wasn't just his younger brother before him, but a man whose genius caused him to grow up too soon and gave him achievements he could never share.

"Why did you push so hard for the symposium to happen?"

Tristan sighed as he walked to the fireplace. He rested his forearm against the mantle while he stared at the flickering flames. The room filled with quiet chatter as other patrons came in to enjoy their pre-dinner brandy, but they gave the brothers a wide berth.

"I know it seems purely selfish, but I wasn't trying to be. I thought I was being helpful," he said with a mirthless laugh, turning back to Will. "I thought if the world knew, then you would be free. I wasn't too far off. Look at how you've blossomed with Jane in your life."

"What do you mean?" Will said, shifting in the chair. This one wasn't as narrow as the one that had been in their room, but it was still a tight fit.

"We're sitting together in a public room having a conversation face-to-face. You barely looked at me a few months ago."

As Will looked around the room, he noted most of the chairs were filled. It was a combination of men and a few couples. There were people he knew from being around the hotel, and also total strangers. Not a single one looked his way.

"I never imagined that no one would stare."

"This is all I ever wanted for you. I knew you could have a normal life."

"I didn't think it was possible," he said, clearing his throat. "What else were you hoping to achieve?"

His brother was silent for a long time as they both sipped their drinks. The crowd dissipated as the dining room opened for dinner.

"Some of it was to feed my ego," Tristan started. "I wanted to show everyone the miracle I achieved. But it's still so much about the science. We can learn how the body heals and how blood flow works. Look at how far we've come in the area of anatomy in the twenty-odd years since autopsies have become normalized. This could be our chance to advance medicine."

Will nodded, downing the rest of his brandy and placing the empty glass on the table beside him. Tristan's ideals were right, even though his previous plan was flawed.

"I don't want just to be your laboratory subject. I want to have a life outside of being poked and prodded. No townspeople or journalists, keep it to a small number of academics."

Tristan looked up at him, startled. "Of course."

"And only me. Jane needs to be kept out of it."

"Shouldn't that be her choice?"

"Involve her behind the scenes if she wants, but news of her can't get back to her brother."

His hands shook with a tremor as he thought about what he was doing. This would leave him exposed. Everyone would know his life was unnatural, but he had to do it not just for Tristan and Jane and the pursuit of science, but for himself as well. He didn't know what his life would look like in ten, twenty, or even one hundred years, but he didn't want to spend his life running from the truth of what he was.

Will stood up, buttoning his suit jacket. "I'll do it, but not until the end of the school year. I don't want to interrupt Jane's schooling."

With his mind finally made up, he wished his brother a good night and went upstairs to see the woman who had made him see the value in science.

CHAPTER 33

*T*hursday was Jane's least favorite day on campus. Her two classes were more than three hours apart, and even worse, she wasn't allowed in the library on Thursdays.

"Are you going to sit down or do you plan on marching back and forth all day?" Will asked, sprawled on the bench. His head was tipped back, and his eyes were closed.

"I'm not marching," she said as she stopped. She had been walking, but it wasn't even a pace, let alone a march.

Will lifted his head. "You definitely are. Soldiers aren't half as dedicated as you."

"I don't march!" She huffed. "If anything, I'm strolling."

"Well, you're strolling a divot into the grass."

She plopped down next to him. "Are you happy now?"

"Quite," he said before resuming his previous position. One arm was across the armrest while the other was draped on the back of the bench. His knee rested against her thigh; he was encroaching on her space by taking up more than half of the bench, but she didn't mind.

He was so much taller than the back of the bench that she couldn't imagine it was comfortable. Still, she envied how he could relax anywhere while she could barely relax in her own bed.

"Are you going to fall asleep?"

"Maybe." His long eyelashes settled down on his cheek. "I won't be able to if you keep shaking the bench with your fidgeting."

"You're the one who wanted me to sit!" She huffed, adjusting her position yet again.

"What's bothering you?"

"Nothing." It was a knee-jerk reaction, a side effect of relying on herself for so many years.

"Liar," he said, the side of his mouth ticking. "Let's try that again. What's bothering you?"

"What am I doing here?"

"Going to school."

"But what will I have to show at the end of this? I can't sit for exams or receive a degree. Do I go to school for years while I wait for my rights to catch up? Eventually, someone will notice I'm not aging."

"That will take at least a decade, if not longer. You're young and stay indoors. Besides, no one knows how old you are right now." Will frowned. "I don't know how old you are."

"I'm twenty-nine." She had never been a person who shied away from her age, but she never had to be concerned with such vanity again.

"I would have guessed younger. We could probably get close to fifteen years in one place."

"I don't know if I can do fifteen years as a student here."

"You don't have to. We can be here for as long as you want."

"But where would we go? What would we do?"

Suddenly, she had so much time she couldn't even think of how to fill it. There were so many things she wanted to do, but the options also felt paralyzing.

"We could stay here for a year or two or go back to York. I have a flat in London, or we could go to Tristan's townhome in Munich. We could do a tour of the continent or even go to the Americas."

"I still want to be able to work. I don't think I want to travel right now."

Will shrugged. "That's fine with me. I've spent most of my adult life traveling, so it would be nice to put some roots down for a while."

Jane smoothed her black skirt. "I like working with Tristan. After I'm done with school, do you think we can go with him?"

"Of course."

"You're very agreeable."

"Your demands are easy. It's not exactly an imposition to spend time with my brother."

That was a foreign feeling to her, but she hated sullying her new life with thoughts of Robert. He had no power over her life anymore, so she wouldn't give him power over her feelings.

"Is there anything you want to do?"

"Actually," Will said, sitting up straight. "I do have something, but it can wait until the summer. I want to do Tristan's symposium."

"Really?" This was the one thing Will could have said to shock her. He detested being poked and prodded.

"Yes. I've learned the importance of science. Plenty of innovations and discoveries could be made with this information, so I figured I might as well help as much as I can. But only me. I don't think you should be revealed on stage."

Her face fell into her familiar scowl. "Why not?"

"You deserve your freedom." Will reached out and placed his hand over hers. "If people knew you had died, they would want to experiment on you. Maybe even in worse ways. I can handle it, but I want you to have the option to go off and have a life of your own. Besides, I won't make it easier for Robert to find you."

Her scowl fell because it was undeniably sweet. She knew the idea of her leaving bothered him, but he always supported her. It made her not want to leave.

"I suppose I can accept that. However, I want to help Tristan any way I can."

"I would expect nothing less."

Blushing, her eyes dropped to the grass. "If only everyone else believed in me as you do."

His hand brushed against her cheek, causing her to look up into the warm, honey-yellow eyes she had come to know as well as her own. Leaning into his touch, she soaked up the support he offered that was nothing to him, but everything to her.

"They will. One day they'll see how smart you are and how much work you've been putting in."

"But how long must I wait for the world to catch up?" Tears welled up behind her eyes, but she willed them to dissipate because she couldn't cry in front of the building that housed her next class. She would never break into the boys' club if they caught her crying.

"I don't know how long it will take, but I do know that it *will* happen."

"Even if it takes one hundred years?"

"Even if it takes one thousand," he murmured, leaning down and brushing a soft kiss against her lips. It was chaste, but still scandalous for the middle of the courtyard.

Though it wasn't even close to the most scandalous thing they had done on school grounds.

"If it takes one thousand years for me to become a full student, I'm pitching myself into a volcano."

Will laughed, his eyes crinkling at the corners. If she had to spend forever with anyone, she was glad it was him.

* * *

THE SCHOOL LABORATORY didn't look anything like what she had expected. She imagined it to be a sterile white room with two long tables that housed a dozen microscopes each, but still left enough room for a notepad so they could scribble down their observations. Glass beakers and flasks would line the walls filled with various liquids, ready for experiments.

However, this room was a smaller lecture hall with most of the seats removed. The walls might have once been white, but they had faded to a dirty grey. A cracked wooden podium stood at the front of the room that looked too unstable to hold a stack of papers. Most disappointingly, there were only two microscopes.

The two microscopes sat on the table next to the sad podium:

one shiny, brass microscope and one tarnished silver one that looked to be many years out of date. Two microscopes for a class of twenty-five people was a travesty in time management. Three slides were stacked beside each microscope, but these weren't the clean glass slides she had used in Tristan's lab. These were chipped and yellow.

"What's wrong?" Will asked. They were still arm in arm, but she had stopped in the doorway to take in the disappointing scene.

"It's nothing like I dreamt it would be," she sighed, walking over to the desk nearest the microscopes. If she would only get a few moments with one, she would make the most of her time.

They were the first in the room, which wasn't unusual because they were typically the first arrivals for the lectures as well, but it made her nervous all the same. Logically, she knew she was in the correct room—the notice on the door confirmed she was—but it still felt like it could be a cruel joke from her classmates.

"It certainly doesn't look like much," Will said, frowning as he surveyed the room. "Harris has bemoaned the lack of funding from the department. It looks to be even more dire than we imagined."

"I suppose working in Tristan's lab has spoiled me."

There was no comparison between the two. Tristan's lab was clean and modern, while this was a relic of a bygone era.

Will snorted. "Certainly, I don't think he has ever spared a single expense in his entire life. Private funding makes all the difference."

Walking around the desk that held the microscope, she took them in from every angle. The brass one looked similar to the one in Tristan's lab, but the ocular lens was shorter. The other was older; the metal had been tarnished in places where the students had held it over the years.

"Do they pass your muster?" Will asked.

She shrugged. "I'm no expert, but they both look like they work. I'll have to wait until I use it to declare if they're both satisfactory."

The door opened, and Jane saw Dr. Harris enter. Tension melted out of her at his sight as her irrational fear of being in the wrong place had been quelled.

"Oh, Hello, Mrs. Byrne." Dr. Harris stopped when he spotted her.

"Good Afternoon, I was starting to worry we had the incorrect location."

"No," he said as he continued to the podium. His eyes were fixed on the papers in his hands. "You've found the correct location."

"Good." Her voice pitched up as she tried to keep her tone casual, noting his strange behavior. "I'm excited to learn how to use these microscopes. I've never worked with either model before."

The professor slowly shuffled his papers on the podium, keeping his eyes downcast. Dread curled inside of her since he hadn't met her eye since he entered the room.

"Are you here to drop off my next batch of research?"

"No, I wasn't aware there was a deadline." She had already returned the stack he had given her the other day, and when he gave her the new stack yesterday evening, he didn't mention a deadline. "I can get them to you by Saturday."

"That will be fine," he said, rubbing the back of his neck, and finally looked up. "I suppose I'm curious as to why you're here then."

That simple statement rocked her. Her hands curled into fists at her side, not to control any violence, but because she had to keep from showing a reaction. Will had gone completely still, and she could feel the rage emanating from him. She prayed he would stay out of the confrontation to come.

"I'm here for class, of course." It was a miracle she kept the tremor from her voice. She gave him a bland smile even as bile gathered in her mouth.

Dr. Harris cleared his throat before returning to fiddling with his papers. "I thought you were aware of the policy."

"What policy?" Her mouth felt like sandpaper. Oh, she was going to be sick, but she prayed against all hope that it didn't happen in this room. One humiliation was plenty.

"Women aren't allowed to be in the lab."

"Oh." It felt like her heart had been ripped out of her chest. Her fists tightened, pushing her fingernails deep into her palm. The pain was almost a relief as it gave her something else to focus on.

"And who decided to ban women from the lab?"

Her head snapped to Will, who glowered at Dr. Harris as he waited for the answer to his question. Jane could see him prepare his defense of her as if he were a knight riding into battle to save her.

"Don't." She hated that he was a witness to her humiliation; she didn't need him to get involved as well. "It doesn't matter who made the policy."

"No," Will walked towards Jane. He reached for her arm, but she shook him off. "He needs to tell you, he owes you that much."

Dr. Harris's annoyed expression burned the numbness away, leaving rage in its wake. How dare he expect her to accept this injustice?

The door opened behind her with a cacophony of sound that meant her classmates had arrived. Fantastic, an even bigger audience was what this moment lacked.

"This is precisely why many of my colleagues and I believe women have no place at Cambridge."

"If women are such a burden in academics, then why have my wife work for you?"

Jane flinched at Will's use of wife. She wanted to throw it back in his face that she was not and never would be his *wife*, but she was forced to hold her tongue.

"Women aren't without their uses. I've found they're best utilized for clerical work, which is the work I have provided Mrs. Byrne." Dr. Harris looked up at Will with an arched eyebrow, challenging his ire. "Work that she asked for without complaint."

"Only because she saw you as a mentor and thought you would teach her. Instead, you used her as free labor." Will took a step forward, and her hand shot out to stop him, gripping his black suit jacket so hard the fabric stretched.

The room was so quiet that all she heard was the hammering of her heart. It was the only time her classmates had ever been silent.

She knew the moment class was over, this juicy piece of gossip would spread around the school like wildfire.

"Stop it," she hissed. "I don't want your help."

"I hoped she would be easier to deal with since she was married, but that's clearly not the case."

"I don't need anyone to control me," she snarled. Her vision clouded as she shook with rage. She released Will's sleeve and pushed him away. "You're nothing more than a mediocre academic in the twilight of his career. Your research is incoherent and uninspired, yet you expect the world to be handed to you because you've been in this job for far too long."

Turning on her heel, she stormed off without another word because she was too angry to remain in that room for another moment. She was sick of Dr. Harris, her classmates, and all the men who thought they were better than her just because they were men.

The door slammed behind her, startling everyone in the hallway and causing more men to stare at her. She wanted to scream, to pitch a fit, and smash one of the wooden chairs against the ground until it splintered. If they wanted to stare, then she could give them a show.

Instead, she briskly walked out, throwing the doors open to the courtyard. Will would come after her any minute, and she didn't want to deal with him either. It didn't matter that he tried to defend her because he went all growly and possessive after she repeatedly told him she didn't want him to do so. Technically, she wasn't supposed to be unchaperoned on campus, but if anyone had a problem with it, they had to catch her first.

Will was right. That was the single worst part about all of this: she had been warned and didn't listen. No, instead she laughed him off. Told him he was paranoid when in reality she was blindingly naive. Again.

Weaving through the buildings, she wanted to make it difficult for Will to trail her. As far as she was concerned, he was part of the problem, so she needed to get as much distance between them as possible before she burned their relationship to the ground as well.

She wanted to be alone. It was better that way. Safer.

Stone pavement gave way to soft grass as she passed from the campus to the road. It hadn't yet rained that day, but the many previous days of rain kept the grass soft and the road muddy.

When she reached the road, she turned back, frowning as she scanned campus one last time before she left. No one had come after her. It was both a blessing and something that hurt her irrationally. She stomped off down the road. She wanted to be alone anyway.

A gust of wind blew towards her, causing her to blink away the tears caused by the sharp chill. She clutched her wool coat close. Manic laughter bubbled from her at having to walk against the wind in addition to everything else.

Nothing she did had any effect on her life. She killed herself only to be brought back immortal. She excelled at her schoolwork just to be dismissed by teachers and students alike. She shrank herself in every way, only for the world to carve more flesh from her.

A carriage rolled past her, the wheels spraying her with cold, wet mud from her head to her hem. Wiping mud from her face, she tried to rescue the worst of it before the stain set. It was her favorite cloak, her warmest cloak, and now she'd have to wash it, and it would take days to dry.

She stared at the mound of mud in her hand, mud that became her problem because the carriage was moving too fast on the road. The driver saw her, and the considerate choice would have been to slow down, but he declined to do so.

The tears she held on such a tight leash finally broke through, which made the inferno inside of her burn brighter. Now she was angry, cold, dirty, and crying in the middle of the road.

The glob of mud taunted her. She needed to clean her hands, but her handkerchief was in her book bag, which she had left behind with Will. The offending carriage was still in sight, not too far in front of her. Before she could think better of it, she took a few big steps and lobbed the mud at the carriage. It hit the lacquered black wood with a satisfying slap before sliding down, leaving behind a filthy trail in its wake.

The carriage rolled to a stop, which made her bravado waver. She was a sobbing, mud-covered woman clearly in the midst of a breakdown on the side of the road, and she prayed her clear instability was enough to defend her from a prissy lord's anger.

The door to the carriage opened, and her heart thumped. She was ready to run. Once again, her impulsiveness was coming back to haunt her.

"Jane! Jane Montgomery, is that you?" Her heart stuttered, and her blood ran cold as one of her worst fears materialized.

" $\mathcal{I}$ can't believe you're really here. Everyone thinks you're dead." Eleanor's lip quivered, making Jane terrified that the woman was about to burst into tears.

"I don't know who you're talking about," she lied, shifting her eyes to try to find the best escape route. Unfortunately, they were on a rural stretch of road with vast open fields on either side.

Eleanor walked towards her. She wore a pale blue dress with a thin wrap over her shoulders. Her hem dragged in the mud with every step.

"Oh Jane, it is you!" The woman threw herself into Jane's arms, bursting into tears as Jane awkwardly caught her so she didn't face-plant into the mud.

"Oh, um, I'm terribly sorry, but I'm actually Mrs. Byrne. I'm very sorry to hear about your friend," she said while woodenly patting Eleanor on the back.

Dealing with tears had never been one of her strengths, but it touched something deep inside of her to know these tears were for her.

Eleanor lifted her head to look at Jane with puffy red eyes. Her brow furrowed as she studied Jane's face. "What's your first name then?"

Jane hesitated. Using her real first name would be a problem, but Will swore it would be easier than training to use a new one. Now she couldn't even think of another name.

"Well, it *is* Jane, but I'm a different Jane."

"It is you," Eleanor wailed. "I couldn't believe it when they said you died. Then Robert started behaving so strangely, and I knew something had to be going on."

"Ah." She didn't know how to respond since it didn't feel right to keep trying to convince her of the lie, but coming clean wasn't an option because she had someone to think of other than herself. No one would get to Will if she could help it.

"What happened?"

She shimmied out of Eleanor's grasp. "Not here, if we must talk, we need to go somewhere private."

Running wasn't an option, not when Eleanor would follow. Besides, she needed to know what Eleanor knew about Robert. It had been too easy for her to forget the troubles of her past life, but now she needed to know what Robert was up to. If he believed she was alive, he would stop at nothing to find her.

Eleanor nodded. "Of course, I'll tell my driver to keep going in circles so we can speak for as long as you need. My husband is traveling separately, so we'll be alone."

Jane followed Eleanor into the carriage. The outside was finished in a shiny black lacquer, but the inside felt cozy. The black wood continued inside, but the seats were upholstered with a rich purple fabric that felt soft beneath her fingers. Jane cringed at the thick streaks of mud she tracked in, but Eleanor didn't seem to notice the mess. Matching purple curtains tied back with gold tassels hung over the windows, framing the view of the countryside.

"That's how I saw you," Eleanor said, motioning to the windows. "At first, I thought you were a hallucination because it seemed like wishful thinking to spot you here of all places, but I would recognize that scowl anywhere." Tears gathered in her eyes, and her voice wavered. "But then I heard the mud hit the carriage, and it was an action that was so *you* I knew I had to stop. And there you were."

"I apologize for throwing mud at your carriage. It was incredibly childish."

Eleanor waved her off. "Oh, don't worry. It's only a bit of mud." Eleanor pulled a lace handkerchief from her bag and dabbed her eyes. She then reached back into the bag to pull out a sturdier handkerchief and handed it to Jane.

"Thank you," Jane murmured.

The handkerchief was a thick white cotton, free of any embellishments or embroidery, so she didn't feel bad about using it to wipe away the muck.

"What happened, Janie?"

Jane wiped her face first before methodically cleaning her hand, taking care to dig out the mud from beneath her fingernails. She wasn't sure where Eleanor would take her, but she wanted to look presentable when they got there.

"What was Robert's story?" She knew Robert tried to find her because he showed up at the Gardner home, but that was weeks after she left the house. What she didn't know was what happened both before and after her brother's visit.

"He said you had contracted an illness and died before a doctor could get there. He rushed a funeral, claiming his grief was too great to waste time."

Jane stifled an eye roll. She wasn't surprised that Robert's plan was bad, but she was disappointed. How had he so thoroughly outmaneuvered her in life, but then gotten sloppy after her death? Unacceptable.

"After the funeral," Eleanor continued. "Your lawyer came forward with your will, and that's when his story changed. He said he only *thought* you had died, but he wasn't sure because you were missing and he assumed you were dead because that's the only way you would be missing without a trace."

"How did he explain burying a coffin?"

Eleanor snorted. "He said he filled it with rocks. The constable had it exhumed and confirmed there wasn't a body inside. It was a fairly pathetic showing."

She was grateful that someone else thought Robert's plan was idiotic. Pivoting from a bad lie to the truth was risky when the truth also sounded like a lie.

"Why did he say he faked my death?"

"He said he had reason to believe you had killed yourself, and decided to lie because he didn't want the shame of your suicide tarnishing your memory."

Jane squeezed her hands; the idea that her brother saw shame in her desperation made her want to scream. "Did people believe him?"

"Mr. Anderson fought against it. He worked with the watchmen to determine you went missing the same day you updated your will, which everyone found highly suspicious."

"What did Robert have to say to that?"

"He had been successfully stonewalling the authorities until then. He hid behind his grief, and they didn't push too hard at first. That is, until your fiancé came back." Eleanor folded her arms across her chest. "Why didn't you tell me you were engaged?"

Jane grimaced; she had nearly forgotten about Lord Percy. "There was nothing to tell since I never agreed to marry him."

The corner of Eleanor's mouth twitched. "I figured as much, but I wanted to make sure. Everyone was shocked when a *baron* showed up, saying you were to be wed." Eleanor grimaced, eyes turning down. "I mean no offense by this, but we were shocked a lord would be interested in you."

"I'm not offended. I had similar thoughts when I was told the news."

"That made your solicitor even more suspicious, because then two men had financial interest in you, and maybe even a motive."

"A motive? Did they investigate Robert for murder?"

Not even in Jane's wildest dreams did she think her brother could be arrested for her murder.

Eleanor shook her head. "There hasn't been an arrest because

Robert now insists you ran away. Lord Percy says he wants you returned to him or your body found."

"I'm not Percy's. I never was," Jane grumbled. She had assumed once he learned of her death, Lord Percy would move on to find another woman with a sizable inheritance.

"He left York before I did, so there's a chance he's given up on you after all. Most of what I hear is from gossip, and the people in town are far more interested in your brother than the lord who's a stranger."

Jane understood because gossip this good was rare up there. The Montgomery Mines were one of the largest employers in the area, so she was well known despite being a reclusive spinster.

"What happened?" Eleanor asked softly.

"I need you to promise you won't discuss this with anyone, not even your husband." Jane folded her arms across her chest and set her jaw in a hard line.

Jane knew it was a big ask, but she had people to protect. After a short deliberation, Eleanor gave a sharp nod, and Jane told her of the mess her life had been. She told her about the fake will, Robert burning her library, and Percy's threats.

"Since I couldn't trust anyone, I planned my escape. I created a will because I knew I would be presumed dead, and then I ran away."

It was enough of the truth that she didn't feel bad lying to Eleanor. The only details she needed were that Jane had successfully escaped a bad situation.

"Leave it to Jane Montgomery to perfectly plan her disappearance. I can't say I'm surprised you would be able to pull off something like this, but I am impressed."

"So you understand my need to remain hidden? I can't go back."

Eleanor shook her head hard. "I won't, I promise. Especially now that I know what a snake Robert is."

It would be easy for her to be mad at the fact that it had taken so long for someone to see how she suffered at her brother's hands. No one cared to notice until she had been pushed over the edge, but Jane only felt relief. She had finally been seen, and Eleanor would never betray her. Eleanor had been a better friend than Jane ever deserved, but she was thankful for the opportunity to improve.

"What are you doing out here, Eleanor?"

"I'm interested in attending next year, so I thought I would visit to see what it's like. I have a meeting with a professor and was promised a campus tour." Eleanor clapped her hands. "Oh! We'll be able to attend school together just like we dreamed about when we were girls."

Jane gave her a tight smile. "Great," she said with fake enthusiasm as a knot formed in her stomach. "Which professor are you meeting with?"

"Dr. Harris, I've heard he's the best scientist at Cambridge."

Eleanor's excitement was so pure she didn't want to taint it, but Jane knew she had to burst her bubble to save her friend from future heartbreak.

"He's deeply mediocre," she said, fighting through her bitterness. "Even worse, he has a problem with female students. He thinks we're less capable than our male counterparts."

"There really is no escape from men, is there?"

"No."

"Well," Eleanor sighed. "No one said this mission of ours would be easy?"

"What mission?"

"Gaining women the right to an education. We'll do the hard work now so it will be easier on the next generation."

"I'm not sure if I'm doing much for the advancement of women here." The memory of this afternoon reared its ugly head.

"You are."

The women settled into a comfortable silence, and Jane watched Eleanor as she dug through her bag looking for something. Removing a pair of spectacles, Eleanor put them on before picking up her book.

"Are the glasses new, or were you better at hiding them when you were younger?"

"They're new," Eleanor said, her cheeks turning red. "My eyes have gotten worse this year to the point where I could barely read. You should consider yourself lucky that you don't need a pair yet. Time comes for us all."

They'd known each other for twenty years, growing together from children to women. Eleanor would continue to change; the years would put lines on her face, and her blonde hair would turn grey, while Jane would remain the same.

Eleanor worked for a future she would never see, while Jane would be able to see this through. It didn't matter how many years it would take; one day, she would not only become a full student but also earn a degree and even become a doctor. Progress may take time, but people like Eleanor would never rest until every woman had been uplifted.

Squaring her shoulders, Jane decided she would take on the task as well. Eleanor might never see the fruits of her labor, but Jane would do it for them both.

CHAPTER 35

*W*ill wanted nothing more than to throttle Harris until he saw the life flicker from his eyes. That stupid, cruel man. Humiliating Jane in front of her peers was a new low, even for a man Will did not like or respect.

When she finally left the room, he was relieved that Jane's terror was over. Part of him wanted nothing more than to follow her. He wanted to take her in his arms and hold her as she grieved, but he couldn't let this fool's abhorrent behavior stand.

Stalking towards the cowardly man, Will let all of his hatred for the man bleed out onto his face.

"Listen here, Harris," He didn't care to keep his voice low since he knew the entire room was hanging onto his every word. "I've let a lot of what you've done slide because my wife wanted me to, but you have lost all of that goodwill. If you ever speak to my wife like that ever again, I will *end* you."

Harris' eyes widened until the full whites of his eyes could be seen through his spectacles, and he went to say something, but Will cut him off.

"I know you only think that means hitting you or some other physical altercation, but remember, I come from a powerful family, and I can end you in so many more devastating ways. No one would even hire you to polish slides when I'm through with you."

Will was sure it would have felt great to hit him, but the look of fear in the professor's eyes was far more satisfying. Especially since this was an ongoing threat, and he could only hope to see the fear in his eyes each time he saw the man from now on.

"And all of you," he said, stepping back to look around the room so there was no question that this warning extended to all of them as well. "I expect you all to treat my wife with the respect she deserves. You fools could learn a thing or two from her if you took the chance to talk to her. The world is changing, and you'll be left behind if you don't change."

Some of the boys had the good sense to look chastened, but he knew that many wouldn't care. That wasn't his problem, since the only thing he cared about now was that Jane was somewhere out there hurting.

* * *

RUNNING his hands through his hair, Will knew he looked crazed standing in the muddy road. He hadn't been too far behind Jane, but he couldn't even find a hint of a trail. There were a few muddy imprints that might have been footsteps, but he wasn't sure if they were hers. Or if they were really even footsteps. Tracking was not one of his strengths.

When he didn't find Jane anywhere on campus, he decided to walk back to the hotel. While they frequently took the carriage to campus, Jane preferred to walk. Besides, he couldn't imagine her having the patience to hire a carriage when she was that angry.

When the hotel came into view, the sky opened up and poured rain down on him. Lovely. The mud already made his steps difficult, but now his boots were sticking with his every step, causing him to fling mud when he finally got them free. By the time he returned to the room, his boots, trousers, and cloak were all a travesty, but he ignored the looks he got as he tracked mud through the lobby.

"Jane," he exclaimed, bursting through the door, searching for her scowling face, but the room was empty.

On the walk over, he had convinced himself she was in the room, but now that she wasn't, he grew concerned. Jane was highly independent and liked her space, but she wasn't one to run off. She was hurt and embarrassed, but he didn't think she would leave without a word.

Unease filled him as he searched the room for clues to whether she had been there. The small brown bag she used as a suitcase was in the closet, and all of her clothes seemed to be there. It wasn't until he found her new copy of *Grey's Anatomy* that he relaxed. She would leave her clothes—and maybe even him—behind, but she would never abandon a book.

Stomping back to the lobby, he received more glares from the hotel's employees. He supposed he could have changed or at least wiped down his boots, but Jane had so consumed his thoughts that he had forgotten about the mud.

"Mr. Byrne!"

Will turned to see a red-faced Oliver bounding towards him.

"Oliver, have you seen Mrs. Byrne?" He doubted the boy had seen Jane, but he needed to be sure.

"No, sir, but I've been trying to find you. Someone checked into the hotel today with a lot of questions, but I didn't tell him anything. None of us did."

"What kind of questions?" Will asked, heart pounding as fear sparked within him.

"A man came in wanting to know if we had seen a woman who looked like Mrs. Byrne. He said his sister had run off, and he worried she was being taken advantage of. He said she was rather innocent and easily tricked by someone trying to get her fortune."

"How are you so sure it's Mrs. Byrne?"

Will felt like he was going to be sick. Never once did he think Jane's brother would find them.

"He knew how tall she was and how she's always got her head in a book or writing in a journal." Oliver hesitated, but he could see the sympathy in his eyes. "He also looks just like her. His room is on the bottom floor, and he's not here right now. Though I'm not sure how long he'll be gone."

"Thank you, Oliver. I appreciate your discretion. Keep me posted on his movements."

Will dug in his pocket, pulling out several bills that he shoved at Oliver before turning back to go out to the veranda. He prayed he found Jane before her brother did.

Gravel crunched as he walked down the drive. Jane had gone on more of her independence trips to bookstores, the modiste, a bakery, and she had even picked up some trousers Will had sent to the tailor to be repaired. Her next mission was to go to a pub on her own, but she had been putting it off because it made her nervous. If he had the day she had, he would have high-tailed it to a pub, but he wasn't sure if she would break that barrier or not.

A black carriage rolled down the driveway, and his heart pounded in hope that she would get out so he could whisk her away to safety. Before the driver had even fully stopped, the door was thrown open, and a dark blur shot out like a cannon.

It was Jane. He opened his arms in preparation for the hug that was sure to come. He had never expected her to run into his arms, but he certainly wouldn't complain. Before he could gather her into his arms, she stopped short of him.

"Have you ever met Eleanor Campbell?" She asked quietly, throwing her arms around his neck so she could lift his hood. His face wasn't covered like it used to be, but he was shadowed.

"What?" The name wasn't familiar, but he couldn't be sure because he had always been terrible with names.

"Eleanor Campbell. I don't remember her husband's first name, but I'm pretty sure he's a sailor. She knows your brother, and I need to know if you have ever met."

"Oh." He looked up to see a blonde woman exit the carriage with a bemused look. She didn't look familiar. "I don't think so. Who is she?"

"A friend I've known for many years." Jane looked behind her and smiled, but her eyes were tight.

He frowned. "I didn't think you had any friends."

It sounded rude, but in all the weeks of stories they shared, she had never once mentioned a friend. All of her stories were marked with a sense of loneliness.

"It's complicated, but she's never taken no for an answer, so I have finally accepted we are friends. There's no time to go over this with you. She doesn't know we're pretending to be married, and I told her I ran away from Robert. Let me do all the talking."

"Janie, I don't think I've ever seen you move quite so fast before," the blonde woman said as she approached them.

"Yes, well, I knew Mr. Byrne here was worried, and I wanted to assure him that I was fine."

The other woman's lips twitched. "I see," she said, craning her head to look up at him. He pushed back his hood so she could get a better look.

"You're quite tall."

He wasn't sure if Jane didn't want him to talk a lot or if she expected him to be completely silent. "I am," he said after Jane remained silent. It felt rude not to answer.

She smiled before turning her gaze towards Jane. "I like him. You make sense together."

"It's not like that," Jane said quickly. He would be offended at her diminishing of their relationship if it wasn't for the fact that she was bright red and stammering.

"I said you needed a tall man. I'm glad you finally listened."

"We're friends. He's been helping me around school as my chaperone."

"Well, whatever you're calling it these days, I'm glad you've found someone." She turned to Will with a brilliant smile. "I'm Mrs. Campbell. Miss Montgomery hasn't told me nearly enough about you, but I hope we can remedy that immediately."

"Don't use Montgomery," Jane hissed. "I'm using a different name here."

"What name should I use?"

Jane turned a deep, deep crimson. "Byrne," she choked out.

"What an interesting name," Mrs. Campbell said with a grin.

"I'm sure you need to get ready for dinner, and we have an

engagement as well," Jane said, pulling him away before either he or Mrs. Campbell could say another word, and she didn't let go until they were locked inside their room.

They silently stood before each other, and he didn't know what to say. Will was so thankful that he had gotten to her before her brother did, but so much had happened since he saw her last that he wasn't quite sure where to start.

"You're dripping on the rug," Jane said.

Will looked down to see that his cloak had created a sizable puddle on the green rug. "Oh."

He removed his coat and gloves, setting them both out to dry. While he could no longer get sick, sitting around in wet clothes wasn't comfortable.

"I'm surprised you're not leading with 'I told you so,'" she said, careful to look anywhere but at him.

"I would rather have been wrong."

"I know," Jane sighed.

"How did Mrs. Campbell find you?"

"On the road. She drove past me, and I threw mud at her carriage. I tried denying it was me, but she saw right through me."

Unease traveled through him because two people from her past had shown up on the same day. He wasn't sure if it was a coincidence or part of a larger plan.

"Do you trust her?"

"Implicitly. Eleanor is many things, but she has always been a good friend. Even when I didn't deserve her loyalty, I always had it."

Will was pleased she had at least one friend. Clearly, they weren't close, but there was a bond between them. He trusted Jane when she said she believed her to be loyal.

As the silence stretched between them, his thoughts returned to that afternoon. Her face was tight, and it was clear that what happened in class was still at the forefront of her mind.

"I'm sorry."

Jane sat on the green velvet couch. Her posture was stiff, but there was color in her cheeks again.

"It's not your fault." He hated the idea of her blaming herself for falling for predatory behavior.

Her head snapped up, and her narrowed eyes stared back at him. "What do you mean?"

"You had every reason to believe he really supported you. This is all on him. It has nothing to do with you."

"I know that," she snapped. "I'm not mad at myself for being taken advantage of."

His brow furrowed. He was glad she didn't blame herself, but he didn't follow.

"I'm angry at him, but the foolishness I feel isn't for believing him, it's for thinking that this time would be different. That men would be different." She let out a mirthless laugh. "I was so confident you were borrowing trouble that your warnings never even gave me pause."

"I never wanted to be right. I would have much rather looked like some crazy, jealous husband than to be right."

"What happened after I left?"

Will stiffened. "I threatened him."

Jane groaned. "What did you say?"

"I told him I would end him."

"Murder?" She sputtered, her eyes wide as she gaped at him.

"Of course not. I meant professionally. I told him I would use all of my connections to end his career."

Jane stared at him until his chest went tight. Truthfully, he had acted on instinct when Dr. Harris disrespected Jane. It was unacceptable for many reasons, but one of the dozens of reasons was that she was *his*. It was the truth that flowed in him, but now he wasn't sure if that was the best reasoning after all.

"I would have loved to see his face. I imagine you were the only person who could have gotten through to him anyway." Jane sighed, leaning her head on his shoulder. "Today was the most embarrassing day of my life, but at least it can now be a memory. The worst thing that could have happened today already did."

Will stiffened; it wasn't as if he forgot that Robert had found them, but he had been so worried about Jane that it slipped his mind for a moment.

"Lord, I can feel you spiraling over there. What happened?" Jane asked, balancing her chin on his shoulder as she looked up at him through her eyelashes.

"Robert's here."

"What do you mean?" She furrowed her brow.

"Oliver told me that someone checked into the hotel asking for you. He described you well and said he was your brother. Oliver didn't give him any information, but he knew it was you."

"Did you see Robert?"

"No."

Jane shot up and began to pace across the room. "So, it may not have been him after all."

He knew she was working through her panic, so he kept his voice even. "I think it is him, even though I wish it weren't. Oliver said he saw the resemblance, and I'm sure the other staff did as well. Besides, he had your real name."

"I don't know how he found me. Though I suppose I have been underestimating him for ages."

"If he knew for sure you were here, he would be in the room. So while he is too close, he hasn't yet caught you. As long as there is breath in my body, I will make sure you never have to return to him."

Luckily, there wasn't much that could steal the breath from his body anymore.

"I know," she said with a small, sad smile. "But I think we should leave Cambridge no matter what."

CHAPTER 36

*J*ane couldn't believe she was the one to suggest leaving Cambridge, but the words felt right as soon as they left her mouth.

"No," Will said. "I won't let you change your dream because of him. His presence complicates things, but it's nothing we can't handle."

"His presence changes everything. There's no way he doesn't find us. I'm one of four female students, and you're at least a head taller than everyone, with a very memorable face. It won't take him long to find us."

"I told you I should have worn the hood up. That would have helped."

"The hood does nothing to mask your height. You are just as memorable with or without it."

"Still, you shouldn't have to give up your dream. We can lay low for a while, and I'll get you another chaperone. Oliver said that neither he nor the rest of the staff will cooperate with his search. He'll move on eventually."

She stopped pacing and stood before Will. Her heart rate calmed as she looked at him. Closing the distance between them, she reached for his hand. Her thumb brushed against the smooth knuckles of his big, warm hand.

"Cambridge was always part of my dream, but do you know what the most important part of it was? Being respected for my intelligence. I wanted to be taken seriously. My highest aspiration was to be a research assistant. I didn't even have it in me to dream bigger."

"You are a research assistant."

"Precisely. I found someone who respects my intelligence and my abilities and pushes me to want things I never thought were possible. Now, I dream beyond being a student. I want a whole life in science. I even want to become a doctor because I've finally found someone who believes in me."

"Tristan will keep helping you, don't worry about that. You can keep working with him, and he'll do whatever he can to make you a doctor. He's a good person to have on your side."

"Tristan isn't who I'm talking about." Will was her heart, but sometimes she wanted to shake some sense into him. "It's you. You gave me this beautiful gift of becoming a student, but you've also given me the room to grow into who I was always meant to be. I want to learn more about her, and I want to do so with you."

Will's yellow eyes widened as he looked shocked at her declaration. If she was honest with herself, she was a little surprised too, but when she was faced with Robert's return, it was the easiest decision she ever made. She loved Will and never wanted to let him go.

As his shock faded to panic, her declaration of love died on her tongue. Nothing good could come from the way he looked at her.

"I had Oliver spy on Dr. Harris for you."

"What?" Jane's smile faded with the pleasant buzzy sensation in her chest.

"I hired Oliver to watch for correspondence from him and to take note of any time you met to work together."

"How long has this been going on?" The inside of her mouth felt like ash. She wanted to scream, run, or do anything to get away from this moment, but she was stuck because her brother could be downstairs at any moment. She was forced to keep living in this moment before it could become a memory.

"Within the first few days of arriving. I had him stop right after Tristan showed up. I realized it was wrong."

"So, Tristan knows about this, too?"

Jane never expected Tristan to choose her over his brother, but it hurt that they had both lied to her.

"Yes, but he only helped me stop it. He almost certainly thinks I already told you. I know I should have. The right thing to do would have been to never start, but I was so worried that he would take advantage of you and—"

Jane raised a hand to cut him off. "So, when I begged you not to interfere, you were already interfering."

Will looked like he was about to argue, but she quieted him with a glare.

"Yes."

Jane closed her eyes. Everything was unraveling like a nightmare. She should have known that all of this was too good to be true. That Will was too good to be true.

"So, not only did you have someone spy on me, lie to me about it, but you did all of this, and today still happened."

"Yes."

Will's eyes dropped to the floor, and the tips of his ears were red. At least he gave her the courtesy of looking ashamed of his actions.

"When I woke up alive in that room, I was angry that my plans were foiled, but I never once blamed you. It was a misunderstanding, not a betrayal." Jane took a shaky breath. Tears gathered in her eyes, but she wouldn't dare let them fall. "But this... this is a betrayal."

"I'm sorry."

Taking a step back, she finally let go of his hand. She hadn't even realized she was still holding it. Tears gathered in his eyes, and she knew he was sincerely sorry.

"I'm going to lie down."

Jane turned to go to the bedroom without another word. She

couldn't even give the excuse of having a headache or an upset stomach since they were both past such things. What she really wanted was a safe place to cry.

After she gently shut the bedroom door behind her, part of her wanted to push the chestnut armoire in front of it to deny him access, but that was childish. They could sleep in the same bed without issue. Even after his omission, she didn't like the idea of him sleeping on the floor.

The extra pillows were still lined up against the wall, unused for quite some time, but she picked them up and rebuilt the wall, needing the barest sliver of privacy. Only after the pillow wall was remade did she finally give in to her tears.

* * *

GOLDEN SUNLIGHT STREAMED into the room. She hadn't meant to go to bed so early, but it had been easier to cry herself to sleep than she expected. The one difference this time was that she didn't have a headache or a scratchy throat from her tears.

The steady breaths behind her told her Will was on his side of the pillow wall. She was glad he was on the bed rather than acting like a martyr either on the floor or the couch, but she didn't know what would happen next.

Jane still loved him. Obviously, if her love had been so fickle, then it wouldn't have been love at all. Though she didn't know how to move forward.

Quietly, she got dressed, pulling on her brown tweed dress that the modiste had talked her into despite not being Jane's usual style. Her hair was a mess after sleeping in her updo, but she tucked in some of the stray hairs.

The first step was to confirm that Robert was at the hotel. It wasn't that she didn't trust Will, but her new philosophy going forward was to confirm everything herself. Running away would be easier, but she no longer wanted the easiest way out.

She slouched as she walked through the hall, both to make herself seem shorter and because good posture was typically important to her. If Robert saw her face, it would all be over, but she hoped that by making herself look different, her brother wouldn't recognize her at a glance.

Her heart pounded in her ears as she reached the lobby. Part of her expected Robert to be waiting for her with a whiskey tumbler in hand, but when there were no other guests in the lobby, she let out a shaky breath.

She asked for Oliver at the front desk, but was told he wouldn't be coming in until later. Briefly, she considered questioning this unfamiliar man, but she didn't want to draw attention to herself in case Robert had gotten to him first. Will said no one there would betray them, but her trust wasn't high at the moment.

The dining room was quiet as she peeked inside, careful not to draw attention. Most of the tables were empty as it was still early for breakfast, but a few tables were occupied.

In the back corner sat Robert Montgomery. Her vision swam as her fingers squeezed the wooden door jam to keep her legs from collapsing. He was reading the paper with a cup of tea in front of him, like she had seen him do thousands of times.

With Robert's presence confirmed, it was time for the second part of her plan, but it took her body a few moments to gain the strength to move. Her quick, shallow breaths evened out as she reached the second-floor landing.

In all of her worry about escaping Robert, she hadn't been paying attention on the staircase and nearly ran into someone. It was a shorter man, and the second-worst person for her to see that morning.

"Ah, Mrs. Byrne," Dr. Harris said.

"Pardon me, I wasn't looking where I was going."

"I do hope you return to class despite yesterday's unpleasantness. You produce good work."

"Not good enough," Jane snorted. Sure, he may want her to return, but only so he could continue using her intellect.

Or due to Will's threats.

The man stammered as he tried to find his next words, but Jane found she did not care about anything this man had to say.

"Pardon me, but I must return to my husband."

Jane moved past him without looking back. Only once she had locked the door behind her did she relax. Her hands shook as her adrenaline crashed. The man probably would have thought her discomposure was because of him, but she had worse demons to fight.

Will exited the bedroom, eyes wide. "You're back."

"I am. I had to see if Robert was here myself."

"And?"

"He's in the dining room."

Will ran a hand through his hair, eyes darting, and she knew he was trying to formulate a plan. It was time for the second step of her plan.

"I want to go home."

"What?" Will's face paled. "You wish to go with your brother?"

"No." Jane recoiled. "I suppose I don't really have a home, but I wish to return to York."

"You have a home," he rushed to say, stepping towards her. "You'll always have a home there. Even if we aren't anything to one another, or you want me to leave. I promised to take care of your future, and now I swear this to you."

Jane swallowed. Logically, she had known such things, but it was nice to hear.

"I do appreciate it, and I want to return there for a bit while I plan where I want to go next." Jane took a deep breath. Step three was the difficult one. "I forgive you."

"I'm—" Will started before she cut him off.

"I forgive you, and I even understand, but I want to go out on my own. I wish to explore my independence. For a while at the very least."

"I understand." Will's face shuttered. "How long do you want to be in York?"

"A few weeks, maybe. I want to be able to plan my next step without as much pressure. Robert has scared us into moving twice, and I don't want to give him the chance for a third time."

It would also give her more time with Will. Her feelings were confused, but she wasn't ready to lose him forever.

A knock sounded at the door. Both she and Will froze. Her heart pounded as she was convinced Robert was on the other side. Will may have sworn that he would never let her go back, but her brother was slippery.

"It's Tristan."

She could have collapsed in pure relief. Will let out a similar deep breath before opening the door for his brother, careful to only open it wide enough for Tristan to slip inside.

Tristan turned to her, his gaze filled with such sympathy that it made her stomach turn.

"How are you doing?"

"I'm fine," Jane snapped. "I assume you know what happened yesterday?"

"I did, and I quit Dr. Harris' service right then. His students can teach themselves how to use microscopes. Not only were his actions inappropriate, but he never should have done so in front of the entire class."

"He won't get another chance," she said. Tristan's head tilted in question before she continued. "I'm not returning to class."

"You can't let this stop you. Their old-fashioned minds will change with time."

"Her brother is here."

She was thankful Will was there to help her with the conversation, even though it made her feel like a hypocrite. How could she like his interference sometimes, while other times it felt like a betrayal?

"What's your plan?" Tristan asked, looking at Will instead of Jane.

"Ask her, my days of scheming are over."

Jane squared her shoulders with the confidence that she could move on to the next step of her plan. "First, Tristan, you need to return to your room to gather your stationery. We also need to ask Oliver where we can get a serviceable wig on short notice."

* * *

HOURS LATER, Jane was physically exhausted but mentally too wired to even consider resting. It turned out espionage was rather fun.

Will latched their final trunk, stacking it near the door with the others. They were leaving Cambridge with more luggage than they arrived with, but it would still fit comfortably on the small carriage. Her small brown bag would be traveling on her lap.

"I still don't understand why I have to wear so much padding in my shoe," Tristan grumbled as he stuffed his feet into Will's extra pair of boots.

"You wouldn't have to if you weren't so short."

"I'm not short," Tristan snapped. "You're just the size of a building."

"You barely have any stuffing in your shoes. I'm wearing heeled boots and several balled-up handkerchiefs," Eleanor said, fussing with her skirts in the mirror.

Rather, fussing with Jane's skirts as she was wearing the dress Jane had died in. The one Will had been so desperate to throw away. Jane hadn't worn it since they arrived, but she was glad she hadn't gotten rid of it.

"You'll both be fine," Jane said. "You'll only have to wear the disguises for one day. Two at most."

Jane carefully dipped her paintbrush into the pink powder, careful to pick up only a small amount, before painting a scar on Tristan's face.

"Think of how much fun you'll have pretending to be us," Will said. "If you really want to, you can get back at us by saying outlandish things."

"Careful, or I'll start telling people about how interested you are in science. I'll get you invited to seminars," Tristan pouted, but at least he didn't move as Jane finished the shading on the scar by his lip.

"Try not to get stuck in conversations, but be visible and loud." She stepped back to look at her work. Up close, it was clearly makeup, but it didn't look bad from a distance. It would be perfect with the hood up. "Draw some attention, but not too much. Don't be afraid to mention your plans until you get to London, and then you can break away and do whatever you need to do."

"Yes, yes, we get the idea, Janie," Eleanor said as she fussed with her wig in the mirror. "I do look rather good as a brunette."

Eleanor wore the long brown wig Oliver had procured half an hour earlier. When she saw the styled wig in his hands, she didn't bother asking where it came from. Sometimes it was better not to know.

"You do look dashing, Mrs. Campbell," Tristan said as he pinned back one of the sleeves of Will's cloak.

"Please," she said in an exaggerated tone. "Call me Jane."

"I don't sound like that."

"You kind of do," Will said, passing Jane's cloak to Eleanor.

She huffed. There was no use arguing when they would keep needling her.

A knock sounded at the door in the pattern they told Oliver to do once the dining room was full. Robert was out for the day, but Eleanor and Tristan—dressed as Will and Jane—would go downstairs, discussing their plans to leave for London as they walked past the busy dining room before leaving for the train station. Their goal was to create a false trail while Jane and Will snuck into a different carriage to return to York. They would be skipping the train this time, instead switching out horses as needed so they could head straight to the Gardner home.

All things considered, it wasn't a bad plan, especially on such short notice. Jane was endlessly lucky that Tristan and Eleanor agreed to it. Eleanor's husband would be staying at the hotel. Jane wasn't sure what she told him to get him to agree, but Eleanor swore she didn't divulge any of Jane's secrets. She also swore he wouldn't be asking further questions. Jane accepted she would never understand their marriage.

"That's our cue," Jane said. She and Will were leaving first.

Eleanor walked over to Jane with open arms. It was eerie to see the woman dressed like her, even if they didn't look alike. The wig and heels helped, but their similarly colored eyes made the disguise work even though Eleanor's were a true blue to Jane's grey.

"I'm so glad I got to see you again," Eleanor said. "I hope this will not be our last meeting. Please write me when you can. Do it under any name you choose, but I want to hear from you."

Eleanor squeezed her so tight Jane couldn't help but reciprocate.

"I promise. Thank you for everything. You've been a better friend to me than I've ever deserved. I swear I'll write."

One day, Jane would break her promise and disappear, but until then, she would cherish the time they had.

Eleanor released her, stepped back, and Tristan took her place.

"I know we will see each other soon, but I do wish you luck."

"You too," she said before hugging Tristan as well. "We'll get the preparations started."

"Mrs. Jones will be endlessly thrilled to know we're hosting another symposium so soon."

They broke their hug, and Will said his goodbyes to the pair as well. Soon, the four of them stood before each other like a bizarre mirror image.

"Try to keep it believable and not too over the top," Will said.

Tristan held out his arm for Eleanor. "They're obsessed with touching, so it may be something we want to practice."

"You know I am married," Eleanor said with a glare, taking his arm.

"Don't flatter yourself," Tristan snorted. "My laboratory is my wife, and she is very, very jealous."

"Tell me more about your laboratory."

Jane couldn't help but smile as they drifted off in conversation.

"Are you ready to go?" Will asked, his own arm outstretched.

"I am."

Jane took his arm, and they snuck out of the room and back down the back staircase into the dark blue twilight.

CHAPTER 37

*H*ome had lost its appeal to Will. He loved his garden, Mrs. Jones, and the familiarity of his own bed, but what it lacked was Jane. She was no longer at the desk on the other side of the room, she wasn't beside him as he worked, and, worst of all, she no longer slept beside him.

She was still in the same house, but they felt more separate than ever.

Digging his hand trowel into the wheelbarrow, he collected the last of the mulch, spreading it around the rootstock of his beloved Yorkshire rose bush, and giving the dirt a gentle pat to tuck it in for its long winter's nap. It took five days of backbreaking work, but his garden was fully winterized. He had done his part, so now it was up to his flowers to survive the season.

Besides saving his garden, the five days of work gave him something to do besides waiting outside the laboratory for the chance to catch a glimpse of Jane. They still shared meals and sat together in the evening, so it wasn't as if they never saw one another.

However, there had been a distinct lack of kissing. Last night, they had been on the couch while she flipped through his sketchbook, sitting so close their thighs brushed. When she looked up at him, she stared at his lips for so long that he was convinced she would kiss him, but then Tristan came in, and the moment passed.

Sitting back on his heels, he surveyed his garden one final time to make sure he hadn't missed anything. The blooms were long gone, the leaves were withered and brown, and the stems had drooped. His once vibrant rose garden looked dead, but he knew better.

This was yet another season of life. The roots were still strong, sucking up nutrients from the dirt until the ground thawed, the weather warmed, and they could show off come spring.

Satisfied that his plants were taken care of, he took off his gloves and shook them free of dirt. The only thing left on his to-do list was to oil his gardening tools before hanging them in his shed for their seasonal rest as well.

Tonight was the symposium.

Tonight, Jane was leaving.

Not forever, as she never failed to mention when she discussed her plans. She never gave him an exact timeframe, just leaving it at not forever.

However, forever was a loaded term for two people who wouldn't die.

Grabbing his tools, he walked to the shed. The door squeaked as it opened. He would have to make sure to tell Mr. Morris so it could be fixed. He picked up the jar of cleansing oil and an old rag and got to work.

Humming a tune as he worked, he tried to keep his shaking hands from slicing himself with the shears. Today was the last day he would live in secret. This time tomorrow, a group of scientists would know he had died. It would take time for that information to spread, but it would slowly creep through academic and scientific circles.

Will did his best not to think about what would happen after the symposium. He was dedicated to staying in York through the winter at least. Partly to help Tristan continue his work, but also because he didn't know where else to go.

There was his flat in Chelsea, but he couldn't imagine returning to his former life. Even when the truth about him was out there, he couldn't imagine returning to the old clubs he used to haunt or seeing his friends who had left his body behind in Paris. No, he was better without them.

The only thing he knew for certain was that when he did leave, Mrs. Jones would be going with him. The most significant change that occurred upon their return was that he hired a full staff to assist the aging housekeeper. At first, she grumbled about being replaced, but he saw the relief on her face when tasks were being completed, and she wasn't exhausted every day.

"What are you doing?"

Turning, he saw Jane leaning against the door frame, clad in the simple black frock she wore while working in Tristan's lab.

"Working."

"You have such a big night, I thought you'd be getting ready."

Jane stepped inside the shed, looking around his workspace. He liked seeing her in his space, but he was also wary of why she was there. It was the first time she had found him during the day, let alone linger in his shed.

"I could say the same about you, since you're leaving tonight. Are you all packed?"

"I am. Morris packed my trunks on the carriage. I'm ready to go whenever." She gave him a small smile that felt like the golden rays of sunshine despite the overcast skies. "I found the envelope you left me."

"Ah."

"Is that all you have to say for yourself? Are you not going to explain this?" She asked, holding up the stark white envelope he hid in one of her packed trunks while she was at breakfast.

"I didn't think you'd find it until after you left." His tools were clean enough that he replaced them on the hooks. Jane remained silent, and he sighed. "I wanted to make sure you would be taken care of no matter where you went."

"Slipping me some bills is making sure I'm taken care of. This isn't only all of your bank information, but also letters from your solicitor about how to get more money and approval to buy whatever property I want."

"I didn't buy anything for you. If you don't want any help, you can ignore the letters or even burn them if you wish. I hate the idea of you sleeping between scratchy sheets in some seedy inn because some brilliant scientist who can't manage his finances hasn't paid you in weeks."

Emotions flitted across Jane's face so quickly that he couldn't keep up. Chances are, he had overstepped her boundaries again, but he had held his tongue so much over the last few days that he had earned the right to be a touch overbearing.

"Every day I waited for you to ask me where I'm going."

"I didn't want you to feel like I was planning to follow you. If you wanted to share your plans, I figured you would."

And she hadn't, so instead he memorized her face and would wait until she found him again.

"Why didn't you ask me to stay?"

Her eyes were wide as she looked at him, worrying her bottom lip with her teeth. She looked as though she thought the answer would be because he didn't care enough, when the opposite was true.

"I wanted to every moment of every day because I love you." He never thought this would be how he told her, but he needed her to understand. If these were the last words they had for a while, he would make them count. "I love you, and I don't care if I go with you or if you stay with me as long as we're together. I don't want the only reason you're with me to be because I begged you to."

"So that's all you want? To be someone's first choice?"

"Not someone's, *yours*. I don't give a damn if I'm your first choice or twentieth. I just want to be *your* choice."

"You speak of choices now when our relationship only began because you took the choice of my life from me." She hit her hand against her chest; her breathing was ragged.

"Which is why I will never steal another choice from you again." He took a step towards her, his heart pounding both from their argument and just being near her. "You deserve to have the life you desire, and I'm not selfish enough to demand to be part of it."

Jane's grey eyes were wild like a brewing tempest, but she looked conflicted, not angry. Even after looking at her for weeks, he was struck by her beauty. He would miss her with the same brutality if they were separated for a single day or one hundred years.

Before he could react, she grabbed his face, kissing him with a ferocity that momentarily surprised him before he wrapped his arms around her. She was soft and warm against him, even as their kiss was a furious battle of lips and tongues, telling each other everything they couldn't speak aloud.

Every moment he spent with her was a gift beyond measure. Even arguing with her was a privilege. She never shied away from his scars or borrowed parts, so Will would be hers forever.

Jane wrapped her legs around him, and he lifted her easily, walking her to his workbench.

He broke their kiss to look at her, his thumb stroked her flushed cheek, before she turned her head to kiss his palm. If this were their goodbye, he would make every moment count.

CHAPTER 38

*T*here were a million rationalities as to why she kissed him, but the only one that mattered was that she wanted to more than anything. As they were arguing, she was struck by the fact that she couldn't remember their last kiss. The memories of their past encounters had melded together, but she wanted one clear memory if this was their last time.

Will pulled away, looking at her with such tenderness it made her chest ache. This man *loved* her, but he was willing to let her go. She grabbed the lapels of his jacket and pulled him to her again. They both knew what this was, and she didn't want to waste time on melancholy before they had even parted.

The workbench was custom-built for him, so she was at the perfect height. Eager hands traveled up her bodice from her waist to her breasts. He swiped his thumb over her nipple, but she felt only the ghost of sensation through all her layers of clothing.

Her own hands traveled over his body, memorizing him. Her hand cupped his cock over his black wool trousers, feeling him swell beneath her touch.

"Are you certain?" He rasped.

"Yes."

They fumbled together, moving her skirts up and unbuttoning

his trousers to free him before he slid into her in one smooth movement.

Throwing her head back, her hands went to his shoulders to hold onto him. The tools on the wall rattled with each forceful thrust. With one hand on his hip, he moved the other to circle her clitoris.

Leaning back, she used her arms to brace herself against the onslaught. Will looked down on her with a tortured tenderness she surely echoed.

"I can't wait until high necklines are out of style."

Will's finger ran down the line of buttons that started at her throat.

"You can't rip my clothes every time they get in your way."

He growled, telling her what he thought of that, but he didn't rip her favorite day dress after all.

Pleasure welled within her as Will's pace grew erratic; she knew he was close to his climax as well. His steady hand between her thighs made her squeeze around him.

"Oh, Will," she moaned as her pleasure crested, euphoria flooding her veins.

Time seemed to stretch out in those few moments before Will followed her, and then everything felt sublimely perfect.

It was madness that she was going to walk away from the man she loved, but he was right. It would be too easy for her to stay forever, and while that was what a large part of her wanted, she was terrified she would grow to resent him if she stayed. She needed to prove to herself that she didn't need him, that she didn't need to be dependent on others to live.

Will murmured her name in between kissing her forehead, temple, nose, neck, and ear. Any place he could reach was kissed. In return, she ran her hands through his thick, dark hair, grazing her fingernails over his scalp in the way that made him shiver.

It would have been so easy to stay wrapped up in one another.

"You should probably get ready for the symposium."

The spell between them broke. Will silently cleaned her with his handkerchief before she slipped off the workbench. There were no more words to share between them, but it wasn't an uncomfortable silence.

Jane opened the door to the shed and hesitated. She couldn't just leave it at that. A final goodbye with Tristan and Mrs. Jones as well would come later, but this could be one of their last moments alone.

"I'm going to Scotland."

"What?"

"Edinburgh." Jane turned to face him. "Eleanor told me women are going to medical school up there. I don't wish to enroll, but I'm interested in seeing what the academic culture is up there. Maybe there will be other opportunities for women."

Jane left before Will could respond, walking quickly to the house. Once she got settled in Edinburgh, she would write to him. Maybe invite him up to visit if she managed to build a life she wanted to show off.

* * *

JANE FOUND Tristan alone in the library, sitting in one of the old armchairs with his head in his hands. He was sharply dressed in a black tuxedo, but his hair stuck out like he had been pulling at it for hours. This was the side of Tristan most people never saw. He wasn't always the self-assured genius he pretended to be around company.

"You look like hell," she said.

"I don't know how I'm supposed to do this," he said, looking at her with swollen, bloodshot eyes.

She poured him a bit of Will's good brandy and placed it in his shaky hand.

"Do you have a comb?" He nodded, gesturing to the table beside him. She picked up the fine-toothed black comb and began fixing his hair. "You've done this before. All you need to do is share your research. Then, Will does the exercises to demonstrate life and cognitive ability. Finally, it's the audience questions, but we can cut that portion if you so wish."

"How am I supposed to tell them that I experimented on my own brother? That I challenged the natural order of life? They're going to want to run experiments on him. He'll be nothing more than a test subject." Tristan barked a laugh. "But that's exactly how I've treated him since I brought him back."

"Will knows that's not all he is to you." Grease would have been useful for taming Tristan's rakish waves, but she was making it work with the comb and a lot of patience. "What was your plan last time?"

"I was so blinded by the idea of glory that I didn't have a real plan. I wanted my brother to be able to live openly without fear, but it was nearly as important that everyone knew I had harnessed the power of God."

Jane sighed. As brilliant as Tristan was, he struggled with the human side of his work. His intentions were good, but his execution could use work. A *lot* of work.

"I thought forcing my brother to reveal himself was what was best for him." Tristan shook his head, taking a sip of brandy. "God, he would have hated me for all time if I had put him through that."

"This time, he's ready, and you have an actual plan. You're only introducing this to scientists you trust." When Tristan had laid the false trail for them in London, he visited some of his friends at various scientific societies and academic journals to invite them to the symposium. "It will no longer be a secret after tonight, but the people you've invited know the gravitas of your discovery. It's not as if you decided to throw a ball to announce to hundreds of people from all around Yorkshire that you had unlocked the secrets between life and death."

"That wasn't one of my better ideas, was it?"

"No."

Even thinking about his ridiculous plan made her anger flare with how unfair it was to Will. Luckily, he had seen the error of his ways.

"The ball was for Will. He was so heartbreakingly lonely that I would have done anything to fix him."

Satisfied with Tristan's hair, she returned the comb to the table.

She gave him a reassuring pat on his shoulder despite the twinge in her heart. "You were trying to take care of him the best way you knew how, but it's not up to you to fix him."

It wasn't up to either of them.

"I'm sorry. For what I did to you." Tears filled his eyes as Tristan looked at her. "I only considered Will's happiness; I never thought about yours. Despite having every reason to hate me, you've been such a good friend."

"I've already forgiven you."

There were so many things in this world for her to be angry about that she couldn't sustain her anger against the man who had given her everything.

"Do you mind if I ask you something personal?" Tristan asked.

"Of course."

"What was dying like?"

Over the course of working together, Tristan had conducted countless interviews with her, studied her blood, listened to her heartbeat, and devised dozens of tests to measure her abilities. He looked at her skin under microscopes and observed her healing capabilities in real time. In all of their time spent together, he had never once asked about dying.

"It was like falling asleep." Truthfully, she didn't think about dying much, but it had never haunted her. "My last thoughts were those of love. I thought that maybe I would finally get to meet my mother, which felt quite nice."

"I'm so sorry I took you from that," he said, squeezing his eyes shut. His knuckles were white as he gripped the fine fabric of his trousers.

"Don't be, because while it was such a lovely feeling to leave this world on, I don't know if anything happened between that final thought and waking up. You didn't rip me away from anywhere."

Jane knew his greatest fear was that he had ripped them away from heaven and damned them to live forever on Earth. Maybe there was some mythical afterlife she was missing where everyone she loved was waiting for her, but if there was, she had no memory of it.

"Did it feel like a long time?"

"It was only the blink of an eye."

"Thank you, that was very comforting." Tristan released the firm grip on his legs, wiped his eyes with his sleeve, and pulled himself back together. "For so long, I thought death would be the last thing I had to worry about. Then, when I brought Will back, he was so convinced I damned him that I worried I did."

"There's no way to know everything that can happen. There are things we learned today that were unimaginable yesterday, and we will learn more tomorrow. It's up to us to have faith that we'll make the best of it."

"I thought I would be ready by now, but I don't know if I am." Tristan smoothed out his white waistcoat and straightened his tie. "I know that must sound ridiculous since it wasn't like you were ready. Or Will."

"Maybe it isn't something you can ever really be ready for, but you also don't have to worry about it now. We have all the time in the world."

"I have been threatened with being thrown in the lake for asking this next question, but if you don't tell my brother, then I won't."

"You want to know where I'm going?" She asked, and Tristan nodded. "I'm going to Edinburgh."

"That's a good choice. Some of the best medical schools in the world are up there."

"I'm hopeful the academic culture is more amenable to women. I'm rather put off from being a student right now, but I would like the chance to build community."

"It's been a few years since I've been there, but I think you'll enjoy it. I purchased a home between Edinburgh and Glasgow, but I haven't had the chance to go there yet."

While she didn't agree with all of Tristan's choices, he was a good scientist. She couldn't even fault him for what he had done. As with all human innovations, love fueled Tristan's discovery.

The door opened, and Will stepped into the room wearing a tuxedo that matched Tristan's, but he filled it out very differently. His white waistcoat showed off the broad expanse of his chest, while his tailcoat drew her eye down his body to his thick thighs hidden beneath the black fabric. It looked as if his arms would burst the seams of his tailcoat if he flexed, but somehow he had his full range of movement as he closed the door behind him. His hair was combed back so his whole face was in view, and his honey colored eyes glowed in the light of the gas lamps. He was so handsome it almost hurt to look at him.

"Don't tell me you have cold feet."

Will gave Jane a questioning look to see if she thought Tristan would be okay to do the presentation tonight. Jane nodded. Will might not know it, but Tristan had pulled himself together well enough that there was no question he would be ready when the time came.

"I'm fine. Although I'm feeling a lot of sympathy for trying to push you through this before."

"You're finally getting what you want, so no backing out now. People will be here soon, and we need to be ready. The blackboard is on stage. Do you have the chalk?"

"It's on the table," Tristan said, eyeing Will with a grim determination, and Jane took that as her cue to let the brothers have a moment alone.

"I'll take it out. I'll leave one piece at the board and the rest on the podium." Picking up the chalk, she closed the door behind her so the brothers could hash out whatever they needed to. The tension between them when she first arrived was gone as they had repaired their relationship.

Walking out to the ballroom where the makeshift stage had been set up felt like deja vu, but this time the symposium would happen. With the white chalk set on the wooden tray beneath the blackboard, she checked to ensure everything else was ready. Erasers were on the podium shelf, and she placed the chalk box beside them. Tristan's speech was on the top shelf of the podium beside a glass of water. Everything was ready.

Looking out at the empty ballroom from the podium, she imagined a crowd gathered for a presentation of hers. There were only twelve chairs arranged around the podium. It was barely more than a handful of people, but they would all be a part of history.

"Are you going to watch the symposium or will you be using it as your distraction to leave?"

"I'm going to watch. Mrs. Jones found me a good hiding spot."

Jane walked Will over to her hiding place just inside the doorway to the servant's entrance that was hidden in the ballroom. It was angled so she could see the stage, but remain hidden from the audience.

"This is a good spot," Will said, examining the small hallway. "I was worried you would leave without saying goodbye."

"No." Her cheeks burned because she had considered it. Goodbyes were difficult. "Morris is waiting in the carriage. I told him he didn't need to wait out there for me, but he insisted."

"If it makes you feel better, his staying out there is less about you and more because he likes to smoke his pipe and nap under the stars."

They were forced to be inches apart in this small hallway. This close, his scent overwhelmed her, smelling of his usual dirt and flowers, but also of the lavender soap she bought on one of her independence outings in Cambridge.

"As long as he's having a good time."

"I have a gift for you." Will held out a voluminous soft parcel she hadn't noticed. "A going-away present, I suppose."

Jane took it from his grasp, gently unwrapping the brown paper. It was his cloak.

"I know it's kind of silly," Will blathered. "If you don't want it, you can give it back, and we can pretend this never happened."

"No," she said, unfurling the heavy wool cloak. "I love it."

"Good," Will said, lips turning up some, but the smile didn't reach his eyes.

Earlier, it hadn't been awkward between them, but now it was. A countdown hung between them, perilously close to zero.

"Let's wait to say goodbye until after."

"All right." Uncertainty flickered across Will's face. "Could I hold you for a moment?"

Jane threw her arms around him, pressing her ear against his chest as his heart hammered and the cloak fell to the floor between them. He hugged her tight, his head buried in her neck as he took deep, even breaths. Whispering her reassurances to him, she rubbed his back until the tension released from his muscles.

A sharp rap at the door told them it was time for Will to get in place. Reluctantly, he let go, but took her hands in his.

"Wait for me here." Will kissed both of her hands. "I'll come to you as soon as it's over."

Jane nodded, her throat was too thick with emotion for words. Will turned, leaving her alone in the narrow hallway. She picked up the abandoned cloak, wrapping it around herself, taking a deep breath. It smelled of dirt, flowers, open air, and a hint of his sweat. It was nearly as good as being enveloped by him.

The murmur of voices told her that doors had opened. Most of the audience was hidden from her, but she could see the first row. She didn't recognize anyone, but that wasn't a surprise, as Tristan didn't invite anyone from Cambridge. The scientists were from his most trusted circles in London.

Tristan took his place at the podium. His earlier nerves had been eased, and he wore his typical easy grin. The slight tremor in his hands was the only tell that he was nervous.

Will was behind the makeshift curtain she had set up earlier. It felt like a good idea earlier, but now it felt unnecessarily theatrical. Burrowing herself into Will's cloak, she found comfort in the familiarity even as her unease grew.

"Good evening, gentleman. Thank you for coming out here on such short notice. Without further ado, let's begin."

$$* * *$$

Will

The gas lamps lining the stage were bright enough that Will could barely see the crowd, which greatly helped his nerves. His part of the symposium began with a brief overview of his musculature and calisthenics to show how he moved. Slides were shown comparing dead tissue to his living tissue. Tristan then gave a lengthy explanation of some of the science involved in the reanimation process, but Will's mind had wandered during that section as he found it to be terribly dull.

Nearly all of his secrets were spilled to the silent crowd, but he and his brother decided to leave out his regenerative healing abilities. Reanimation was daring enough without a room of people wanting to know if he would be able to regrow a limb like a lizard's tail.

Instead, he answered logic riddles and memory puzzles to demonstrate his cognitive ability, and wrote some lines of poetry on the blackboard to show his fine motor skills.

The presentation ended with an arithmetic display. Writing sums on the board was his least favorite part of school, and he couldn't believe he was living out his boyhood nightmare once more. Six plus two was nothing, and twelve and eighteen were easy enough.

Thirty-five and twenty-seven gave him pause, but he solved it before an uncomfortable amount of time passed. Setting the chalk down, he itched to wipe his sweaty, chalky palm, but making a mess of his tuxedo would do little to impress his audience. Turning to Tristan, the relief in his brother's face told him they made it to the end of their demonstration. He did it. Now it was time for audience questions, but soon he would be free to return to Jane.

It would be to say goodbye, but at least he could hold her one final time.

"That concludes the demonstration portion of this evening. Does anyone have any questions?" Tristan said, tucking his hand into his trouser pocket. Will knew it was his nervous tic, but it seemed casual enough to the audience.

No one raised their hand.

The room was so quiet, Will would have thought it to be empty if he couldn't hear their breathing and a few rapid heartbeats. Conversation erupted when Tristan announced the subject of the presentation, but the crowd fell silent as soon as Will walked on stage. It unnerved him, but it was better than being jeered at for an hour.

"I have a question," a voice boomed from the back of the room.

"Go ahead. Come closer so it's easier to hear." Tristan shaded his eyes with his hand to better see the speaker.

"I want to know what you did with my sister."

Will looked at the man approaching the stage. He was tall, with broad shoulders and a swoop of chestnut-brown hair. Angry grey eyes looked at him with a mask of revulsion that felt quite familiar. So this was Robert Montgomery.

The family resemblance was evident in their height and coloring, but he also commanded the room in the same way as Jane. His presence was so strong that Will didn't notice the man beside him at first, but he did take notice when the man stood beside Jane's brother.

He was a bit shorter, with a slighter build, making him look insignificant beside Robert. However, Will recognized both his icy blue eyes and his hateful sneer because they played back in his memory so often. Robert Montgomery had arrived at his home with the man who had gutted him in an alley in Paris, leaving him to bleed out beneath the stars.

347

*H*orror spread throughout Jane's body, locking her in place. Her brother had found her, and Lord Percy was with him. There was no way either man would ever let her go. She had to run.

The carriage was outside, packed with her belongings and instructions on where to take her. Will and Tristan could bluff their way out of this, inadvertently giving her the time she needed to escape. They would even be telling the truth when they said they had no idea where she was.

"What did you do with my bride, you fiend? We know you kidnapped her," Lord Percy said as he pointed at Will.

Despite the worst acting she'd ever seen, Will was frozen, his face chalkier than she had ever seen before. His nerves had been shot from the demonstration, and this surprise must have pushed him too far.

Carefully, she backed away from the crack in the door, lifting Will's cloak so she didn't trip on the hem as she made her escape. Her steps were silent, but she barely risked breathing in case anyone heard her.

Halfway down the hall, she stopped, far enough away that she couldn't hear the commotion in the ballroom anymore. If she left now, they would take Will into custody while they tried to find her. When they couldn't prove she was alive, they would charge him with murder, likely sentencing him to death. And when they couldn't kill him, the real torture would begin.

She couldn't do that to him. Will was the only thing she loved more than her freedom.

Running down the hallway, she burst from her hiding spot. Will's cape billowed behind her as her angry footsteps echoed off the marble floor. Everyone turned towards her, Robert sneered, and Percy's eyes widened. "If you have anything you wish to say about me, I would rather you do so directly to me."

"Sister, I'm so glad to see you," Robert said with that stupid smirk on his face. "You have no idea how much I've worried about you."

Will looked at her, as if he was holding himself back from throwing himself between Jane and her brother; she shot him a harsh look to stop him. She could handle her brother on her own.

"I'm so touched to hear that, *dear brother*," she spat as she stalked towards the stage. "Although I'm not sure if it's me that you missed or the money you stole from me?"

Even from a distance, she saw his nostrils flare. "Of course, I missed you. You were engaged to one of my dearest friends before you disappeared right before the wedding."

"I'm sure this has been one big understanding," Tristan said, moving his hands to his pockets as he always did when he was nervous. "If you gentlemen would follow me to the study, I'm sure we can sort this out."

"Don't think we've forgotten about you. I am exceedingly curious as to how my sister got here," Robert said, waving his walking stick at Tristan.

"I walked through the door over there." Jane pointed behind her before crossing her arms in the way her brother always hated. If anyone was going to spark her brother's temper, it had to be her. She was the only one he wouldn't whack with that stick. Probably. "Really, Robert, I thought you could keep up."

"Not only did I find my sister had been taken in by a pair of *bachelors,"* Robert thundered, ignoring Jane. "But then imagine my shock when I find they have been engaged in the worst type of witchcraft." Robert pointed his cane again, this time at Will.

Jane snorted, finding the accusation of witchcraft to be beyond absurd. Magic wasn't real. Her brother had never appreciated science. She expected to hear similar guffaws from the scientists in the room, but as she looked over the audience, she didn't see the same incredulity she felt. Their faces were weary, and more than one person looked at Will in terror. Her stomach dropped. Perhaps the room wasn't on their side after all.

"I received an interesting letter from my younger brother not long ago," Percy said, his icy mask of those born into the aristocracy firmly in place. "He told me of a man with a ghastly visage escorting his tall wife to class."

Bile collected in Jane's mouth as she fought the urge to be sick. Although maybe getting sick in the middle of the ballroom would provide a decent distraction from this horror.

"Most intriguing," Percy continued. "Is that my brother is studying at Cambridge, the very same institution you begged me to allow you to attend. Not only were you a student, but you were reportedly *married.*"

"Oh, Janie, you ran off with a nobody?" Robert shook his head. "How very pedestrian."

Her blood boiled as she surged forward, ready to wipe that awful smirk off his face, when she felt iron hands hold her in place. Her shoulders dropped because she knew who it was, despite not noticing Will leave the stage. His thumb discreetly rubbed the back of her arm in a small act of comfort.

"Your sister is more than capable of making her own decisions." Will's voice was even, but she could hear his simmering rage. "If you would like to discuss any specifics, we can go to another room like civilized people, but if you're not interested in that, I suggest you leave."

"I was disappointed to miss you at Cambridge, but imagine my surprise when I heard one of the brutes who kidnapped my fiancée returned to York. There was talk of scientists staying at a nearby inn for a symposium. I expected a boring slideshow about plants, but imagine my surprise when I saw the man who cheated me out of my winnings at cards in Paris last year."

Will's grip tightened as she rocked back in shock at the news. She was surprised he could remain so calm when faced with the villain who had murdered him.

"You killed him," her voice was quiet as Percy's cavalier attitude stoked her rage.

"How could I have murdered him if he's standing right here?"

"I know Dr. Gardner used some big words, but if you paid attention to the demonstration, you would know he was brought back from the dead."

"So they claim." Robert stalked across the room, waving his walking stick for emphasis. "However, I have another theory of what happened here. I think you saw my pathetic sister and thought she would make the perfect victim for all of your sick fantasies."

Unease grew in the crowd, and a stone settled in her stomach. Her brother's story was equal parts ludicrous and compelling, especially since the crowd had already heard another unbelievable story.

"You know that's a bald-faced lie." Her hands were in fists at her side. She didn't know how to win the crowd back, but she prayed the truth was enough. "You tried to sell me to Lord Percy, but I ran off when it was clear my consent didn't matter to the marriage."

"Interesting, I do like your story. Of course," Robert said as he stalked closer. "I do think the story of Mr. Gardner drowning you in the river so he could make you his undead bride is a touch more compelling."

Color drained from her face at the reveal that he knew about her death in the river. For the first time, she wasn't sure if she would be able to talk her way out of this.

"And if we aren't careful," Robert continued. "They're going to be wandering the countryside killing indiscriminately to add to their undead army!"

He punctuated his point by waving his cane as he shouted. It was a shame he missed his calling as an actor. They were in a room full of scientists who might fall for the theatricality, but they wouldn't be moved to action.

Jeers sounded behind her, and she turned to see the crowd her brother was feeding. It wasn't the scientists, no, they were fear-stricken and silent in their seats. The jeers were coming from a crowd of men filing into the ballroom that must have been led here by her brother and Percy.

Damn.

"Let's all take a step back here before we get too riled up. There is no agenda to create an *army*. I was already doing similar experiments, and I happened to succeed with my brother."

"Then how do you explain the presence of my dear sweet Miss Montgomery, who was ripped from life days before her wedding?"

Jane snorted. Lord Percy was playing to the back of the room, but if anyone in this crowd knew her, they would know he was lying since no one would ever describe her as dear or sweet.

"Especially after she had waited so long to find her perfect match, and to a titled lord no less," Robert added.

Will's grip on her tightened as the crowd grew angrier.

"Leave her out of this," Will started. "Your quarrel is with my brother and me. Let her go, then we'll talk."

Jane whipped around to face Will. His eyes were fixed on Percy. His face was drawn, but she could see the grim determination.

"No." It came out rougher than she meant it to, but she wasn't going to leave him.

Will's eyes flicked to her, and he lowered his voice. "Run, you were going to leave anyway. This is your chance to be free."

"Not without you, *never* without you. I love you." Jane turned to face her brother. She wouldn't let Robert rip this beautiful life from her when it was only now within her grasp. "The only thing that happened here is the advancement of science. No one has been harmed, so we can be on our way. You never have to see us again."

"Of course, you think running away is a viable option," Robert said, walking along the stage. "But how are we supposed to rest knowing that people like *him* exist?" He pointed his cane at Will.

"How can we forget the monster waiting in the shadows, ready to take our wives and daughters to turn them against God and the natural world. No, there is no place on this Earth you could hide where we would not hunt you."

The crowd gave an angry cheer, and Jane knew she had lost.

"I would have done anything for a lifetime with you, but the time we had together was better than I could have ever dreamed," Will whispered into her hair before placing a kiss on the crown of her head. "You make me feel *alive.*"

"No, we're getting out of here together," she whispered as the crowd crept closer. There was no way in hell this would be their end. "You're *mine.* I will accept nothing less than forever with you."

"Get her away from the monster!" Lord Percy shouted as he charged towards them.

"Run!" Will pushed her aside to put him in the direct path of the disgruntled lord.

"Go!" Tristan shouted.

The scientists tried to flee, but the entering crowd blocked them. Tempers were high as shouts ran across the room. Chaos surrounded her. Will managed to continue blocking Percy from getting to her, but he kept looking back at her.

Her presence distracted him, and he needed his full attention so they could get out of there. Wood splintered behind her as the mob destroyed the stage, likely targeting Tristan's research.

Holding up both her skirts and Will's cloak, she ran for the servant's door. It was no longer a secret since she burst into the room through there, but the dark hallway was difficult to maneuver if you didn't know the way.

Her heeled boots echoed through the hall as she ran faster than she had ever run before. The door at the end of the wall was closed, but she didn't slow down, bruising herself as she broke through the wooden door and fell into the kitchen.

"Mrs. Jones!"

The housekeeper was the only other person she cared about in the home. She wasn't sure where she was, but they would never leave her behind.

A crash came from the hallway, and she knew someone was trying to follow her.

A different servant's corridor went upstairs, and she made a run for it. This time, the door was better hidden.

Reaching the second-floor landing, she knew exactly where she needed to go. If the mob thought there was power in destroying Tristan's notes downstairs, she needed to make sure his actual research was rescued. Even if no one ever used it again, there was no way this incredible achievement could be lost to time.

There was no movement on the second floor yet, but she was still careful to keep her footsteps on the thick carpet where her steps were muffled. She would get Tristan's research, go to the carriage, and pray everyone joined her.

The laboratory was as she had left it earlier. Tristan's cup of tea still lay abandoned on a stack of books on his messy desk. Her own cleared desk was the only tidy spot in the entire room. It was likely the last time she would ever be in there. Her heart ached, but it wasn't the time to let nostalgia bog her down.

She grabbed an empty messenger bag before going to Tristan's desk.

To an outsider, Tristan's desk was chaos, but she had learned it was *organized* chaos. The books containing the instructions for the procedure were stored in different volumes, but each was discreetly numbered so he wouldn't lose track of them. She shoved all of the numbered books in the bag.

Dozens of notebooks were left on the shelves, but she wasn't sure what else was important. Anything left out went into the bag, as did the newer book he had started for his blood typing project. The leather strap of the bag dug into her shoulder, but she added the dark blue books that held notes on her and Will after the procedure. The bag was too full to close, but it was a shame she couldn't save more.

As the mob grew louder downstairs, she knew it was time for her to leave. The loss of the beautiful brass microscope was a shame, but it was nothing that couldn't be replaced.

"I shouldn't be surprised that you ran off again."

Ice shot through her veins as she turned to see Robert smirking at her from the doorway. Mercifully, he wasn't holding his cane, but she didn't trust him not to hurt her.

"Can't we agree that I'm more trouble than I'm worth and you let me go?"

"No."

"Well, it was certainly worth a try." She shrugged while covertly scanning the room. She was too far from anything to throw, but a heavy bag full of books rested on her shoulder.

"You know I prayed for years that you would run away, never to be my problem again. I can't believe you finally did so the moment I needed you around."

"Well, you know me. I live to disappoint you." Slowly, she gathered the bag straps in her hand so she could hit him to make her escape. "What was your grand plan anyway? I'm almost impressed you got Percy to return for your farce of a confrontation."

"He's here because I *own* him. His family lost their fortune due to overspending and poor planning before he gambled the rest away. I've never seen a more hopeless financial situation."

Robert sauntered towards her, not quite in hitting range, but he was getting close. She had to be careful since he would only afford her a single chance.

"What could he possibly be giving you in return?"

"He's going to have a peerage created for me once you're married."

"And how would he achieve that?" Jane asked, biting the inside of her cheek to keep from laughing. "Traditionally, that's not a power barons have."

"Obviously, he won't be the one to do it, but he has favor with the queen since he attended school with the Prince of Wales."

The metallic tang of blood filled her mouth as she chewed the inside of her cheek raw. It was almost unbelievable that this was the same man who had bested her so many times.

"I'm sure the queen will do a favor for him," she said, unable to keep the mocking tone out of her voice.

Robert turned deep red before lunging at her. However, she was prepared and swung the overfull bag at him, connecting with his head. He let out a grunt before falling to his knees. He was still between her and the door when she swung the bag at him again.

"You bitch." After blocking her hit, he lunged at her from his knees in an attempt to catch her legs.

Jumping back, she avoided his grasp, but fell into the table holding the microscope. The momentum caused her to let go of the bag, tossing it in the opposite direction. While her escape was paramount, she wouldn't dare leave the research behind. It was too important.

"I can't wait until Percy locks you away and I can watch the life slowly drain from your eyes."

Propped against the table, she blindly groped behind her for something to throw at him. "You will never get me, but even if you did, I already died once, and you'll never have the pleasure of seeing me do so again."

"Only according to that doctor, but we could always test his theory a few times. After all, isn't that what scientists do?"

Finally, her fingers grasped the microscope behind her. Swinging it around, she smacked him across the face. His head turned at an unnatural angle with a dull thwack as he crumpled to the floor. Blood pooled on the worn rug beneath him, but she hit him again for good measure. This time, his skull crumpled beneath the force, exposing his light pink brain to the open air.

"Burn in hell, you miserable bastard," she spat at Robert's body as she grabbed the book bag before running from the room.

Her hand shook with a slight tremor at the fact that she had taken a life. Her brother's life. Still, she couldn't quite feel sorry for what she had done. If it were between her and him, she would choose herself every time.

Stealth was no longer her priority as she heard fighting beneath her. Her goal was to locate Mrs. Jones and then wait in the carriage for Will and Tristan. They would all make it out together.

CHAPTER 40

*W*atching Jane walk away had been one of the hardest things Will had ever done, but he was glad she was gone. Hopefully, Morris took her far away. In the end, she told him she loved him, which was more than enough for him. It gave him the strength he needed to stare down the man who killed him.

Lord Percy.

He'd been too foxed to know the name of his killer, but he shouldn't have been surprised that he belonged to the aristocracy. That entitlement had to come from somewhere.

"First, you steal my jackpot," Percy sneered, stalking towards him. "Then you bespoil my bride. You've crossed me for the last time."

Percy lunged at Will before he had time to react, hitting Will in the cheek with a poorly formed fist. Pain bloomed for a moment before quickly fading.

"What's the matter, Percy?" he taunted. "Didn't anyone teach you how to throw a punch?"

Will landed a jab of his own to punctuate his point. It was clear Percy had never been in an actual fight since the man couldn't take a punch. His head snapped back, and his body pinwheeled as he staggered back. It was an overreaction to a soft hit, but Will would never complain about winning a fight.

"You didn't have near this much fight in you in Paris," he said, spitting blood on the black-and-white checkered floor.

Will's vision clouded with the deepest rage he had ever felt. His killer's nose crumpled beneath his fist, but he couldn't even feel the satisfaction through the haze of his anger.

"Why?" Will barked between hits. Bones cracked beneath his fists, but nothing could stop him. "Why did you have to kill me? You could have robbed me. I would have given you everything."

Will let Percy shove him away, the answer to the question that haunted him was more important than his bloodlust.

"You drew cards instead of folding, stealing a straight flush from me." Percy's face was contorted in hatred as he spoke of a night that happened more than a year previously, but Will didn't even remember that hand. "As far as I'm concerned, you stole from me."

Percy swung at him, but Will easily blocked the hit despite the chaos that reigned around them. The stage had been ripped apart. There were far more angry townspeople than people to rage against. Their pitchforks ripped paintings apart, windows were smashed, and curtains were torn from their rods.

"What did you need the money for?"

"I had to pay some debts before I was allowed to leave Paris."

Finally, he had the reason for why he was killed, but it truly was senseless. If the money were for a sick child or a starving family, he would have understood his sacrifice, but it was all for naught.

"You're a pathetic excuse for a man."

"At least I don't have to kill a woman to find someone to fuck me."

"That means next to nothing coming from someone who tried to force a woman into marriage."

Will grabbed him by the collar. Percy's icy blue stare had lost its menace with both eyes so swollen they could barely focus on Will. A trail of blood ran from his nose, over his split lip, before dripping onto his starched white shirt. Bruises already formed beneath his eyes, acting as a frame to his crushed nose.

"Semantics," Percy said before headbutting him.

Will dropped him, grabbing his head as pain radiated through his skull. It felt like his nose had been pushed into his brain. Blood poured from his nose. It would heal quickly, but was a nuisance in the meantime.

"So you do bleed after all."

"If you think that's going to stop me, you have vastly underestimated me."

Will rushed him again, getting a few good hits into his body. Percy socked him in the stomach, but Will barely felt it. He wasn't sure if it was the head injury that still rang in his head or his rage, but he was glad to be unencumbered.

"You think fighting me is giving you a chance, but Montgomery is collecting his slattern of a sister now. If you give up, I'll make sure your death is swift."

"We left a few things out of the presentation. I've lost the ability to be killed. Everything you do to me will heal, and I promise you that I will never, ever stop coming for Jane. The biggest mistake you ever made was going after her."

Will swung his fist and connected with Percy's hard jaw. His hand throbbed from the contact, and he heard the man's jaw crack. Collapsing, he fell on what remained of the stage, knocking some of the gas lamps together. Two of which shattered as they hit the wooden stage, immediately setting the structure on fire.

Percy tried to pull himself up, but he was shaky and clattered to the ground. The man was dazed, but conscious. A shrill scream sounded from across the room, causing Will to quickly turn to see the source.

Tristan evaded being struck with a club as another man hit him from behind. His brother wheeled around and punched the man who had hit him in the face. Will was glad he took the time to teach his brother how to fight when they were kids.

Pain radiated throughout him as he felt a crack on the back of his neck. Percy simply wouldn't give up.

"Do you think there is any hope of escaping me? I will ruin you and your entire life. You haven't even begun to taste my vengeance."

Percy stumbled, holding Robert's cane, knocking over more lamps to feed the fire. The fire was a problem, but he didn't care if the entire house burned as long as his family got out.

"You may not be able to die," Percy continued. "But I'm pretty sure your brother can. And we can always test that theory on Jane a few times. I know that would help me feel better after the trouble she's caused me."

Will had enough of this man for either of his lifetimes. It was time to end it.

Placing his hands around Percy's neck, he squeezed using all his strength. The baron thrashed in his grasp as his face turned bright red. He was able to suck in some air, but Will squeezed harder.

There was a commotion behind him, but he didn't dare look away from Percy. His only hope was that Tristan would win his fight.

Glassy eyes stared up at him as Percy ceased his struggle, but Will still didn't let go. He wasn't going to take any chances. Percy fumbled with something in his coat, but Will didn't take his eyes away. Percy's face was amongst the last things Will saw before he left this world, and he would return the favor.

"Will!" Tristan shouted.

It took everything in him not to turn to see what his brother needed. He could only pray it wouldn't be too late. Percy's eyes moved, the beginnings of a smirk forming on his dying face, when Will heard a booming noise.

Looking back, Will saw his brother stumble backwards, holding his stomach. A flintlock pistol rested in Percy's grasp. Will dropped his hands from the man's neck, running to his brother as Percy sputtered for breath behind him.

"Tristan! Are you all right?"

"Ah, it hurts a bit," Tristan responded, doubled over as he tried to stop the blood flow.

Will took his hand and eased him to the ground so he could check his brother's wound. Blood soaked his suit jacket as he found the entry wound in Tristan's gut. Will felt his back for an exit wound, and Tristan winced when he found it.

"It's not in a great location, is it?" Tristan asked with a short laugh.

"No."

Even though there was an exit wound, a shot to the gut wasn't something you could survive, but he used his own jacket to try to stop the blood flow all the same.

"It's all right. Go find Jane and get out of here."

Smoke filled the room as the fire spread from the stage to the broken wooden chairs littering the room.

"No, I'm not leaving you. I'll take you to the carriage, and if Jane isn't there, then I'll look for her while you wait out there."

"Will, the fire's spreading. If it gets to the storage room, the lamp oil will cause an explosion."

"Which is why I won't leave you here. This gunshot wound doesn't mean it's the end, but there is no coming back from an explosion."

He needed to get Tristan out of there. His brother was going to hate dying, but he would get past it.

"I think fire can kill you if it can burn through you at a higher rate than you can heal yourself."

"Well, we'll just have to think of this as an experiment then."

Tristan was slumped over, trying to stop his own bleeding as Will looked for a way out. The servant's entrance would get them to the carriage faster, but the fire had nearly engulfed that area, and he didn't want to risk getting stuck in that hallway with the flames.

He turned his head and saw Percy approach him with Robert's discarded cane drawn like a bat.

"I told you there was no way out of this," Percy wheezed as he stumbled towards him.

"Why won't you stay down?"

Will walked to him, ripping the cane from his hand before breaking it over his knee. He was sick of fighting this man. It had been cathartic at first, but now he just wanted to be free of the man who had killed him and, now, his brother as well.

He thrust the broken cane into the same place on Percy's stomach that Tristan had been shot. The broken cane stayed in his gut as Will twisted the handle to make sure Percy did not get up again.

"Your brother's going to die, and Montgomery has his sister by now. Even if you kill me, you'll have to live without either of them."

Will didn't dignify him with a response. The man had done enough damage to his life. Now he could spend his final moments alive drowning in his own hatred.

Using the broken cane as a handle, he pushed the man into the flames. Percy's screams pierced the air as Will picked up one of the intact gas lamps from the stage and threw it at Percy. The flames that already covered him burned brighter.

Will returned to Tristan, crouching beside him on the floor. His breaths were shallow, and his skin was pale with a light sheen of sweat.

"I'm sorry about that."

"You had something to take care of, I understand." Tristan took his hand, smiling up at him. "I want you to know that my proudest achievement was being your brother."

"Don't waste your breath on goodbyes."

Flames crawled up the wall, likely spreading to the second floor through the floor. The exit to the front door was blocked by fire as well. They were almost surrounded.

"Jane told me that dying didn't hurt. I didn't believe her at the time, but the pain is ending. You have a better chance of getting out of here if you leave me behind. Find her and Mrs. Jones."

"If you think I would ever leave you behind, you don't know me at all. You and I are stuck together forever, either here or somewhere else."

As he looked down at his dying brother, he finally understood Tristan because Will refused to live without him either.

This was going to hurt, but Tristan would pass out soon. Will stood up, throwing Tristan over his shoulder. When he only gave a muffled grunt, Will knew he wasn't much longer for this world.

He attempted to leave through the front, but the flames were so intense that his hair singed. He didn't care if it made him completely bald, but he didn't want to chance Tristan catching on fire in case his body was too damaged for the procedure.

Eyes watering from the smoke, he went back to the middle of the room. All of the exits had been blocked by the fire that crept closer and closer to the lamp oil.

This couldn't be how his life ended. In his desperation, he turned again, seeing the stained glass windows that the stage had blocked.

Dodging the fire, he made his way to the windows, rattling the pane to see if there was a latch he had never noticed, but they were solid. He looked around for a heavy item to throw through the glass, but everything he could have used was on fire. Adjusting Tristan on his shoulder, he climbed up on the windowsill and kicked the window.

Glass pierced his boot, impaling his foot with shards, but he kept kicking. Those injuries would heal, the same way the burning in his lungs from the smoke was only temporary as well. Once the hole was big enough, he jumped through, not caring about the lacerations he got on his head or arms as he fell onto the back garden.

Rolling through the bushes, he was thankful to have pruned them earlier. He took one last look at his beautiful garden, but he would far rather remember it in its glory rather than its waning moments. One day, the land would heal and return even stronger than before.

Tristan was silent over his shoulder. Will no longer heard his shallow breaths or his pained groans. His brother was dead.

Jane would know what to do. They had worked together enough that Tristan had to have taught her the procedure. She was somewhere out there waiting for him. No matter how much he begged her to leave, he bet she wouldn't have left without him.

He prayed she made it to the carriage, but he hadn't seen Robert, which made him deeply nervous after Percy's threats.

As he rounded the corner, the carriage was still there, but Jane wasn't beside it. The mob had convened close to the carriage.

Though now that the mob was outside, they looked more like a concerned crowd as they watched the fire spread.

If Jane wasn't watching the fire, then she had to be in the house. There was no third option he could stomach. At least if she were in the house, he could save her.

He just needed to find a place for Tristan to wait while he searched for Jane and Mrs. Jones. Morris was watching the house with the mob, so at least there was one person he didn't have to locate.

The carriage was the obvious spot to put Tristan, but he doubted the crowd would let him through with a body in his arms, seeing as death is how this whole ordeal started. The shed was the better option to store his brother before he walked back into the burning house.

* * *

Jane

Bounding down the servant staircase, Jane clutched the bag to her chest. Smoke lingered in the kitchen, but fire hadn't yet made it there.

Grabbing a discarded rag, she held it over her mouth in an attempt to keep from breathing in smoke. While her body would heal itself, smoke inhalation still hurt.

Black smoke poured from the door to the servant's corridor, making her eyes water as she coughed. It was foolish to run through smoke too thick to see through into what would most definitely turn into an active fire, so she closed the door, blinking away the tears the smoke caused.

Running in the opposite direction, she threw open the kitchen door and was greeted with clean air. Big gulps of fresh air hurt her ravaged lungs at first, but breathing was easier every passing moment. Blessedly, the carriage was still there. Morris held the reins as he stood next to the horses, making sure they didn't get spooked despite the fire and the small crowd around the carriage. The moment he saw her, his face crumpled in relief.

"Mr. Morris, make sure you watch over this bag." She threw the book bag into the carriage. "Has anyone else made it out?"

"Not yet."

The horses were growing restless from the fire, and she saw the strain it took to keep them from bolting.

"We can't leave without them."

"If the fire spreads,—"

"No, we aren't leaving anyone behind. If anyone comes out, make sure to keep them here."

Morris didn't look convinced, but he gave her a reluctant nod. "I'll wait as long as you tell me to."

Jane fought her way through the crowd pouring from the house, leaving the mob to fend for themselves. They didn't deserve to be let off the hook of sowing chaos in her home, but there was no time for revenge. Glass popped as the windows rattled in their frames.

The night was quiet for a few moments as if the world was taking a deep breath before a loud boom sounded that shook her teeth. The fire had reached the fuel storage.

Glass rained down on her, slicing open her face and arms, but she didn't feel the pain as her blood trickled onto the grass beneath her.

Fire was a problem because it could damage them at a rate greater than they could heal, whereas an explosion would leave nothing to heal. Falling to her knees, she waited to see Will run from the house with Tristan and Mrs. Jones slung over his shoulders. They would all get into the carriage, and Morris would drive them away from this nightmare.

The fire blazed on, but no one left the house.

Pain radiated from her palms as she pushed herself up from the ground. Her hands were a bloody mess that glittered in the light of the flames. Her skin was already healing over the foreign objects embedded in her hands.

A hand dropped on her shoulder. Hope surged in her, but when she looked up, it wasn't Will.

"We need to leave. Now," Mrs. Jones said, tugging on her arm.

"No, he's coming out. I know he is," she sobbed, but even as her heart begged her to stay, she knew she was only wasting time.

"He would want you to leave. They both would."

Looking up at the pleading housekeeper, she saw tears in her eyes. The housekeeper loved them like her own sons, but even Mrs. Jones knew if they were both still inside, the chances weren't very good.

"Maybe they already got out." Her voice was scratchy from emotion and smoke damage.

It went against everything in her heart, but she took Mrs. Jones' hand. The glass burrowed itself further beneath her skin, but the pain was all that anchored her.

CHAPTER 41

"This is as far as I can take you, Miss," the driver said as he stopped the cart.

"Thank you for taking me this far," she said, handing him the fare before grabbing her bag and hopping onto the dusty road.

The wind blew a chill that had her hugging Will's cloak to her as she shivered, but she was exceedingly grateful it had not yet rained. Searching for a needle in a haystack was difficult enough without the haystack being sopping wet.

Two weeks had passed since the symposium, and she still hadn't found Will and Tristan. After the fire burned out, she searched the smoldering ruins of the house, but there wasn't a sign of either of them.

They had been in Edinburgh for a week, as that was where she had told both Will and Tristan she would be. Her days were spent searching for Will while Mrs. Jones wrote letters to everyone she could think of in an attempt to find the brothers. Every night when Jane returned, the housekeeper looked at her with such hope that it was a stab to the gut each time she dashed the older woman's dreams.

A few days prior, she had managed to charm a list of homes sold in the last few years from a real estate broker. She first tried to gain the list using her feminine wiles, but when that didn't work, she burst into tears, and he gave her the list almost immediately.

She thought the list would hasten the process, but she had been proven wrong at every turn. Even when offered double the rate, city coaches didn't want to go so far out only so a woman could knock on someone's door. This morning, she had managed to persuade a sheep farmer to take her most of the way since it was on his way home. She still had to walk nearly a mile to get to the house, but it would have taken her all day to get there if she hadn't gotten the ride.

Relief coursed through her when the house came into view. If a stranger opened the door, she would burst into tears again, but she hoped she could at least get a cup of tea out of it. Yesterday, the homeowner she startled didn't give her anything, but someone gave her a biscuit the other day.

This house was a modest two-story stone structure. It was just enough space for a couple of bedrooms and a laboratory. Maybe a reading nook if she were fortunate. The house was dark, but she was undeterred. This was the first place she had been to that *felt* like it could be right. Hope invigorated her every step, and she prayed that this time she finally had something to walk towards.

Cupping her hands, she put her face against the dark window. The curtains were shut, so she couldn't see anything inside. No smoke curled from the chimney, nor did candlelight flicker inside. It looked truly, properly empty.

She let out a shaky breath as she rested her forehead against the cool glass. This was her best lead, and it had been a waste. Dread swirled inside of her; there was an outcome she refused to think about, but every day she went without seeing him, that quiet part of her grew louder.

Lifting herself from the glass, she grabbed her bag and swung it over her shoulder as she started the long walk back. There wasn't a cart waiting for her, but maybe once she got back on the main road, she could hitch a ride.

Right as she was about to step off the front stoop, she heard a thump from inside and froze. It sounded like a heavy book hitting the floor. It echoed in her ears since it wasn't the type of sound that came from an empty home.

She slapped her open palm against the door. It would have wasted too much precious time to close her fist to knock. She paused to put her ear against the door. There wasn't a sound inside, but that didn't discourage her.

"It's me! It's Jane."

He had to be in there; she wouldn't accept anything else. She would kick the door down if necessary.

"Please!" She cried, her voice ragged as she blinked back tears.

She stopped knocking. Perhaps the sound was a hallucination caused by wishful thinking after all. She didn't know what to do now that Scotland was a bust.

Maybe Will and Tristan had gone to Munich to put as much distance between them and England as possible. Or maybe they had gone to London, or the Americas, or a thousand other places that were important to them that she didn't know about. Letters had been left with Morris as he supervised the rebuilding of the house, as well as with Will's solicitor in case he ever reached out to either in an attempt to locate her. Staying in Edinburgh felt like giving up, but it also might be the best option.

The canvas strap dug into her shoulder as she walked down the stone steps of the porch. The bag wasn't heavy now, but who knows how it would feel once she hit her third hour of walking. At least blisters on her feet weren't a concern.

Gravel crunched under her feet when she heard the squeak of hinges behind her. She didn't dare turn because her fragile heart couldn't take it if a stranger stood at the door. She stayed frozen, not even breathing, as her world stopped in anticipation of what could happen next.

"Jane."

The tears she had kept at bay now flowed freely as relief rocked her. Turning around, her bag flew off her arm before landing in the dirt. Standing on the porch was Will, *her* Will.

Rocks sprayed across the drive as she ran up the entry, taking the steps two at a time before she threw herself into the arms of her love. He caught her because he always had and always would. Burying her head in his neck, she cried.

"It is you, you're really here," he whispered before pressing a kiss to the top of her head.

She pulled back from the hug to see his face. Yellow eyes shone down on her, glassy with tears. Several days' stubble lined his jaw, and his hair was mussed as if he had been repeatedly running his hands through it. He wore only a wrinkled white shirt, filthy and ripped black trousers, and scuffed black boots. It looked to be the same outfit she had last seen him in, minus the vest and suit jacket.

"What happened?"

"I worried I would never see you again." He cupped her face in his big hands and placed his lips against hers. She surged against him, deepening the kiss in the need to feel him against her to prove he was really there. "When the house went up the way it did, I thought for sure you were still inside. The only thing that played in my mind for days was telling you to run through the passage that caught fire. I thought I had killed you."

He rested his forehead against hers, breathing in her presence the same way she did his.

"You know I never follow directions."

His laugh was a quiet sound that made her heart soar.

"I'll keep that in mind if I ever make the mistake of trying to tell you what to do again." He kissed her on the forehead in what felt like a benediction before grabbing her hand and leading her inside. "We have much to discuss."

They ended up in a small parlor, sitting twisted to face each other on a spindly loveseat. She told him of hitting Robert over the head when he tried to take her. How Mrs. Jones found her and left together after the final explosion that engulfed the house in flames.

"It was smart of you to leave word with my solicitor. I wish I had thought of that. I merely hoped you would someday make your way to Scotland."

"It all worked out in the end." There was no room for regret, not when they had found each other again. "Now, tell me what happened to you. I didn't see you again after I left the ballroom."

Will's eyes dropped to their clasped hands as he recounted his own story. He told her of his own fight with Percy and how he had stoked the fire before Will had finally killed him.

"I'm proud of you for standing up to him. I know how difficult that must have been for you," she said, rubbing her thumb over the rough edges of his hand.

His breath hitched. "I kept worrying you would be incredibly upset with me for killing him. I suppose I don't have to worry about that anymore."

"They made their decisions to stoke hatred in the end. Neither cared how many had to die for their greed."

"I keep thinking that perhaps we are aberrations. Maybe we belong dead after all."

"No." She brought his hand to her lips, brushing a kiss against his knuckles. "We belong together. Not even the natural order of the universe could keep us apart. This means something. *We* mean something."

Their entwined hands dropped to the couch between them. She was resolved to never let him go again.

"I'm sorry I didn't wait for you. I tried looking for you in the house, but the flames were too bad, and I didn't see you outside. I was worried the mob was going to catch me, so I ran." He stopped, choked up. His eyes were downcast as he absent-mindedly rubbed circles on the back of her hand.

"It's all right, I don't blame you. We found each other, and that's what counts. Where's Tristan?"

She felt unbelievably rude that she hadn't asked about his brother yet, but she had been too overrun with relief to realize it until now.

"He fought against the mob for as long as he could. Percy shot him in the gut."

"I'm so sorry." She squeezed his hand. "And how is he now?" The question came out in a whisper, dread curled inside of her like a lead stone.

"He's dead. I brought him here because I thought I could... I had seen him do it. Helped him. I thought I could remember, and at the very least, he would have notes here, but I've read all of his journals and I can't find anything."

"Is he here?"

"Yes, he's downstairs on ice. I'm doing all I can to buy us as much time as possible, but I'm worried this knowledge died with him."

"I need to get my bag."

She wanted to shake herself for being so careless as to let it lie forgotten on the drive. Will followed, apparently unwilling to let her go as well. Relief flowed through her when the bag was where she left it. Will picked it up and slung it over his shoulder.

"Take me to the lab."

The laboratory was in the cellar of the house, and she shivered at how cold it was. In the middle of the room, a shroud lay on a metal slab, surrounded by large blocks of ice.

"Hand me my bag, please."

Will handed her the bag, and they finally let go of each other as she set it on the table to open it.

"After I ran from the ballroom, I figured we wouldn't be able to return to the house, so I went up to Tristan's lab and grabbed all that I could. That's where Robert found me, I bashed his head in with Tristan's brass microscope."

She removed journals and loose pieces of paper, setting them in stacks on the desk. They held the most significant discovery of the modern age. Maybe it should have died with its creator, but the good doctor's creations were far too selfish to let that happen.

Will sucked in a sharp breath. "You mean you have—"

"Yes."

"And you'll be able to do it?"

She turned to look at Will, the man she loved. The look of hope he had wasn't questioning if she was capable, but because he couldn't stand to get his hopes up.

"Yes, but I'll need an assistant."

"I can help."

She nodded, walking over to the hooks where Tristan kept his laboratory coats. Even though she had never been in this lab, the layout was almost the same as the one where she had spent some of the best times in her life. Passing one coat to Will, she tied the other around her

Nerves prickled at her, but she knew she could do this. Every moment she hadn't been searching for Will was spent studying Tristan's work. She opened the journal that held the instructions, written in great detail by a neat hand, almost as if he knew that one day someone would need them without having him as a resource.

"Let's begin."

ACKNOWLEDGMENTS

Writing a book is a solitary experience, but it isn't something you do alone. I want to thank my parents for their support every time I come home with a new dream. At least this one is easier to stomach than improv comedy.

Thank you to Kelsey and Kendra for generally being the kind of siblings that I would also fight the natural order of life and death for.

Jamison for being my best friend for [redacted] years. I know you think I don't listen to you, but you got me to cut things that not even my writers group or editor could get me to let go of. Love you.

I may be biased, but I have the best writers group in the world. Anna, Ariel, Kyra, and Whitney, thank you for reading this from its earliest version and helping it come to life! It's so exciting that we all get to be on this journey together.

Molly, thank you for my beautiful cover! I love it so much, and thank you for not murdering me when I would give you vague notes or make you change something just to change it right back.

Grace, thank you so much for your phenomenal editing skills and for listening to me yap endlessly. Everyone can also thank you for championing sweet baby Tristan to get his own book.

Thank you to The Ripped Bodice for creating the community that led me to some of my very best friends. I love yapping with all of you. Thank you to Jeanne for always allowing me to corner you after book club!

There are truly too many friends and family who have been endlessly supportive of me on this endeavor, and I love you all!

Thank you for the years of listening to me talk about this. And thank you even more for preordering, reading, and liking all of my social media posts. I appreciate all of your support more than you will ever know.

Lastly, I want to talk about my Grandma Violet. She wanted to be a writer, but her father told her that she could only choose between being a teacher or a nurse since she was a woman. Because she chose to be a nurse, I get to be a writer.

ABOUT THE AUTHOR

Kate Crow is a gothic romance author and lifelong monster lover. When she isn't writing, she loves going to the movies, knitting, and being very loud with her friends. She lives in Los Angeles with her cat, Lombard, and her physical media collection. Keep up with her at www.katecrow.com.

facebook.com/katecrowauthor
instagram.com/katecrowauthor
tiktok.com/@Katecrowauthor